Alienated

MELISSA LANDERS

HYPERION

LOS ANGELES   NEW YORK

Copyright © 2014 by Melissa Landers

All rights reserved. Published by Hyperion, an imprint of Disney Book Group. No part of this book may be reproduced or transmitted in any form or by any means, electronic or mechanical, including photocopying, recording, or by any information storage and retrieval system, without written permission from the publisher. For information address Hyperion, 125 West End Avenue, New York, New York 10023.

Printed in the United States of America
First Hardcover Edition, February 2014
First Paperback Edition, January 2015
V475-2873-0-15104

This book is set in Bembo.
Designed by Tyler Nevins

Library of Congress Control Number for Hardcover Edition: 2013032977
ISBN 978-1-4231-8525-3

Visit www.hyperionteens.com

10 9 8 7 5 4 3 2

To the best parents in the universe, Ed and Kathy Beckett,
for being my earliest and most fervent fans

Chapter One

Winning. Cara Sweeney had made it her business, and business was good. Honor Society president? Check. Young Leader Award? Check. State debate champion two years running? Double check. And when the title of valedictorian had eluded her, she'd found a way to snag that, too.

Over the summer, she'd staged an academic ambush of such epic proportions, Midtown High's geek-elite were still chewing their pencils in shock. Sneaky as a senator, she'd retaken AP Calculus, raised her grade from 92 to 100, and usurped Marcus Johnson as valedictorian. Her stealth attack had caught him with his Hanes down, and unless her grades tanked this year—which was *so* not going to happen—the sulking loser had no chance of reclaiming his rank.

But she had a feeling Marcus would laugh his lacrosse pads off if he could see her now: slumped in the principal's wingback guest chair, mouth agape as she tried to form a coherent response to the "awesome news" Mr. Ferguson had just tossed into her lap like a live grenade. "I don't think you understand what a big deal this is. Not only for you, but for the whole school." Principal Ferguson's brown caterpillar eyebrows inched toward a receding hairline. "The L'eihrs chose you over every other valedictorian in the country. We're talking thirty thousand seniors!"

"Mmm-hmm." Cara nodded blankly, trying to make sense of it. Maybe there'd been a mistake. She'd cut soccer, track, volunteer tutoring, and chess club a couple years ago when Mom got sick, and it took a lot more than academics to impress a scholarship committee these days. So why hadn't they chosen someone more accomplished?

"I know the money comes with a few strings attached, but this is the opportunity of a lifetime." Mr. Ferguson pointed a marble fountain pen at her and "fired" it like a tiny pistol. "Especially for a budding journalist. Think of the blog potential here."

A few strings attached? Holy Mary, mother of all understatements! Cara shifted in her seat, the backs of her thighs sticking to the warm leather. "Oh, right—yeah, of course I'm happy. It's just a shock. I didn't even apply."

"No application. Every high school submitted its top candidate, and the L'eihrs took it from there. You'll never guess why they picked you." Without giving her a chance to try, he announced, "They saw your footage from last year's state debate finals. They admired your"—he held up two fingers and made air quotes—"passion."

"What?" Cara scrunched her brows. Passion? She'd hammered the opposing team until their captain had cried and run off stage. The L'eihrs, who had the emotional range of tree bark, liked her atomic temper?

"This is huge!" Pausing a moment, Mr. Ferguson twisted his mouth while jabbing his index finger at a closed manila file folder. "And you don't seem thrilled. Last year you said you were interested in exchange programs."

Well, yeah. But there was foreign, and then there was *foreign*.

Mr. Ferguson leaned forward, resting his arms on the desk's polished mahogany surface. His eyes softened behind thick glasses, voice lowering to a whisper. "You're not afraid of the L'eihrs, are you?"

"No!" Cara scoffed, wiping her clammy palms on the front of her skirt. "Of course not."

Okay, maybe a little. She'd been as fascinated as everyone else when the aliens made contact two years ago, but their secretive nature made her stomach feel heavy, like she'd eaten a dozen Taco Bell double-decker burritos in one sitting. And as much as she wanted to travel, leaving Earth wasn't what she'd had in mind.

"Good. I don't want you doing anything that makes you uncomfortable. The young man—uh, I mean the young . . . uh, well, technically we have the same DNA, so I guess I could call him—"

A sharp voice barked, "Student ambassador," and Cara jumped in her seat. The old military guy lurking near the corner had camouflaged so perfectly into the green curtains that she'd almost forgotten he was there.

3

Mr. Ferguson nodded. "Right. The ambassador who'll stay with your family sounds just like you—a top student, even by L'eihr standards, which is saying a lot." He picked up a small photograph and handed it across the desk. "He just turned eighteen. His name's Aelyx."

He pronounced it *A-licks*. Cara gave the photo a perfunctory glance and handed it back. Whatever. They all looked the same to her.

"Wow, this scholarship is a lot more . . ." What was the right word? Lavish? Excessive? ". . . generous than the others I've applied for, but I don't know how my parents will feel."

What a bald-faced lie—she half expected her nose to grow. Mom and Dad would streak the Super Bowl halftime show just to meet a L'eihr, let alone live with one.

"No problem. I called your folks this morning, and they're totally on board."

Frick. Of course they were. Mom was probably emptying Troy's old bedroom at that very moment, finally clearing out his tacky, testosterone-fueled shrine to heavy metal and Harley-straddling bimbos.

Mr. Ferguson stood and pulled some papers from his file. "And from what the colonel says, your brother's over the moon"—he let out a hearty laugh—"to be the first human on planet L'eihr."

"Wait." She bolted forward, gripping the armrests. "Troy's going *there*?"

"He didn't tell you?"

She shook her head.

"As soon as he heard you were selected, he volunteered to

4

serve as human liaison for the program. He'll get acclimated to the L'eihr culture now so he can help you and the other two exchange students adjust when it's your turn next year. Think of him as your intergalactic mentor." He grinned. "A big brother, no pun intended."

If this were Mr. Ferguson's idea of a few strings attached, she'd hate to see what he considered complicated.

The colonel came to life again, stepping forward and giving a curt nod. "Your brother's a fine Marine. He's never turned down an opportunity to serve his country."

Exactly. Which was why Cara hadn't seen the jerkwagon in almost two years. Apparently the Middle East wasn't far enough away for Troy—he needed to leave the galaxy now. What was next, time travel?

Principal Ferguson strode to the door, bouncing on the balls of his feet and happier than a pigeon with a French fry. "I'll make some copies of the exchange contract while Colonel Rutter explains the details."

Cara turned her head and caught a glimpse of her dazed reflection in the debate team trophy cabinet. The blue eyes of the concavely distorted girl staring back looked haunted, like the stuffed owls in science lab, and long wisps of fiery auburn hair made her cheeks look even paler.

Get a grip, she chided herself. *Maybe it won't be so bad.*

Sure, living with a L'eihr for the rest of the year would blow chunks, but she'd get a full ride out of the deal—anywhere she wanted, even Dartmouth! She'd never dreamed she could afford the Big Green, considering Mom's treatments had knocked the family into a black hole of debt six figures deep.

And Mr. Ferguson was right about the blog potential. Humans knew next to nothing about L'eihrs, and she'd be sharing a bathroom with one. That gave her an instant leg up on every other journalist in the country.

What if she started a brand-new site, something with a catchy title and an outer-space theme? If A-licks would open up and spill some tidbits about life back home, she could run a special-interest series and attract followers from around the globe. And when it was her turn to visit L'eihr, all the photos and news she'd gather could land her a book deal. She might even be able to sell her proposal to a publisher before she left.

The more Cara thought about it, the more she realized the scholarship wasn't the real prize here. This exchange could launch her career into the stratosphere. When she looked at it that way, putting up with a creepy houseguest was totally worth it.

"Buck up, Miss Sweeney." Colonel Rutter's firm voice brought her to attention, and she jerked upright like a soldier. He stood tall and lean behind the principal's desk, narrowing his shrewd gray eyes as he spoke. "You look shell-shocked, and you should be. This program's not for namby-pambies. I'm gonna lay it all out, and if you can't handle this, you'd better say so. Understood?"

"Uh, yes."

He glanced at his shoulder and smoothed a derelict wrinkle into submission before sitting down. This man didn't take any crap, not even from his clothes. "The World Trade Organization chose me to head the LEAP: the L'eihr Exchange Ambassador Program. America, France, and China will each get a student ambassador. The goal is to help humans and L'eihrs understand each other better. Now let's be frank. We want an alliance with L'eihr."

Cara nodded. Unlike most of her classmates, she made it her business to know what went on in the world beyond the school's graffiti-stained walls.

"Our polls show Americans don't support it. Too many suspicions. But the LEAP's gonna change all that."

"Seriously? How?"

"Aelyx will be your shadow. Where you go, he goes. Do you work?"

"I waitress on the weeken—"

"Quit."

She cleared her throat. "Just quit?"

"The LEAP pays a small stipend, so consider it your job. Full time. You'll represent the whole country, so you gotta go all in." He leaned forward and raised his brows as if expecting a reply.

"Understood." That seemed fair. The higher the reward, the greater the responsibility. She'd rock this exchange like a hurricane. Besides, she wouldn't exactly miss slinging footlongs at the Dreamy Weenie. "I'll give my two weeks' notice after school."

"Make it one week." Then he added, "Every other Wednesday, a camera crew will come to your house to tape interviews. They'll air Fridays at nineteen hundred hours."

"Whoa, whoa, whoa." Televised interviews? Cara wiped her palms on her skirt again, rethinking a career at the Dreamy Weenie. "We'll be on TV?"

"You asked how we're gonna ease suspicions. This is how. By bringing a harmless L'eihr into everyone's living rooms. People fear what they don't understand, so they're gonna get to know Aelyx. More importantly, they'll see you"—he pointed an index finger at her nose, just like the old Uncle Sam poster—"at ease beside Aelyx, showing the world there's nothing to fear."

"But—"

"Now back to your responsibilities. You need to help Aelyx collect water and soil samples. Their scientists want to analyze contaminants. And I'll expect you in Manhattan for the LEAP gala in three weeks."

"An excused absence, so don't worry." Principal Ferguson breezed back into the room, oblivious to the fact that Cara's pulse was pounding at the base of her throat. Probably because he wasn't the one going on camera in front of eleventy billion people. He handed her a stack of papers still warm from the copier. "Here's the contract and the scholarship details. Read this over with your folks tonight, then sign it and bring it back in the morning."

Colonel Rutter thrust a business card at her chest. "Call if you have any questions. See you in three weeks." Then he stood, turned on his heel, and left the room before she could ask if skipping the interviews was a deal breaker.

This was happening so fast. She could barely catch her breath. Less than five minutes ago, her greatest dilemma had been which movie to see Saturday night with her boyfriend, Eric, and now . . .

Oh, no! Eric! She'd forgotten all about him. He and his

friends hated L'eihrs—not just a pinch of ignorance and a dash of mistrust, but serious loathing. He'd go full-on banana sandwich when she told him.

"You look a little overwhelmed." Principal Ferguson sat on the edge of his desk, smiling down at her with such tenderness it made her heart pinch. "But I know you'll do great. I'm so proud of you."

That nearly undid her. For some ass-backward reason, she could take any criticism, but kindness made her blubber like an infant. Digging a fingernail into her thigh to keep from crying, she whispered, "Thanks."

"And this gives you a chance to thank the L'eihrs for what they've done." He tilted his head, delivering a pointed look that shamed her. "I hope you don't take that gift for granted."

With flaming cheeks, Cara stared into her lap and brushed her thumb over the frayed hem of her jean skirt. The fact that she questioned this opportunity just proved she was the most unappreciative jerk on the planet. Her whole family owed an enormous debt to the scientists of L'eihr. Two years ago, as a gesture of goodwill, they introduced humans to the *asheem*— a potent medicinal root native to their planet, which could isolate and kill cancer cells. It had come just in time to save Mom's life.

Standing, she summoned all her courage and extended her palm to shake the principal's hand. It was time to woman up. This wasn't the end of the world.

"This feels like the end of the world," Syrine said, pressing her fingertips delicately against the spaceport window as if trying to capture the distant, backlit planet glowing in the darkness.

Aelyx glanced over the top of her head at Mother L'eihr. He'd never traveled off-terrain before, and he couldn't deny the pang of longing that settled beneath his breastbone when he viewed their home from five hundred miles above the ground. Why the Elders had chosen to send them away—and to a primitive, foul planet such as Earth—was beyond him. Perhaps his leaders really had gone soft in the mind, as many of the other clones suspected.

"I wish they'd reconsider," Eron whispered, glancing over his shoulder to ensure the ambassador hadn't returned. "This alliance is madness."

"Which is exactly why we need to go," Aelyx told his friends. Unwilling to risk speaking aloud any longer, he locked eyes with Eron. *Did you bring the* sh'alear?

I sewed it into my tunic lining with a sprig of nilweed, Eron assured him. *Just like you said. And I helped Syrine do the same. The canines at Earth's customs checkpoint won't smell a thing.*

Good. Aelyx leaned against the cool metal wall, trying to look innocent. *Just make sure you don't launder your tunic while we're aboard the ship.*

Eron laughed. *Like I'm that deficient. You're the one who left a ration of* l'ina *under his bunk for a week.*

A grin curved Aelyx's mouth. *Gods, that was awful. I'll never forget the stench.*

None of us will.

"Stepha's coming," Syrine warned them. "Guard your thoughts."

Ignoring the urge to flinch and whirl around, Aelyx

leisurely turned to face the ambassador, who crossed the steely corridor with exaggerated, slow steps.

Stepha smiled at them, but it didn't reach his eyes, dulled by the malaise that plagued all the Elders. His ancient form stooped under the weight of lethargy, his words slow and deliberate when he droned, "I've had your luggage delivered to the main transport. Did you bring your student visas?"

Aelyx nodded, struggling to block his anxiety. It didn't work. Stepha's rheumy gaze caught with Aelyx's and held.

Don't be afraid, Stepha told him privately. *Your human is a dedicated hostess. She's already sent me several messages asking about your personal preferences.*

Cara Sweeney wasn't the root of Aelyx's concern, but he was grateful that Stepha thought so. Aelyx would face execution if the ambassador discovered his treachery, and he preferred to return home alive.

"How fortunate," he replied aloud. Deception was impossible through Silent Speech.

"Before we board," Stepha told the three of them, "I want to warn you that humans have unusual standards for sentimental expression. Try not to be offended by their ways. Integrating with them will be a challenge, but I know you're fit for the task. You three are the finest in your Aegis. Remember that and be patient with your hosts and their peers. We'll all benefit from an alliance, both humans and L'eihrs. Do you understand?"

They all nodded, avoiding one another's eyes.

"Excellent." Stepha swept his hand to indicate the boarding platform. "Then we're ready."

Aelyx glanced out the port window again. The sun had just begun to eclipse L'eihr in a brilliant pinprick of light that forced him to shield his eyes. Right now the Aegis would begin to stir, the communal washrooms filling with his yawning peers. Vero, the house pet, would awaken in an empty bunk and wonder where his master had gone. Would he remember Aelyx when the exchange was over? Probably not.

Syrine tapped his forearm, returning his attention to present company. She must have sensed his agitation. It was one of her many gifts.

We can do this, she promised, then gestured out the window and added, *for them*.

I know. After all, the *sh'alear* had been his idea, and when the rest of the Aegis had learned of his plan, they'd declared him a hero. But that didn't mean Aelyx looked forward to spending eight months on Earth among savage aliens. He shook his head and glanced once more at his home planet before assuring Syrine, *You're right. We can do this*.

The two of them followed behind Eron and Stepha, making their way toward the main ship. The station was virtually empty at this early hour with the exception of a lone vendor peddling his wares near the boarding gate. A hiss of steam from the spaceport's ventilation system punctuated the echo of clicking boots. Aelyx noticed the recycled air had a distinct odor to it, akin to the stale scent of *H'alar* cave, his favorite hiding spot as a child. How many hours had he and Eron spent exploring those narrow, frigid passages? Hundreds at least.

The memories sent a prickle of worry through his chest. Humans would ruin it, just as they'd destroyed so many of their own natural wonders. Mankind didn't regulate their population growth as L'eihrs had done. Aelyx had studied human history. He knew what would happen if these aliens ever settled on his planet. Something American humans called "Manifest Destiny." They'd take whatever suited them and outnumber the L'eihr within decades. He couldn't let that happen.

"Here, brothers," the vendor called to Aelyx and Eron. "You can't travel to Earth without these!"

"I'm certain that I can," Eron said with a laugh.

Aelyx glanced at the man dangling a black cord from his fist. A twinkling object reflected the overhead light, and upon closer inspection, he found the man had affixed a faceted *ahib* to the cord as some form of adornment.

"What's this?" Aelyx asked him.

"A neck-lace." The vendor brought the cord to his throat in demonstration. "I've heard that human females cannot resist shiny objects. They wear stones around their necks and even embed them into their ear flesh. If you buy this for your hostess's *Sh'ovah* Day, you honor the Sacred Mother while presenting a fine gift to your human."

Aelyx pressed his lips together to contain a smirk. He doubted a common pebble from beneath his feet would impress anyone. Not even humans were that foolish.

"It's true," Stepha said. "Stone jewelry is considered the preferred gift by many females, though they don't observe *Sh'ovah*. Instead, they celebrate the anniversary of their birth."

"Interesting," Aelyx muttered. Perhaps he should bring a gift. It might give the impression that he cared. "I'll give you thirteen credits."

The man wasted no time in wrapping the neck-lace inside a fabric pouch. Aelyx extended his wrist for the vendor to deduct the credits, and after a quick scan of the data embedded beneath his skin, he pocketed his "treasure" and jogged to catch up with Eron and Syrine.

"Earth girls really covet stones from the ground?" Syrine asked in disbelief. "My human's a male. I wonder if he'd enjoy a nice satchel of dirt."

"Or perhaps a parcel of animal droppings," Eron added with humor in his eyes. "What odd beings."

As Stepha shuffled within earshot, Aelyx quickly changed the subject, asking Eron, "Is your *l'ihan* aboard this transport?"

"I wish," he said. "But no. She's assigned as medic on the—" Eron bit short his reply as Syrine broke into a sprint. Her boots rattled the metal grates beneath their feet, ponytail swinging between her shoulder blades as she left them behind.

"*Fasha,*" Aelyx swore, watching her disappear through the ship's doors. Maybe Syrine's affections for their roommate ran deeper than he'd thought. "She's still upset about you and Elyx'a?"

Eron dropped his gaze. "They were friends once. I think that makes it worse." He glanced up just long enough to add, "If you and I wanted the same female and she chose between us, I imagine we'd become enemies, too."

"Don't be so sure." Aelyx had never felt that level of attachment for anyone. He elbowed Eron lightly in the ribs. "Perhaps I'd show mercy and simply let you have her."

Eron laughed, but still he looked troubled. "Syrine cares

for you," he said as if probing for a reaction. "Maybe not the same way she feels for me, but you could—"

"Wait," Aelyx interrupted. "Are you saying I should make her my *l'ihan?*"

"No! Well, perhaps. Just think about it. Sooner or later, we all have to choose. Why not her? You know the two of you are compatible."

Why not Syrine? Aelyx couldn't say with any degree of certainty. He simply didn't see her that way. "First of all, you assume she'd have me as your substitute."

"A poor one at that, but yes, I think she would."

Aelyx shot him a burning look.

"And second?" Eron asked.

"It would feel unnatural. You might as well ask me to partner with a human."

Eron shuddered and opened his mouth to speak when the ambassador interjected from behind, "Keep an open mind, brother. There are worse things The Way could ask of you."

Aelyx gripped the icy railing with both hands, feeling his eyes widen to the size of *sh'ad* patties. His friends were right— the Elders *had* spent their wits. If he'd ever felt a moment's hesitation about his plan, it was gone now. Aelyx closed his eyes and focused, slowing the rush of blood to his head and steadying his pulse. In a deceptively calm voice, he assured Stepha, "I will follow The Way to glorify Mother L'eihr."

Chapter Two

Alienated

MAY THE SOURCE BE WITH YOU

Thursday, September 3

Greetings, Earthlings!

Welcome to *ALIENATED*, your exclusive source for close
encounters of the nerd kind. I'm Cara Sweeney, and I'll be your
intergalactic tour guide this year. As I host the nation's first
L'eihr exchange student, I'll be dishing out all the juicy tidbits
you always wanted to know about L'eihrs but were afraid to ask.
And nothing's off-limits, folks. When it comes to unearthing a
story, I'm not afraid to boldly go where no girl's gone before! It
all kicks off in two weeks, so check back soon and check back
often. Want my posts delivered to your inbox? Subscribe to my
RSS feed! In the meantime, please join me in extending a big
Homo-sapiens welcome to Aelyx, who should be piercing the
ozone right about now.

Can't wait to meet you in Manhattan, Aelyx! And don't worry—
I come in peace. ☺

Cara scheduled her post to drop at six o'clock the next morning, which gave her more than enough time to spring the

news on her boyfriend. Since she hadn't considered Eric in her decision to accept the scholarship, the least she could do was give him a head start on blowing a gasket. Which he undoubtedly would. But she didn't want to think about Eric right now, not when she could distract herself with debate practice instead.

She closed her laptop and leaned forward in her seat to tune in to the mock debate taking place on the other side of the World Studies classroom. Joss Fenske was arguing for the benefits of treating water as an economic resource to be traded across international borders while his opponent checked her watch.

"Uhh," he began, "water is a, uhh, naturally occurring commodity, no different than, uhh, oil or natural gas—"

Cara interrupted him by shooting a rubber band at his neck. When Joss heaved a sigh and cocked his head as if to ask, *Seriously?* Cara shrugged and lectured, "Those *uhh*s are killing us. Same goes for saying *like* after every other word." She pointed at Kaitlyn Ray and said, "I'm looking at you, Kaity."

"Like, gag me with a spoon," the little smart aleck replied.

Ignoring her, Cara returned her attention to Joss. "This time I want you to counter the argument that, unlike oil and natural gas, water's necessary to survival, and without controls in place, we could see wars break out as the population continues to explode."

Joss licked his lips and nodded, then began yammering with all the confidence of a deer staring down a speeding Mack truck. Cara slumped at her desk and propped her chin in her hand. This team was toast after she graduated. She could coach them into the ground, but she couldn't give them the fury that won championships. Fight came from within— either you had it or you didn't. Even the L'eihrs recognized passion when they saw it.

Which reminded her, the L'eihr ambassador had finally answered her e-mail asking what Aelyx's room looked like back home. His response: gray walls, beige floor, basic cot, one storage unit per resident, no decorative embellishments. In other words, prison chic. At least it wouldn't take long for Mom to transform Troy's old bedroom—just a few coats of paint and a new area rug. Cara could swing by Lowe's and pick up supplies after debate practice. If Aelyx felt comfy and secure, it might loosen his tongue for a blog interview.

Her eyes darted to the clock above the SMART Board.

"Let's break a few minutes early," she suggested. "I've got a physics lab due tomorrow." Not to mention an essay for AP English, an alien exchange student to prepare for, and some explosive news to dump on Eric. Looked like another all-nighter.

"Hey, babe." Eric brushed shreds of grass and dried mud from his lacrosse jersey, littering Cara's front porch with debris, while darting a glance over her shoulder into the living room. He kicked off his cleats and stepped inside, then closed the door behind him. "Where's your dad?"

She plucked a leaf from his sweaty blond hair and used it to tickle beneath his chin. "In the kitchen. Why?"

"'Cause he'd kill me for this." Hooking an index finger,

he pulled back the top of her T-shirt and peered inside. When she smacked his hand away, he flashed a lopsided grin and nodded toward the kitchen. "Feed me. I'm dyin' here."

"Boobs and snacks?" Cara folded her arms while a smile tugged the corners of her mouth. "Is that all you want from me?"

She was only half joking. Ever since junior prom, when a few of Eric's buddies had gotten lucky, he'd been trying to play catch up, like sex was a race and he didn't want to come in last place. He didn't seem to care that she wasn't ready to cross the finish line.

"I'm so offended right now. How could you think that's all I want?" Then the sly grin curved his lips again. "I'm after way more than that."

"Jerk." She laced their fingers together and tugged him toward the kitchen. "C'mon, I'm starving, too." Right on cue, Cara's stomach gurgled in response to the scent of spicy marinara sauce. She hadn't eaten a bite at lunch, too unsettled by the prospect of telling Eric they'd have a third wheel for the rest of the year. Well, a fourth wheel if you counted her best friend, Tori, but Eric didn't hate her as much as L'eihrs. Close, but not quite.

"Your mom making pizza?" Eric slipped his other hand up the back of her skirt, and she smacked that one, too, wishing he'd give it a rest already.

"No, it's—" All coherent thoughts ceased and Cara froze in place when she walked into the kitchen and found her parents entwined against the refrigerator, lost in a deep kiss.

She cringed and raised a hand to shield her eyes while Eric

spun a clumsy pirouette and bolted from the room like it was on fire.

"Gross." She peeked through her fingers. "Why can't you guys keep that stuff private?" Really private—like behind closed, dead-bolted, soundproofed doors.

Mom broke from the kiss with a smack and pushed a tangled black lock of hair away from her face. "Hey," she said through swollen lips. "When did you get home?"

Dad didn't bother looking up. Only his mussed strawberry hair was visible as he nuzzled the side of Mom's neck.

"Just a few minutes ago." Cara wrinkled her nose. "Really, Dad, can you give it a rest?"

A dismissive wave was his only reply. Dad was captain of the Midtown fire department, and he and Mom were always . . . amorous . . . when he came off a forty-eight-hour shift. Why couldn't she have normal parents who hated each other, like everyone else?

Her appetite crushed, Cara decided to abandon the snack-finding mission. But first she completed her daily scan of Mom's face, checking for pale, waxen skin or the gray semicircles that used to haunt her eyes. Finding everything smooth and rosy, she released a quiet sigh and turned away.

Even after all this time, it was hard to believe Mom was really cured, that some celebrity prankster wasn't waiting to jump out of his tricked-out media van to yell, *Boo-yah! Your mom still has ovarian cancer. You got served!* She wanted to trust the L'eihr plant, the *asheem*, but it wasn't so easy. Turning away, she gave her parents the privacy they obviously wanted and returned to the living room.

"What, no food?" When Eric clutched his stomach in mock agony and played dead, collapsing onto the sofa with a *thud*, she saw a glimpse of the old Eric—the dorky, beanpole freshman who'd made her laugh, even when the heart of her family was dying. Now he seemed out of place on her shabby furniture, like a young, blond Zeus come to wreak havoc among mortals. She missed the string-bean boy and his jokes.

"You've got two legs," she teased. "Walk 'em back in there if you're hungry."

He cringed like he'd tasted anchovies. "Geriatric porn doesn't raise my flag."

Cara giggled. The old Eric was still in there. "Hey, let's play Total Zombie Massacre—battle to the death, just like old times." When he shook his head, she pleaded, "C'mon. I'll go easy on you."

"I have a better idea." Grabbing her wrist, he gave a mighty tug, sending her careening into his lap. The pungent odors of musky cologne and sweaty boy pummeled her nostrils, and then his mouth was at her ear, his fingers dancing up the length of her inner thigh. "Let's go to your room. Your dad's not coming up for air anytime soon."

Palming his damp chest, she pushed away and tried to breathe through her mouth. Why couldn't he understand that all this pawing only pushed him further from his goal? "Unh-uh. Tori's coming over."

He heaved a sigh against the side of her throat while his fingers halted their advance toward third base. "Great. Just what I need. Why can't the clinger get her own life?" He pushed Cara away and moved to the other end of the sofa, but not before she slugged him in the bicep.

"She *has* a life. She's skipping student council for me." And Tori hadn't missed a meeting yet—mostly because her longtime crush, Jared Lee, was class president.

"Why'd you ask her over?" Eric said, rubbing his arm. "Trying to get rid of me?"

"Maybe I should." Heat rose into Cara's cheeks. The endless groping, the insults—she couldn't take much more of the new and "improved" Eric. Closing her eyes, she counted backward from ten to one and tried to recall the bulleted list of suggestions in *Anger Management for Imbeciles*. Deep breath in . . . deep breath out. Oh, to hell with it. If this didn't get rid of him, nothing would: "I signed the contract."

"What contract?" It took a few seconds for her words to sink in, and then Eric's lips parted with an audible *pop*. "That LEAP thing you talked about at lunch?"

"Yep."

"You're screwing with me, right?"

"Nope." Stiffening her resolve, she added, "We bring him home in two weeks."

"Are you insane? You'll have to actually go there! No amount of money's worth that!" Eric reached into his back pocket and pulled out a wet, crumpled leaflet, but his hand froze in midair before it reached her. "Wait. Did you say *him*? It's a guy? No effing way!"

Three sharp knocks sounded at the door, and Tori let herself in, turning their attention away from the argument for a few seconds.

Tossing her long black braid over one shoulder, Tori dropped her goalie gloves haphazardly onto the floor before tugging her Midtown soccer T-shirt over her head and using it to wipe her sweaty face. Then she slung the shirt around her neck and stood in her sports bra and shorts, gripping her waist like Wonder Woman.

Tori shot daggers at Eric. "Hey, *culo*." She flipped him the bird, and he returned the gesture. Their hatred had always been mutual.

She was the yin to Cara's yang—teakwood skin, jet black eyes—an academic underachiever with ten tons of nuclear energy driving her miniature four-foot-nine-inch frame. But they had one thing in common: they didn't hold back.

In an unusual move, Eric spoke directly to Tori, waving her over to the sofa. "You're not gonna believe this."

"Let's see. Something I'd never believe . . ." She tapped one finger against her chin. "You finally took your nose outta Marcus Johnson's butt crack?"

"You won't be laughing when a L'asshole crashes your next slumber party," Eric said darkly. "Have fun braiding his hair, or whatever you girls do at those things."

"What's he talking about?" Tori pulled a chair up to the sofa, then turned it backward and straddled the seat while Cara filled her in on what she'd missed.

"*Puta madre!* Slow down. You gotta read this before you decide for sure." Tori held one hand forward while using the other to pull a sweaty wad of paper from her bra. She smoothed it out against her thigh and handed it to Cara. "They were giving 'em out after practice."

"Us, too," Eric added, flinging his leaflet onto the sofa cushion. "Marcus's dad is president of the local chapter. I already joined."

Cara held the nasty thing at a distance and glanced at the front cover. HALO: Humans Against L'eihr Occupation. The Patriots of Earth. "Seriously? Since when does anyone listen to HALO?" The kooks had thousands of members in every nation, but they were known extremists—the kind of people who stockpiled weapons and looked forward to the apocalypse. "Did they offer you any Kool-Aid? I hope you didn't drink it."

"You're the one swallowing poison." Eric grabbed his pamphlet and held it in the air like a gospel. "If you believe what the government says."

Tori leaned forward in her chair and pointed one purple fingernail at the opening paragraph. "This part's kinda scary."

With a resigned sigh, Cara scanned the sheet. *"The L'eihrs, at least the few we've been permitted to see, possess technology, intelligence, speed . . .* blah-ditty-blah-blah-blah *. . . And that begs the question: What could they possibly want from us? Their freakish physical advances are the result of an ancient breeding program, and now that we know humans and L'eihrs are genetically compatible, we believe it's our women they're after, to spawn a race of mutants."*

What utter lunacy. She could teach HALO a thing or two about proper persuasive writing techniques. "Oh, come on," she said. "This is total propaganda. Who takes this stuff seriously?"

"This isn't a joke." Eric's jaw clenched and his eyes hardened in a way she'd never seen before. It sent frost skittering down her spine to see the boy she'd once loved disappear inside the furious stranger glaring at her now. "They won't talk about anything, especially not their weapons, and that telepathy crap they do is—"

"Creepy as hell," Tori finished.

"Look, it's done. I already signed—"

"It's not the only scholarship in the world, you know." Eric pushed off the sofa, propelling himself to his feet with the force of his anger. "This program's only for valedictorians. So if you say no, the freak goes to another school. But if you say yes, we're all stuck sitting next to him in class, in the lunchroom, sharing a bathroom. . . . What if they let him play sports?" He raked a hand through his hair, setting it on end. "Think about it. Everyone'll hate you for bringing him into our lives. And they'll hate us"—pointing to himself and Tori—"by association."

Cara studied both of them in shock. "You won't want to be seen with me?"

Eric's hot gaze darted to the scuffed hardwood floor between his feet.

"I'm not gonna ditch you, but think about it." Tori rocked back in her chair. "We don't know anything about them. What if they're up to something? What if they don't let you come home when it's your turn?"

"They healed my mom. Why bother with that if they just want to wipe us out?"

"Oh, grow up, Cara." Eric charged to the door and snatched his cleats off the front porch. "They want something for that cure. Nothing's free. It's time to take one for the team. Shred the contract or whatever. Undo it."

"No!" How dare he order her to do anything? "This could make my whole career."

"No? Just like that? God, you're so selfish!" Eric was shouting at her—for the first time in all the years they'd known each other. "Putting yourself and the whole town at risk, and why? So you don't have to take out student loans?"

"*I'm* the selfish one? You arrogant pri—"

"What's the problem?" Dad strolled in from the kitchen, his hair wildly tousled from Mom's fingers. He gave Tori's shoulder a playful squeeze, then scowled at Eric and offered a curt nod of acknowledgment. "Bet you've got some homework to do."

Eric took the hint. "Yeah." He leaned in to kiss Cara's cheek, but instead delivered a whispered warning in her ear. "You better figure out what's important." And then he turned and left without saying good-bye, pulling the door shut so softly it barely made a sound. Somehow it stung her ears worse than a slam.

Eric's HALO pamphlet had fallen to the floor, and Cara picked it up, glancing at the last lines. *It is better to die proud Patriots of Earth than to live in quivering supplication to an alien race. Take care that you recognize the L'eihr enemy. He may look human, but he is not.*

She shook off a chill. It terrified her to think Eric actually believed this drivel and that Tori wasn't far behind. What if he was right about the whole student body despising her for bringing Aelyx to school?

Cara pulled a deep breath in through her nose and held it.

No, she couldn't believe that. Reasonable people would have doubts, just like she did, but they wouldn't come after her with pitchforks and torches. And Tori was crazy to think the L'eihrs wanted to lure her to their planet and trap her there to make babies. If that was their goal, why not abduct her now? They had the technology to do it—easily.

So why did her palms feel clammy again? Why was her heart trying to escape her body by way of her throat?

Cara released a loud puff of air and tried to ignore the prickles of dread that tickled her skull—the same ones she felt mid-debate when she realized she'd picked a losing argument.

CHAPTER THREE

Narrowing his eyes, Aelyx peered at the lofty banquet hall ceiling, where thousands of faceted chandelier crystals refracted the light and illuminated the hall in prisms of color. How completely garish. Just as the spaceport vendor had claimed, humans were fixated on shiny objects to an extent that bordered on delirium. And that was just the beginning.

The smoky scent of meat permeating the air was rank and unfamiliar. Between the click of shoes against polished marble floors, echoes of conversations and laughter, and clinking champagne glasses, the noise overwhelmed him. It seemed humans had made overstimulation a way of life.

He leaned against the wall—an extravagant tile mosaic depicting soldiers mounted on horseback—and observed his host family from a distance. They hadn't been formally introduced yet, and he already dreaded sharing a home with these people. Bill Sweeney, the father, laughed loudly with his wife and pinched her rear end when he thought no one was looking. Troy Sweeney, the family's oldest child, seemed intent on eating his weight in an appetizer called shrimp cocktail. It certainly didn't look appetizing.

He recognized Cara Sweeney easily from her photograph. Tonight, however, she wasn't smiling. She stood rigidly with her arms crossed over her chest while casting hostile glances at her brother. Considering what he'd learned about her hobbies—solitary activities such as reading classic novels, video gaming, and journalistic writing—her closed-off body language came as no surprise. This female seemed to prefer isolation to the company of others, possibly a defense mechanism resulting from her mother's near death. All the better. That meant she might not follow his activities too closely.

Was this girl truly the best the humans had to offer? He supposed Cara was an attractive female, a bit tall perhaps, but her blazing copper hair and blue eyes assaulted his senses. Vibrant colors didn't exist naturally on L'eihr, and she reminded him of how alien this new world was. When his retinas couldn't tolerate any more abuse, he glanced away and found Syrine in the crowd.

Syrine wore the same tan and gray uniform that he did, but she appeared far less relaxed in it as she conversed with her host student, a lanky Frenchman with deep black hair. While Syrine's shoulders tensed so visibly they crept to her ears, the boy propped one hand against the wall and leaned toward her in an obvious mating ritual.

Sacred Mother, how disgusting. The imbecile either failed

to notice or simply didn't care that Syrine had no interest in pairing with him. No L'eihr of their generation would sink to sharing genetic material with a human, not even if The Way demanded it.

As if called, Syrine glanced toward him. She ducked beneath the human's arm and scurried to where Aelyx stood, concealed in an alcove.

Locking eyes with him, she complained, *Great gods, I can almost see the hormones rolling off his filthy body. I nearly vomited my supper.*

Establish boundaries now, Aelyx advised, *before it goes too far.*

Have you seen him? She glanced over her shoulder at the boy, who'd already moved on in an attempt to entice a new female. Tipping back his head, the Frenchman honked a laugh through his hooked nose. *He doesn't understand nonverbal social cues.*

If all else fails, an "accidental" knee to the groin should deliver the message.

At least your human seems tolerable. Quiet and reserved.

Aelyx studied Cara Sweeney, feeling his brows pinch together. A pained expression distorted the girl's ivory features, and she pressed one hand against her stomach as if she might become physically ill. Tolerable? He doubted it.

And Eron, Syrine continued. *His female observes personal boundaries. Such luck!*

They peered across the room at Eron's host, who stared at the floor, both hands clasped behind her back as if meditating. Her parents spoke above her head while a young boy pushed a die-cast vehicle across the marble tile at her feet. The child bore a slight resemblance to the girl, but considering China's population restrictions, he probably wasn't a sibling. Too bad Earth's other nations hadn't implemented similar policies. With their limited resources, humans were mating themselves into extinction.

Don't worry, Aelyx told Syrine. *If the* sh'alear *works, we won't be here long.*

It'll take one month at least, Syrine complained. *And if we're caught . . .*

If we're caught, we die, he warned. *Failure's not an option.* He could feel Syrine's unease seeping to the surface, eroding her courage. Perhaps they'd better go over the plan again—all three of them. *Go tell Eron to keep his com-sphere close. I'll contact you both in three days.*

Don't lose faith in me. I can do this. Syrine placed her fingertips against the left side of Aelyx's throat in a farewell gesture of esteem. *For the Sacred Mother.*

And her children. Aelyx returned the gesture and pulled his hand away, then backed into the shadows of the alcove.

Once, when Cara was ten years old, she and Troy had gone exploring in the woods behind their house. He'd held a tree branch out of the way for her, and then—thinking it would be hilarious—he'd let it go too soon so it smacked her right across the belly. She'd had to breathe in tiny gasps for the next hour. Kind of the way she was breathing right now.

Like the leather pumps contorting her toes, her black cocktail dress was a size too small, and Mom had bought inexpensive Spanx to avoid paying for a new outfit. Unfortunately, the spandex was three sizes too small, and she hadn't been able to sit down (or inhale) all night.

"Are you gonna stop giving me the stink-eye and talk to me yet?" Troy had finally torn himself away from the buffet station, and he had shrimp between his teeth. Some things never changed. "I won't see you for another year."

Cara opened her mouth to speak, but then shut it again as a tug-of-war raged inside her. She wanted to throw her arms around Troy's neck and beg him not to leave, to tell him how the house was too clean and quiet when he was gone. Crazy as it seemed, she missed his white tube socks scattered across the living room floor and the way he finished all the milk so she had to eat dry Cheerios. She wanted to demand he find another job, one that didn't require a Kevlar vest and an anthrax vaccination.

And she wanted to punch him in the stones for abandoning the family once again.

Instead, she asked, "Are you scared?"

"What, of going to L'eihr?" He snorted and flashed an easy smile. "Hell, no! I can't wait. I get to be the first person to travel at light speed. That's huge, Pepper."

"Don't call me that. I'll be seventeen next week." When she was a newborn, Troy had taken one look at her red hair and compared her to a chili pepper. The nickname had stuck ever since, despite her repeated efforts to kill it.

"Hey, I just thought of something." His blue eyes widened in amazement. "If Einstein was right about light speed, then you'll be older than me when I come home to visit."

She thought that would be fitting but didn't say so. Instead, she nodded toward the other side of the ballroom where three L'eihrs stood huddled together: the official ambassador, who lived in Manhattan, and two visiting students. The third student had wandered away more than thirty minutes ago. "They haven't opened their mouths once—I've been watching. They just look into each other's eyes. I'll bet L'eihr's a really quiet place."

Troy shrugged and began picking his front teeth with his pinkie nail.

"I wonder which one's mine." She hoped it was the short one "talking" to the ambassador. He was the only one who smiled—the only one who looked human.

"Go find out."

Part of her felt like she should, but the way they tipped their heads and stared at one another seemed so intense. She got the feeling they didn't want to be interrupted. And maybe it made her a speciesist or whatever, but watching them together made her wonder how Troy would tell them apart once he got to L'eihr.

All of them, men and women alike, wore their shoulder-length light brown hair tied neatly behind the neck. It blended perfectly with their russet skin, and when combined with the tan uniforms, they were a monochromatic solid wall of brown. Like walking paper bags.

Supposedly, their planet was way older than Earth, and all races sort of blended together thousands of years ago. Then they started evolving. Or mutating. Scientists claimed the same thing would happen here one day, but she doubted it. And anyway, why did they try so hard to look alike, right down to their six-inch ponytails?

Before she had a chance to ask, the inside of Cara's throat tickled. She tried to cough, and the elastic band digging into her waist practically spliced her liver in half. "Ow!"

"What's with you?" Troy ran a hand over his cropped black hair and cocked an eyebrow. "*Female* problems?" He whispered "female" like it was a dirty word.

"No," she said with an eye roll. "This underwear's killing me."

"So take it off. Big whoop."

"Oh, sure. I'm all about keepin' it classy like that."

"You need to unclench, dorkus. Go to the bathroom and stuff it in your little handbag or something. No one'll ever know." With a shake of his head, he added, "Jesus, you're such a *girl*."

An unexpected glow radiated inside her chest at Troy's casual insults, and she bit her lip to hide a smile. Yeah, she'd missed this, too. Glancing to the side, she noticed a restroom sign and began to take his suggestion seriously. Maybe it wasn't that big a deal. Without "support lingerie" sucking in her curves, the dress would fit tighter than a wet suit, but she could live with that.

"Okay. I'll be back in a minute."

While skirting around the buffet table, Cara caught a whiff of prime rib and her stomach rumbled. Maybe she could manage to eat something after removing the organ grinder panties. She hobbled toward the ladies' room door, but a middle-aged man wearing a black suit stopped her before she could enter.

"Sorry, miss," he said while scanning the room. "You can't go in there." He wore an earpiece and touched it as if receiving a message. She glanced at his badge: Secret Service.

"Why, what's wrong?" It was getting harder to breathe.

He continued surveying the ballroom, never making eye contact while he spoke. "The president's using the facilities. You can't be inside with her unless you have security clearance. I need you to back up."

"How much longer will she be in there?"

Silence. Still no eye contact. But it made sense that a president who didn't care about the Constitution didn't care how long she monopolized the ladies' room, either.

"You know where another bathroom is?" she asked, shifting her weight to one hip.

A soul-piercing glare was his only reply. Tempting as it was to exercise her right to free speech, she held back, remembering her new role as student ambassador. The L'eihr group still huddled nearby, and she didn't want their first impression of her to be of the psychotic variety.

So now what? She spun around and looked for an open office or any space that might offer a few seconds of privacy. She spotted a large mural that led into a darkened alcove. It could work if she was quick. Glancing over her shoulder to make sure no one was watching, she strolled into the dim recess.

Without wasting a second, she kicked off her pumps, hitched up her dress, and hooked her thumbs beneath the stiff elastic waistband. But the spandex didn't go down without a fight. She jerked and tugged at the stretchy fabric, grunting and swearing quietly to herself for what seemed like an hour. Finally, she rolled the material down over her hips, past her thighs, and stepped free, feeling a breeze of frigid air from a nearby vent raise goose bumps on her naked backside. She was pulling her dress down when she heard muffled laughter from behind. Still barefoot, she gasped and whirled around.

"Sorry," said a voice in the darkness. "I didn't mean to startle you. I only wanted to make my presence known before you removed any more clothing."

Cara's heart pounded against her ribs while she scrambled to pick up her Spanx and cram them inside her purse. She cleared her throat. "I was just . . . um . . . really uncomfortable. I'm not taking anything else off." She slipped her shoes on and backed toward the hallway, feeling her whole body flush red-hot with embarrassment.

"You don't have to explain yourself. I've come to expect the unusual from humans."

The owner of that buttery voice stepped into the light, and Cara stood face-to-face with one of the most stunning individuals she'd ever seen—the missing third student. She clenched her teeth and tried not to gawk, but it wasn't easy.

From a distance, he'd seemed unremarkable, but up close, his appearance intimidated her. Taller than any of Midtown's athletes, his fitted uniform outlined every solid curve of muscle in his chest and arms, the fabric straining visibly against his broad shoulders. One strand of long honey-brown hair had escaped his clasp and fallen against the outside of his angular jaw, and when he glanced at Cara, her stomach dropped to the floor. It was his eyes that'd left her stunned—not brown like the rest of him, but the most exquisite shade of silvery gray. Holy crap, did they selectively breed for looks, too? That just wasn't natural.

"S-Sorry you had to see that," she stammered while stepping out of the alcove. "I don't usually go commando." Oh, God, did she just say that out loud?

He chuckled again, then shrank back as if he'd startled himself with his own laughter. His brows drew together. "It's none of my concern, *Cah*-ra."

"Uh, I'll just let you get back to . . . whatever you were doing." Which was lurking in the dark like Chester the Molester, but after her display, she could hardly criticize.

She teetered all the way across the crowded ballroom before she realized he'd called her *Cah*-ra. If he knew her name, it probably meant the L'eihr she'd flashed was her student ambassador. Awesome. So much for representing America and making a good impression. And so much for convincing Eric to give the LEAP a chance. He'd take one look at Aelyx and start making ultimatums again. Eric didn't even like it when she hung out with the spindly guys from the Honor Society, so he'd freak when—

"Took you long enough. You fall in?" Troy interrupted her musings, his face bright with excitement as he gazed over her head, searching for someone. "Where's the L'eihr ambassador? He's supposed to take me to my ship." Troy was practically bouncing in place while her heart sank like a boulder. Another year apart, and he didn't seem bothered at all.

"I dunno." She shrugged. "You say good-bye to Mom and Dad?"

"Huh? Oh, yeah. They're by the punch bowl with Colonel Rutter. You're supposed to go meet up with them." Troy grabbed her into a crushing bear hug. "*H'aleem*, Pepper. That's L'eihr for good-bye." Then he turned and disappeared into the crowd. Gone without a care, just like always.

"Love you, too, asshole," she muttered to herself.

She released a heavy sigh and made her way to the beverage table to meet her parents. Even from a distance, she noticed Mom's eyes were puffy and red, but Mom smiled up at Dad while he caressed her arm and kissed her forehead.

Mom stood on tiptoe and waved to her. "Colonel Rutter went to get our exchange student. Isn't this exciting?"

"Yeah," Cara mumbled while chewing her thumbnail. "I can't wait."

"Here he comes!" Mom bounced the same way Troy had just done, more excited than a kindergartner at snack time.

It was him, all right. Time for damage control. Pulling her shoulders back, she plastered a confident smile on her face.

Colonel Rutter began the introductions. "Aelyx, I'd like you to meet the Sweeney family: Bill, Eileen, and Cara. Troy Sweeney's taking your place on L'eihr."

Aelyx shook Dad's hand and said something in another language—something beautiful and flowing, like a cross between French and Hawaiian. "It's an honor," he translated in English.

"Believe me," Dad said, practically beaming with pride, "the honor's mine."

Next, Aelyx extended his hand to Mom. "Mrs. Sweeney, thank you for opening your home—"

Before he could finish, Mom jumped forward and pulled Aelyx into a hug. Cara noticed his back stiffen for several beats too long before he returned the embrace and gave Mom's shoulder an awkward *pat, pat, pat.* Either people on L'eihr didn't hug, or he found humans repulsive. Probably both.

Finally, he turned to Cara. She offered her hand, and he took it in both of his. While his grasp was warm and strong, there was an eerie vacancy in his gaze, almost robotic. She hadn't noticed it before, and the last line of HALO's pamphlet suddenly rang in her ears: *He may look human, but he is not.* Some long-buried, primal instinct screamed, *Danger!* but she tightened her grip and resisted the urge to pull her hand free.

"*Cah*-ra," he began. His voice was alluring, but his eyes were dead. "Your name is the Irish word for friend. I hope you and I will be great friends." It sounded rehearsed and completely insincere, almost backhanded in its delivery.

Her palms were sweaty—there was nothing she could do about that—but she was determined not to let her voice shake. Flashing her most diplomatic smile, she replied, "Your name means 'son of Elyx,' which doesn't give me much to work with, but it's nice to meet you, too." At his startled response, she added, "Looks like we both did our homework."

He released her hand, stepped back, and didn't make eye contact for the rest of the night. It was going to be a long plane ride home the next day. And a very long year.

Chapter Four

Aelyx felt a brief crush of claustrophobia when he entered the Sweeneys' modest home. An oversize, overstuffed floral sofa dominated the living room, while a dark wooden coffee table claimed the remaining floor space. But it was the sixty-inch television mounted on the opposite wall that commanded the most attention. Dozens of family photos splayed outward from either side of the flat black screen like vines run amok.

Eileen Sweeney linked her arm through his again, and his muscles twitched from the contact. He wished she wouldn't touch him so frequently, but to say so might be rude. He also wished Bill Sweeney would cease his endless prattle. Sacred Mother, when the man wasn't speaking incessantly, he was practically copulating with his wife in public. During the flight from Manhattan, Bill and Eileen had rained kisses on each other nonstop. The ambassador had warned him about this, but still, were these humans incapable of self-control? Cara was the only member of the family to give him any peace.

"Your room's down here." Eileen pulled him through a short hallway. "I decorated it in the natural colors of L'eihr."

When Aelyx stepped into his bedroom, the tension in his shoulders evaporated. Nothing, not even a single picture frame, adorned the freshly painted gray walls. A standard bed draped in beige stood opposite a simple chest of drawers. The space was open and uncluttered. Perfect. He set his duffel bag on the floor and sighed with relief.

"Mrs. Sweeney—"

"Eileen." She smoothed a lock of hair behind one ear and smiled.

"Thank you for your hospitality."

Beaming, she waved a dismissive hand. "I'll let you unpack while I heat up the pizza." Without another word, she left the room and closed the door.

Aelyx felt a quick pang of remorse for his harsh assumptions about the Sweeneys, but he pushed it to the back of his mind. He unzipped his bag and surveyed the clothing Colonel Rutter had provided for him. While he understood the importance of dressing to assimilate with humans, he'd worn the L'eihr uniform all his life. Parting with it felt abnormal, like shedding his skin. With a quiet groan, he changed into a pair of blue denim pants and a gray cotton shirt. Then he folded his uniform and brushed his fingertips against the smooth fabric before placing it in the chest of drawers with the other garments.

The scent of strange food began to permeate the air, and he wondered how he'd choke it down without retching. He'd practiced eating Earth fare, but he couldn't tolerate the overwhelming flavors. Seasonings were used far too liberally here. Aelyx let his mind wander back to L'eihr, to the tranquil mountains, the quiet companionship of his peers, and his favorite meal—tender, juicy meat braised with root vegetables. But in the end, he knew reminiscing wasn't helpful. He needed to focus on his mission—the sooner he achieved his goal, the sooner he could return home.

A nearby door slammed, and seconds later, the wall that divided his bedroom from Cara's began thumping in time with her speakers. Cara's voice sang out, far too muffled to interpret her words but clear enough to highlight her flagrant tone-deafness.

An involuntary smile curved Aelyx's mouth. Leaping gods, there it was again—though he found nothing particularly entertaining about the girl, she'd already elicited this reaction in him several times, starting with the moment she'd removed her undergarments and revealed her bare, round bottom. Her skin was even paler than he'd thought possible, so translucent it practically illuminated the darkness, and he'd finally understood why humans called the act *mooning*.

He reached into his duffel and retrieved Cara's photograph, studying the wide smile that parted her lips and crinkled the skin around her bright blue eyes. Those eyes hadn't appeared as friendly today after the third time he'd defeated her in chess. He'd laughed then, too, and she hadn't seemed to appreciate it.

From what he knew, Cara was a competitive student, the

top in her class. Losing to him so consistently must have been torture. He considered allowing her to win a game or two but decided it wasn't in her best interest. Besides, she wouldn't believe the victory was genuine. She was only human, but brighter than most of her species. Maybe some coaching would help. At the very least, he should make an effort to show interest in her life. It would seem suspicious otherwise.

Yes, he'd seek her out and initiate dialogue . . . as soon as he found the will to leave his bedroom.

Subscribe [Archive] [Recent Entries] [About Me]

Alienated

MAY THE SOURCE BE WITH YOU

FRIDAY, OCTOBER 19
The Eagle Has L'anded!

That's right, gentle readers, Midtown's booming population of 21,096 just grew by one. Maybe now we can justify that new traffic light on Main Street. Anyway, Aelyx is in the hiz-ouse!

Sadly, our trip wasn't devoid of HALO hijinks. The whack-a-doodles took to the streets in protest, clogging traffic for miles—sorry, Manhattanites!—and making us miss the first leg of our flight home. They even overturned a (fortunately vacant) car. Luckily the National Guard didn't hesitate to step in and gas the rioters.

But enough of that. Let's get back to Aelyx. How was our first meeting, you ask? In a word:

With her fingertips poised above the keyboard, Cara slouched in front of her computer, feeling mocked by a half-blank screen. The cursor blinked at the top of the page with a clock's rhythmic precision, teasing: *tick-tock, you're blocked, tick-tock, you're blocked.*

Writer's block wasn't the only problem. After arriving home, she'd rushed to her room to blog about the gala while each sensation from last night was still fresh in her memory. She wanted so badly to spin a riveting tale of meeting Aelyx for the first time, but what could she say? She'd mooned him before even shaking his hand.

And instead of charming her with stories of life on L'eihr, Aelyx had snubbed her for six hours of in-flight hell. The details of their budding friendship would've made such interesting reading . . . if there *were* a friendship.

In reality, she didn't have anything remotely pleasant to say. Aelyx was so strange. He refused to eat or drink anything but water, spoke only when asked a direct question, and the emptiness in his—albeit stunning—eyes gave her the shivers. Sharing that information with the world? Not the best idea. And she definitely wasn't blogging about what an idiot she'd been during their layover at the airport.

To pass the time, she'd pulled a 3-in-1 magnetic travel game set from her backpack and challenged Aelyx to a game of chess. He'd won in less than five minutes—seriously, five minutes—even though he'd never played before. Completely shocked, not to mention pissed, she'd demanded a rematch, and with a smirk that practically said, *As you wish, stupid human,* he'd creamed her again, easily. Had she let it go? Of course not. There were other games to play: checkers, backgammon, rock-paper-scissors. In the end, she'd left her dignity at Concourse B and boarded the plane in silence.

After shutting down her computer, she decided to see if Mom needed help with dinner. It wasn't a service Cara usually offered, but anything was better than staring at a blank screen. Well, anything except spending time with Aelyx. She peeked down at the end of the hallway and noticed his door was closed. He was probably still unpacking. Quiet as a nun, she stepped into the hall and tiptoed to the kitchen.

"Mom, is dinner almost—" She stopped short, grasping the doorframe for balance.

While a box of leftover Domino's lay open on the counter, Mom stood wrapped in Dad's arms, her cheek buried against his chest while her shoulders hiccupped with the silent quakes that came from too much crying.

Likely because of Troy. They only saw him once every couple of years now, and it always took Mom a week to recover when he left again. Not that the selfish jackass noticed or cared.

Cara stepped closer and patted Mom's arm. "It's only eight months, and then he gets to come home for a visit. It'll go by fast."

Mom's voice sounded muffled when she said, "And then you'll both leave."

"That'll go by fast, too." Or at least Cara hoped so.

But there was no reasoning with Mom when she was like this. She mumbled something about wanting her family together under the same roof while Dad glanced at Cara and shook his head as if to say, *Not now.* He whispered in Mom's ear, and they swayed together to the drone of the microwave.

Nodding, Cara turned and walked into the living room, but she didn't expect to see Aelyx on the other side of the doorway. Her breath hitched, and she placed a shaky hand over her heart.

"Hello, *Cah*-ra." He raised his hands in a nonthreatening gesture like a robbery victim. "Sorry to startle you."

She noticed his clothes right away. Aelyx had finally stopped wearing his uniform, and she was shocked at how appealing he looked in jeans and a snug-fitting T-shirt. It almost compensated for his strangeness. Not quite, though.

"Don't go in there." She gently pushed him away from the kitchen, but his shoulder muscles tightened beneath her hand, and he jumped back as if her fingers were tipped with spikes. Whoa. What was his problem with physical contact? Did L'eihrs have too many nerve endings in their skin?

"Did I hurt you?" she asked.

As if to erase her touch, he rubbed a hand over the top of his shirt. "Of course not."

"It's just, my mom's upset." Cara tipped her head to the side and raised an eyebrow. "And when my dad tries to make her feel better, they usually end up kissing. A lot."

He hesitated, eyes darting to the kitchen, clearly repulsed by the idea. A moment later, he gestured toward the living room. "Should we play chess while your parents . . . finish dinner?"

Losing to him for the forty-seventh time sounded about as enjoyable as bathing in sweaty gym socks, but she couldn't think of a convincing excuse to get out of it. So she grabbed the chess game and set up the board on the coffee table, then knelt on the floor opposite Aelyx.

"You first." He pointed at the board. "Your parents seem unusually affectionate, even for humans."

Snorting a laugh, she moved a pawn two spaces forward. "Yeah. I hope you've got a strong stomach. It wasn't always like this. Believe it or not, they used to be normal. Before Mom got sick."

"Cancer, right?" He mirrored her move and she advanced another piece.

"Mmm-hmm. I guess it was a wake-up call. Dad was a hot mess. He spent all his time at the hospital with Mom and didn't eat or sleep. Then Mom lost her job at the bank, and the insurance company dropped her." Cara didn't mention this, but it was a miracle the fire department hadn't let Dad go, based on how much work he'd missed. Mom's cancer had set the family back, but it could've been a lot worse. "That's when I started waitressing."

Aelyx captured her first pawn and rolled it between his fingers. "That's terrible." His expressionless eyes didn't match his words, but at least he'd made an attempt to sound sympathetic.

"It was." She moved her knight within range of his bishop as a lure, but he didn't take the bait. "Especially when Troy left. Mom kept getting worse, and I don't think he could stand feeling helpless, so he joined the Marines and deployed right away."

"You were alone?"

"Sort of." She thought about Eric and Tori, wondering how long she could delay their first meeting with Aelyx. "My boyfriend checked up on me, but he was just a friend back then. We didn't start dating till Mom was better. And sometimes my friend Tori brought me dinner. But other than that, yeah, I guess I was alone."

Aelyx captured a third pawn and began stacking the pieces into a little tower. "I'm sorry to hear that."

"It's okay. On the bright side, I learned to pay bills, do laundry, cook for myself . . . well, kind of. I'm not a great cook." Sucktacular was more like it.

While she took his first pawn, she worked up the nerve to ask a question, something she'd been dying to know for years. The problem was how to phrase it in a way that didn't sound insulting. Clearing her throat, she leaned toward him and looked directly into his cold, steely eyes. "If I ask you something, will you tell me the truth?"

He hesitated, obviously caught off guard, and then nodded with exaggerated slowness like he knew this wouldn't be a casual, friendly sort of inquiry.

"The cure from the *asheem*—it's permanent, right? Like, it's not a trick that'll wear off one day, is it?"

With a quiet sigh, he relaxed his posture and flashed a quasi-smile. "No." He seemed so relieved that she wondered what kind of question he'd been expecting. "But if it were a trick, do you think I'd admit it?"

"Probably not." Still, she believed him for some reason. Aelyx didn't strike her as a very good liar. "Hope I didn't offend you."

"Not at all." He snatched her rook off the board and replaced it with his knight. "I would have been skeptical, too."

Well then, they had something in common.

They played in silence for several minutes, and then Aelyx made a careless move—he left his queen unprotected. For the first time, Cara felt hope that she might actually win. She paused to analyze the board, making sure it wasn't a trap, and then took his queen with her bishop. Sweet victory seemed so close that her pulse began to quicken and she felt tingly all over. Who needed drugs when winning felt this good?

"Sure you want to do that?" Aelyx asked. "I'll checkmate you in two moves."

She was pretty sure he was bluffing but scanned the board one more time just to be safe. Aelyx shrugged a shoulder and pushed his rook forward five spaces.

"So tell me about your family," she said while moving her next piece. "I'll bet your parents are better behaved than mine."

"Technically, they've been dead two thousand years. I was cloned from the archives."

Cara froze in place, her hand still curled around the bishop. "Cloned? As in a genetic copy of someone else?"

"Yes, that's typically how it works."

"But what about the genetics program?" L'eihrs were known for their meticulous, organized breeding. Why would they want to clone people who lived thousands of years ago when they'd achieved so many advances since then?

Aelyx's voice was guarded when he said, "Our geneticists terminated the program."

"Why?"

"Because we all started growing tentacles."

Her eyes opened wide. "Really?"

"No," he said, totally deadpan. "Not really."

Damn, she'd walked right into that one.

Smirking at her expression, Aelyx continued. "The program was deemed obsolete twenty years ago. It's as simple as that."

She wanted to ask why L'eihrs didn't procreate the natural way, but the idea of discussing sex with Aelyx skeeved her out. "Does that mean everyone younger than twenty is a clone?"

He nodded, considering his next move.

"So you don't have parents?" As soon as the words left her mouth, she cringed. What a stupid, insensitive thing to say! "I mean, you're adopted—not that you don't have parents."

He studied her for a few moments, the expression on his face unreadable. "All citizens of L'eihr are my family." His clipped tone told her the subject was closed, and to confirm it, he slammed his knight down like a gavel. "Checkmate."

Her victory tingles morphed into the sick weight of disappointment. Not only had she lost—again—but their conversation had taken a hard right turn into Awkwardville. One thing was certain: she'd never complain about her parents to Aelyx again. *Oh, boo-frickety-hoo, my mom and dad love each other too much.* He'd probably kill to have that "problem."

Uncertain of what to say, she slouched forward and cleared the board in silence.

A few minutes later, Dad leaned through the doorway and announced supper was ready. It was about time. She needed something to cover up the sour taste of defeat that lingered on her tongue.

They took their seats at the table, and Cara leaned over her plate to inhale the mingled scents of pepperoni and mozzarella—pure, greasy goodness from above. If anything could make her feel better, it was this. She leaned toward Aelyx and tried to lighten the mood.

"Prepare to have your taste buds rocked," she told him. "The ambassador said L'eihr food is really simple, so you're going to love this."

"What is it?"

"*Piiiii-zzzza*," she said reverently. "Otherwise known as culinary Nirvana."

He wrinkled his nose, casting a dubious glance at his slice.

"Trust me, it's amazing." She tapped a nail against the golden crust. "There's bread on the bottom, then a layer of tomato sauce—that's a vegetable, by the way—"

"Fruit," Mom corrected.

"Yeah, yeah. Then it's topped with cheese, which is made from cow's milk. But the best part is pepperoni sausage."

"And how is sausage made?" Aelyx asked.

Dad laughed dryly from across the table. "Ignorance is bliss in this case."

"Just try it," Cara prompted.

Aelyx gripped the slice with stiff fingers and held it away from his face for a few moments before lifting it to his mouth to pull free a tiny bite. He worked his jaw cautiously as he chewed, like the pizza might explode if he bit down too hard. Just when Cara expected his expression to transform in rapture, his eyes widened and began watering like he might get sick. Quick as a cobra strike, he snatched a napkin and pressed it to his lips while gagging and swallowing at the same time.

"Are you okay?" She shot a hand out to comfort him, then drew back, remembering how he'd reacted to her touch in the living room.

After swallowing hard a few times, he nodded.

"Wow, you really hate it." Which was putting it mildly. The way Aelyx glared at his plate told Cara he wanted to torture that pizza until it begged for death. "I'm so sorry. I had no idea." She pushed away from the table and offered, "I'll make you a sandwich."

"No!" He flashed his palm at her in desperation, napkin still clutched against the corner of his mouth. "Please, no more."

"You have to eat something."

"My supplements can sustain me for weeks."

"Pills?" Cara asked. "You can't live off pills."

"Injectables, actually, and I can. For a while, at least."

"Out of the question." Part of her job was to keep Aelyx comfortable and happy, and no exchange student of hers would resort to freebasing nutrients. "There has to be something you can handle, and I'm going to find it."

Aelyx pulled the napkin free long enough to warn, "Your 'culinary Nirvana' was bad enough going down, *Cah*-ra. I don't want to taste it again coming up, which is what will happen if you force anything else on me tonight."

"Oh. I didn't think about that."

Her cheeks heated as she realized pushing unfamiliar food on Aelyx was just as bad as not feeding him at all. The way his skin paled reminded her of the time Tori had double-dog-dared her to try raw oysters, which had looked exactly like mucus. Turned out they'd tasted like mucus, too. Cara had upchucked afterward, and the sight of those half-digested mollusks had spurred a pukefest that'd lasted the whole evening.

"You know what?" Cara said, sliding her plate aside. "I'm not hungry, either." It was time to take her hostess swagger to the next level. "Let's talk about something besides food. Tell me about your trip from L'eihr to Earth. How long did it take?"

For the next twenty minutes, Cara nodded intently, pretending to understand Aelyx's tutorial on traveling at light speed and using wormholes as intergalactic shortcuts. By the time he finished, she was no closer to grasping the exact science of "space chronology," as he called it, but at least his complexion had transformed from green to beige.

Mission accomplished.

CHAPTER FIVE

Aelyx awoke in a sweaty haze, the same way he'd begun each morning since his arrival on Earth. He pulled off his dampened T-shirt and used it to blot the perspiration from his forehead, wondering when his body would adjust to this unfamiliar climate. Probably just in time for his departure.

The bare taupe walls of his bedroom bathed in the gentle glow of the early morning sun reminded him of his quarters on L'eihr, exactly as his human hosts had intended. He indulged for a moment, closing his eyes and pretending he was there now. His longing for home made his chest ache and stole his breath. After eighteen years in the bustling Aegis, he couldn't even sleep properly without his roommates snoring and rustling in their bunks an arm's length away. Gods, he missed them.

Fortunately, three days had passed, so he could finally reconnect with Syrine and Eron. Even though he had no progress to report, his heart raced in anticipation of glimpsing their faces.

Aelyx pulled the com-sphere from beneath his pillow and whispered the passkey to unlock it. The brushed metal buzzed to life, tickling his palm as he spoke his friends' names and waited for their own spheres to summon them.

Eron's hologram was the first to appear on the bed-spread, his miniature fingers stretching toward Aelyx's throat in the standard greeting. Judging by the tile wall and shiny chrome fixtures in the background, he'd locked himself in the bathroom.

"Quiet," Eron said, stepping into the porcelain tub and pulling the shower curtain closed behind him. "My human's young cousin has taken a liking to me. I think he's listening at the door."

Syrine's image flickered to life. Shadows darkened the skin beneath her heavily lidded eyes, and her mouth sagged— obvious proof that the French boy hadn't given her much peace.

"Mother of L'eihr." She rubbed her face with one palm. "Kill me now."

Aelyx offered a sympathetic grin. "Remember what I suggested if he refuses to observe boundaries?" No living creature could tolerate a kick to the reproductive organs.

"I'll never earn his trust that way." Syrine shook her head. "What about your female? Is she as tolerable as I predicted?"

He considered a moment. Cara had made an obvious effort to be sociable in the past two days, filling their schedule with activities and conversation. He supposed talking with her was preferable to spending time alone.

"Yes," he finally decided. "Fairly tolerable."

"How about you?" she asked Eron.

"I can't complain. My family is quite welcoming. I rather like them, especially little Ming. He looks at me like I hand-carved the moon."

Syrine flashed an obscene gesture, not bothering to hide her jealousy. "When do you integrate with the others?"

"Next week."

"I start tomorrow," Aelyx added. He looked forward to his first day of school with all the enthusiasm of a man facing a lobotomy.

"I haven't been able to sneak away yet," Eron whispered. "Have you?"

Aelyx and Syrine both shook their heads. "We expected this," Aelyx said. "But our host families will relax once we settle into a routine. I'll try to plant my *sh'alear* in the next few days."

"So will I," Eron promised, "if the child will give me a moment's rest. I swear by the Mother he wants to play alien invaders all—" Three quick knocks sounded from Eron's bathroom door, followed by a child's high chirp. After muttering a good-natured curse, Eron shut down his sphere, disappearing from view.

"We'll have to do it soon." Syrine paused to yawn. "It'll take weeks to see results."

"Get some rest," Aelyx told Syrine. "This will be over before long." She nodded and her hologram vanished into the air like a wisp of smoke. With a sigh, he stuffed his comsphere into his top dresser drawer.

Raising his chin, he sniffed the air and recognized the stench of something humans called *bacon*. It was harsh, salty, and dripping with animal fat. He shuddered with disgust and grabbed his clothes. A cool shower would restore his body temperature, and if he hurried, he could claim the bathroom before Cara monopolized it for one of her hour-long grooming sessions.

He turned the doorknob as quietly as possible and stepped into the hall. He was within two paces of the bathroom when Cara rounded the corner and met him face-to-face. She sucked in a startled breath, clutching the front of her bathrobe. Her eyes widened, traveling slowly down the length of his exposed chest while a burgundy flush spread across her cheeks.

Fasha. What was he thinking leaving his room half dressed? Now he'd made the girl uncomfortable. He held the folded clothing high against his bare flesh, but that only seemed to make matters worse as her gaze darted to his abdomen and held there.

He glanced down, wondering what had caught her attention. "Ah." The answer came, and he smoothed two fingers over his lower stomach. "I don't have what you call a belly button."

"Oh, right." She cleared her throat and stared down at her slippered feet. "Because of the clone thing."

"No. Because we're all born from artificial wombs. Even the Elders."

"Really? So it doesn't matter how— Oh!" With a gasp, she pointed at his feet. "And your toes!"

He'd forgotten humans still had five toes, and Cara probably didn't realize hers would appear just as odd to him.

"You'll lose the smallest one in a couple thousand years," he said. "Maybe sooner, if you stop mating like animals and reproduce with purpose."

"What the—" When her eyes turned to slits, he knew he'd said something wrong. Perhaps *mating like animals* had sounded too harsh, even if it was true. She kicked off her slipper and pointed to her ivory foot. "I like my pinkie toe just the way it is, and I'd rather grow a second head than let the government tell me who to sleep with!"

"Of course." He spoke in low tones, the way he'd seen humans placate domesticated canines. It seemed to work, because when he added, "Please forgive my rudeness," she fingered her furry robe and gave a pardoning nod.

"I made breakfast," she said curtly. "It's just the two of us."

Aelyx didn't want breakfast, especially if bacon was involved, but he hated to anger Cara again so quickly. Besides, today marked the seventeenth anniversary of her birth, so he postponed his shower and prepared for the worst.

"Happy birthday," he told her while pulling on a clean T-shirt.

"How'd you know?" Turning, she glanced over her shoulder and led him toward the kitchen. A symphony of unfamiliar odors mingled with the bacon to assault his nose and turn his stomach before he reached the doorway.

"I requested a portfolio on your family several weeks ago." When they reached the kitchen, he stopped short. The surface of the oak table was barely visible beneath dozens of breakfast dishes: bacon, eggs, cold cereals, a scorched assortment of breads, and clumsily chopped chunks of fruit.

He stared at the smorgasbord in open-mouthed surprise. "This is a lot of food for two people. Where are your parents?"

"At mass. They never miss it. I'm more of a cafeteria Catholic—I pick and choose when to go, what to believe. Drives Mom crazy."

Ah, yes, their God, whom Christians referred to as Father. Interesting that several galaxies away, his people prayed to the Sacred Mother and her children, the gods of L'eihr.

Cara shrugged and nodded toward the table. "You can try a little of everything till you find something you like."

"You made all this for me?" Surely she didn't expect him to sample each foul dish. He might not survive it.

"Don't panic. You don't have to eat it all. But I can tell you don't like the food here, and it's my job to make sure you're comfortable and happy."

Comfort and happiness: two states of being he'd never achieve on Earth.

"You shouldn't have," he managed.

She smiled and stood a bit straighter. "It was no big deal."

But clearly it was a "big deal." She must have spent hours preparing the meal, and on her birthday, no less, so he forced a grin, took a plate, and spooned out a small serving of each food on the table.

Twenty minutes later, he simply couldn't take any more.

"I'm sorry." He tried to hold back a grimace. "I appreciate the effort."

"No biggie. But we have to find something you like before you lose weight."

"Actually, I've gained weight by default. L'eihr is slightly smaller than Earth, so my body is heavier on your planet."

"Really?" Her auburn brows rose toward her hairline. "How much heavier? Is it harder to move around?"

"No, the difference is negligible, only a few pounds. But don't worry about my nutrition. The supplements really do supply my body with most of my dietary needs."

Cara pursed her lips and tapped them with her index finger. "What do you eat for breakfast at home?"

"Usually *t'ahinni*. It's a basic grain and protein dish made with *larun*, my favorite flatbread." Aelyx sighed, remembering the nutty, slightly smoky flavor of warm flatbread, freshly baked and crisp from the oven. He could almost taste it.

"Does lar-uhn compare to anything here?"

"Well . . ." He glanced around the table. "It's difficult to explain, but maybe a cross between your wheat toast and that corn bread over there."

"Hmm." Cara's gaze shifted to the side and she fell silent a moment. A slow smile spread across her mouth. He wondered, a little nervously, what she was thinking.

"Okay." She pulled a folded piece of paper from her robe pocket and slapped it on the table. "I made a list of things we can do today." She pointed a red fingernail at each item as she spoke. "We can go hiking. I thought about swimming, but I don't think it'll be warm enough. Or—"

"Wait," he said. "Isn't it customary to celebrate your birthday with friends and family? Don't worry about keeping me entertained. Do what you like; I can stay here and read."

"Eric and Tori have away games." The corners of her mouth drooped into a scowl. "You'll meet them at the party tonight."

The prospect didn't seem to excite her. Before he had the chance to ask why, she pushed her chair away from the table and tossed the list into the recycling bin. "Let's just take a walk. I'll go get dressed."

Aelyx moved into a patch of shade and gazed at the silvery undersides of the leafy canopy shielding him from the sun. A light wind caressed his skin, offering a temporary reprieve from the oppressive heat. He pulled back his dampened hair and fastened it behind his neck.

"We should've gone swimming." Cara used a hand to fan her cheeks. The breeze shifted a branch from above, allowing the sunlight to touch her hair. The metallic strands seemed to ignite, glistening like a flame, and he glanced away. It was too much color, a sensory overload.

"Is this what you'd call an Indian summer?" He squinted at the vivid green grass. No matter where he trained his gaze, he couldn't escape Earth's vibrancy.

"No, because we haven't had the first freeze yet. But this time of year's always wonky. Next week we'll probably be wearing sweaters." She sat on a thick patch of grass and leaned against an oak tree. "Tell me about the weather on L'eihr. You have seasons, right?" Before he had a chance to respond, she said, "That's a stupid question. Your planet revolves around a sun, so of course you have seasons."

"It's not a stupid question." He sat down in the cool grass opposite Cara. "Temperatures on L'eihr would fluctuate with the planet's rotation if we didn't manipulate the climate."

She leaned in his direction, eyes wide. "You control the weather?"

"Of course. That shouldn't surprise you."

"Well, what do I know about L'eihr? There's not much information out there."

"That's the point of the exchange. And humans are fairly close to achieving climate control. I'd say within the next two hundred years."

"Or sooner, if your scientists decide to share the secret." She smiled and plucked a blade of grass from the ground.

"Perhaps. You never know." Everything had a price. The cancer cure had served its purpose, and he was certain humans would do just about anything for more of L'eihr's technology. In fact, his Elders were counting on it, the shortsighted fools.

"So tell me about your weather. I'll bet it's sunny and warm every day." She swept the blade of grass absently back and forth across the side of her calf, and for an inexplicable reason, Aelyx's breath caught at the top of his lungs.

"Not quite." Glancing at Cara again, he trained his eyes on hers, away from her body. "We maintain a mild temperature, around seventy degrees, but we don't manipulate cloud cover. The main purpose behind our weather control is to prevent destructive storms. Our oceans are larger than yours, so there's greater potential for damage."

"How much larger?" she asked. "Is there less land mass?"

"About forty percent less." L'eihr boasted only two continents, and most of the land remained uninhabited. "But we control urban sprawl, so it's not an issue."

"I wish you'd brought pictures. I've got no idea what to expect when it's my turn to come visit you. What's your planet look like?"

He leaned back and closed his eyes, smiling as he summoned his favorite images. "Well, for starters, our sky isn't blue, it's gray. The shade changes as the day goes on."

"Shut up!"

"Pardon?" Had he said something wrong again?

"It's just an expression," she said with a wave. "You surprised me, is all."

"Oh. Anyhow, the gases in our atmosphere are different from Earth's, which affects the color of our sky. We have three moons, but the third is so small it can only be seen at certain times of the month. And photosynthesis doesn't exist on L'eihr. Our plants derive nutrients from the air, like your Spanish moss, so there's no green. Everything is gray and brown. Imagine how Earth's northern hemisphere looks in the winter. It bears a slight resemblance to L'eihr."

"Dreary and lifeless?"

Laughter bubbled up from deep within his belly. Gods, her rudeness astounded him sometimes. "I suppose it would seem that way to you." He glanced at Cara, whose cheeks flushed even more deeply than before. It was hard to believe her red face belonged to the same body as those long, fair legs.

"Sorry, I guess beauty's subjective, huh?" She grinned sheepishly.

"Well, I guess we both . . ." He trailed off, trying to remember the human expression he'd heard on the television yesterday. "Eat our feet sometimes."

Judging by the puzzled expression on Cara's face, he didn't get it quite right. After a few seconds of reflection, she burst out laughing. "Oh! You mean 'put your foot in your mouth.'"

"That's it." What an odd description for verbally embarrassing oneself. "Where did that expression originate, anyway?"

"No idea, but come on." Still laughing, she gestured toward the house. "We'll Google it."

They both rolled to their feet. "It's too hot out here any . . ."

Aelyx trailed off as Cara accidentally brushed the inside crook of his arm, a touch that was barely a touch at all, and stunned him into silence. If the sunlight in her hair overloaded his senses, it was nothing compared to her casual contact. This time the feeling wasn't altogether unpleasant, but he chafed one hand over the spot as he strode behind her to the back door.

Four hours and one Google search later, the doorbell rang and he introduced himself to Cara's prospective mate, Eric. When they shook hands, Eric's grip was tighter than necessary, his thin lips pressing together in a scowl.

Aelyx studied the human Cara found so enchanting. Eric

stood tall for a male of his age, with the sturdy build of an athlete. He seemed intelligent but not on her level. And like Cara, his eyes were blue, but less vivid and much less friendly. Aside from his physical attractiveness, what could have drawn her to a boy like this?

"So." Eric slid an arm around Cara's waist and pulled her tightly against him. "How do you like Earth so far?"

Aelyx smirked and wished he could answer truthfully. *I loathe your pathetic planet, and I don't like you any more than you like me.* "This is my first experience with interplanetary travel, so it's a shock, but so far I'm enjoying myself."

"That's great," Eric said, clearly lying. "I'll see you around school this week. We have a lot of classes together." In other words, *I'll be watching you.*

Suddenly, the front door swung open and a dark, petite female entered, dropping her handbag onto the wood floor. Without offering a greeting or even closing the door behind her, she strode to Cara's side and locked eyes with Aelyx. Her narrowed gaze swept over him for several awkward seconds before she finally said, "So you're him."

"This is Tori." Cara cleared her throat. "My really rude best friend."

Now Aelyx understood Cara's reluctance to celebrate her birthday—all her companions despised him. An unexpected swell of compassion stretched his rib cage as he watched her face blanch. His peers would undoubtedly object in a similar way if he'd brought her to one of their social gatherings, and like Cara, he'd feel torn between his duty to her and loyalty to his friends.

Maybe he could help. "It's a pleasure to meet you, Tori. Cara's told me—"

"Save it." She rolled her dark eyes. "We're cool, but I've got a lot of questions for you."

"Who wants cake?" Cara asked in an unnaturally high-pitched voice. "Red velvet!"

"Which reminds me." Aelyx played along, reaching into his back pocket. "I have a present for you." He handed her the silvery pouch with the neck-lace inside. "Happy birthday."

She tilted her head while her mouth formed a perfect oval. "You didn't have to do this." Her smile sent an unexpected ripple of pleasure through his belly, definitely worth the thirteen credits he'd spent.

When she opened the drawstring and lifted the black cord from inside, her eyes widened. "Is this from L'eihr?"

"Yes, it's called an *ahib*. A common gem in the same 'dreary and lifeless' colors of my home." He flashed a teasing grin, darting a glance at Eric, whose jaw clenched so tightly he'd probably just cracked several molars.

"There's nothing dreary about this." She held the cord to the light, watching the dangling stone cast gray and beige sparkles across the back of her hand. "It's amazing. I love it." She unfastened the clasp and started to put it on.

"Yowza." Tori bounced back and punched Eric in the shoulder. "What'd *you* get her?"

Eric grabbed Cara's wrist, halting her movement. "She can't keep that."

"What?" As Cara froze in place, the dangling pendant swung to and fro, throwing tan prisms against the wall. She jerked from his grip. "I sure as hell can!"

"Dude, what's your problem?" he asked Aelyx. "You don't buy jewelry for someone else's girlfriend!"

Aelyx shrugged and glanced from person to person for guidance. Finding none, he asked Cara, "Do you like it?"

"Yes," she declared, almost defiantly.

"Then I don't see the problem," he told Eric. "The fact that you purchased an inferior gift hardly seems like any failing on my part. It's common knowledge that shiny rocks are preferred among human females."

That rendered everyone speechless. While Aelyx stood there wondering if he'd put his foot in his mouth again, Eric cupped his palm over Cara's lower back and guided her to the opposite side of the small living room.

Eric glared at him in silence as if waiting for something.

"Would you like some privacy?" Aelyx asked.

"Nah," Eric drawled. "Why don't you come closer so you can watch?"

"I'd prefer not to." He glanced at Cara.

"It's fine. Just give us a minute, okay?"

"Of course." Aelyx joined Tori in studying the black-framed photos peppering the wall, but faces and landscapes blurred into obscurity as his attention remained focused on the argument brewing six feet away.

"I said I'd give it a try," Eric whispered harshly, "and I did. I'm not putting up with him for the rest of the year. He's gotta go."

"Well, you didn't try very hard."

"He's. Gotta. Go."

"Maybe you should go." Was it his imagination, or did Cara's voice tremble on the last word?

A soft rustling of fabric sounded from behind, and when Aelyx turned, it was just in time to watch Cara disappear down the hallway with Eric towing her by the shirtsleeve in a rough manner. Before he thought better of it, he started after them, but Tori brought him to his senses with a quick tug of his own T-shirt.

"Don't." She chewed the end of her braid and stood on tiptoe, darting a glance around his shoulder toward Cara's bedroom. "Maybe she'll really do it this time."

"Do what?"

"Dump the *pendejo*."

Aelyx hadn't studied Spanish as thoroughly as English, so he didn't understand her last word. However, the sentiment behind it was clear. The narrowed glares Tori had fired at Eric showed she loathed the insufferable dolt even more than he did.

Several minutes of silence passed between them before Eric tore into the hallway and continued straight out the front door, slamming it behind him without a backward glance.

When Cara padded silently into the living room blotting her eyes with a tissue, Tori bolted across the room to embrace her. Arms encircled waists in a tangle of contrasting dark and ivory limbs as the girls clung to each other. Aelyx felt he should contribute in some way, but he knew nothing about the emotional distress of human females.

"I can bring him back," he said. "I'm not sure why you partnered with a male like that, but I can find a way to tolerate him if it's what you want."

"No," she said while scrubbing away a tear. "Let him go." Cara seemed to recover quickly. She made her way into the kitchen, where she devoured two slices of cake. There were no more tears. If anything, her laughter seemed a bit too loud. But when she returned to the living room to fasten her necklace, her fingers shook, and she couldn't manage the task.

"Can I help?" he offered.

She gave him the neck-lace and turned to gather her thick red waves. Aelyx approached her bare neck with caution, though he couldn't discern why. Something about the warmth from her body and the citrusy scent of her shampoo unnerved him, and he accidentally snagged a lock of her hair three times before fastening the clasp. Careful to avoid further contact, he moved back into his own safe space and told her, "All done."

She spun around and touched her chest to straighten the neck-lace, then pulled the crumpled tissue across her nose, giving him a small smile. "Thanks. It really is beautiful."

Aelyx averted his eyes. A knot lodged deep in his belly when he considered what his plans would do to Cara. Judging by the set of Tori's stiff, folded arms and her avoidance of his gaze, Cara would lose her closest friend next. But what could he do? The fate of one human paled in comparison to the fate of an entire planet, especially one as extraordinary as L'eihr.

"It's only a common pebble," he said, more harshly than he'd intended. "But I'm glad you like it."

Then he left her with a flicker of confusion behind her eyes as he returned to his room for the evening.

CHAPTER SIX

MONDAY, OCTOBER 22
Take Me to Your Cheerleader.

Today, Aelyx has reached an important human milestone:
his first day of school. And my mom stepped in like a boss,
commemorating the occasion with a dozen embarrassing photos
of our guest. Which I am TOTALLY posting here, because I'm a
good friend like that.

So here we are, armed with backpacks and lunch boxes, ready to
embark on the perilous journey through high school. (Actually,
the not-so-perilous journey through the private, gated woods
leading to high school.) But I know Aelyx will never forget this.
It's going to be a great day!

Posted by Cara Sweeney 7:02 a.m.

What a crock—this was going to be a craptacular day.

But nobody would ever know it, because Cara lived by the
first rule of debate: never let 'em see you sweat. She also lived

by the first rule of getting over your asshole ex-boyfriend: never let 'em know it hurts.

She cranked up the stereo until her teeth vibrated in time with each screaming guitar riff, then tipped her head back and squeezed a few eyedrops beneath her lids to hide the evidence of her heartbreak. A little dab of skin cream smoothed the puffiness around her eyes, and after a heavy layer of makeup, she looked human again. No, not just human. Polished. Unaffected. She added a third coat of mascara—but not the waterproof kind. If she cried today, her face would look like a mudslide, and that was a pretty frickin' good incentive to fight back tears.

Finally, she checked her reflection in the mirror—glossy auburn hair curling gently past her shoulders, nearly flawless skin, snug black top, gray plaid miniskirt, and the pièce de résistance: black leather riding boots. Eric's eyes had nearly bugged out of his head the last time she'd worn this out-fit. She wanted that jerkwad to know exactly what he was missing. After fastening the necklace Aelyx had given her—another silent *screw you* to Eric—she grabbed her backpack and ran outside.

Aelyx faced the woods and stretched his lithe body, raising his arms so high they lifted his T-shirt and gave her a peek at the strong planes of his lower back. Cara nibbled her thumb-nail, remembering how she'd caught him shirtless on his way to the shower yesterday. He'd tried covering his magnificent chest with a pair of folded pants, but that'd drawn her atten-tion to his flat, bronzed belly, somehow even hotter without its "button."

Too bad his attitude didn't match his looks, but then again, if it did, he wouldn't be a L'eihr.

Deciding she would give him a fresh start today, she skipped down the steps, joining him at the head of the wooded path. "Ready to roll?"

When he whirled around, a spark flashed behind those silvery eyes, like flint striking steel, but it died in an instant, snuffed out by his inner zombie. He lowered his head and peered at her. "Are you all right?"

"It's your first day of school on an alien planet, and you're asking if *I'm* all right?"

"Losing a mate can be traumatic for hu—"

"Whoa." She raised one brow and an index finger to match. "He was my boyfriend, not my mate. We never . . . mated."

"All the same, it's understandable—"

"Look, it's sweet of you to ask." Hitching her book bag over one shoulder, she nodded toward the path, and they began walking at an easy stroll. "Yeah, I'm bummed, but it had to happen sooner or later. I'll miss the old Eric, but that's not the guy I broke up with last night. Does that make sense?"

Aelyx shrugged. "To be honest, I don't know what qualities you ever saw in him. I can tell why he chose you, but—"

"Oh, yeah?" Cara's spirits lifted as she sensed a compliment coming on. "Why do you think he chose me?"

"It's obvious." He swept a hand to indicate her loose curls. "Your long, shiny hair, healthy skin, and bright eyes show that you're well-nourished."

"Uh, thank you?"

"I'm not finished."

"Go on, then."

"You're clearly intelligent." Then he felt the need to add, "For a human."

"Gee. That's so sweet."

"But Eric was probably most attracted to your waist-to-hip ratio." For a split second, Aelyx resembled a human boy as he leaned back and peered at her caboose. "Hips of that width are likely to pass live offspring without complications."

Cara nearly swallowed her own tongue. She didn't have big hips, did she? More importantly, had she really expected a genuine compliment from a L'eihr?

"Let's not talk about me anymore," she said, resolving to lay off the carbs, starting tomorrow. Wait, tomorrow was pasta night. She'd lay off the carbs Wednesday. "Let's talk about you."

"What would you like to know?"

"How can you be so calm? I'm secondhand nervous for you. I couldn't even eat breakfast." And that tragically neglected breakfast had been Mom's throat-choking, triple chocolate chip pancakes—manna from heaven, proof that God loved her and wanted her to be happy.

To hell with cutting carbs. Life was too short for that nonsense.

"It's predictable for humans to fear the unfamiliar," he said. "I'm not human."

"Oh, please. You're not just a little scared?"

"I'm fine." He favored her with a glance, empty and cold. So he wouldn't admit he was nervous. Typical guy. He had more in common with humans than he realized.

The distant sound of shoes slapping against the dirt path caught Cara's attention, and she glanced over her shoulder to see Tori slow to a jog, waving one arm as if hailing a cab. This was unusual. Tori never walked to school—it cut ten whole minutes from her sleep schedule.

"Hey." A light breeze tossed Cara's hair into her face, and she tucked the locks behind her ears. While she paused, Aelyx continued walking, picking up his pace to either give them some space or to avoid Tori. Maybe a little of both. "Did you get towed again?"

"Nope. I'm your personal jock-blocker, baby." Tori reached into her jeans pocket and handed over a half-eaten Snickers bar. "Happy Douche Liberation Day." Then, nodding at the chocolate offering, she added, "I started celebrating without you."

"Just finish it." Cara's stomach was already full. Of butter-flies on meth. "Do I want to know what a jock-blocker does?"

Linking arms, they scrambled to catch up with Aelyx, who had already put the distance of half a soccer field between them. "I'm here to make sure you don't let that *carajo* sweet-talk you into getting back together."

"Wait, what?" *Would* Eric want her back?

"Don't even think it," Tori warned.

"Easy for you to say. You'd take Jared Lee back in a hot second."

"Assuming we were together—which we're not—and assuming he was a raging asshole—which he's not—I'd dump his carcass and move on." Tori tugged her brows low and leaned to the side, scanning Cara's outfit before clicking her tongue in disapproval. "Speaking of which, what's with the date bait?"

"What's with the third degree?"

"Here's a question for ya." Tori pointed her Snickers at the honey-brown ponytail hanging between Aelyx's shoulders. "Does the Outer Space Creep probe you in your sleep?"

"Shh!" Cara couldn't help giggling, but she gave Tori's arm a hard bump, sending her candy bar sailing into the underbrush. "I hope Aelyx doesn't have friends like you, or my turn on L'eihr is gonna suck."

Something in her words must've upset Tori, because she grabbed her braid and used the end like a paintbrush against her lips, a nervous habit she'd picked up in the seventh grade. With one corner of her mouth puckering into a frown, Tori watched Aelyx silently for a few seconds before announcing, "I wanna talk to the A-Licker."

"Fine, but play nice or take your ball and go home." Cara flashed an *I'm not screwing around* look. "This is hard for him, and it's my responsibility to—"

"Yeah." Tori rolled her eyes. "I bet he cries himself to sleep every night. Right before he sticks alien trackers up your butt." After tugging free, she jogged to catch Aelyx, and Cara sprinted along, preparing to tackle her best friend and clap both hands over her mouth if she got too saucy.

"Hey." Tori panted after catching up with him. "I need to know something."

Aelyx slowed his pace, heaving a sigh that contradicted his next words. "Good morning, Tori."

She ignored the greeting and got right to it. "How am I supposed to let my girl here," she said, nodding at Cara, "jet off to some planet we know nothing about? How do we know it's safe?"

"Safe?" Aelyx repeated with a smirk. "Last year, your tri-county reported sixty-seven murders, one thousand cases of assault, and over two hundred rapes. There hasn't been a violent crime on L'eihr in ten generations, and you're concerned about her safety *there* as opposed to here?"

"You're joking, right?" Cara scanned his face for any hint of teasing but found none. "That's impossible."

"I assure you it's not." He raised one haughty brow.

"How'd you do it, then?" Tori circled one finger around her temple in the universal gesture for crazy. "Alien miiiiiind control?"

Aelyx parted his lips to reply but hesitated a moment as if deliberating how much to reveal. "Let's just say it's due to evolution and breeding."

"Uhn-uh." Cara shook her head. "Not buying it. Violence is part of human nature. You can't just—"

"But you keep forgetting, *Cah*-ra." Aelyx stopped, turning to face her and narrowing his cold chrome eyes. "I'm not human."

A prickling of goose bumps raised the hairs on her forearms and along the back of her neck. Aelyx began walking again as if nothing had happened.

"W-well," she stammered, "I'll see for myself." And strangely enough, she wasn't afraid. She couldn't wait to see how his people lived—and whether he'd embellished their greatness.

"I'm not reassured." Tori kicked aside a twig and openly glared at Aelyx. "You talk, but you don't really say anything."

"Tor-*ri*!" Cara chided.

"No, don't *Tor-ri* me! Why won't he answer the question?"

"I did. You simply didn't like the response." Aelyx started to say something more, but his head snapped up as if on high alert. Soon Cara understood why. A distant clamor filled the tranquil woods, growing louder as they approached the end of the trail.

Cara froze and stared blankly across the street at the Midtown High parking lot, where a swarm of demonstrators chanted and pumped their handmade signs into the air: HONK IF YOU SUPPORT HALO! It was like watching an anthill under attack—bodies scurrying in every direction without any leadership. Random car horns blared as morning traffic crawled past, and two uniformed police officers shouted at the protesters while shaking their heads and pointing to the clogged street.

She turned to Aelyx, who maintained a calm expression but clutched his notebook in a white-knuckled kung-fu grip.

"Not a very warm welcome," Tori said.

Cara drew Aelyx's attention to the vacant lot adjacent to the school. "At least you've got groupies."

A much smaller crowd of around fifty men and women held signs that read ALL ARE WELCOME! and WE L'OVE YOU, BROTHER! The supporters swayed from side to side and sang with wild flower-powered abandon, but HALO's disorganized chants drowned them out.

"Come on, we'll be late." She reached out to pat Aelyx's shoulder, but then pulled back. She kept forgetting he didn't like to be touched. "Just ignore the freak show."

Tori led the way, waving to the crowd like Miss America and taking their focus off Aelyx, if only for a few moments.

After a tight nod, Aelyx lifted his chin, and they walked briskly toward the school's entrance. Cara kept her eyes forward, pulse racing and in total awe of Tori's brass *cojones*. She heard a few isolated shouts from the protesters, mostly "Don't trust him!" and "You're a traitor, Sweeney!" When feedback from the police bullhorn pierced the air, she cupped her hands over her ears. It was still easy to hear the officer tell the crowd to disperse, that they couldn't legally protest on school property.

When she made it into the building, she heaved a sigh, rolling her shoulders to release the tension. Tori promised to find them at lunch and then rushed off to her first class.

"You okay?" Cara whispered to Aelyx, standing on tiptoe to reach his ear.

"Of course. Why wouldn't I be?" But his stiff posture and clenched jaw gave him away.

"It's normal to feel a little shaken up, you know."

"For *your* kind, perhaps."

"Oh, gimme a break; you don't have to pretend that noth—"

"Sacred Mother," he said, skidding to a halt in the middle of the crowded hallway.

"What?" She followed his gaze to a group of girls squealing

and bouncing toward them. She glanced back at Aelyx's gaping mouth and laughed. It was about time something cracked his stoic veneer. "Aw, look. You have a fan club."

Five freshmen danced around one another, hopping up and down as if their heels were made of springs. Each L'eihr wannabe, or L'annabe, as people called them, wore her poorly dyed brown hair in a low ponytail and dressed in a beige top over gray pants. Cara shook her head at their orange-streaked faces. Friends didn't let friends abuse self-tanning spray.

The L'annabes giggled and pushed the group spokesperson forward. "What's your name?"

"Aelyx." He took a step back, and Cara pressed her lips together to stifle another laugh.

"Aaaaaa-licksssss," the girl repeated above a chorus of screams. "Omigosh, a real L'eihr right here in Midtown, I can't believe it, welcome to Earth, we think you're so amazing. Can you tell us about your planet, and space travel, and are there other aliens with special powers, and maybe you can hang out with us after school today at my house, and can you really read minds?"

He blinked a few times and shook his head. "No, I can't read minds."

As perversely entertaining as it was to watch him squirm, it was time to be a good little hostess and intervene.

"Stop." Cara stepped in front of Aelyx, holding her palm toward the group. "Don't get too close."

The girls glanced at one another, stupefied.

"This is really important. Did you guys color your hair in the last three months?"

"Maybe," the group's leader conceded. "Why?"

"Oh, no!" Cara pushed Aelyx farther back and shielded him with her body. "Don't you know the chemicals in hair dye are toxic to L'eihrs?"

"What? I never heard that." The fan girl bit her bottom lip and wrinkled her forehead.

"Hmm, maybe it's not common knowledge yet. They can handle most of our chemicals, but not dye. If you get too close, he'll have some kind of freaky respiratory reaction." She leaned forward, trying to look stern. "You don't want to be responsible for killing our exchange student, do you?"

Shaking her head, the girl backed away and rejoined her friends. "Of course not. I'm so sorry!"

Thank God for gullible freshmen.

Aelyx glanced at her with a flicker of amusement in his eyes and then turned to the girls with a generous smile. "It's all right. You didn't mean any harm."

The L'annabes nodded vigorously and said good-bye, giving him a wide berth to navigate the hallway as Aelyx and Cara walked to class.

"Spanish military leader El Cid's real name was . . ." Mr. Manuel's voice trailed off into a question. "Anyone?"

Cara knew the answer, but she didn't feel like participating. Instead, she rested her chin in her palm and gazed out the window at the parking lot. The last remaining protesters had left hours ago, and things were calm. Well, calmer, anyway. Things inside were pretty dull, too. Apparently, Eric had changed his entire schedule to avoid her, which was both good and bad. While she didn't have to look at his smug jerkface, that meant he couldn't see how much she pretended not to care about his smug jerkface.

"Yes, Aelyx?"

The sound of his name brought her to attention.

"Rodrigo Diaz de Vivar," Aelyx said. "He's known as the national hero of Spain—a warlord, like so many of Earth's idols."

"Impressive." Mr. Manuel crossed his arms. "You don't even have a textbook yet."

"I studied your history while I was still on L'eihr." And with a smirk that had become his own personal signature, he added, "It didn't take long." He returned his attention to the copy of *Advanced Binuclear Theories* the science teacher had lent him. Maybe he should read *How to Avoid Acting Like a Pretentious Ass* instead.

"Why is it," Mr. Manual began loudly, "that an alien knows more about your planet's history than you do?" He pointed an accusing finger at the class and raised his voice. "The average grade on the last test was forty-six. Forty-six! Does anyone even care?" While he ranted, several students turned in their seats and narrowed their eyes at Aelyx. Someone whispered, "Nice going, L'asswipe."

When the bell rang, Cara decided to let the classroom clear out before heading to lunch. Why risk getting jumped if she didn't have to? She nudged Aelyx's desk, and he glanced up from his book.

"You're not doing any favors for yourself," she said. "You'll never make any friends with those little digs."

"Digs?"

"Oh, you didn't study *that* before you left L'eihr?" she asked. "A dig's an insult. You know, like announcing your gift is superior to Eric's, or telling me my hips are huge, or saying it didn't take long to study our planet's pathetic history."

"Well, in all honesty, it only took three—"

"Look. You're some kind of genius. We get it. Whoop-de-do." She twirled one finger in the air. "But honesty is overrated. We've got a long year ahead of us, and the whole student body will hate you if you don't lay off."

"That won't happen. You're forgetting"—he closed his book and pointed it at her—"that I have a fan club."

"You made a joke!" Progress! "I'll make a human out of you yet."

"That's an ugly threat, *Cah*-ra."

"Very funny. The halls should be empty now. Let's go eat."

As Cara had feared, the garlicky reek of sloppy joes was the only thing greeting them inside the cafeteria. A slow hush permeated the room, spreading from person to person like a rolling fog of silence. Ignoring the freeze-out, she scanned the crowded space for Tori, who caught her eye and waved from an open table all the way in the back.

While crossing the lunchroom, Cara noticed a few eyes widen when Aelyx passed. Brandi Greene, the dance team captain and one of Cara's ex-friends, spat orange Gatorade onto her tray and sat there staring with her mouth hanging open like a 7-Eleven. Cara laughed inwardly, but she'd had the same reaction the first time she'd met Aelyx. The boy was chocolate for the eyes. But for every dreamy sigh, there were ten openly hostile glares.

Pseudo tuberculosis broke out at Eric's table of jocks as they passed. *Cough, cough.* "L'asshole!" *Cough, cough.* Cara kept her eyes trained forward and studied Eric from her peripheral vision. He seemed too focused on his hatred of Aelyx to notice her. She knew that shouldn't bother her, but it did. Why couldn't he suffer, just a little bit?

One thing was clear: lines had been drawn. She'd run track, played soccer, debated with and tutored many of the people who now leered at her like she had an STD. Eric had been right. She'd just set the world record for Fastest Freefalling Social Status.

"Sorry about this," Aelyx whispered from behind her, tickling the back of her neck with his warm breath.

"I should be the one apologizing." She sat beside Tori, facing the wall, while Aelyx took the seat across the table. "I bet your friends back home will treat me better than this."

Aelyx's shoulders slumped a couple inches while he took a sudden interest in the chipped tabletop. Maybe she'd been too hard on him back in the classroom.

"Yeah." Tori shook her apple at him. "You made quite an impression. I took a lotta crap for you today."

"Whatever," Cara said. "You don't take crap from anyone." She pulled a Ziploc bag from her mini-cooler and handed it to Aelyx. "Here's a slice of provolone and some of those wheat crackers you liked."

Aelyx perked up. Poor thing, he had to be starving. "Thank you, *Cah*-ra."

"And by the way," Tori mumbled with one cheek stuffed full. "You're sayin' it wrong. It's *Care*-ah."

"Don't listen to her." Cara slid a bottle of unsweetened iced tea across the table. "I like the way you say my name."

"Oh, barf."

Just as Cara geared up to elbow Tori in the ribs, Brandi Greene slipped into the seat beside Aelyx. She tucked a blond curl behind her ear and rested one hand on his shoulder. She didn't even notice when he flinched away. "You," she said, "are literally the most gorgeous thing I've ever seen."

Cara fanned a notebook to disperse the scent of cheap floral perfume, a noxious odor she hadn't endured since Brandi joined the dance team and nixed their friendship freshman year, upgrading to a new set of friends. "Well, that's one way to introduce yourself."

"Hmm?" Brandi asked, still gazing at Aelyx.

"Aelyx, this is Brandi, who, like the rest of Midtown High, lacks social skills."

"Hey, I heard you and Eric are splitsville." Brandi blinked her clumpy, tarantula-leg lashes, feigning innocence. "You don't care if I ask him out, right?"

A ten-ton bomb filled with sulfuric acid exploded inside Cara's stomach. Of course Brandi would want to move in on Eric—he'd become popular practically overnight after joining the lacrosse team, and the little social climber hadn't made it to the top of the ladder yet.

Cara dug a fingernail into her palm and smiled sweetly. "Go for it. I'm sure he's looking for an easy rebound."

The insult slipped off Brandi's shoulders like she was

coated in social lube. "He's got that worked out. The whole team's taking Marcus to The Ho Depot for his birthday on Friday."

Cara's jaw slackened while her heart sank into her lap. The Ho Depot—a nickname for the skeevy strip joint that just went up outside city limits. Ever since word got out that the girls sold "services" in the back room, the place had become an XXX version of Chuck E. Cheese's for barely legal birthday boys.

A lump formed in Cara's throat, and all the swallowing in the world wouldn't push it down. Eric was tired of waiting for her to put out, so he was going to get it somewhere else. She shouldn't care—it was none of her business anymore. So why did she want to vomit and cry at the same time?

Tori's hand gripped hers beneath the table while Brandi turned back to Aelyx. "Everyone says you're crazy smart. Are all the L'eihrs like you?"

Aelyx moved a few inches in the opposite direction and said, "We've been bred for advanced cognitive skills, among other things."

"Bred? Literally? Like your babies are planned and stuff?"

"Not anymore, but pairings were carefully planned for the last ten thousand years."

Brandi licked her top lip. "Are you all this hot?"

Instead of responding, Aelyx shoved four crackers into his mouth. It seemed like a good time to change the subject.

"Hey," Cara said to Aelyx, "can you make it home by yourself later? I've got to go grocery shopping."

He nodded, mouth still full.

Brandi clapped her hands together while bouncing in her seat. "I know where you live—I'll walk him home!"

Aelyx shook his head and waved her off, which Brandi took as an enthusiastic *yes!*

"It's no problem," Brandi insisted, even as Aelyx held one palm forward.

"Better watch out," Tori said. "No one's gonna want his sloppy seconds."

"For you, I'll risk it." Brandi gave Aelyx's ponytail a playful tug. "See you later, gorgeous."

Cara hid a smile, even as guilt tugged at her stomach. She probably shouldn't abandon Aelyx, but he'd appreciate it later. She had something special planned that just might salvage this terrible day for both of them.

"They're every bit as loathsome as I'd anticipated," Aelyx whispered, unclasping his hair as Syrine's miniature hologram nodded in agreement from atop his chest of drawers. "Completely worthless as a species." Especially the sex-obsessed female who'd followed him home after school. When she wasn't fondling his chest, she'd badgered him with questions about L'eihr weaponry. As if he'd discuss such things with her. It had taken nearly an hour to make her leave.

"Praise the Sacred Mother I'm educated privately in the home." Syrine's host attended an all-male school, the only perceivable benefit of living with him. "I only socialize with the youth during—"

A metallic clatter from the other end of the house rang out.

"What was that?" Syrine asked.

"My human. I think she's preparing a meal." His vacant stomach rumbled in protest, no longer satisfied with nutritional supplements and the occasional cracker. He'd give anything for a bowlful of *l'ina*. But no matter what Cara was cooking, he knew he couldn't eat it.

Cara. One thought of her brought an invisible weight crashing down upon his back. She didn't know it, but she'd never see a penny of her scholarship. She'd never set foot on his planet and, worse yet, her peers would hold her accountable for his actions.

Suddenly, an earsplitting series of shrill beeps rang out from the circular white device affixed to his ceiling—the smoke detector.

"We'll talk later," he mouthed before shutting down his com-sphere and stuffing it inside the top drawer. Pressing his palms over both ears, he ran through the hallway and toward the kitchen, where tentacles of foul-smelling smoke curled from the open doorway.

He darted inside and found Cara—her face streaked with sandy-colored muck—waving a broom to clear the hazy air.

"Are you all right?" he yelled over the alarm.

With a vigorous nod, she threw open the back door while he opened both windows to allow a cross breeze to ventilate the room. Eventually the air cleared, and sweet silence resumed.

The lingering stench burned his nostrils. "What happened?"

Cara pushed a greasy lock of hair away from her face and pointed to a plate of charred flatbread by the stove. "I made *larun* for you."

Larun? At first he didn't understand, but after scanning the countertop and identifying several varieties of grains and oils, it all made sense. Yesterday he'd said his favorite breakfast tasted like a cross between wheat toast and corn bread, and she must have tried replicating it for him. Great gods. She'd done all this for *him*—right after she'd lost her mate and half her peers.

She cleared her throat and glanced down at her pink-polished toes. "I know you're hungry. I wanted you to have a taste of home."

Something warm swelled inside his lungs until Aelyx feared he might take flight right there in the cluttered kitchen. If there was a name for this emotion, he didn't know it, but he wished he could summon the feeling at will.

Nodding at the plate, he extended his palm for a sample.

"But it's burned," she objected, "and totally vile."

"I'll judge for myself."

Hesitantly, she broke a piece in half and offered it to him.

She was right. *Vile* didn't begin to describe what he'd just put into his mouth. The texture reminded him of chewing soil, gritty and thick, and his taste buds could discern nothing but carbon. When he bit down too hard, a sharp edge of grain sliced his gums and he winced, holding one hand against his cheek.

"Oh, Cara, it's so . . . good."

"Yeah?" Her eyes sparkled with amusement. "Then you probably can't stop at one." She held out the plate. "Go on. Finish the rest."

"No, that's okay," he said, holding up his hands. "I don't want to be greedy."

"I insist."

"Really, I should save some for your parents." It was getting harder to keep a straight face. "They'll love it."

"That's true." She tilted her head in mock contemplation. "I know! I'll make a fresh batch every single day until you leave. Then I'll bring the recipe to L'eihr . . . so you can eat it *forever!*"

He couldn't hold it in another second. Laughter erupted from his chest, so he had to clap a hand over his mouth to keep from spraying the floor with the half-chewed bits he hadn't managed to swallow. Cara joined in, tossing the plate into the sink before collapsing against the counter in a wild fit of giggles. She kept pointing at him and trying to speak but couldn't manage to get out the words. After a dozen tries, she snorted and said, "I wish you could've seen your face when you put that bite in your mouth. It looked like you were chewing glass."

"It felt that way, too," he barely managed.

She threw an oven mitt at his head, which he dodged by ducking behind the kitchen island. He doubled over in another bout of uncontrollable laughter. Soon his muscles ached, and he pressed both hands over his abdomen to still the pain.

"Either you'll starve," she said, "or I'll kill you with my cooking. Either way, you're screwed."

"Completely *fashed*," he agreed.

"I can see the headline now," Cara choked out. "Midwest girl slays exchange student with flatbread, ends alliance negotiations."

"L'eihrs retaliate by forcing humans to eat Sweeney's creation," he added, "ending all life on Earth."

She burst into another fit of giggles at that before gasping, "What a terrible way to go."

"The worst," he agreed. But at least he'd be in good company.

CHAPTER SEVEN

C ara lifted one leg from the water and watched tendrils of steam swirl up from her reddened skin. The bath was one of the few places she could be alone now. Colonel Rutter wasn't kidding when he'd called the LEAP a job—she'd worked overtime making Aelyx feel at home these last couple of weeks.

With her laptop perched securely on the tub's porcelain ledge, she tapped the screen with a dry index finger and pulled up her blog. Her eyes automatically darted to the followers— a whopping 120,467—before skimming the comments from that morning's post.

Subscribe [Archive] [Recent Entries] [About Me]

Alienated

MAY THE SOURCE BE WITH YOU

WEDNESDAY, NOVEMBER 5
The good, the bad, and the useless: it's Trivial Wednesday.

A special thanks to Vegan_Mandy for suggesting the following theme days. I'm sending you an extra gooey, totally vegan, home-baked virtual cookie. Can you taste the love? Anyhoo, here's what my esteemed followers can expect when they visit my page:

• Culture Clash Mondays: tidbits on how L'eihr customs differ from ours.
• Trivial Wednesdays: a sampling of pointless L'eihr trivia.
• FAQ Fridays: I'll try to answer the most commonly e-mailed question that week. Notice I said *try*. Despite what my best friend might've told you, I don't know everything.

So, without any further ado, here is a fact that will benefit you in no way whatsoever: L'eihrs do not have facial hair. No, really, I'm serious. Geneticists bred the stubble right out of their cheeks about three thousand years ago after deciding it didn't have the same benefits as body hair. Um, scientists of Earth, can you get to work on that? I don't have a mustache—not that there's any shame in that—but I'd love a break from shaving my legs. Please and thank you.

Posted by Cara Sweeney 7:07 a.m.

28 comments

<u>Amanda</u> said . . .
You're so lucky! I wish our school had gotten him.

<u>Olca</u> said . . .
Beam me up, Hottie!

<u>Ashley</u> said . . .
He doesn't shave? That's so cool. No wonder his skin looks sooo soft. ::swoon::

<u>Keith</u> said . . .
STFU, Ashley. I have three classes with the smug jerk, and it sucks.

Marcus said . . .
True dat, Keith. Dude's a total douche-guzzler. HALO meeting tomorrow @3pm.

Humanist said . . .
Who gives a damn about beards? What about weapons? Ask him that, you stupid BITCH.

Tori said . . .
@Humanist: Post that under your real name, coño. So I can come put my foot up your ass.

From there, it got *really* ugly. Who knew an innocent bit of trivia could incite so much drama? She changed her blog settings to suspend comments pending her approval and closed the computer screen.

After plunking a grapefruit-scented bath fizzy into the water, she sank down and tried to decide what to wear when she got out of the tub. Tonight the camera crew would film the first round of interviews—nationally televised interviews—so millions of people could kick back in their recliners, crack open a cold Bud, and laugh at the idiotic things she'd undoubtedly say. At least it wasn't live, so the film editor could delete any incidents of projectile vomiting.

A knock on the bathroom door interrupted her solitude. "Hey, Pepper," shouted her dad. "Tori's here."

"Okay. Tell her to hang out in my room."

"Already did." The *thud* of Dad's heavy work boots retreated toward the kitchen.

Cara dried off and wrapped herself in a fluffy blue bathrobe before padding to her bedroom, but Tori was nowhere to be found. Just as Cara started toward the kitchen, she heard a *thump* against the wall coming from Aelyx's bedroom. A quick peek down the hall showed his door ajar—odd, considering he'd never left it open before.

On tiptoe, she peered into his room and found Tori rifling through the dresser drawers, hunched over piles of clothing like a bargain bin shopper on half-price day.

"What the hell!" Cara glanced over her shoulder. Luckily, Aelyx wasn't within earshot . . . yet. "Get outta there!"

Without bothering to turn around, Tori held up something that looked like a metal golf ball. "What's this?"

"I don't know, but put it back!" Clearly she'd have to haul Tori away by force before Aelyx discovered them snooping through his things. She rushed forward, snatching the ball from Tori's palm. It felt lighter than she'd expected, and she couldn't help taking a closer look. The brushed, steely surface felt cool to the touch, not conducting her body heat the way metal should. She gave it a light shake, but nothing rattled inside. "Where'd you get this?"

"Top drawer, under his boxers."

"Seriously? You went through his underwear? You're deranged." Cara opened the drawer and shoved the sphere beneath Aelyx's . . . personal articles. Then, after hastily refolding the shirts Tori had rumpled, she grabbed her friend's hand and hauled her out of Aelyx's room, closing the door behind them.

She had barely enough time to shove Tori across the threshold to her bedroom when Aelyx rounded the corner and strode into the hallway. He stopped short when he noticed her, eyes wide as if she'd caught him doing something wrong instead of the other way around. Cara hoped she didn't look as guilty as she felt.

"Hey," she said casually, pulling her robe's belt a little tighter. "What's up?"

"Nothing." He folded both arms across his chest, which drew her attention to his dirt-streaked sweater. "Just getting some fresh air before the interview."

"Again?"

This made three days in a row he'd gone out for "fresh air" and returned looking like he'd face-planted into the lawn. A scrap of brown peeking out from beneath his shoe revealed an oak leaf he'd tracked inside. Maybe he'd been secretly meeting a girl in the woods. A surge of completely irrational jealousy swelled beneath her rib cage before she reminded herself Aelyx didn't have any girlfriends. That she knew of . . .

He studied the floor when he mumbled, "Yes. The colors don't bother me as much now."

"Right. The colors." He was the world's worst liar. But as much as she wanted to press him for more information, it wasn't any of her business. It's not like she wanted Aelyx for herself, so who cared if he was hooking up on the sly? Cara shoved down her irritation, suddenly feeling extra naked beneath her thin blue bathrobe. "Hope you had a nice walk," she chirped, scooting inside her room.

Once safely behind her own closed door, she refocused, gearing up to tear her best friend a new one. But then Tori turned around, and all those reprimands slid down the back of Cara's throat. Redness rimmed Tori's bloodshot eyes, half concealed by puffy lids. She'd been crying. Only Tori didn't cry. Ever.

"What happened?" Cara crouched down to study her friend's face as if the answer might be written across her forehead, but Tori backed away with a casual shrug.

"I got impeached."

"From student council? They can't do that!"

Tori dragged her feet to the bulletin board and began fidgeting with Cara's awards and ribbons, rubbing the satiny fabric between her fingers. "They can call a vote if I miss three meetings."

"But you didn't—"

"They switched the last two meeting times and didn't tell me." Grabbing her braid, Tori swept the frayed ends back and forth across her lips. "Then I skipped one last month when you asked me to come over. Y'know, that day you dropped the bomb about—"

"The exchange." The real reason for this little *coup d'état.* Damn it, Tori shouldn't have to suffer for sitting next to Aelyx in the lunchroom. "They can't do this. We'll call Mr. Ferguson."

"Forget it. I don't wanna be there if they all hate me. What's the point?" Tori belly flopped onto Cara's polka-dot bedspread. She rolled onto her side and traced an embroidered black circle with her fingernail. "I heard Jared Lee was gonna ask me to prom before all this, but he changed his mind. And my team's givin' me hell, too."

"Well then Jared's a tool. And soccer season's almost over. Just hang in—"

"Don't you think it's time to send the A-Licker somewhere else?" Pushing upright, Tori hugged her knees. "I mean, I know you want the money and all, and it's not like I care what anyone thinks . . ."

"You sure about that?" Of all the people caving to pressure lately, she hadn't expected this from Tori, the firecracker who used her middle finger like a calling card. Cara walked to the closet and fingered through her meager wardrobe without seeing a thing, blinded by disappointment. "Look, I committed to this, but it's not *all* about the money." Which was true. She'd kind of grown to like Aelyx, or at least to tolerate him. "Give him a break; he hasn't done anything wrong."

"Hasn't done anything wrong that you know of. Come on, Care. He's a total creeper and he's up to something. Besides, I don't like the way he looks at you."

"Huh?" Cara spun around with a belt in one hand and a skirt in the other. "How does he look at me?"

Tori raised a black brow. Then she made a circle with one hand and stuck her index finger through it in an X-rated puppet show. "Like he wants to dock his ship inside your spaceport."

"You've cracked. I think he's seeing someone."

"Not a chance." Tori shook her head. "Don't tell me you haven't noticed. He watches you like a stalker—everyone's talking about it."

Great. That meant the rumor mill would proclaim her pregnant with alien twins by next week.

"It's just because I'm his only friend."

Tori narrowed one eye. "You're defending him? Maybe he's drugging you. You pour your own drinks, right?"

"Don't be ridic." She held up two tops—one pink, one green. "Which one?"

Tori pointed to the sleeveless pink V-neck and scooted off the bed. "Let me know if you wanna ditch him some night. It sucks that you're single now and I still don't get to see you."

Thinking about the breakup still sent pinpricks skittering across Cara's body, but they stung a little less each time. This one barely hurt. "You can see me whenever you want."

"Alone. As in, without *him* lurking around the corner." Tori dug through Cara's makeup bag and inspected a couple shades of lip gloss. "I'm takin' this," she declared, holding up Gritty in Pink.

"But you don't even wear makeup."

"I do now." She nabbed a tube of mascara, too. "Maybe it's time for a change."

"What's that supposed to mean?"

But she just waved the pilfered cosmetics and left without another word. Cara stared at her zippered bag in confusion, then shook her head and dressed for the interview.

Cara leaned back and enjoyed the soft tickle of a foundation brush while the makeup artist worked her magic. The stylist ran his fingers through her hair, and the sensation brought goose bumps to the surface of her skin. She sighed and listened to the flurry of activity coming from the living room. The air was thick with excitement and hairspray.

"Ugh," said a sharp female voice. "That sofa's hideous. We'll need a solid neutral drape. Have three chairs brought in from the kitchen and cover them in the same fabric." The sound of clicking heels approached. "Tell the lighting crew to set up in the corner and crank up the air conditioner. This tiny dump will get hot fast."

Dump? Cara's eyelids flew open, and she scanned the room for the source of the voice. Sure, the sofa was hideous and her house was small, but it wasn't a dump.

"Seat Bill Sweeney on the outside," said a woman with chin-length, platinum blond hair. She wore a C-emblazoned pink suit and had an annoyingly exquisite face. "He's a total dud."

"Hey!" Cara protested from her seat at the kitchen table. Strangers couldn't insult her dad. Only *she* could insult her dad.

"And the mother—head shots only," the woman said to her assistant. "She's a chunky little thing."

"I'm right here, you know." Was this lady missing her internal filter? Maybe she thought beautiful people didn't need one. Feeling a full-scale firestorm brewing, Cara held her breath and counted to twenty.

"I see that." The woman picked a piece of lint from her shoulder. "Sharon Taylor. I'm interviewing you tonight."

Pursing her red lips, she made a "shoo fly" motion with one hand. "That's what you're wearing?"

"Yeah."

Sharon shook her head. "Auburn hair and pallid skin—the worst combination. Don't wear pink, sweetie. Redheads can't pull it off." Then she clucked her tongue in sympathy.

Screw twenty. Cara counted to a hundred. In Spanish.

"How about a nice kelly green top?"

"Don't have one," Cara lied, deciding to wear pink tonight out of spite.

"Oh, well." Sharon waved her fingers at the makeup artist. "Play up her eyes. She's got great eyes, at least."

When Aelyx entered the kitchen, Sharon froze in place. "Sweet baby Jesus! You're going to make my job so easy." She sashayed over to him and cocked her head to the side, appraising his face. "Very nice features," she said, talking to herself. "Strong jaw, full mouth. Excellent wardrobe choice. You're breathtaking."

No kidding. Aelyx had cleaned up nicely since Cara had seen him in the hall. The fitted ivory shirt he'd chosen highlighted his bronze skin while clinging to the contours of his chest, and he'd smoothed his long brown hair to perfection and secured it at the nape of his neck with a leather cord.

But then Sharon scowled. "What's with the face? You look like a cyborg."

Aelyx walked to the sink and filled a glass with water. "I don't know what you mean."

"You know, a robot. You've got no sentiment, no spark.

Can you try to look a little animated?" She gripped her waist with one well-manicured hand.

Aelyx stared at her while Cara's cheeks burned hot enough to fry eggs.

"If you're so advanced, then you can manage to look alive. That empty stare's disturbing, and it's not going to help you fit—"

"Stop!" Cara stood from her chair. Unfortunately, the stylist still held a lock of her hair, sending her head snapping back. She rubbed her throbbing scalp and glared at Sharon. "There's nothing wrong with his face."

Sharon froze for a few seconds and brought her hands together in prayer. "I just had an epiphany. Cut the parents. They're boring." She pointed back and forth between Aelyx and Cara. "*This* is what people want to see." Smiling and nodding like a dashboard bobblehead, she added, "Friendship, maybe more?"

Cara rolled her eyes. "Friendship, period." She stalked into the living room and plopped down on the sofa. Her stylist followed and shellacked one last section of hair in place while Cara tried to steady her pounding heart.

Aelyx sat beside her, so close his sleeve brushed her bare arm. When he leaned in to whisper in her ear, a spicy-sweet scent filled her nostrils.

"And you say our breeding program is a bad idea," he teased, nodding toward the kitchen. "I give you irrefutable evidence to the contrary."

"What? You mean Sharon?" Was he wearing cologne, or

did all L'eihrs smell this good? And how had she never noticed before?

"On my planet, she'd never be allowed to reproduce, and no one would clone her. She's awful."

Cara couldn't argue with that. "I think she left her soul at home. Maybe it didn't match her shoes."

Sharon took the seat opposite the sofa, and her crew filed into place. With the living room at full occupancy, Mom and Dad came in from the porch and settled in the kitchen doorway to watch, giving Cara encouraging waves.

"Don't be nervous," Sharon said. "We're not live, so mistakes are no big. Ready?"

She turned to the camera and flashed her flawless white veneers. "Good evening, America. I'm here with Cara Sweeney, host to a very special exchange student . . . from planet L'eihr!"

Sharon pointed a golden pen at the sofa. "Cara, tell us about your role in the program."

"Well." Cara paused to clear her throat, even though it didn't need clearing. "I take Aelyx everywhere I go and help him understand how we live. He shadows me in school—we even share a locker." She covertly wiped her sweaty palms on the cotton slipcover.

"How do the other students feel about that?"

"Um, there were a lot of stares the first day. But it's been almost two weeks now, and things are mostly back to normal." It was the Mount Everest of lies. Protests continued each morning, usually ending in fistfights, and students openly recruited new members for HALO right there in the hallway as she and Aelyx passed. They wore little gold pins in the shape of angel wings, but their whispered insults were anything but saintly.

Sharon crossed her legs. "Aelyx, how were you chosen for this program and what did you do to prepare?"

"I have a special talent for learning languages, so The Way selected me to represent our people." He spoke fluidly—no hint of anxiety—and for the first time, Cara envied his ability to shut off his emotions.

"The Way?" Sharon asked.

"Our wisest leaders. They make all decisions on L'eihr."

"I must say, your English is impeccable," she said. "No trace of an accent. How long did it take you to learn?"

"One week."

"Excuse me?" Sharon leaned forward, cupping one ear, while Cara questioned her own hearing. Maybe a week didn't mean the same thing on L'eihr. "You learned English in a week, as in seven days?"

"It took one week to master English," he said. "As languages go, yours is rather uncomplicated. I spent my remaining time studying Earth's history, particularly reoccurring themes of warfare. We take academics seriously on L'eihr, unlike Midtown's students, who seem content to learn as little as possible."

Cara discreetly kicked him in the ankle while smiling for the camera.

"Ow— Well," Aelyx corrected, "only some of them. Others are quite dedicated."

Sharon froze with the golden pen wedged between her

lips. "Uh . . . what was your first impression of our planet?"

While Aelyx leaned back on the sofa, tilting his head in contemplation, Cara braced herself for a tsunami of complaints. She didn't expect to hear him say, "Amazement. The colors of my home are neutral and muted, so Earth's vibrancy was a shock. To be honest, sometimes the beauty is overwhelming. It's a shame you're allowing industry to destroy it." He folded his hands in his lap. "And I was impressed by the hospitality of my host family. They've amazed me, especially *Cah*-ra."

"How so?"

"I'm not sure she'd want me to share the most recent example." He glanced at her, eyes bright with amusement.

"Oh, no." He meant The Great Barley Debacle. She couldn't believe he'd brought it up. On national television! Cara laughed nervously as her cheeks went up in flames.

"Now I'm intrigued," Sharon said.

"I've had trouble finding food I can consume here. *Cah*-ra keeps trying to re-create my favorite L'eihr flatbread from ingredients on Earth to stop me from going hungry." He laughed and shook his head. "It's such a kind gesture."

Cara tried to pull herself together. "I'm going to find something you like or die trying. You can get me back by making disgusting fake Pop-Tarts when it's my turn on L'eihr."

Sharon smiled knowingly at the camera before turning back to Cara and Aelyx. "That's a beautiful necklace," Sharon said. "Very unusual."

"Thanks. Aelyx gave it to me for my birthday."

"Oh, really?" Sharon's voice dripped with implication. "Give us a look."

With a little reluctance, Cara lifted the silk cord so the cameraman could zoom in on the *ahib*. She hoped Sharon didn't try to spin this into something romantic.

Sharon quirked an eyebrow. "So he gives you jewelry, and you spend hours baking for him? Sounds like you're getting along really well. That's what I call interplanetary relations!"

Holy God, why did she have to take it *there*? The woman really was missing a soul.

The interview continued until Sharon said she had enough material to edit into a thirty-minute show. Cara felt a cold weight in her stomach when she thought about the national airing on Friday. The exchange program's goal was to make people trust Aelyx, but she doubted anyone with a serious prejudice against L'eihrs would like what they heard. In fact, it would only feed their paranoia.

Later that night, Cara hovered over her laptop to perform some damage control.

Sex sells, she typed. *And a certain journalist wants you to think I'm letting Aelyx stun me with his laser, if you know what I mean. Don't buy it—we're just friends. And speaking of Aelyx, let's cut him some slack. Try to put yourself in his four-toed shoes and—*

A clatter from outside startled her, jerking her fingers away from the keys and drawing her attention to the back wall. This sound was different from the customary raccoon assault on their garbage cans—muffled and farther away.

She turned off her bedroom light and tiptoed to the

window, where she pushed aside the curtain and peered into the darkness.

The moon's dim glow illuminated the backyard, but nothing seemed out of place. She swept her gaze across the shorn grass; past the old, rusted swing set; and into the trees, finding nothing out of the ordinary. Just as she was turning away, something moved in her periphery, and she spun back into place in time to see the shed door swing open.

Cara's heart pounded. Someone was in the shed . . . where Dad kept the chain saw and a variety of other mass-murderous tools. Her overactive imagination conjured pictures of a hockey-masked lunatic kicking in the back door, armed with a cushion-gripped awl. Pressing her nose to the glass, she squinted at the intruder's long ponytail and his broad shoulders as he closed the door and refastened the latch. She released a loud sigh of relief, fogging the windowpane in the process. It was only Aelyx.

But relief soon mingled with concern. Why was he in the shed, all alone at midnight? If Cara focused hard, she could barely make out the shape of a small box in his left hand. He glanced over both shoulders, as if he sensed her watching, but before she could drop the curtain, he jogged toward the woods and disappeared into the blackness.

What the hell? Cara stood frozen, her head tipped in confusion. So if Aelyx wasn't meeting a girl for frisky-time in the woods, what was he doing out there? She ran down a mental list of what could be inside the box he'd taken from the shed. Birdseed, insecticide, nails, grass seed, fertilizer, screws. What would he want with any of that?

Was Tori right? Could Aelyx have an ulterior motive on Earth? Cara felt silly even considering the possibility, but that didn't stop her from chewing on her thumbnail and staring out the window for the next hour, where she fell asleep waiting for him to return.

Chapter Eight

"Hey, Dad," Cara called into the kitchen before peeking inside. If her parents were getting jiggy against the fridge, she wanted to give them time to unlock their lips before she walked in on something that couldn't be unseen. "You in there?"

"Yup." He was all alone, leaning against the counter and elbow-deep in a bag of Doritos.

"Where's Mom?"

He muttered around a mouthful of chips, "The grocery."

A man of few words, her dad. But those were the words she'd wanted to hear. Cara whipped out her cell phone and sent Mom a text. *Can u make roast tonite?*

Seconds later, Mom replied, *U hate roast,* which was absolutely true.

For A, Cara clarified, *not me.* She still hadn't found a meal Aelyx liked, but she was getting closer with each attempt. The key was flavor—his taste buds couldn't tolerate as much as hers. Unsalted crackers, air-popped popcorn, dry toast: these were the foods he tolerated best, so she needed to think bland. And when it came to bland, not even Introductory Statistics could compete with Mom's roast.

Will do.

Cara sent a quick *Thanks!* and pocketed her phone. She noticed Dad's work duffel discarded by the back door. "Is your medic stuff in there?" she asked.

He nodded.

"Can I borrow your stethoscope?"

Another nod.

"We're studying auscultation in health class," she lied.

He swept a hand toward his duffel and quirked a *go ahead* brow.

"I just want to listen to my valves."

He scrutinized her above the Doritos bag. "Really."

Before he had a chance to change his mind, she rifled through his supplies and grabbed the scope.

"I'll bring it back in a few minutes," she called over one shoulder as she retreated to her bedroom.

Once there, she locked the door and knelt at the wall that separated her from Aelyx. Then she tucked the stethoscope tips inside her ears, pressed the chest piece to the wall, and shamelessly tried to eavesdrop on the speakerphone conversation taking place in the next room.

She heard three muffled voices—Aelyx's, another male, one female—and in keeping with her rotten luck, they were all speaking L'eihr. Or at least she thought so. The stethoscope didn't amplify as much sound as she'd hoped. The voices sounded young, though, and they spoke with more inflection than the droning ambassador from the gala. So she assumed these were the other exchange students, the short, friendly-looking guy they sent to China and the girl who ended up in France. After a couple minutes, Cara still had no clue what they were saying, but their tone didn't sound secretive. The girl was obviously bitching about something, and the boys seemed oblivious as they laughed and carried on their own side discussion. In other words, they were normal teenagers.

Cara didn't know whether to feel relieved or frustrated.

She'd spent every minute of the last several days watching Aelyx for strange behavior. Well, strang*er* behavior. But nothing had changed. He still rearranged the plates in the dishwasher so they lined up in meticulous order, and he still turned up his nose at doughnuts and Froot Loops. If anything, his attitude had improved. She'd suggested that he observe other teens for social cues, and he'd done the job in spades. Yesterday after spending the afternoon with the track team, Aelyx had smacked her on the back and yelled, "Good hustle!" after she'd jogged up the front porch steps.

What he hadn't done was sneak out to the woods again, which made her wonder if she'd overreacted. For all she knew, he could've been rummaging in the shed for the same reason she snooped through medicine cabinets when she used other people's bathrooms—pure curiosity. Maybe his trips into the woods really were innocent strolls. *Or maybe he's gathering information out there,* her inner nutcase whispered, *to identify human weaknesses.*

No, it didn't make sense. Humans had plenty of weaknesses; that was no secret. Following all those political blogs had made her paranoid. And a jerk. While Aelyx was in there making time for his friends, she was huddled on the floor taking the plaster's heartbeat. She should be with Tori, who'd just lost her spot on the soccer team. Enough of this douchebaggery.

Cara tossed the stethoscope onto her bed and dialed Tori's cell. When it went to voice mail, she tried her landline and got the same result. Weird. Maybe the team had reconsidered. Cara was about to send a text when the garage door sounded from the other end of the house, and she headed to the kitchen to help bring in the groceries. If she couldn't reach Tori, at least she could lend a hand in fixing supper for her only other friend in the world.

A couple hours later, when the kitchen was thick with the scents of potatoes and carrots, Cara dished up a plate and made her way to Aelyx's bedroom in hopes of enticing him to the dinner table. Since he couldn't stand the smell of their food any more than the taste, he hadn't joined them for many meals.

With mad waitressing skills, she balanced the plate in the crook of one arm while knocking on his door. After he shouted, "Come in," she peeked inside and found him stretched out on the bed reading *Thermal Physics*. He'd unclasped his long brown hair so it spilled around his face like a satiny veil. Truth be told, he looked hotter than the stoneware burning through the arm of her sweater.

"Thermal physics, huh?" she asked. "I breezed through

that last night in the bath, right after Advanced Biotech."

He shot a cold glare over the top of his book. Ouch. His mood sure had shifted since his lighthearted phone call that afternoon. "What's that?" he asked, nodding at the plate.

"This, my alien friend, is pot roast." She made a show of inhaling the steam wafting up from the dish, even though she didn't like it. "I know I've said it before, but I think this is the one."

"Mmm-hmm," he said skeptically. "Just like chicken noodle soup. Honestly, *Cah*-ra, I'm not—"

"Just come to the table and try it." She backed into the hall and beckoned for him to follow. "It's only meat and vegetables. No seasonings. Mom didn't even salt it." To further convince him, she added, "If you don't like this, I promise I won't make you try anything else."

"Really?"

"No, not really." Like *that* was going to happen. "But I'll leave you alone for a whole week."

He gave a resigned sigh and closed his book, then sat up and refastened his hair at the base of his neck. "Fine."

"That's the spirit."

Mom and Dad were ready and waiting when they joined them at the table. Mom had even busted out the Merlot, something she only reserved for celebrations or really lousy days. Judging by her silence while making supper, though, Cara guessed it was the latter.

"Giving it another shot, eh?" Dad asked Aelyx.

Aelyx settled in his chair. "*Cah*-ra can be very persuasive."

"Damn straight," she added, sliding in beside him.

Mom shot her a warning glare while pouring Aelyx a glass of iced tea. "I picked up some tofu while I was out—that's tasteless protein—so I'll fry some if you don't like the roast. Just let me know, hon."

Cara gestured at Mom's wineglass. "What happened?"

"Nothing."

"You look like you want to rip someone's face off."

Mom opened her mouth to speak but stopped and glanced at Aelyx just long enough for Cara to understand it had something to do with him. "It's been a long day."

Then Dad blurted, "Her numbnuts volunteer coordinator tried giving her the ax because—"

"Bill!" Mom whispered, not so discreetly kicking Dad under the table. "We have a guest!"

"How can the library fire a volunteer?" Cara asked. "They don't even pay you."

"I didn't get fired. The head librarian stepped in." Mom flapped one hand in the air in a message to let the subject drop. "Now let's eat." Then she dug right in before insisting they say grace. Wow, she must really be pissed.

Following Mom's lead, Cara speared a forkful of beef and signaled for Aelyx to do the same. He stabbed a small bite.

Cara lifted her fork in a toast. "Ready?"

"No."

"C'mon," she said. "We'll do it together on the count of three. One . . . two . . ."

Before she finished, Aelyx wrinkled his nose and shoved the bite into his mouth. He clenched his eyes shut and chewed while Cara braced herself to admit failure once again.

But then something phenomenal happened.

Mom's pot roast brought Aelyx to life. He glanced at Cara and smiled—a real smile that reached all the way to his eyes and lit them up like a supernova. Even his body responded, relaxing against his chair the way hot wax conforms to the curves of a votive holder.

"You like it?" Cara asked.

"It tastes just like *l'ina!*"

"Please tell me that's not someone's name."

He laughed in a warm, low chortle that made her want to say something funny so she could hear it again. "It's my favorite dish from home."

"That's a relief." She wiped imaginary sweat off her forehead. "Hey, maybe my brother's eating *l'ina* right now and comparing it to Mom's roast."

"Possibly." Wasting no time, he shoveled in another bite and spoke with one cheek full. "It's a staple on my planet."

"If Troy ever decides to e-mail, we'll ask him," Dad grumbled.

"I heard transmissions from L'eihr are delayed because of signal problems on the main transport," Aelyx said. "They should've given Troy a com-sphere—that's our newest technology. But e-mail is antiquated, so it's only as reliable as the ships conveying the electronic data. Think of it as an intergalactic Pony Express. All it takes is one ship to disrupt the chain. That's probably why you haven't heard from him."

That wasn't why, but Cara didn't want to further upset Mom, so she kept quiet.

She couldn't quit watching Aelyx for the rest of the meal.

It made her smile to see him eat with so much enthusiasm. He'd never looked more human.

After they'd finished, she asked Mom to make pot roast every night that week. Bland or not, Cara would gladly suck it up if it meant seeing Aelyx glow that brightly each night.

Because, you know, it was her job. Nothing more.

Chapter Nine

The next morning, Cara pulled on her blue knitted cap, grabbed her backpack, and headed outside to wait for Aelyx.

A gust of wind from the east sent hundreds of burnt orange leaves bursting from their branches and whirling through the air. She lingered on the back steps to watch the sheets of foliage flutter to the ground like sunset-colored rain. Aelyx was right—sometimes her planet's beauty overwhelmed the senses.

Soon he joined her.

"Ready?" His breath condensed, lingering in the air, and he immediately wedged both hands deep inside his coat pockets and shivered. He didn't seem to tolerate the cold any better than the heat—probably spoiled by L'eihr's controlled climate.

They traveled the wooded path a while, chatting over the

crunch of fallen leaves, until a girl's shrill voice called out from behind.

"Wait!" Brandi Greene jogged toward them, blond curls bouncing around her deceptively angelic face.

"Hey," Cara said, making an effort to play nice. She should have known better.

"Hi, Aelyx." Brandi ignored Cara's greeting and flashed her pearly whites at Aelyx. "I watched your interview three times! Literally!"

Aelyx didn't give Brandi the slightest glance. Cara knew because she watched his face. Not that she cared or anything.

"Wonderful." With an eye roll, he turned and marched onward.

"Tell me more about babies on your planet." Brandi cozied up to Aelyx, and he veered away, colliding with Cara's hip. Since he needed a wider berth, she fell back on the narrow dirt path and walked behind them.

"You said there's no unauthorized breeding," Brandi said without missing a beat. "So you have to have, like, a license or something? 'Cause I think it's messed up that I have to get a permit to have a yard sale, but any idiot can have a baby."

"No, there aren't licenses for reproduction. You need to remember that our societies are different. On Earth you procreate for love—"

Cara scoffed. Midtown High boasted a dozen teen pregnancies each year, and most of those babies were conceived via sloppy drunken hookup, not love. "Or because we're wasted."

Aelyx quickened his pace and heaved a sigh. "As I was saying, before we abandoned the breeding program, scientists tracked each citizen's genetic material to determine which pairings would yield the most favorable result."

"No way!" Brandi's voice sounded delightfully scandalized. "So they literally told people who to have sex with? What if the guy was ugly or something?"

"Sexual intercourse wasn't required."

"What?" Cara and Brandi said in unison.

"Genetic material from the male and female was combined artificially." Aelyx turned and glanced at Cara. "This shouldn't be surprising. You've had this technology on Earth for many years." He faced forward and continued walking. "Then the embryo was developed in an artificial womb, same as the clones. Our females haven't been burdened with pregnancy in over nine hundred years."

That last part sounded pretty cool. Mom loved to tell labor and delivery horror stories, and sometimes Cara wondered if it was Mom's passive-aggressive way of trying to scare her into abstinence. Which was totally working. To have a baby without any pain sounded perfect. Women on L'eihr were lucky—well, if you didn't count the weird clone thing and the total lack of individuality.

"Whoa, that's wild. But you still have sex, right?" When Brandi tried to lean against Aelyx's shoulder, he darted away.

"Some of our citizens choose to engage in physical intimacy, but it's rare. That kind of connection sometimes causes complications."

That sparked Cara's interest. "Wait a minute," she said. "How's it possible for a whole planet full of people to avoid sex?"

"Most take advantage of the hormone regulators."

"Hormone regulators?" Brandi asked. "Like birth control pills?"

"No. The regulators suppress reproductive urges."

Holy frick, that was creepy as hell.

"Do you take the hormone pills?" Brandi's voice oozed seduction.

"Not anymore. They're weaning my generation off of them." Aelyx turned around and gave Cara a look that said, *A little help, please?*

Jogging forward, Cara wedged herself between the two. "You feeling better, Aelyx?" When he shot her a questioning look, she added, "I heard you sneezing like crazy last night."

"Oh, right." He played along, sniffling and dragging a hand beneath his nose. "I don't know what's wrong. Allergies, I guess."

"Remember not to touch anything," Cara said darkly. "Especially after what happened *last time*."

He gave a slow nod. "I'd almost forgotten about that."

Brandi studied him for a moment before taking the bait. "What happened?"

"When we were at the exchange party in Manhattan," Cara said, "Aelyx shook this guy's hand. No big deal, right? But half an hour later, the guy's palm turned red and splotchy with little white blisters all over it."

"And?" Brandi asked.

Cara shook her head seriously. "It took forever to figure it out. Aelyx had sneezed into his hands and didn't get a chance to wash up before he met that poor guy. Apparently, L'eihr saliva's super acidic. Who knew?"

"Well," he said, "you have to remember I'm not human. My body, including the pH level of my fluids, differs from yours."

Nice one.

Cara cupped a hand over her mouth and whispered in Brandi's ear, "Can you imagine kissing him?" She shuddered in mock disgust. "Anyway, that's why he needs to keep his distance." She pointed to Aelyx and asked, "Hey, when was the last time you washed your hands?"

Aelyx stared at his palms. "You know, I can't remember."

Brandi almost tripped over herself darting ahead of him on the path. This new development didn't drive her away, but at least she gave Aelyx a few inches of personal space as she started asking about L'eihr drugs.

Cara smiled. It turned out Aelyx was almost as good of a liar as she was.

"Conflict's a natural part of life. It exists on L'eihr—I know it—and I won't believe anything you say till I see it for myself." Cara brought a pencil to her lips and shrugged one shoulder casually, but her cerulean eyes flashed with passion. Aelyx loved it. His spirited debates with Cara and her World Studies instructor were the only pleasurable activities taking place for him inside Midtown High.

"I'm inclined to agree." Mr. Manuel perched on the corner of his desk, ignoring the other students, who had turned their attention to the cellular phones concealed beneath their desks.

"I never said conflict was nonexistent," Aelyx told her. "Only violence."

"But that's natural, too," she countered.

"You're only half right." Aelyx leaned back and stretched out his legs, resting his feet on the steel bookrack beneath Cara's desk. "Physical aggression is natural. We use rigorous sports to tame it." The clones did, anyway. Aelyx didn't mention his Elders had stopped feeling aggression decades ago, when they'd virtually died inside. "Violence isn't tolerated. Tempting as it may be to resolve conflicts with our fists, the promise of harsh consequences keeps us compliant."

"Consequences?" Mr. Manuel asked, sitting a bit straighter.

Cara perked up as well, giving a little sneer. "Like what? They chop off your hands for fighting?"

Aelyx held both palms forward. "I still have mine."

"*You* were in a fight, Mr. Perfect?"

"Just once." Only a fool would repeat an infraction after twelve lashes from the *iphet*. He could almost feel its blazing electricity stinging his flesh, and half a lifetime had passed since the incident. "Yes, our punishments are harsh, but we're also trained from infancy to follow The Way. And don't forget, my generation is cloned from the archives, so—"

"So," Mr. Manuel interrupted, "they hand-selected a generation of ideal L'eihrs? That has disaster written all over it."

Aelyx didn't see the problem. "Why regenerate flawed citizens?"

"Newsflash," Cara said. "You're flawed, too."

"Big time," someone muttered from behind.

"Perhaps, but still evolved. Our last war ended thousands of years ago. Your wars in the Middle East have barely ceased, and already there's conflict simmering again. Humans have yet to move beyond the cycle of aggression." And they never would. He'd wager his life on it. "That's the main difference between us." The reason their societies should never coexist.

Before the debate could continue, a bell chimed in three short bursts through the loudspeaker, and noisy chatter erupted as students filed out of the classroom. In their customary fashion, he and Cara waited until the room emptied before departing for lunch.

The clamor of a hundred simultaneous conversations reverberated through the halls, joined by the squeak of rubber-soled shoes against tile floors. The acrid scent of tacos weighted the air, and he inwardly thanked Cara for packing his lunch again. He only wished it were pot roast instead of cheese and crackers.

"Keep putting 'em up, assholes," she muttered as they passed a HALO recruitment poster taped to the wall. It proclaimed, HELL, NO! L'EIHRS GOTTA GO! Not very creative, but then again, they weren't the brightest among humans. "Because this feels great." She tore it down and shoved it into a nearby recycling bin.

"See? There's a healthy way to—" Aelyx stopped, distracted by the odd behavior of several students around him. As soon as they caught a glimpse of his face, they'd fling themselves from his path as if his touch might turn them to stone.

Not that he was complaining—he preferred this to humans like Brandi clinging to him like religion.

While Cara charged forward, ripping posters off the dingy cinder block wall, a dark-haired female *click-click-click*ed over in platform heels and tugged Cara's sweater. It took Aelyx a moment to recognize the girl as Tori. She'd cut her long hair last week and now wore it cropped at an angle that followed her jawline. A revealing skirt had replaced knee-length gym shorts, and she'd rimmed her eyes in jet-black goo, no doubt in an attempt to attract a mate. He wondered which male she'd targeted.

"I just found this in my locker." Tori thrust a folded note at Cara, and he moved in to peer over her shoulder. TRAITOR BITCH was all it said.

Cara glanced at him and away just as quickly. "Yeah. I got that, too."

"What?" Aelyx dropped his notebook and fumbled to catch it. "When?"

"Right before World Studies."

"And you didn't tell me?" His chest expanded with . . . what? Anger? Fear? No, this was a new emotion, something he couldn't quite place.

"It's no big deal. I've been called worse."

Tori raised her chin—now four inches higher than usual due to her ridiculous shoes—and glared at him. "I got kicked off student government and the soccer team." She blew a lock of hair out of her eye. "But for some reason, I'm still hanging with you. I hope you appreciate this."

Tori clearly wanted him to return to L'eihr. He wanted to

leave even more than she wanted him gone, but he couldn't very well tell her that.

"I'm sorry, Tor," Cara said, snatching another poster off a metal locker bank. "If it's any consolation, you're doing the right thing."

"Yeah," Tori said flatly, "it's so rewarding. I feel all warm and fuzz—"

"What the hell?" shouted an enormous male with a mop of mahogany hair. The boy used one hand to shove his way through the crowd while tugging Brandi Greene along with the other. He wore a Midtown lacrosse sweatshirt and a fierce scowl. Nodding at the poster in Cara's hand, the boy growled, "You're gonna put that back up."

"Sure, Marcus." Cara flung the paper into the bin and shoved it down with her textbook. "Just hold your breath and wait."

So this was Marcus Johnson—lacrosse captain, HALO recruiter, and recently dethroned valedictorian. Aelyx had heard volumes from Cara about this hulking animal, none of it positive. Even Brandi seemed subdued around him, dropping her gaze to the tile as if to make herself invisible. The closer the boy moved to Cara, the more Aelyx's muscles tightened against his will.

"I know you wrote this." Tori shook her note at Marcus. "Grow some berries and say it to my face next time."

If a smile could be described as evil, that's precisely what curved Marcus's lips. "I dunno what you're talking about."

Tori flashed one of her fingers in what Aelyx assumed was an insult and told Marcus to do something anatomically impossible. Meanwhile, Cara ripped another flyer off the wall, crumpled it into a ball, and launched it into the recycling receptacle.

Marcus's grin faded, jaw tensing visibly as he dropped Brandi's hand and pointed to the bin. "Get it out."

Cara stepped within an inch of the boy and lifted her face to his. "Get bent."

"I'm not fu—" His eyes darted over Cara's shoulder to Aelyx, seeming to notice him for the first time. "Brandi says his spit can eat your face off like acid." Marcus cocked his head to the side and sneered at Cara. "But for you that'd be an improvement."

Despite the heat rising into his skull, Aelyx reminded himself that violence and anger were markers of the weak. He was above it. But then Marcus put his hands on Cara, roughly shoving her to the floor, and Aelyx's mind emptied. His body trembled. Without thinking, he struck back with all his strength and slammed Marcus's shoulder with the heel of one hand, sending the boy spinning into the locker bank, where he landed with a loud metallic *clang* that stung Aelyx's eardrums.

Aelyx's body flushed with fever. He couldn't believe what he'd done . . . or how natural it had felt. He wanted to do it again. Great bleeding gods, what was wrong with him?

The hall fell silent as a hundred pairs of eyes widened in shock. Marcus grasped his upper arm and howled in pain. In seconds, an instructor rushed into the hall demanding to know what had happened.

Aelyx and Cara spent the rest of the hour in the office,

where the secretary, Mrs. Greene, glared at them while answering calls and writing hall passes. A pity the woman didn't share her daughter's fascination with him, because Aelyx could have used some help. If the ambassador discovered what he'd done, it would mean the *iphet*—six lashes, at least.

Fortunately, his consequences were far less severe than he'd anticipated. Marcus's coach interceded on the cretin's behalf, begging the principal not to suspend the boy and "punish the whole team over a stupid scuffle," and the principal assigned both Marcus and Aelyx after-school detention.

They released Aelyx for his next class, but he didn't go. Instead, he left Cara without a word and charged out the side exit, then jogged across the parking lot and into the woods.

He evacuated his mind until all he felt was his feet striking the soft, leaf-carpeted ground. He didn't know how long or how far he ran, but eventually Aelyx stopped and sank onto his haunches, leaning back against the rough surface of a tree. He closed his eyes and breathed deeply in meditation until his heartbeat slowed and his skin cooled.

Being in this place—surrounded by human lust and violence—had changed him. He had to get away. Glancing over his shoulder to be sure no one had followed, he pulled his com-sphere from his pocket and brought it to life.

A minute later, Eron's hologram appeared. Syrine was nonresponsive.

Eron leaned forward and scanned him. "Something happened. Are you all right?"

"Yes." Thank the gods he couldn't use Silent Speech from

a distance. He'd hate for Eron to know what he'd done. "But I can't tolerate another month here."

"Is it really so bad?" Judging by the skepticism in Eron's voice, he'd had a more positive high school experience.

"No," Aelyx told him. "It's worse."

"Just hold on a while longer. If we rush, we could botch everything. Or make Stepha suspicious."

"*Fasha*," Aelyx swore. "There has to be another way . . ."

But he couldn't deny Eron had a point. Aelyx needed to think logically, stop allowing his emotions to drive his behavior. It wouldn't benefit him to leave Earth now if the Elders decided to pursue the alliance. A few more months among humans to avoid a lifetime in their presence—it was a worthy trade.

"Remember what Stepha said about patience," Eron told him. "Humans are overly expressive. It's their way. You can't allow them to offend you so deeply." He paused for a few moments and then smiled to himself. "You made the same mistake the first time we played sticks."

A hesitant grin curved Aelyx's lips. "Well, you kept accusing me of cheating."

"I know. I did it to unnerve you, and it worked."

It'd worked, all right. Aelyx had knocked his friend to the ground, where they'd engaged in the fistfight that had earned them each a dozen lashes.

"Don't let them provoke you," Eron said. "Otherwise you'll reward their bad behavior and encourage them to do it again."

Aelyx nodded. "You're right. I was an idiot."

"What's that?" Eron asked, cupping his ear. "I didn't hear you. Say it louder."

Aelyx laughed and flashed a rude gesture. "Too late. I need to get back to class."

Eron returned the gesture with a smile and disappeared, leaving Aelyx to make his way back to Midtown High—to the only human he didn't want to leave behind.

Chapter Ten

Cara snapped a square from her chocolate bar and held the bite inside her mouth, letting it melt slowly on her tongue. The flavor came gradually, building into a rich, creamy sweetness and releasing a faint earthy aroma. She sighed with pleasure, opened her favorite novel—a tattered copy of *Jane Eyre*—and nestled deeper into the sofa cushions.

Before she'd finished the first page, Mom drifted into the room and settled at the other end of the sofa with one of those heavy sighs that said, *I don't want to bug you, but I'm going to keep making these little noises until you ask me what's wrong.*

So Cara cut to the chase. "What's wrong?"

"Oh, nothing."

Cara gave her mom a couple beats to change her mind, then reopened her book.

"It's just . . ." Mom began.

Cara put her novel down with a sigh of her own. "It's just what?"

"I think I'm being forced out of my own book club."

"How does that happen?"

"Mindy Jordan keeps changing the meeting time and forgetting to e-mail me."

Looked like Mom's friends had stolen a move from the student government playbook. "That's exactly what happened to Tori."

Mom tucked a black curl behind one ear and made a sour face. "And they keep pushing to read that unedited fan-fiction book with all the spanking. They know how I feel about it."

"I'm sorry," Cara said, giving Mom a gentle nudge with her foot. "But you don't want to hang out with people who treat you like that. You can do better."

"I know." Mom slumped back and rested her heels on the coffee table. "I just worry sometimes. I didn't expect people to stay angry about Aelyx this long. He's such a sweetheart. I just heard about a riot in Canada, of all places. Who riots in Canada?"

"Canadians?"

Mom didn't seem to appreciate the joke. "You're being careful at school, right?"

If *careful* meant antagonizing the student Patriots, then yes. "Really careful."

"Good," Mom said. "And by the way, *SqueeTeen* called again."

"No interviews." Between TV features, blogger e-mails, and now requests from magazines, Cara was feeling overwhelmed. Besides, it was really Aelyx they were after, not her.

"That's what I told them."

The doorbell rang, and Mom pushed off the sofa to answer it while Cara tugged open *Jane Eyre*.

"Mrs. Sweeney?" said a man's low voice. "I'm Ron Johnson. This is my son, Marcus. Our kids go to Midtown High together."

Cara dropped her book and sat up.

"Can we come in for a few minutes?" he asked. "It's important."

"Is there something wrong at school?"

"Yes, there sure is."

Uh-oh. Marcus must've tattled to Daddy about the incident a couple of days ago. Cara stood and crossed to the other side of the room.

She watched Ron step inside, followed by Marcus, and she caught herself rubbing her backside, remembering how hard she'd fallen before Aelyx had nearly punched Marcus's arm out of its socket. She couldn't believe Brandi was actually dating this jerk. Reigning king or not, a seat on the homecoming court wasn't worth swapping spit with Marcus Johnson.

Father and son had dressed identically in white buttondown shirts and black ties paired with black slacks. Marcus's hair had been neatly parted and slicked into submission. They looked like Mormon missionaries, minus the name tags and friendly smiles. Marcus slumped forward with both hands in his pockets and kept his eyes trained on the carpet.

Ron nodded a quick greeting to Cara. "Miss Sweeney, Marcus has something to say to you." He elbowed his son in the ribs.

"My behavior the other day," Marcus recited like a stiff, petulant child, "was not befitting a true Patriot of Earth. Please accept my sincere apology."

Sincere her ass. But she'd say anything to get rid of these losers. "Don't worry about it."

Ron grinned and turned to her mom. "The kids had a misunderstanding." He reached into his breast pocket and handed Mom a small pamphlet—the same one HALO members gave out at school. "But that's not why I'm here. The government overstepped its bounds with this exchange program. A lot of us don't want a L'eihr around our kids. It's time to send him back where he belongs."

"Oh." Mom held up a hand. "We're not—"

"Now, listen." Ron darted a glance around the living room, wrinkling his nose. "I understand the money's . . . tempting." Translation: *Clearly you schmucks are broke as a joke.* "But let's think of the whole community, not just what's best for you."

"Well, I think it's a wonderf—"

"How could you bring him here without knowing anything about his kind?" Ron made himself at home, perching on the arm of the sofa while Marcus continued sulking by the front door. "I saw the interview. A total fluff piece! That idiot reporter had a chance to ask the boy about real issues, and she spent the whole time talking about his favorite food and how 'advanced' he is." He made little air quotes. "I wouldn't be surprised if she's working for the government."

Oh, brother. Looked like this guy had a crazy sandwich for lunch—a footlong. Mom was too sweet to dropkick this jerk into next week, but Dad wasn't. In the genetic lottery of life, Cara had scored two things from her father: flaming red hair and a temper to match.

"Hey, Dad," she yelled down the hall. "Company!"

Ron turned his little weasel eyes on her. "And I can't believe you let an alien sleep under the same roof as your daughter. He probably wants to breed with her. I've already heard some stories about those two . . ."

Cara's head snapped up. *"What?"*

Dad strolled in from the hallway, rubbing his weary eyes. He'd just finished two back-to-back shifts, which meant epic sleep deprivation. Awesome.

"Look who's here." Cara used a pseudo-cheerful voice. "The Patriots of Earth!"

Dad groaned and pinched the bridge of his nose. "Not interested."

"Just hear me out." Ron didn't give him a chance to object. "Our country's gone to pot since the L'eihrs made contact. All that looting and rioting filled up our jails, so nobody's enforcing the drug laws. Now there's a dealer openly doing business a block from my house. You know what that does to property values?"

"The L'eihrs brought my wife back from the dead, and you think I give a damn about your property values?" Dad barked. "Get the hell out of my house."

"But look at the ramifications of the cancer cure," Ron said, foolishly refusing to budge. "Smoking's increased three hundred percent, and don't even get me started on the surge in chemical pesticide use."

The whole room fell silent. Had this guy seriously complained about a universal cure for cancer?

All heads turned as Aelyx entered the room wearing a confused expression. He slipped a small gadget into his sweater pocket and glanced from person to person, narrowing his eyes when they settled on Marcus.

Dad hooked his thumb toward the back door. "You two go for a walk or something."

In other words, he didn't want their guest to witness the fury he was about to unleash.

Cara grabbed Aelyx's sleeve and tugged him into the kitchen. "Hurry," she whispered. "You don't wanna be here when he explodes, trust me."

As they scurried outside, she heard Ron's hysterical voice calling, "He has a weapon! I saw him hide it in his sweater!"

What a lunatic. No wonder Marcus was so screwed up. Her dad's voice boomed from inside the house. "I've got a Glock, a shovel, and five acres of woods, Johnson!"

The crackle and crunch of crusty dried leaves delighted Cara's ears. She stomped through the windblown drifts like a child playing in a rain puddle.

"I love this sound. And the smell." She raised her face to the sky and inhaled deeply through her nose. "The air's so sweet this time of year."

But Aelyx wasn't listening. He leaned against a maple tree, engrossed in a handheld electronic game. A juvenile tune rang out from between his palms, followed by a computerized bark.

"Hey," she said. "Is that Puppy Love?"

He glanced up with a pouty expression. "Something's wrong with your game. My canine died again."

"I haven't played that since I was nine. Where'd you find it?"

"I don't understand," he said, ignoring her question. "I fed the thing, allotted a reasonable amount of time for exercise, kept it well-hydrated. Why did it die?"

"Let me see." She leaned over his arm to study the screen. "Oh. You didn't give him any love."

"Love?"

"Yeah. I don't remember all the options, but you do little things to love your puppy. Like letting him sleep in your bed, or rubbing his tummy, or giving him hugs and kisses."

"*Cah*-ra, that's absurd." He turned off the game and shoved it back in his pocket. "All canines, even the ones humans have domesticated, respond to an intricate social hierarchy, not affection. I asserted my status as the alpha male so the animal would know its place. Then I gave it everything it needed to survive. It shouldn't have died."

"Um . . . it's just a stupid game for little girls, Aelyx. My mom bought it for me because I'm allergic to real dogs. How long have you been playing it?"

He hesitated and mumbled something unintelligible.

"What? I didn't hear you."

"Three days. It's the only game in your collection I haven't mastered yet."

"Well, it's nice to know I can beat you at something." Waving him forward, she reached into her pocket for her half-eaten chocolate bar. She broke off a piece and handed it to him.

"What's this?" He brought the brown square to his nose. "It smells musty."

"It's chocolate. You'll love it."

"That's what you said about Skittles. I vomited a rainbow afterward."

"True, but I was right about the pot roast, wasn't I?"

With a dubious sideways glance, he popped the bite into his mouth. Seconds later, his face contorted in disgust, and he ran off the narrow trail to spit the chocolate onto the ground. "That's horrible!"

"You can't be serious. Chocolate's the food of the gods."

Aelyx wiped a hand across his mouth. "Not my gods."

Cara laughed. "Do you worship gods on L'eihr?"

"Yes and no." A yellow leaf spiraled into view and he caught it between two fingers, then paused to spit on the ground once more. "The Ancient Ones believed that L'eihr itself was the creator of all life—our Sacred Mother. Her children were the gods and goddesses of the weather, harvest, fertility, and so on. Like your Greek gods. But nobody really believes that anymore. Worship is more tradition than religion for us, if that makes sense."

"Total sense." She shivered, rubbing her palms together to create warmth. "I'm getting chilly; let's head back. The Johnsons are probably gone by now."

"And you?" he asked. "What do you believe? I'm sorry, my research indicated this is a rude question, but you did initiate the topic."

She imagined him poring over books and electronic data to learn about her customs, and the mental picture made her smile.

"I don't mind. I don't go to mass that often, but I believe in God. A lot of people quit believing when your Voyagers showed up, because aliens aren't mentioned in the Bible. But that kind of thinking doesn't make sense to me. If you believe God's powerful enough to create the Earth in seven days, then why can't He create other worlds, too?"

Aelyx nodded. "That sounds reasonable."

"Anyway, churches all over the world are half empty now. Donations are down, and there's a lot less compassion going around. Not that there was a ton to begin with. It's kind of sad."

A cool wind shook the trees, sending vibrant red foliage fluttering through the air. She gazed up in awe, despite the chill. It was beyond beautiful. "The colors amaze me every single year. I could look at these leaves for hours."

"They're not so bad. But for me, the real beauty's down here." He motioned to heaps of desiccated brown leaves carpeting the ground. "In the colors of home."

A hint of wistfulness tugged at the edges of his full mouth, and she felt that same tug deep in her belly like an emotional sympathy pain. She reached out and plucked a curled brown leaf from its branch, then handed it to him. "Here, a small reminder of home. And better than the *larun* I tried to bake."

He laughed and admired his gift, sliding it over his index finger like a ring. "This leaf would probably taste better than your bread."

With a gasp, she shoved his shoulder and clutched her chest in mock outrage. He retaliated by bending down, scooping an armful of brown leaves, and tossing them into the air over her head. Cara darted to the ground, grabbed two handfuls of ammunition, and a full-blown leaf war erupted.

He darted among the trees, dodging her every attempt to nail him, until he tripped over a rotting log and fell backward. Heart leaping at her imminent victory, Cara dropped to her knees and used both hands to bury him up to his neck in foliage.

"I surrender." Laughing, he rested both hands on his chest and fought for breath. His leather cord had come loose, and his long honey-brown locks spilled across the ground, tangled with debris.

Cara propped on her elbow beside him and pulled a twig from his hair. She'd just opened her mouth to gloat when a sudden movement caught her attention, and she glanced up to find Tori stomping toward them from the house.

Side-swept bangs concealed half of Tori's face, but her one visible eye didn't seem too pleased. Probably because she'd texted earlier about wanting to hang out, and Cara had asked for a rain check. Now here she was, romping in the woods with Aelyx. This couldn't look good.

"Hey," she whispered to Aelyx, "you mind heading back to the house? I'll meet you inside in a few."

He seemed to understand. "Sure."

As Aelyx jogged away, Cara shot to her feet and began dusting herself off, then offered Tori a tentative grin. "I didn't think you were coming over."

"Yeah. 'Cause you were tired and you wanted to read." Her gaze hardened and shifted to Aelyx, now entering the house. "Musta been a boring book."

"No, I *was* reading, but then—"

"Looks like you wanna be alone with him." With a flip of her hair, Tori spun and charged away like a power walker in peep-toe flats.

"Hold up!" She jogged after her best friend, who refused to slow her frantic pace. "Wait, it's not like that." Cara grabbed Tori's wrist, but she shook free. "I swear I really was reading, but then Marcus showed up—"

Tori whirled around, bringing Cara to a clumsy halt. "You're into him."

"Who, Marcus? He's not my type." Cara's pathetic attempt to lighten the mood didn't work.

"That's the real reason you won't quit the exchange."

"We're just friends, Tor."

"He's playing you. I hope you know that. When it's too late and he's wrecked your life, remember this moment"—she pointed at the grass—"right now, when I warned you."

"Look, I know you're not Aelyx's biggest fan, but—"

"I don't trust him, and neither should you." Tori shifted her weight to one hip while studying the tips of her own toes. She fell silent for a few beats before asking, "Remember when I said Jared Lee might not ask me to prom because of all this?"

"Yeah. And I said you can do better."

"Well, I decided to make a move and ask him myself."

Tori's darkening cheeks said it all. "Let me guess. It didn't go well." When Cara extended a tentative hand to comfort her friend, Tori shrugged back.

"He couldn't get away from me fast enough. He kept looking over his shoulder like he didn't want anyone to see us talking."

"Then he doesn't deserve you."

Tori's mahogany eyes locked with Cara's. "Or maybe he knows Aelyx is hiding something, and he thinks I'm in on it. In that case, I wouldn't wanna be seen with me, either."

"Not this again." This was why she hadn't told Tori about Aelyx's visits to the woods or catching him in the shed. She knew Tori would spin it into something sinister. "Look, I've been keeping an eye on him, and he's really not—"

"No, *you* look." Tori jabbed an index finger in the air. "I won't hang around him anymore. So think about what that means." Without another word, she stalked off to her Prius and climbed inside.

It's either him or me. That's what it meant.

Cara didn't know this stranger masquerading as Tori Chávez. A lump the size of a tennis ball rose in her throat as she watched her oldest friend speed away. They'd fought before, many times, but never like this. Cara sank onto the front porch steps and rested her chin on her knees. She'd give Tori a day or two to cool off, then call and make things right. It would be okay. She had to believe that . . . despite the sick tingles forming in her stomach.

CHAPTER ELEVEN

"Hey, come check this out."

Aelyx watched Cara press her face to the living room window, one hand cupped above her eyes, the other sweeping aside the sheer white curtain. Early morning sunlight streamed inside, bathing her fair skin and illuminating the tiny blond hairs that sprinkled her forearm. As he approached the window, chants from the sidewalk grew louder, and he could finally make out what the protesters had been droning for the last hour: *They say allies; we say ALL LIES! They say peace pact; we say EXPULSION ACT!*

When Cara moved aside, he squinted against the brightness and peered across the street, where a fervent mob of hundreds marched a circuit under police supervision, waving signs to advertise the L'eihr Expulsion Act, which would revoke his student visa if it passed. He hoped it did.

"Not that." Cara pointed to the ground in front of the house. *"That."*

Aelyx glanced down. "L'osers." Someone had bleached the word into the grass. A heavy fog settled inside his lungs. The protests had grown more violent with each day. Human paranoia hadn't quite peaked yet, but he wouldn't have to wait much longer. This was what he'd wanted, so why did he suddenly have to struggle to catch his breath? Why did he feel that invisible weight stooping his shoulders again?

"Crazy, huh?" Cara's stomach rumbled and she pressed a hand over it. "I need to eat before we go."

They'd decided to spend the weekend collecting water samples from a nature preserve in the next county. Soil samples, as well. The Elders had asked him to compile a variety for scientific analysis, though they hadn't explained why. Regardless, he was eager to escape Patriot scrutiny and spend a tranquil day with Cara.

He followed her into the kitchen, where the smoky scent of sausage and eggs filled his nostrils. The smell of human food no longer turned his stomach, but that didn't mean he enjoyed eating it. Wheat toast topped with a few slices of beef, already on the table for him, was the only breakfast he could tolerate.

"'Morning, you two." Eileen bent over the sink, her arms immersed to the elbows in sudsy water. Bill stood beside his wife, one arm wrapped around her waist while he rinsed an iron skillet with his free hand.

"'Mornin'." Standing on tiptoe, Cara placed a brief kiss on

her father's cheek while reaching into the cabinet for a bowl. Casual, affectionate touches seemed as natural to this family as breathing, and although the Sweeneys had gone out of their way to make him welcome, Aelyx always felt like an outsider during these moments. He sat at the table and focused on his toast.

"Hey, Dad, you think we should call Colonel Rutter? The protest's pretty tame now, but he might want to send some guards to—"

"No!" Aelyx shouted before thinking better of it. All three Sweeneys turned to look at him. "The, uh, Elders think a military presence will cause more fear among humans. If you feel threatened, I'll join the colonel at the nearest military facility."

"I wouldn't worry about it anyway," Bill told Cara. "This is Midtown, not Manhattan. Nothing happens here." He and Eileen returned their attention to breakfast dishes, but Cara wasn't so easily placated. She studied him for several seconds before pouring cold cereal and milk into her bowl and joining him at the table.

When he couldn't meet her eyes any longer, he pulled the Puppy Love game from his pocket to feed canine number twelve. And though it went against all logic, he changed the settings to allow the animal to sleep in its master's bed. Hopefully this one would survive.

Cara glanced over his shoulder at the screen. "You've killed eleven puppies?"

"Clearly your game is flawed. But not to worry. I'll master it."

She shrugged, muttering over a bite of cereal, "Whatever you say, dog slayer."

Cara watched a dragonfly settle delicately on the water and ride the current downstream. It zigzagged around a protruding cluster of moss-conquered green stones and coasted out of sight. She closed her eyes, skimming two fingers along the stream's icy surface, and enjoyed the gurgling, babbling music of flowing water.

"So tell me why you need these samples," she said.

Aelyx crouched near a patch of cracked mud. He pierced the earth with something that looked like an oversize hypodermic needle. "I'm not sure, but I think our scientists want to analyze pollutants and counter the damage."

"Why?"

"Isn't it obvious?" He smirked and shook his head. "Judging by these preliminary readings, you've contaminated your planet quite thoroughly."

"No, I mean why do L'eihrs care about the environment? Why do they want to help?"

"I guess for the same reason we gave you the cure. A gesture of friendship." He turned the needle tool on its side and tapped a glossy gray information screen.

But friendship involved give and take. What did humans have to give? Besides, judging by how cold L'eihrs acted, she didn't imagine friendship topped their priority list. She decided not to press the issue, though. If she put him on the defensive, he might not answer her other questions.

Aelyx squinted at the screen. "Did something happen here?"

"Like what?"

"Chemical spill or some other contamination?"

"I don't think so." She found a dry patch of gravel and sat down cross-legged. "Hey, can I ask you about something you said in the last interview?"

Aelyx dismantled the tool and reached into his bag for another needle. "Of course." He reassembled the device and dipped it into the stream.

"Well, I'm mostly curious about life out there in other galaxies. You said your Voyagers searched for ten years to find people like us. What else did they find?"

He shook the water-filled instrument and tucked it into his bag. "If Sharon were a decent journalist, she'd have asked that." He climbed the riverbank and sat on the gravel beside her. "Exploring the universe for living beings is harder than you could possibly imagine."

"But your ships are so fast. Didn't L'eihr just send a bunch of them in every direction?"

"It's not that simple." Aelyx picked up a fallen branch and snapped it in half. He used the pointed edge to draw a large circle in the mud. "I want you to imagine this circle as a tiny fraction of our universe. The universe itself would take up all the land around us, as far as the eye can see. You with me so far?"

"Yep."

"Within this circle are billions of planets. Some of these can be eliminated as sources of life because their climates are too harsh, but millions remain to be explored. Even with hundreds of ships, imagine how long it would take to survey all of them."

"Wow."

"Yes, wow." He picked up a handful of pebbles and scattered them inside the circle. "These represent the few life-forms that exist in our small section of the universe. Keep in mind that *life-form* doesn't necessarily mean intelligent life. Some planets, especially the younger ones, support only bacteria and single-celled organisms."

She fidgeted with a smooth stone, suddenly feeling very small and insignificant. "How much intelligent life is out there?"

"Honestly, I don't know. Our Voyagers found less than a dozen cognizant life-forms, but who knows how many more exist outside the circle. Finding humans was equivalent to winning the lottery, even after ten years of searching."

"Those intelligent life-forms—can they travel to other planets?"

"Not any that we found." Aelyx pushed off the ground and slung his bag over one shoulder. "We passed a clearing on the way to the stream. I'd like to go back for some more samples." He offered his hand to help her up.

She hesitated, caught off guard. Aside from their first handshake, Aelyx had never initiated physical contact with her. Not even once. She reached for his hand, but he changed his mind at the last second and turned to continue on his way.

"Did the other aliens look like us, too?" she asked, standing on her own.

"Yes and no. From what I learned, they all walk upright, but their limbs and facial features are different."

"But if you don't count evolution, L'eihrs and humans are practically identical. Our DNA is almost the same. What're the odds that two species light-years apart would be so similar?"

"The odds are infinitesimal," he said with a grin, "unless you believe the ancient legends."

"Oh, ancient alien legends." She paused to hop over a fallen log. "That sounds creepy."

"According to old stories—and by old, I mean thousands of years ago—a legion of L'eihr soldiers were taken from their camp on the eve of an important battle."

"What happened to them?"

"Supposedly, an enormous spacecraft descended from the heavens and hovered above the soldiers' camp. Then they all disappeared inside the ship. At the time, we didn't have the technology for interplanetary travel, so our ancients blamed their gods. Anyway, some of my people believe the abducted soldiers' descendants were scattered throughout the galaxy, and humans are the offspring of ancient L'eihrs."

"But L'eihrs have evolved so far beyond humans. How do they explain that?"

"Simple." He stopped to smooth his hair back and resecure it. "The breeding program is largely responsible for our advances. You humans procreate with no regard for the betterment of your species, which accounts for your weaknesses. No offense."

"None taken." She rolled her eyes.

"But here's the most interesting part. A few of the Ancient Ones had blue eyes."

"Really?"

"Just like yours. According to your scientific community, all humans had brown eyes until about ten thousand years ago, when they believe a mutation occurred. Some of my people believe there was no such mutation, that our Ancients brought that trait to Earth." Nudging her lightly with his elbow, he added, "You and I might be related."

"Oh, sure. I can see the family resemblance. But why aren't your eyes blue?"

"It seems the trait died out."

"But how can any of this be possible? What about the theory of evolution on Earth?"

"*Cah*-ra," he said with a laugh, "it's just an old legend. Hardly anyone believes it."

"Oh, right." She felt foolish for getting worked up over a silly story, but for some reason, the tale had brought chills to the surface of her skin. Luckily, another question came to mind and pushed aside thoughts of creepy legends. "You told me the clones are kind of incubated in a machine, right?"

"You've oversimplified the process, but that's basically it."

"But what happens afterward? When the baby's born, or fully grown, or whatever? Who raises it? Are there enough parents to go around?"

Aelyx stopped at the edge of the clearing, scanning the ground looking for the best place to take his next sample. "Our population's carefully controlled, so each generation perfectly replaces the last. Because of that, yes, there are enough caregivers to go around. But we're all raised and educated in a large commune called an Aegis until we turn twenty-one and leave for the occupational barracks. Each precinct has its own Aegis, and most of us go there after we're removed from the artificial wombs."

"Is a precinct like a town?"

"More like a state, and there are only five of them. Remember, we're not heavily populated. Everyone on L'eihr could live inside Texas." He glanced at her and grinned. "With plenty of room to spread out."

"You said *most* of you go to the Aegis. What about the ones who don't go?"

"Some citizens might want to foster a clone if they share blood ties with him. They're permitted to house the infant for two years, but it's pretty rare."

"Wait. Wouldn't that be like raising your own ancestors?"

"No." He shook his head and gave a soft laugh. "Some human twins are genetically identical, right?"

"Right."

"Does that mean they're the same person?"

"Point taken." Still, it was hard to wrap her mind around this whole clone business. She couldn't imagine changing diapers for the infant replica of her grandpa. "So after two years, parents aren't allowed to see their . . . foster-clone anymore?"

Aelyx glanced up, his silvery eyes warming. "Of course they can see the child. But families as you know them on Earth don't exist on L'eihr." He knelt on the ground and pushed the needle tool into the dirt.

Joining him, she sat with her legs crossed at the ankles. "Were you fostered by anyone?"

"No. I went from the womb straight to the Aegis."

"Oh!" Suddenly everything made sense.

"What's wrong?" He darted up in alarm and glanced around.

"That's why you can't stand to be touched."

"What?"

"You were practically raised in an orphanage. You didn't have a mother to hug you or a father to hold your hand. That explains why you hate to be touched."

She reflected on her most cherished childhood memories: riding atop Dad's shoulders, curling up with her parents under thick blankets during a thunderstorm, cocooning in Mom's lap during story time. She couldn't imagine growing up without that.

Aelyx laughed dryly and knelt on the ground in front of her. "I don't hate to be touched."

"Don't be ridiculous, of course you do. You flinch every time my mom lays a hand on you." She snorted a quick laugh. "You couldn't have been placed with a more touchy-feely family, you know."

"My upbringing wasn't completely devoid of physical contact. Our caretakers know some touch is required for proper brain development."

"Right. And I bet they didn't hold you a second longer than they had to. Look, you don't have to get defensive. I'm just glad I finally understand why you are . . . well, the way you are."

He grinned and shook his head. "There's nothing wrong with me."

"Okay, then," she said. "Prove it."

The gleam behind his eyes said he welcomed the challenge. "How?"

"Touch me." That gleam died real fast, just as she'd expected. She was obviously right, so why wouldn't he admit it? "Go on." She leaned closer and held her palm forward. "What're you afraid of?"

He hesitated and then reached out for her with a tentative hand. But instead of lacing his fingers among hers, he wove them through her hair. Chills danced across the back of her neck, and she closed her eyes automatically.

"I admit physical affection is foreign to me," he said, "but that doesn't mean every contact is torturous. See? I'm touching you right now."

"Not quite." Hair didn't count. She wanted to feel him on her skin. But when Cara opened her eyes and geared up to tell him, she saw a tall shadow move in her periphery. She flinched back with a gasp.

"What's wrong?" Aelyx's gaze followed hers to the wooded area opposite the field.

"Someone's out there."

"Are you sure?" His body tensed visibly as he scanned the vacant landscape.

"Positive." She pointed to the woods, where a group of low branches stirred.

The shadowy figure was gone, but she'd seen him. The chills from her neck spread downward, raising goose bumps on her arms. Someone was still watching them. She could sense it.

"Let's go," Aelyx said, wasting no time in standing and gathering his things.

"Yeah." Cara pushed to her feet and started in the other direction. She tried telling herself it was probably just a hiker out there, but that didn't stop her from quickening the pace.

Chapter Twelve

Subscribe [Archive] [Recent Entries] [About Me]

Alienated

MAY THE SOURCE BE WITH YOU

MONDAY, NOVEMBER 15

Of Mud and Men: it's Culture Clash Monday.

Ever wonder what L'eihrs do for fun? How they say good-bye?
Which hand gestures offend them most? Actually, I'm not
answering that last one. Based on the spirited e-mails I've
been getting (by the way, calling me a ginger whore is totally
unoriginal), many of you would use such information for evil,
not for good.

So instead, let's talk about a rite of passage. Forget Bar
Mitzvahs. On L'eihr you become a man (or woman) during
Sh'ovah. When the elders decide you're ready, which happens
between thirteen and seventeen, you swear an oath to the
"Sacred Mother" (the planet itself), and then all your peers
stand in line and smear mud on your naked body to symbolize
your union with Her. Mazel tov! Sounds more interesting than my
rite of passage: a fully clothed sweet sixteen at the Olive Garden.

That's all for now. Check back for Trivial Wednesday and again
for FAQ Friday. The most commonly e-mailed question last week

was "How have L'eihrs evolved?" I'll ask Aelyx and get back to you. Have a great week, gentle and not-so-gentle readers. All 855,947 of you!

Posted by Cara Sweeney 3:14 p.m.

After uploading her blog entry, Cara left the computer lab to join Aelyx at her locker. But she sensed that something wasn't right. When she opened the metal door, its soft *click* echoed in the crowded hallway. Whispers had replaced the usually boisterous conversations, and even the *squeak* and *click* of footsteps sounded subdued. Weird.

She turned to Aelyx. "Have you seen Tori? She skipped psychology, but I know she's here."

Tori had done a halfway decent job playing hide-and-don't-seek, but Cara noticed her ducking into the stairwell after last period. And after yesterday's creepy peeping incident at the nature preserve, she wanted to keep her friends close.

"No, but I typically don't go looking for her." He leaned against the next locker. "You seem upset. You all right?"

No, she wasn't all right. Despite all the phone messages she'd left for Tori—including several *4giv me?* texts—they hadn't spoken in days. Cara brought her thumbnail to her mouth, but there was nothing left to nibble.

"Tori's still pissed," she said. "I canceled some plans last week, and she thinks it's because I was hooking up with you."

"She despises me."

"No, she doesn't." When he raised one brow, she conceded. "Okay, she does, but only because she doesn't know you like I do. But if—"

154

"There she is." Aelyx nodded at something behind her. He flashed a weak smile and patted her shoulder consolingly, like he knew something she didn't. It reminded her of the time Dad broke the news about Mom's cancer. "I'll wait here, in case you need me."

A flutter tickled her chest as she spun around and spotted Tori leaning against the far wall, her hands wedged into the back pockets of her skintight jeans. Half the lacrosse team, including Eric and Marcus, huddled around her.

Taking a deep, steadying breath, Cara slung her backpack over one shoulder and strode briskly toward the group.

When she stopped in front of them, it was Marcus, not Tori, who spoke first. "We need to talk, Sweeney." He folded his arms and cocked his head to the side in the universal gesture of poseurs trying to look badass.

What a moron. No wonder she'd stolen his class rank so easily. "Come on, Tor, you can't ignore me forever. Let's go somewhere and talk, just us."

But Tori didn't budge. Instead, she studied the pointed tips of her platform ankle boots and mumbled, "Listen to what he has to say."

Then something happened that sent Cara's stomach dipping like a yo-yo. Eric took Tori's hand and gave it a reassuring squeeze. Eric and Tori. Touching. *Does not compute.* Tori's mocha eyes widened, and she jerked her hand away while Eric ran his fingers through his hair, meeting Cara's gaze just long enough to betray his guilt. Wait, guilt?

Eric and Tori—together? No, that couldn't be right. Tori was hot for Jared Lee, not Eric. Tori hated Eric. Cara must've misinterpreted the signals, crossed some wires in her brain.

Marcus tore her away from her muddled thoughts for a moment. "We've been patient with your family so far—"

"Sure. If patient means spewing lies and propaganda and picketing my house every day, you've got the patience of a saint."

A tiny muscle in Marcus's temple twitched visibly beneath his ruddy skin, and she knew he'd love to reach out and choke someone—her.

She hooked a thumb toward Aelyx, still observing them from her locker. "Go ahead. Maybe he'll snap your arm all the way off this time." Was it just her imagination, or had Tori angled her body toward Eric's? Their foreheads were barely six inches apart now.

"Until you send him home," Marcus said, "none of our members will associate with your family in any way." He slashed one hand through the air. "We're talkin' a total shutout."

"Best news I've heard all day. Can you start ignoring me five minutes ago?"

Apparently, Marcus had reached his limit. After giving her a look that would melt the face off a frozen clock, he stalked away with his team, leaving Tori and Eric behind.

The two glanced at each other, cheeks flushing as they fidgeted with bag straps and belt loops. More importantly, Tori wasn't flipping Eric the bird or cursing him out in Spanish.

Oh, God. They really *were* together. Her best friend and her ex.

Posters and banners went blurry. Air thickened until it was

impossible to breathe. The nearby drone of a water fountain rattled her skull. It didn't make sense—they'd always hated each other. And what about Jared? Unless . . .

A snippet of conversation flashed in Cara's mind: *I'm here to make sure you don't let that* carajo *sweet-talk you into getting back together.* Tori had mentioned that right after the breakup. People always said there was a thin line between love and hate. Had Tori's and Eric's anger been attraction in disguise? Was all that talk about Jared simply a diversion? And if that was the case, had Eric ever loved her at all?

With the passing of each silent second, Cara's confident mask evaporated, leaving behind tiny beads of sweat along her upper lip.

"How long?" Cara's voice trembled, and she swallowed hard. "Even before the breakup?"

"No!" Eric held both palms forward. "She started coming to the meetings. We talked a lot, mostly about you, and it sorta . . ."

"Just happened," Tori finished, staring at the floor.

"Unh-uh." Cara shook her head, trying to clear it like an Etch a Sketch. "A zit just happens. My best friend going after my ex doesn't just happen."

"Why do you care?" Eric pointed over her shoulder to Aelyx. "You moved on first!"

"No, I didn't. But that's got nothing to do with it."

The boy she'd once loved was gone, and she'd accepted it. But even if she didn't want Eric back, he'd hurt her. He was the enemy, and the Universal Girl Code stipulated friends should band together in hating the bastard till death.

"This explains your little transformation." Cara swept her hand, indicating Tori's haircut and makeup, including Gritty in Pink. How many times had Tori kissed Eric with that stolen gloss on her lips? "And how you got over Jared so fast. Who *are* you?"

"This," Tori said, tugging at her clothes, "had nothing to do with E."

"Oh, gag! You're calling him *E* now?"

"Maybe I just wanted someone to look at me the way Aelyx looks at you!"

"Right. Or maybe you—" A glint of gold on Tori's low-cut blouse caught her eye, stopping Cara mid-rant. Angel wings. A slow fever scorched her face, her pulse thumping so hard she felt it in her earlobes.

All of HALO's members—which now included Tori—would shun her. So, not only had Tori betrayed their trust, she was about to completely shut her out.

Love, laughter, six years of friendship. It was all over. Something sick and terrible swelled inside Cara's chest, threatening to burst her apart. Tears prickled behind her eyes, and she knew she couldn't hold it together much longer.

"Come on." Tori's own eyes welled with tears. "Don't look at me like that. If you just quit the program, we can find a way to—"

"To what? Pick up where we left off?" No way in hell. Clearing the thickness in her throat, Cara scraped together just enough anger to strike back at them. "I hope he gives you whatever disease he picked up from the Ho Depot."

The knife between her shoulder blades made it hard to turn around, but she did. And with her head held high, she strolled down the hall and out the front door as if her heart hadn't just been pulverized, pureed, dumped onto the ground, and trampled by pigs. By the time she reached the parking lot, she was completely blinded by welling tears.

"*Cah*-ra!" Aelyx called out from behind, but she didn't stop.

He caught her arm and gently turned her to face him. "I'm sorry. I knew this would happen."

"What? You knew about Eric and Tori?" Was she the last to find out? Could this get any more embarrassing?

"Wait. They're a couple?" He shook his blurry brown head. "I expected she'd end your friendship, but I never thought she'd partner with Eric."

"I know, right?"

"Probably united by their hatred of me. I'm so sorry."

"I just want to go home."

He nodded and led her to the wooded path.

Aelyx rested his forehead against the wall he shared with Cara's bedroom and cringed at her muffled sobs. During their walk home, he'd almost had her smiling again until they'd stepped through the back doorway and Eileen had said, "What's wrong, Pepper? You look like you lost your best friend." Cara had grieved without interruption ever since. Each sniffle and hitched breath stung his own lungs as if her pain were his own, but as much as he wanted to console her, he didn't know how.

Frustration tightened his hands into fists. He was a L'eihr—cloned from the archives at the height of his species' perfection. Surely he could think of a way to make Cara feel better.

Before he had a chance to brainstorm, his com-sphere called to him, emitting the low frequency only he could hear. He rushed to his dresser drawer, retrieved the device, and whispered his new passkey, *"Elire."*

Syrine and Eron appeared before him, the former sitting with her legs tucked beneath her on a braided rug and the latter crouched inside a porcelain bathtub, as usual.

"My *sh'alear* is working!" Syrine said, laughing and extending her first two fingers in greeting. "Is yours?"

Aelyx nodded. After several trips into the forest to water and fertilize his seedling, he'd finally noticed the adjacent field of soybean crops beginning to wilt in response to the changes his native plant had enacted in the soil. When the familiar sensation of guilt overcame him, he consoled himself with the knowledge that the changes were only temporary. The crops would resume their regular activity after he uprooted the *sh'alear* and departed Earth. But it wouldn't take long for humans to notice the anomalies and link them to the presence of each L'eihr exchange student, exactly as they'd intended.

"This year's grapes should produce quite the unusual vintage," Syrine gloated, looking happier than she had since leaving home.

Eron's miniature forehead wrinkled. "What if we made a mistake?"

Aelyx felt his brows rise while Syrine recoiled as if she'd smelled something foul.

"Mistake?" she screeched. "Do you know what I discovered my human doing last night? Hiding a video camera in my bedroom! Fortunately, my electron-tracker alerted me before I'd removed any clothing. Or worse—contacted either of you."

"Thank the gods," Aelyx whispered. The lanky Frenchman truly *did* need a kick to the reproductive organs. Brandi Greene had continued pestering Aelyx with longing glances and secret smiles, but at least she didn't invade his bedroom. Yet. "What changed your mind, Eron?"

"My family." He caught himself and corrected, "My host family, I mean. They've made me one of their own. Especially the little one—Ming."

"The one who wants to play alien invaders every day?" Aelyx asked.

A brilliant smile curved Eron's mouth, so wide that it crinkled the skin around his eyes. "Families are only allowed one child here, but Ming was adopted after his parents died. He never thought he'd have a brother, but now he says he has one." Eron shook his head as if in awe. "He calls me his brother."

Aelyx didn't know what to say. He couldn't stop remembering how Cara had squared her shoulders and bravely confronted her peers earlier that day. She'd sacrificed every one of her relationships for him, and much like Eron's host family, the Sweeneys had embraced Aelyx as their own. But that didn't change the fact that the Sweeneys were the minority among humans.

"We can't let our emotional attachments get in the way of what's best for L'eihr," he told his friend. "Analyze your water samples. Look at what humans have done to their own planet. Now imagine what an entire colony of them would do to ours."

"I agree," Syrine announced without a shadow of doubt in her voice. "Eron, you know I've always admired your empathy." When he nodded in response, she softened her tone in comfort. "We're not like the Elders. Our emotions are volatile, but never forget what humans are capable of. Even if one shows potential, never forget the species as a whole is inferior. Watch and see how they react to the *sh'alear*. They're already starting to notice—I've been searching their online discussions. Some of them believe the crops are wilting near us because we've angered their God. Humans have waged wars over less than this."

"But maybe we've created a self-fulfilling prophecy," Eron objected. "Set them up to fail."

Syrine shook her head. "If they were truly evolved, they'd pass the test. Don't you agree?"

Eron didn't deny it, but Aelyx contributed to the argument anyway. "I know our tactics are dishonest, but humans would rise to the occasion if they were capable. The Aegis agreed on this months ago. Are you going to be the one to tell them the plan's changed? That you support the alliance now?"

"No," Eron said, leaning back against the tile wall. "You're probably right. It's only—" A distant knock followed by a child's voice interrupted Eron, who held two fingers forward in a hasty good-bye before shutting down his sphere and disappearing from view. Syrine gave a heavy sigh and followed.

A familiar pang throbbed beneath Aelyx's breastbone. By now, he knew it well. Guilt, his constant companion.

If sabotaging the alliance was the right thing to do, why did it feel so wrong? His instincts told him it had something to do with the red-haired girl sobbing in the next room—Cara, or Elire, as he'd come to think of her. When he returned home, he'd leave her to face the consequences of his actions, alone against all those furious humans. He couldn't deny that was wrong in every possible way.

CHAPTER THIRTEEN

Using her thumbnail, Cara traced the engraving on the heart-shaped sterling pendant Tori had given her last Christmas. "Friendship is one mind in two bodies."

Right. Until your BFF went out of her mind and after your ex-boyfriend's body.

If she closed her eyes, she could still hear Tori's smiling voice. *If we're sharing one brain, it'd better be yours*, she'd said. *Or we're screwed like a* puta *on payday.* They'd laughed and spent the day bouncing back and forth between their houses, gorging themselves on *panetón* and pecan pie, finally crashing in Tori's room at midnight to play dirty Mad Libs.

How had everything fallen apart so quickly? Had they really let something as trivial as a boy come between them? Cara never thought it would happen. She missed Tori already, and a full day hadn't even passed.

She tossed the necklace inside her jewelry box and slumped onto the bed, trying to work up the will to leave for school. As much as she wanted to obey the first rule of debate, she just didn't have the energy. To hell with it. Let 'em see her sweat. Let 'em see her swollen eyelids and reddened nose, her sloppy ponytail and frumpy track pants. Who cared anymore?

Three soft knocks sounded at the door. "*Cah*-ra?"

"It's open."

Aelyx peered inside for a moment, gauging her mood before joining her in sitting at the foot of the bed. His added weight shook the mattress and tipped her sideways until their shoulders touched and he scooted away.

He handed over a blueberry muffin. "Want to stay home today?"

"No." She brought the muffin to her nose, but the sweet scent turned her stomach. "Yes. But I won't."

"We could go in late. Avoid the morning protest."

"Here." She passed the muffin back to him. "Let's just get it over with." But when she stood, he remained seated, fidgeting with his sweater's zipper pull.

He glanced up beneath a fringe of dark lashes, his eyes intense with some unspoken message. "Maybe it's time I left."

"What do you mean, left? *Left* left? To another family?" His slow nod confirmed it. "No! Don't be silly."

"*Cah*-ra, your walls don't block much sound. I heard you last night."

"Oh." Under any other circumstances, the idea of someone listening to her cry would have bothered Cara, but for some reason, she didn't mind Aelyx seeing her at her weakest.

It felt kind of liberating to show how much she ached inside.

"Things will only get worse. I know the scholarship is—"

"I don't care about the money. I don't want you to go. Besides, I can't come visit you if I quit the program, and if I'm not mistaken, you promised me some kick-ass *larun*. So don't try backing out on me now."

He laughed softly but wouldn't meet her gaze. He probably felt responsible for what'd happened, especially after listening to her cry all night. Maybe she didn't have the energy to put up a brave front for the rest of Midtown, but she could do it for Aelyx. He didn't deserve to feel low because of her personal problems.

"Come on, I'll let you escort me to my very first shunning." That earned a half smile from him. "I think this means I'm a woman now."

"And me with no gift for the occasion."

Another joke. He'd changed in the last couple of months. "Guess I picked the wrong day to dress down. A girl's gotta get her glam on when the world turns its back on her."

He shook his head. "I like seeing you like this."

"With no makeup, bad hair, and clothes I found in my gym bag? Yeah, I'm dead sexy."

He pushed off the bed, his face breaking into a warm smile. "You have freckles. Right here." Holding his fingertip an inch from her face, he traced an imaginary line down the bridge of her nose and across the apples of her cheeks. "I can't see them when you wear cosmetics. And look." He brushed his thumb over her lashes, lighter than a butterfly's kiss. "They're gold at the tips."

Before she knew what she'd done, Cara closed her eyes and lifted her face, willing him to keep going. She wanted to feel the warmth of his skin so badly she could hardly breathe. "I'm . . ." *Not wearing lipstick, either. Touch me there.* "Uh . . ." Oh, good God, what was wrong with her? Stepping away, she opened her eyes and plastered on a smile. "I'll grab my Tiara of Shame and meet you outside."

A frosty autumn breeze lifted Cara's ponytail and brushed the sides of her neck. She shivered and plodded ahead on the wooded path. "I need a distraction. Tell me more about the animals on L'eihr. Which one's your favorite?"

Aelyx pulled up his hood and rubbed his palms together briskly. "That would be Vero." He smiled silently for a few seconds as if replaying a memory. "He's our house pet at the Aegis. Similar to a lemur—quick, agile, a good climber—but larger. Like the size of a chimpanzee. He has dexterous hands with opposable digits like a raccoon." He leaned close to her ear and whispered, "I even taught him to write."

"Shut the front door! He must be really smart."

"Well, I may have misled you. I taught him to hold a writing utensil and scribble. But he is intelligent."

"Does he have fur? And how does that work with your controlled climate? Don't your animals with thick coats get too hot?"

"They adapted hundreds of years ago. Most animals on L'eihr have what you'd call peach fuzz instead of true fur. Vero's skin is beige, but he can darken it to gray if he needs to camouflage."

"So let's see if I've got this right," she said. "Vero's a cross between a lemur, a raccoon, and a chimp, but he's hairless? I can't picture it."

"I'll draw him for you sometime, though I'm not a great artist."

She gave a theatrical gasp. "There's something you're not good at?"

"Three things."

"You're joking." She pulled back his hood to gauge his expression. No humor in his eyes. "I don't believe it."

"Every child on L'eihr is tested at age six, then assigned a career based on his or her strengths. I demonstrated superior language skills, so I was chosen to serve as a translator."

She nodded for him to continue.

"But I had a passion for science, not communication, so I appealed to my Elders a few years later. They said my scores were far too inferior to qualify for a laboratory position."

"Sorry." She gave his arm a little pat and quickly drew back. "What's the other thing you struggle with?"

Aelyx kicked a pile of leaves and his smile returned. "Obedience."

She laughed and pointed at him. "You're making this up."

"I promise." He held up one hand. "I rebelled by refusing to participate in my foreign language classes. That earned me five strokes with the *iphet* across my backside."

"Like a paddle?"

"Imagine an electric paddle, more like a whip. And then no meals for the rest of the day."

"Hot damn." L'eihrs didn't mess around.

"Hot damn is a perfect description for the *iphet*. I've experienced it two times, and that was twice too many. Anyway, Syrine—she's the female you met at the gala—snuck food into my dormitory and gave me a lecture on duty and responsibility. After that, we became friends, and a few years later, roommates."

"Wait. Your roommate's a girl?" Cara felt uncomfortable with that for some reason.

"And Eron. He's in China right now. After the three of us were selected for the exchange, we started sharing a room."

"Oh." That made her feel better—less like Aelyx and Syrine were shacking up. "So, are the other two exchange students good with language like you?"

"Eron's a translator. Syrine has . . . other skills." He pressed his lips together, pulled his hood back up, and quickened his pace. Just like that, the mood changed.

"Like what?"

"She's an emotional healer." Then he added in a reverent tone, "I swear she sees into my head, even when we're not together. She's one of my closest friends, similar to your Tori—" He paused on the trail, tripping over his own words, mouth agape for several seconds before he managed an apology. "Sorry. I keep forgetting."

A dull ache spread through Cara's core, like he'd just smacked her in the stomach with a Wiffle ball bat. But when she considered her feelings, she realized hurt wasn't the only emotion threatening to double her over. Syrine wasn't just his roommate; she was his best friend, too? Just how close were they? Close like *that*?

"It's okay," she mumbled.

They continued in silence until they reached the street and witnessed the largest crowd of Patriot protesters to date. Radicals spilled out onto the vacant lot where Aelyx's supporters used to sing and dance, back before fistfights and flying beer bottles had scared away all the hippies.

"I'd half expected them to stay home," Aelyx said.

"Yeah, I'm not feeling very ignored."

At least the government had finally stepped up and sent some troops. About two dozen armed soldiers donned in green camo corralled the demonstrators. Too bad they couldn't contain the cigarette butts, discarded leaflets, and cardboard coffee cups that blew around the parking lot like tumbleweeds.

Cara couldn't help scanning the lot for Tori's Prius, but she quickly forced her gaze back to Aelyx. Clearing her throat, she wiped one dampened palm on her pants. Could she really hold it together? Eric and Tori hadn't even crossed her path yet, and her eyes were already welling up. She faced the frigid breeze and blinked repeatedly until the tears dried.

"You can do this," Aelyx promised.

"I know." But despite that, her feet wouldn't budge.

He studied her for a long moment, then did something she couldn't believe. He reached down and took her hand. His long fingers were stiff, but he laced them between hers and tightened his grip, fusing their palms together in a mesmerizing contrast of skin.

Cara stared at their intertwined hands and went a little gooey inside.

"You don't have to do this," she said. "I know you hate it."

"Quite the opposite." He smiled down at her. "Consoling you brings me comfort. Listening to you cry while I'm trapped on the other side of the wall is what I can't stand."

"You're too good to me."

His smile fell. "I wouldn't say that."

He towed her ahead by their linked fingers, and they faced the crowd as a united front—the two of them against the world. It sparked a flicker of hope inside her chest.

Before they even made it across the street, someone on the fringes of the crowd blew an air horn in four quick blasts. Then, in eerie synchronization, the entire assembly turned to the left and faced the opposite direction. They must've rehearsed it all morning.

Message received: she was invisible. But for the first time since bringing Aelyx to Midtown, Cara felt comfortable gazing into the crowd. She slowed her pace to study the backsides of her would-be foes.

She recognized Mr. McFarland, one of her neighbors and the owner of the Midtown Grocery, and sweet Lord, there was Mrs. Fraker, her old Sunday School teacher. So much for peace, love, and understanding. A lot had changed since HALO's early days, when squirrely radicals dominated the group. Men still outnumbered women, but Cara noticed several high ponytails, French twists, and a few full-length cashmere coats. A little red-haired toddler with wide, curious eyes peered at Cara from behind his mother's hip. She smiled at the boy, but he thrust out his tongue and hid his face.

Inside the school, most students still parted like the Red Sea, while others stopped and stared as she clung to Aelyx's hand. She knew the kind of rumors this would fuel, but who cared? She didn't have a friend in the world except for Aelyx, so his opinion was all that mattered. Strike that—judging by the L'annabe loitering at Cara's locker, it seemed she had two friends.

"*Haleem!*" The girl backed away from Aelyx to avoid killing him via hair dye.

"Actually, that means good-bye," Aelyx said. "*Mahra* is the word you want."

"Maaaa-hraaah." The L'annabe closed her eyes, savoring the exotic greeting in her mouth like a truffle. Half an inch of dishwater-blond roots told Cara the girl had quit coloring her hair, but unfortunately, she hadn't ditched the Quick Tan.

"What's your name?" Cara pried her fingers loose from Aelyx's, then shook her hand to get the blood flowing before entering her combination. "And where's the rest of you guys?"

"Ashley." An unnatural shade of orange darkened her cheeks as she glanced down, straightening the L'EIHR LOVER! button tacked to her sweater. "And it's just me now."

"Oh. Right." Apparently the other L'eihr Lovers couldn't take the heat, so they'd vacated the kitchen. Cara couldn't really blame them, but she admired Ashley's tenacity. A girl with enough guts to flaunt her unpopular beliefs could make a valuable addition to the debate team.

"Hey," Cara said. "You doing anything after school?"

"I don't think so. Why?"

"Want to come to debate practice with me? We only meet once a week now that I've got Aelyx to look after, so it's not a huge time commitment." She sized Ashley up—confident posture, articulate speech, and most importantly, she didn't say *like* or *um* after every other word. "I think you'd be good at it."

"Really?" Ashley beamed bright enough to turn her skin from orange to yellow.

"Really, really."

The warning bell chimed overhead, and Ashley managed a squeaky, "Okay," before waving good-bye and rushing toward the freshman wing.

"That was nice of you," Aelyx said from behind after Ashley had left.

Cara shrugged and popped open her locker. "I admire her guts. Not even my best friend wants to stand up for—" She cut off abruptly as a folded sheet of paper sailed out and drifted to her feet.

She tried hiding it from Aelyx, but he nudged her aside and scooped it off the floor. When he unfolded the sheet, she rested her hand on his forearm and peered around his shoulder. A message penned in meticulously formed capital letters warned, THE COP CAN'T ALWAYS BE THERE TO WATCH YOU. BUT I CAN. —HUMANIST

Humanist? The name sounded familiar. Wasn't that the blog troll who'd ranted about weapons and called her a bitch a few weeks ago?

Cara's mind flashed to the figure in the woods. What were the odds that this note was from the same person? Slim-to-none. But something about the handwriting bothered her, the way each letter imprinted into the paper. The writer had pressed so hard, he'd nearly pushed the ink through to the other side.

This was even weirder than her usual hate mail. "What cop?"

"That one, I suppose." Aelyx glanced over her head, and Cara whirled around to find the school resource officer ambling toward them. She recognized him as someone who'd graduated with her brother. He was fresh out of the police academy and so green he could pass for broccoli.

"Hey, Cara." Barry or Blaine, she couldn't remember which, crossed his arms and let a smile slip before clearing his throat and resuming his mask of super seriousness. "You hear from Troy?"

"No. He only e-mails when he wants something." She reached behind her back, grabbing the note from Aelyx and balling it in her fist. The last thing she wanted was a police escort through the halls because of these letters. "But if I hear from him, I'll tell him you said hi." She slammed her locker shut and started for homeroom, but he stopped her.

"Just so you know . . ." In true police fashion, he paused to adjust his utility belt, something they must've taught all cops in Doughnuts 101. "Someone called in a threat—nothing to worry about, but I'll be walking you and Aelyx to your classes now."

While Cara shut her eyes and groaned inwardly, Aelyx snatched the crumpled paper from her hand.

"Excellent." Aelyx tossed the note to the officer before she had a chance to snatch it back. "Because *Cah*-ra's been getting threatening notes."

"I wouldn't say that, Officer . . ." She trailed off, hoping to catch his name.

"Blake." He smoothed the note and studied it, front and back. "Blake Borsch." Holding the paper in midair, he asked, "Where're the others?"

"There was only one more, and it just said *traitor bitch*."

"Save 'em from now on. I need to see everything." With one hand on his Maglite, Blake extended the other toward the now vacant hall, clearing them for takeoff. "After you."

Cara slouched while trudging to class. It appeared she had three "friends" now: a sexy alien, a crazed fan girl, and a high school cop barely old enough to shave. Oh, and she just caught a glimpse of her former best friend holding hands with her ex. She squeezed her eyes shut, trying to brain-bleach them away. No such luck.

"You really think wars wouldn't break out if water became scarce?" Ashley asked Joss Fenske at practice later that afternoon. With a disbelieving shake of her head, she sat back and tapped an index finger against her desk. "Because countries have been battling over land and water rights for thousands of years."

Just as Cara had predicted, Ashley was a natural. A good thing, too, because Cara hadn't contributed much to the team today. Not that she hadn't tried, but the organized shun had popped her swagger bubble. She couldn't convince a pig to roll in mud today. The team didn't seem to mind—nobody had made eye contact with her that afternoon, not even Mr. Bastian, the faculty adviser. She'd hoped her teachers wouldn't sink so low, but a few of them had abruptly "forgotten" to write her letters of recommendation for her college applications. Speciesist jerks.

Since she was useless for debate, she might as well get her next blog post up. Cara flipped open her laptop and got to work.

Subscribe [Archive] [Recent Entries] [About Me]

Alienated

MAY THE SOURCE BE WITH YOU

TUESDAY, NOVEMBER 16
A Call to Arms!

In case you've been living under a rock and haven't heard, there's a new bill called the *L'eihr Expulsion Act* circulating among our representatives. Anyone with two brain cells to rub together—which is apparently more than Senator Ibis possesses—recognizes this bill for what it is: flagrant xenophobia. He's even stooped to accusing L'eihr exchange students of tainting local crops, which makes no sense. Why would L'eihrs blight a few random fields of soybeans, wheat, and grapes when they have the technology to eradicate all vegetation on Earth? Why not go balls to the wall and leave us at their mercy? Um, because WE'RE NOT ENEMIES, that's why!

Let's stop the crazy and work together to kill this bill. Here's how you can help . . .

Cara paused with her fingertips resting lightly against the keys, unable to continue. She didn't know what to say to rally the troops. Her readers already knew how to write their representatives—what she needed was a fresh idea.

She brainstormed for a few minutes, but nothing came. With a frustrated sigh, she closed her laptop again. It seemed she couldn't debate *or* blog when her give-a-crap was broken.

"Hey, guys." She stood and gathered her things. "I'm heading out early. Think I'm coming down with the flu." *The boo-hoo flu, that is.* "Ashley, you're doing great. See you next week?"

"Okay."

When Ashley continued to gaze at her in obvious concern, Cara flapped a hand and said, "It's probably one of those twenty-four-hour bugs. I'll be fine."

"Oh, I know." She sniffed a small laugh. "Just be careful not to give it to Aelyx."

Awesome. Good to know someone cared.

CHAPTER FOURTEEN

Aelyx assembled the microscope he'd borrowed from the school science lab. It was the most primitive piece of equipment he'd ever used, but the best he could manage considering he'd left his analytical tools on L'eihr. The rudimentary data from his water collection device indicated abnormally high pollutant levels, and curiosity had driven him to investigate.

That and sheer boredom.

He glanced at his bedroom wall. Cara was on the other side of that barrier, but she barely made a sound anymore. She didn't cry, laugh, argue, or debate. He'd allowed her to "win" two chess games, but that didn't help. Now she refused to play. Outside of school, he only saw her at meal times and when their paths intersected on the way to the bathroom. It was as if her glorious flame had been snuffed out, and he wished he knew how to ignite it again. He wanted his Elire back—his beautiful warrior.

With a quiet sigh, he placed a glass slide beneath the scope and removed the lid from his sterile petri dish. After giving the water inside his collection device a thorough shake, he unscrewed the cap and poured its contents into the dish, then squeezed two drops onto the slide. What he saw through the eyepiece made him gasp in shock.

"What the—?" Hundreds of green chunks permeated the water droplets, at first glance appearing plantlike. But he knew with complete certainty he'd gathered no such contaminants in his sample that day at the nature preserve. He isolated one furry bit and studied it under the highest magnification the tool would allow.

Within minutes, he'd identified the matter as *Sphagnum squarrosum*, or as humans referred to it, moss. But how could that be? Even if spores had been present in the water, they couldn't reproduce so quickly under sterile conditions, not to mention devoid of sunlight in an insulated metal tube. He must have made a mistake while collecting the sample—it was the only possibility.

The stereo speakers mounted on Cara's side of the wall broke the silence, vibrating the plaster in time with softly strumming guitar chords. If he listened carefully, he could just make out a man's sullen voice asking, *Please, please, please let me get what I want.* Gods, it was the most depressing song he'd ever heard. Why did humans feed their despondency with music like this?

Enough! If Cara wouldn't pull herself out of whatever hole she'd fallen into, then he would find a way to do it. And if winning at chess wouldn't restore her good cheer, he'd have to find another way to release enough endorphins to improve her mood.

He left his room and marched into the kitchen, where he prepared the richest, most indulgent, and disgusting dish imaginable—a bowl of fudge ripple ice cream topped with chocolate syrup, semi-sweet chocolate morsels, chocolate sprinkles, and, for good measure, a chocolate brownie from the pantry. He even garnished it with a handful of M&M's. This *had* to help. After tucking a spoon inside the bowl, he knocked on Cara's door and asked, "Can I come in?"

"S'open," she called, voice muffled as if she'd pulled the comforter over her head.

He was partially right—a pillow, not a blanket, covered Cara's face when he sat beside her on the bed. With his free hand, he yanked the pillow free, revealing blotchy, reddened cheeks and puffy eyes so bloodshot they nearly matched the rest of her. Tugging on her shoulder, he encouraged her to sit up while waving the bowl beneath her nose. "Look what I made for you. A bowl of diabetes."

She peered at the concoction for a nanosecond, then pulled a wadded tissue beneath her nose and turned away. "Thanks, but I'm not hungry."

"But . . ." Aelyx looked down at the bowl in his hand. "It's full of chocolate."

"Just stick it in the freezer."

Fasha. What now? Perhaps if he complimented her appearance . . .

He set the bowl on Cara's nightstand and surveyed her wrinkled pajamas and the snarled locks of hair framing her face. "You look lovely today." Was that a bit of potato chip stuck to the side of her forehead?

"Thanks, but you're a liar."

"Would you like me to . . ." He trailed off, grappling for inspiration. "Read to you? Or play your favorite video game? I'll let you win."

She released a hitched breath like tiny aftershocks following an earthquake. "I just wanna be alone, okay?"

Aelyx didn't want to go, but he'd run out of ideas. "All right." He pushed off the bed and retreated to his room for research. He had to find another way to help her.

Once seated on his carpeted floor, he turned on the laptop computer Colonel Rutter had given him, waiting patiently as it hummed to life before accessing Earth's web of electronic data. After checking his school e-mail account and deleting half a dozen messages from Brandi Greene, he clicked a search engine icon, then typed the words *how to* and paused, considering what to query. Before he'd decided between *cheer someone up* and *mend a broken heart*, the search engine suggested *how to kiss, how to make out, how to make love, how to boil an egg.*

Sexual reproduction and food—humans' two favorite subjects. He scoffed at their primitive drives, but then curiosity wrapped its fingers around his brain. Most humans expressed affection by pressing their lips together, a simple act, so why would anyone feel the need to research the process? Was there more to it?

He decided to find out.

Aelyx clicked the suggested links, and for the next two hours, he gave himself the kind of education they didn't provide at the Aegis.

Cara felt something gritty against her cheek and lifted her head from the pillow to investigate. Potato chip? She brushed the crumbs onto the floor and snuggled deeper into her cozy flannel bedding. A persistent beam of sunlight had escaped from a gap between the curtains and crept toward her face all afternoon, so she thwarted its efforts by pulling the sheet over her head. *Screw you, sunlight.*

She'd survived the first week of HALO's organized shun, but it left her feeling like a deflated balloon. Of all the students avoiding her, the only one who mattered was Tori, who looked almost as miserable as she was.

Tori clicked through the halls like a tiny high-heeled ghost. Shadows darkened the skin beneath her lifeless eyes, and she stared at the floor while loosely holding Eric's hand, never once looking at Cara. Did Tori miss her? Probably. Did she spend her afternoons crying in bed and listening to her mom's Morrissey collection? Probably not. But as much as Cara wanted to move forward, she didn't know how. She hadn't been able to blog since the day she found out about Tori and Eric. Heck, she hadn't even checked her e-mail.

She heard a sharp knock on the door and threw back the sheet.

"*Cah*-ra?" Aelyx called. "May I come in?"

Again? As much as she appreciated his concern, she wished he'd leave her alone. "Sure."

The door swung open, and he charged inside without hesitation, his hair loose and flowing behind him. He crossed the room and knelt on the floor beside her bed until they were at eye level.

"I made something for you." Teasingly, he dangled a sheet of white drawing paper just outside her reach. "But you can't have it until you get out of bed."

She considered snapping at him, but curiosity got the better of her. She kicked off the covers and stretched out, yawning. Then with a slow roll, she scooted off the mattress and joined him on the floor. "I'm out. Where's my prize?"

When he held up her reward, a tiny giggle rose to Cara's lips. It was Aelyx's pet, Vero, practically coming to life on the page. The animal *did* remind her of a lemur, but with the floppy ears of a Labrador and the thick body of a wildcat. Vero's head was cocked to the side, and he held his paw forward while studying her with enormous black eyes. His skin looked baby soft and delicate, like a hairless cat she'd once petted. Extending her index finger, Cara traced the graceful curve of Vero's tail, looking forward to the day she'd meet him in person. A year seemed far too long to wait.

"You're so full of it," she said.

"Me?" Aelyx said, pointing to himself with lifted brows.

"You said you were a bad artist. This is phenomenal."

"I said I wasn't great, and that's the truth. You don't know what Vero really looks like. I couldn't get his face quite right."

"Well, thanks for my present. Can I go back to bed now?"

"No." He curled his large, warm hand around hers, then seemed to think better of it and tucked it beneath his thigh. "There's more."

She waited for him to elaborate, but he didn't. Instead, his gaze darted back and forth between her throat and her lips while those silvery eyes darkened and jump-started her pulse. Seconds ticked by, but he kept watching her mouth. Was he trying to tell her something? Did she have food stuck between her teeth? She ran her tongue over the smooth enamel but didn't feel anything. That only made it worse. Aelyx swallowed so hard his Adam's apple shifted. He looked ready to choke. Or barf.

"More?" she prompted.

His eyes widened. "What?"

"You said there was more."

"Oh. Yes." Glancing at his lap, he cleared his throat and gathered his loose hair to secure it behind his neck. "I did some research today."

"On?"

"How to mend a broken heart, among other things." He pushed off the floor and brushed imaginary dust off his jeans. "One of the recommendations involved cosmetic procedures. Sorry, but I won't give you a pedicure."

The mental image of Aelyx painting her toenails made her laugh, despite the heaviness in her lungs.

"But I know something that'll help. Get your shoes. We'll have to hurry to make it back in time for the interview."

"Where're we going?"

A small grin curved his lips. "Let's just say we're getting your fight back."

"You're pulling my leg, right?" Cara craned her neck, narrowing her eyes at the sign hanging askew from high atop the crumbling brick warehouse. In peeling paint, it advertised the UPPERCUT BOXING GYM. They crouched behind a Dumpster in the back parking lot like muggers waiting to ambush a jogger. "It's not even open."

"I know." Aelyx pulled something from his back pocket that looked like a chrome key fob. "They're closed for renovations. Come on." He grabbed her hand and they sprinted to the back door. Why? She had no idea. When Aelyx held the gadget near the dead bolt, it emitted two high-pitched beeps, and the bolt slid out of place with a *click*. He pulled open the door and shoved her inside before closing and locking it behind them.

"What *is* that thing?" she asked, taking in her surroundings. The inside of Uppercut didn't look any more impressive than the outside. A low beam of sunlight cut through the windows, illuminating a few tattered black punching bags patched together with silver duct tape and hanging from the ceiling at awkward angles. A boxing ring stood in the distance, its sagging ropes a testament to all the bodies that had bounced against it over the years. Speaking of bodies, at least twenty years of bitter, reeking sweat seemed to seep through the walls, the floors, the weights . . . good God, it smelled like ass in here.

"An electron-tracker. It serves many purposes." He bent over an equipment bin, and Cara tried not to ogle his backside.

After a minute, he surfaced, holding two cracked red boxing gloves and a pair of those circular mitts the trainers wore over their hands in the movies.

"Breaking and entering a smelly gym? This is your plan to cheer me up? What's next, shoplifting used bowling shoes from the Goodwill?"

"Stop complaining and come over here." It wasn't a request. When she reluctantly obeyed, joining him near the water fountain, he held a glove open for her. "Go ahead."

She pushed a hand into one decrepit glove and then the other, trying not to think too hard about how many grimy fingers had curled into their padded depths before hers. Then she rested each glove against his belly while he tied the laces.

"So now what?" She let her heavy hands drop to her sides. "Fight Club: Human versus Alien?"

Aelyx slipped his round mitts on and beckoned her to come closer. "That's basically it." He held both hands up in front of his chest. "Hit me."

"Seriously?"

"Do it."

She rolled her eyes and gave a halfhearted swing at his hand, making contact with the tip of her glove.

"That was pathetic," he scolded. "Do it again. Get angry."

With a sigh, she tapped him again. What was the point? She didn't want to get angry—it took too much energy.

Aelyx shook his head, circling her like a shark in the water. "Again."

When she delivered another lackluster tap, he nudged her arm with one of his mitts and shouted, "Quit *fashing* around."

Her next attempt didn't please him, either. He nudged her in the back, harder. "More!"

She wound up and tried to put some force behind the next punch, but instead of praising her, he bumped her shoulder with so much force she fell back several steps. "Get angry!"

"Did you just push me?" Her pulse quickened and her cheeks flushed hot.

"The *Cah*-ra Sweeney I know"—another little shove—"wouldn't lie around"—and another, harder—"and hide under a blanket." His stunning face twisted into a scowl as he shouted, "Hit me!"

Flames licked Cara's body inside and out, and something in her chest popped like a soap bubble. Pulling her fist back, she tensed every muscle in her body, then delivered a blow with all her weight behind it. Her glove smacked Aelyx's padded hand with a booming *thud* that delighted her ears and stung her knuckles.

"Again!" he shouted.

She swung with the other hand, grunting like a savage, losing herself in a thrill of fury as she pummeled his hand. He didn't have to order her to keep going. With rage exploding from her body like an ignited fuel tanker, she advanced on Aelyx, pounding her fists into his waiting mitts again and again and again. A left jab—*Tori abandoned me*—a right hook—*Eric stole my best friend*—an uppercut—*the whole school hates me*—she only paused long enough to shake back her hair before resuming her attack. She may have even kicked him once or twice; it was hard to tell.

Adrenaline surged through her body, making her feel

invincible, and just when she wound up for another punch, Aelyx darted to the side and grabbed her around the waist, settling behind her, molding his body to hers.

"Good." He guided her to a battered punching bag. "Now don't stop."

And she didn't. It might have lasted thirty minutes or three hours. Time lost all meaning as pent-up hurt and anger spewed out with each frenzied strike of the bag. She pounded it until her breath came in gasps and her heart lodged inside her throat. When she didn't have the strength to lift her gloves anymore, she crumpled to the floor and pushed her dampened hair away from her face. Her lungs burned, her body ached, and she hadn't felt this good in weeks. Tori's betrayal was still fresh, but for the first time, Cara knew it wouldn't break her.

Aelyx crouched down, tossing his mitts to the floor and smiling so widely it would have stolen her breath if she'd had any to spare. "There's my Elire." He pronounced it *eh-leer.*

"What's that?" she asked.

"Your L'eihr name. I think I'll call you that from now on." He pulled a dry washcloth from the waistband of his jeans and sat beside her on the dirty tile floor, scooting close enough to blot the sweat from her forehead. Then he unlaced her gloves and tugged them off.

"*Eh-leer,*" she repeated, trying it on while flexing her stiff fingers. "What does it mean?"

"Beautiful warrior."

She ducked her head, face glowing impossibly hot under his gaze, which had darkened again and dropped to her mouth. He trailed the washcloth down her temple and along her jawline before handing it off.

"Perhaps you should take over from here," he whispered.

"Thanks." The air between them crackled with energy so thick it was almost tangible, his face close enough for her to feel his warm breath. Just when she thought he might kiss her, he rolled to his feet and backed away.

"The interview," he reminded her.

"Oh, right." She scrambled to push off the floor, but her spaghetti-noodle arms wouldn't hold her weight. "I might need a little help."

He hesitated, then reached out a hand. "Of course. What are friends for?"

Aelyx had once heard Bill Sweeney say, *A little knowledge is a dangerous thing.* As he sat beside Cara on the sofa, watching her face tipped toward the makeup artist, her full lips parted to receive a coat of lipstick, he began to understand why. Ever since his research into kissing and other human mating rituals, his mind had relentlessly fixated on Cara, flashing manufactured sensations of how her soft, wet mouth might feel against his own. He could almost taste her on his tongue, and when his traitorous body responded to the fantasy, he had to pull an accent pillow onto his lap and force himself to recite Earth's periodic table of elements. Gods, what had he unleashed? How would he survive the remainder of the exchange like this?

"You know," Sharon Taylor said to Cara, "with your fair skin, you'd look great as a blonde."

"Oh." Cara touched her hair self-consciously and cleared her throat, a nervous habit she displayed during each interview. "I don't think so. The upkeep's too spendy."

"You sure? My stylist's a miracle worker. I can get you squeezed in for an emergency appointment. You're practically a celebrity now. We've had a ton of requests for photo spreads, and I figured you'd want to look your best. But if you don't care . . ." She trailed off, making her judgment clear.

What nonsense. He'd grown weary of humans trying to modify Cara's hair, cover her skin with cosmetics, stuff her into revealing clothes. "I like your natural color," he announced. "It reminds me of the autumn leaves." They'd all fallen now, and strangely enough, he missed their vibrancy.

"Really?" She inspected a lock of her hair and parted her lips again. Those lips . . .

Hydrogen, helium, lithium, what comes next . . . oh, beryllium, boron.

"Whatever." Sharon studied her reflection in a compact mirror and tilted her head from side to side. "We're changing things up tonight." The compact snapped shut with a *click.* "I'm asking questions submitted by the viewers. And I'll warn you, some of them aren't pretty."

Aelyx knew this should please him. All the hate mail he and the Sweeneys had received indicated humans had nearly reached the breaking point, which meant returning home sooner. So why did his stomach sink at the thought?

He wished he could escape with Cara and leave both their worlds behind. Would she go? It didn't matter. There was nowhere *to* go.

The interview began in the typical fashion, with Sharon making thinly veiled implications about his relationship with Cara. He didn't discourage her. The idea of an illicit human–L'eihr tryst would drive extremists half mad, sparking them into action.

"Aelyx." Sharon's voice brought him to attention. "Our first question comes from Jamie in Ohio. She asks, *How do L'eihrs feel about the Expulsion Act, especially considering all you've done for cancer victims?*"

He leaned forward and folded his hands. "We don't harbor any ill will against humans for HALO's actions. We know they make up a small percentage of the population." He smiled. "They're just more vocal than the rest."

"And why is that?" Cara demanded, straightening beside him on the sofa. "Why is it always the crazies who make their voices heard while everyone else shuts up and does nothing?" Her face darkened, pulse thumping at the base of her throat. "This is how discriminatory legislation gets passed—people know it's wrong, but they're too lazy or too scared to take action. Hello? Jim Crow laws, anyone? Not that long ago, it was illegal to consort with a member of another race. What if the civil rights leaders of the sixties had sat back and waited for someone else to fix the problem? Nothing would've changed."

Sharon's reaction reminded Aelyx of a parent patting a youngster on the head. "Well," she said with a smile, "aren't you opinionated?"

"Yeah," Cara said, lifting her chin. "And unlike most of America, I'm not afraid to express it."

Sharon tapped the end of her golden pen against her lips, then pointed it at Cara. "But you've suffered the consequences for that, haven't you? Isn't it true your best friend and your boyfriend of three years have stopped speaking to you, along with most of the school?"

The color drained from Cara's cheeks, but she smoothed a wrinkle from the tan slipcover and gave a quick nod. "That's all right. Just shows who my real friends are."

"Aelyx," Sharon said, "why do you think your presence has sparked such an extreme reaction here?"

"It's biological," he said. "A natural human response to fear something different or strange. It's in your genetic makeup. And when an individual's afraid, it's an equally natural human response to strike out in defense."

"Like the basic flight or fight reflex?" Sharon asked.

"Exactly." Cara had warned him against hurling "jabs," but no one could fault him for delivering a blow disguised as compassion. "I don't believe members of Humans Against L'eihr Occupation are terrible people. I think they're frightened and misguided, and we should pity them. In fact, I believe a quote from your Bible summarizes the situation perfectly."

"And what's that?"

"They know not what they do." He added a sad shake of his head as he relaxed against the sofa. "They're afraid but quite harmless, I'm sure." If that didn't stir their rage, nothing would. He glanced at Cara, who studied him beneath a puckered brow. Perhaps he'd "laid it on a bit thick," as the human expression went.

Sharon nodded in agreement and said, "Our next question comes from Sean, right here in Midtown. *How do you explain the death of crops near Midtown, Lanzhou, and Bordeaux? It only makes sense that L'eihr exchange students are to blame.*"

"I can't explain the anomaly," Aelyx said, "but it's absurd to assume we're killing your crops. What would any of us stand to gain from that?"

Sharon lifted one shoulder. "You have to admit it's quite a coincidence."

"Or not," Cara interjected. "People need to take off their tinfoil hats. I'll bet someone's trying to frame the L'eihrs by blighting our fields. I wouldn't put it past these crazies. I mean, what's a little soybean-murder to someone who threatens people just for talking to us?"

"I guess it's possible." Sharon flashed a loaded grin and said to Cara, "You're quick to come to Aelyx's defense. I can tell he means a lot to you."

Cara turned her soft blue gaze to him, holding there and shaming him with the admiration he saw. "You're right." Then, just when he thought he couldn't feel any lower, she added, "He's an amazing friend, and I'm proud to know him."

Aelyx swallowed hard, trying to push down that old familiar feeling that burned a hole in his throat. He wondered how grateful Cara would be if she knew his real purpose on Earth. He wasn't a friend. Friends didn't deceive each other, destroy lives, and then escape to another galaxy.

For the first time since arriving on Earth, Aelyx felt subhuman.

CHAPTER FIFTEEN

Subscribe [Archive] [Recent Entries] [About Me]

Alienated

MAY THE SOURCE BE WITH YOU

TUESDAY, NOVEMBER 26
Alone in a crowd.

Let's get serious for a minute. These days, my family's not feeling
the love, and it kinda hurts. My dad was banned from his favorite
pub, the one he helped save from an electrical fire last year. My
mom—who insists on "re-homing" captured moles from our
yard and volunteers thirty hours a week at the library—had her
car keyed three times in the parking lot.

As for me, people literally turn their backs when I walk by, most
of my "friends" wouldn't spit on me if I were on fire, and now
I can't even buy a pack of gum in this town. I'm serious. The
owner of the Midtown Grocery posted my picture behind all
the cash registers, right alongside sketchy perps who write bad
checks. Nice, huh? Apparently they don't serve my kind here.
And what is *my kind*, you ask?

Well, I like to think I'm the tolerant, forward-thinking kind. The
decent kind. The kind who believes we can learn a lot from
L'eihrs. And despite experiences to the contrary, I know I'm not
alone. If you're one of *my kind*, it's time to stand and be heard.

There are nearly one million followers on this blog, and if we all work together, we can . . .

"Any suggestions?" Cara asked Ashley, who perched beside her in the empty World Studies classroom where the debate team used to practice before they joined the shun. "I want to bring the hammer down on HALO, but not by stooping to their level."

Ashley chewed on the end of her ballpoint pen, orangey forehead wrinkled in thought. "You could ask your supporters to start a petition against the Expulsion Act."

"True," Cara agreed, "but I'd like to make a bigger impression."

Ashley considered a moment and suggested, "How about an online movement to educate people?"

"Like . . . ?" Cara prompted.

"Like an International L'eihr Awareness Day."

"Huh." Now that was an idea. They could call it L'awareness Day. "I kinda like it. We could do a mythbusters segment, too. Finally debunk the crazy rumors about crop killings and abductions and mutant alien babies."

Nodding vigorously, Ashley continued. "You could ask other bloggers to join in by giving them a discussion prompt, maybe design a logo to grab for their sites."

"You know what'd be cool?" Cara said. "To incorporate some kind of contest and let the winner Skype with Aelyx."

"I'd be all over that," Ashley said.

"Public demonstrations would be even better, but that's hard to organize on a global level."

"Worth a try, though."

"Thanks for the idea," she said, giving Ashley's shoulder a light bump. "Hey, maybe you could guest post for me next week."

Ashley's blond brows shot toward her hairline. "Seriously?"

"Yeah." Then Cara added a dollop of figurative whipped cream and a cherry on top. "You should interview Aelyx for a special feature."

"Omigod!" Ashley squealed, bouncing in her seat. "Omigod, omigod, omigod!"

"Is that a yes?"

"Yes!" She quit vibrating long enough to ask, "So, should I call him? My hair still hasn't grown out from when I dyed it, so maybe I shouldn't get too close."

"Nah," Cara said. "I'm sure the chemicals have faded enough by now. He's probably in the library if you want to get started. I need to wrap up this post, and I don't think anyone's going to show for prac—"

Before Cara could finish, Ashley snatched her notebook in one hand and bolted for the door. The echo of her squeaking sneakers faded as she jogged down the hall, leaving a smile on Cara's face. If the former L'eihr Lovers could see Ashley now . . .

Cara returned her attention to her computer, where she outlined a basic plan for L'awareness Day and scheduled it a month in advance, hoping that would give her enough time to work out the details. Just as Cara hit the publish button, Ashley came dragging through the door with her shoulders slumped.

She tossed her notebook onto the desk. "He wasn't in the library."

"How about the computer lab?"

"No dice."

"Huh," Cara said. "That's weird. I wonder where he is."

"Look at this!" Aelyx used his com-sphere's magnification feature to show Eron the sample in his petri dish. "I collected the water a week ago, filtered it through a micro-strainer to remove contaminants, and then poured it back into the tube. When I opened it today, this was everywhere."

"Impossible." Eron's hologram bent over the dish, peering inside.

"That's what I thought when I analyzed my first sample. It was moss that time. What about yours?"

Eron glanced up. "I never opened my tube. The initial diagnostics were enough for me."

"Go get it." Aelyx wasn't sure what outcome he wanted—if Eron's sample displayed the same characteristics, it would validate his findings. But it would also mean something was terribly wrong with Earth's water supply—or at least the water near Midtown and Lanzhou.

In minutes, Eron returned with a glass bowl. He set it in the bathtub, unscrewed the lid to his collection tube, and poured the contents into the dish. Once Eron magnified the sample with his com-sphere, Aelyx noticed a heap of tangled, filamentous algae in the water.

"Bleeding gods," Aelyx whispered. "What does it mean?"

Eron shook his head in disbelief. "A shame we're translators and not scientists."

"Could the *sh'alear* have caused this?"

"Impossible," Eron said. "It kills plant growth; it doesn't accelerate it."

"You're right. We should probably tell Stepha." Aelyx wasn't looking forward to that conversation. He'd never been skilled at deception, and he feared the ambassador would glimpse his face and immediately know he'd done something wrong. "I'll contact him tonight."

"And I'll ask Syrine to check her sample." Eron disposed of his water by pouring it into the toilet, but instead of flushing it down, he avoided Aelyx's gaze and said, "I'm going to speak with her about something else, too."

"What's that?"

"I'm going to uproot my *sh'alear*. We were wrong about humans."

Aelyx wanted to contradict him, but when he opened his mouth to speak, the words clung to the back of his throat. In truth, he wanted to abandon their plan, too, but not because he'd changed his mind about all humans. Just one. It was at that moment Aelyx realized he didn't want the exchange to end. Ever. Leaving Cara behind would be harder than severing his own arm. But despite that, he felt a duty to put aside his feelings and focus on L'eihr.

Aelyx considered his next words carefully. Eron had always been different—more sensitive than most of their kind. "I know you've taken a liking to your 'brother' . . ."

"It's not just that—"

"But," Aelyx continued, "I'm afraid he's clouded your judgment."

"Do you trust me?" Eron asked. When Aelyx gave a reluctant nod, he added, "Do you think I would do anything to endanger our Sacred Mother?"

"Not intentionally." Aelyx nodded at the miniature toilet. "But look at your water sample. Look what they've done to Earth."

Eron flushed the toilet as if to destroy the evidence. "That doesn't mean they'll do the same on L'eihr. The colonists will be carefully screened."

"You don't know that."

"Please," Eron said, turning up both palms in surrender. "Will you at least consider it?"

For several eternal moments, Aelyx said nothing as his heart and mind battled for dominance. In the end, his heart won. "Fine. I'll consider it. But Syrine won't."

"Don't be so sure. She'd do anything for me."

"Not this."

"I have hope." Eron lifted two fingers in a good-bye. "That's enough for now."

Chapter Sixteen

"'Oh, the weather outside is frightful,'" Mom's soft voice sang slightly off-key, accompanied by the sizzle and pop of hot oil, "'but the fire is so delightful.'"

Cara smiled and glanced at Aelyx, leaning in to whisper, "Mom lives for Christmas carols. She won't stop until February. Enjoy." With the exception of classical instrumentals, Aelyx despised human music.

He pressed his lips close to her ear and made her shiver. "If that wretched noise makes Eileen happy, I'll find a way to tolerate it."

"'And since we've no place to go,'" Mom crooned while flipping a chicken thigh in the frying pan, "'let it snow, let it snow, let it snow.'"

Cara held a slippery, wet carrot in one hand and a peeler in the other. While she carved away the dirty orange exterior, she thought about Christmas, specifically what to buy for Aelyx.

She wanted to give him a special reminder of Earth to take back to L'eihr in the spring, a small memento to keep in his room at the Aegis. Her chest ached when she imagined life without him. Sure, things would go back to normal within the community, maybe they'd be able to grocery shop in Midtown instead of driving an hour away and coming home with melted ice cream, but she'd miss him. Terribly.

She continued peeling the carrot, but her thoughts were still with Aelyx. Given how much he hated Earth, he'd probably never come back to visit, and she couldn't travel beyond the stratosphere until next fall. With a sigh, she turned to watch him.

Aelyx stood at the other end of the kitchen counter dicing a potato with the skill and ease of a master chef. Unbelievable. She studied the misshapen chunks of vegetables on her cutting board.

"I'm starting to feel inadequate," she said. "You slaughter me at chess—"

"But it took eighteen moves last time. That's an improvement." His knife never slowed as he spoke.

"You finished your physics project in ten minutes," she continued. "You just beat my high score in Total Zombie Massacre, and you even outperform me in my own kitchen." A one-armed monkey could outperform her in the kitchen, but that was beside the point. She washed another carrot and then returned to her spot at the counter. "One of these days,

I'll find your kryptonite and win at something besides Puppy Love."

"Actually, I beat your high score last night. Canine number fifteen enjoyed having his ears scratched, so the game awarded bonus points for that. But don't sell yourself short," he said with a smile in his voice. "You throw a mean right hook."

Cara laughed and the peeler slipped in her wet grasp, slicing the side of her index finger. She sucked a loud gasp.

In a flash, Aelyx was there. He pulled her to the sink, turned on the faucet, and held her hand beneath a stream of cool water. The sight of blood and the throb of her finger should have bothered her, but she was far too distracted by the warmth of Aelyx's body pressed against her from behind. His hot breath tickled the skin on the side of her neck, and she unconsciously closed her eyes. The urge to lean into him and rest the back of her head on his shoulder, to mold her whole body to his, was almost uncontrollable.

Mom's voice broke the spell, jerking Cara out of her haze. "You okay?" She inspected the cut. "It's not deep." She wadded a clean paper towel against the wound. "Here, hold this over it for a minute, and you two find something to do until dinner's ready."

"Come on." Aelyx took her arm, leading her out the back door. "I wanted to show you something anyway."

It was a perfect late-autumn evening, with the low sun glowing gently behind the dormant trees, softening the angles of their naked branches. A light chill brushed Cara's cheeks, refreshing but not too frigid, and the sweet scent of wood smoke drifted on the breeze. Aelyx scanned the surrounding acreage using some kind of gadget that detected warm-blooded life-forms. Aside from a few squirrels, nothing was lurking out there, so he took her injured hand while towing her into the woods.

"Let's see." Gingerly, he lifted the paper towel. "No more bleeding. I think you'll live." He tucked the makeshift bandage in his pocket but kept her hand. "Maybe you should pay attention when you're wielding sharp objects."

"Hey, it's your fault. You made me laugh."

Turning her palm upward, he began tracing the lines with his thumb as they walked. His liquid-silver eyes blazed beneath dark lashes. "How can I make it up to you?"

Cara's heart fluttered. She cleared her throat and said, "Teach me your chess strategy." But that wasn't the first thought that came to mind. Not even close.

"I don't know." He stroked her palm in circles. "It might take twenty moves to defeat you then."

The heat radiating from Aelyx's touch was making her dizzy, so she reclaimed her hand and turned her gaze to the forest floor. "So, uh, are you getting tired of all my blog questions yet?"

"I think I can stand a few more."

"Good, because people want to know how L'eihrs evolved. I guess it's a preview of where humans are heading, right?"

He helped her over a patch of mud. "Yes and no. You have to remember most of our advances are due to selective breeding. For example, our brains grew larger over time, but because only those with extrasensory abilities were selected to reproduce, all L'eihrs can use Silent Speech."

"That's your name for telepathy?"

"Right." He tapped an index finger against her temple. "Your brains will grow, but unless you stop procreating for love, your abilities won't change."

"What else?"

"We no longer have an appendix, but that's also a result of organized breeding, not evolution. Let me think . . ." He paused for a moment. "Oh, if I focus, I can regulate my body temperature by several degrees."

"No way!"

"Way," he said with a grin. "Honestly, though, it's easier to put on a sweater. There are a couple others that come to mind, like increased lung capacity and greater endurance."

"This is so cool. I can't believe I didn't ask you sooner." She slid a glance at him and bit her lip before adding, "I wouldn't mind hearing about your weapons, either." She'd wanted to broach the subject for weeks, but she didn't know how. Nobody, not even the highest-ranking military officials, knew about them. She looked up and met his gaze. "Off the record?"

It took a lot to render Aelyx speechless, but this did the trick. He didn't seem offended, more like contemplative, unsure of how much to reveal. They continued in silence, and when they reached a small stream, Aelyx pointed to a cluster of trees and ignored her question. "Look around. I want you to remember this place."

"Why?" Glancing at the barren forest, she noted a few distinct markers: a boulder shaped like a kidney, an old deer blind nailed to the massive oak on her left, and a rotting fallen cedar damming the stream, pooling the water into an algae-coated, mucky pond.

He pointed to the charred remains of a tree, cleaved in half by lightning. "If anything happens and we get separated, I want you to meet me right there."

"What do you mean if anything happens?"

He lowered his head to deliver a solemn look. "One of these days, things could get violent. Your military will probably protect us both, but I've picked this spot as a rendezvous point."

"Okay, but why here?"

A smile curved his lips. "Because this is where the ambassador parked my getaway car."

Before she had a chance to ask what he was talking about, Aelyx took her hand and led her to the split tree. He reached down, scooped a handful of dirt and debris into his fist, then pointed high above their heads with his other hand. "Watch this." With a mighty heave, he threw the dirt into the air, where it did something scientifically impossible: struck an invisible barrier and bounced back, showering them in pebbles and dust.

She brushed off her sweater and face. "What was that?"

Aelyx pulled the key fob gadget from his back pocket, the same one he'd used to break into the boxing gym. Holding it above his head, he shouted, "*Elire*," and two quick beeps pierced the air. Then, like something out of a science fiction flick, a sleek, silvery spacecraft morphed into view, suspended above them like a massive, solidified water droplet. "Cloaking device," Aelyx explained. "Hides it from view."

"Nice getaway car." She grinned at him. "Let's go for a ride!"

Aelyx shook his head, shouting Cara's nickname again, and they watched the craft disappear. "My shuttle is like the credit card your father gave you last week. Only for life-threatening emergencies. Syrine and Eron have one, too. Just in case."

"Seriously? You're gonna show me that and not take me up for a spin?"

"Yes." Chuckling, he wrapped an arm around her shoulder. "If you'd ever experienced a dozen lashes with the *iphet*, you'd understand."

"Oh. Sorry." Once again, she'd forgotten that L'eihrs didn't hand out detention for breaking the rules. And since free speech as she knew it in America didn't seem to exist on L'eihr, his leaders might've forbidden him from discussing weapons. L'eihrs didn't screw around, and she didn't want him whipped with that electric thing. "I didn't think about that when I asked about your weapons."

"Would you really like to know?" he asked hesitantly. "I'll tell you if you promise to keep it off the blog."

"You sure? I don't want you to do anything you'll regret."

"I trust you."

"Okay, then."

He took a deep breath and began. "Our weapons were once like yours—crude projectiles designed to damage the body. But over thousands of years, the weapons evolved as we did. They were designed to be more efficient and humane, and eventually one was created that killed without harming the body or the environment around the body."

"How?"

"We call it *iphal*, which means 'end.' It delivers a concentrated pulse of energy that disrupts the heart's rhythm. The victim dies instantly, without pain and with no destruction to the tissue. There are *iphals* used for individuals—during an execution, for example. And there are larger ones used to neutralize a more comprehensive force, like an opposing battalion."

"Whoa," she heard herself whisper. "You can take out whole squadrons with a burst of energy?" She hadn't expected anything that frightening. No wonder the L'eihrs kept it a secret.

Aelyx seemed to sense her panic. "L'eihrs don't attack without provocation. We really aren't an aggressive people."

Sure, but humans would go ballistic if they learned L'eihrs could end their lives with a simple heart-zapper. She couldn't tell anyone, not even Mom or Dad.

Suddenly her mind shifted gears and she remembered Aelyx's mysterious late-night trips into the woods. Everything clicked. "This is where you've been going—to check on your getaway car!"

His brows lowered in confusion at the abrupt change in their conversation.

"The times you snuck out of the house," she explained. "You've been coming here."

"Oh." Slowly, understanding dawned across his face,

followed by something that looked a lot like guilt. He hesitated long enough to tell her a lie would follow. "Yes, I had to make sure the cloaking device hadn't . . . uh . . . disengaged."

"You *weren't* coming here?"

At that, his chin lifted. "I just told you I was." Then he turned and stalked back the way they'd come.

Cara knew a guy on the defensive when she saw one. Eric used to do the same thing—deflect and get angry with her when he'd done something wrong. So what had Aelyx done wrong? And more importantly, how would his people punish him if they found out?

Chapter Seventeen

Cara hugged herself and shivered against the cold. Pulling her fluffy bathrobe collar around her neck, she shuffled her bare feet along the rough ground of the forest, wincing when an acorn pricked her heel. She knew this place—the kidney-shaped boulder and the blackened tree, split in half by lightning. Aelyx's meeting point. What on earth was she doing there? In her bathrobe?

A loud buzzing vibrated the air above, and she lifted her face to the treetops expecting to see a mutant-sized hornets' nest. Instead, Aelyx's chrome shuttle morphed into view, drifting slowly to the ground like a fallen leaf. She backed away, fearing the heat from its thrusters, but nothing touched her skin aside from a light breeze. The shuttle doors melted open, and Aelyx smiled from inside, strapped into the pilot's seat.

"Come away with me." He extended his hand like Peter Pan, ready to fly her to Neverland.

Forever? The word didn't leave her lips, but somehow Aelyx heard. Still grinning, he nodded and motioned for her to come closer.

But what about Mom and Dad? Before Aelyx could reply, the crunch of footsteps sounded from behind, and she whirled around to find Eric and Tori regarding her. They were younger versions of themselves: Eric, the string-bean boy with bad skin and an easy smile, and Tori, the tiny seventh-grade firecracker wearing her goalie uniform, brushing her lips with the end of her long braid. They both had tears in their eyes.

"Are you really gonna leave us here to die?" Tori asked.

To die? Cara didn't understand.

Someone grabbed her arm and she gasped, jerking awake.

"You okay?" Aelyx leaned over his desk, tilting his head in concern.

"Yeah." She sat up and rubbed her eyes while darting a glance at her math teacher, who had his back to her. She'd never fallen asleep in class before, and she hoped he hadn't noticed.

When the bell rang, Cara thought about the dream while following Officer Blake to her locker. It didn't take a shrink to figure out the symbolism. If she were honest with herself— and she usually tried to be—she had to admit her feelings for Aelyx had moved beyond friendship. She didn't want him to leave without her. The only part of the dream that didn't make sense was Tori and Eric. Why would they care if she left? They had each other now, the backstabbing bastards.

"You look a little pale," Blake said, studying Cara as she entered her combination. "Well, paler than usual, anyway."

"I'm just tired. Couldn't sleep last night." When she turned to check the clock at the other end of the hall, she noticed Tori—the new and "improved" version—staring at her from the entrance to the girls' bathroom.

Tori's red-stained lips pressed into an unforgiving line, her once-laughing eyes narrowed into slits. If looks could kill, Cara would be sporting a toe tag right about now. Tori jerked a thumb toward the bathroom in a rude summons, but Cara shook her head. She had no desire to be alone with her former best friend.

All traces of Tori had vanished, both inside and out, and Cara wondered what she was capable of these days. Delivering a threat for her Patriot friends? Cara didn't want to believe it, but then again, she'd never expected Tori to hook up with Eric, either. Cara's golden-haired ex strolled to Tori's side, taking her hand and towing her in the other direction. As she catwalked out of sight in her high-heeled boots, Tori glanced over her shoulder and burned one more death glare into Cara's forehead.

Just like that, Cara forgot her locker combination. She was vaguely aware of Aelyx speaking, but couldn't interpret his words over the throbbing pulse in her ears. What was Tori's problem? It wasn't enough that she'd destroyed their friendship—she had to declare some lame girlie-war, too?

Aelyx turned her face, meeting her eyes. "Elire, she wants to hurt you. Don't give her what she wants."

His voice boomed painfully inside her head. "Why are you shouting? I'm right h—" Suddenly, it occurred to her that Aelyx wasn't talking. She heard his voice, uncomfortably loud, but his lips remained sealed, just like in the dream. "What the hell *was* that?" She bolted back, slamming her head against the locker door.

"Whoa." Blake's jaw dropped. "What's with you?"

"Uh . . ." Cara rubbed the back of her head and thought fast. "I saw a mouse." She pointed across the hall and clarified, "Over there."

As soon as Blake stalked forward, eyes fixed on the floor, Cara whispered to Aelyx, "I don't know what you just did to me, but we're gonna try it again!"

"Twenty-seven."

"Good." Aelyx rewarded Cara with a fist bump that didn't quite connect. He sat facing Cara on the beige-carpeted floor of his room, which she'd decided was the best setting for their experiment. It's empty and completely boring, she'd said, so we won't get distracted. The house was quiet, with Bill working a forty-eight-hour shift at the fire station and Eileen volunteering at the library.

He touched his forehead to Cara's, stared into her wide blue eyes, and thought of another number.

"One thousand, two hundred and nine," she said. "But can you stop yelling?"

He sat back, wondering why Silent Speech seemed loud to her. Perhaps her human brain wasn't equipped to handle it. That would explain why he wasn't able to fully connect with her cognizant mind. "I'm not yelling. There's no volume control for thoughts."

"So it doesn't seem loud when you talk to other L'eihrs?"

"No."

"Oh." She slouched against the bed frame and swirled her fingertips across the carpet. "What's it like when you hear it?"

"I hear thoughts like they're spoken. But I can feel emotions, too. It's one of the ways we know if someone is telling the truth. And we can project images and sensations." He didn't realize until then how much he'd missed communicating silently with his own people. During these past few months on Earth, he'd been more vocal than in a lifetime on L'eihr.

"Can I try sending you a thought?" she asked.

"Sure, but don't expect too much. Receiving information's easier than projecting. It took thousands of years to refine it."

Cara nodded, setting her long auburn hair in motion. She leaned forward and gazed into his eyes. Several moments ticked by, but he heard nothing.

He shook his head. "Sorry."

"Can you send me a picture? I want to see something from L'eihr."

"Sure." Aelyx stretched out, considering which memory to use. A moment later, he'd found just the right one. "This'll be harder than receiving words or numbers, so try to relax your mind."

"Okay."

Peering deep into her eyes, he recalled a memory from the Aegis—at the end-of-year games when his peers had cheered him on during the obstacle course competition—so Cara could see his home wasn't as cold and inhospitable as she thought.

She sat still and focused. "Hey! I don't see anything, but I feel you. You're totally pumped! What's so—" Suddenly, she grimaced and pulled away, holding her forehead between her hands.

"Are you okay?" Aelyx shot forward and steadied her shoulders.

"Yeah, just a headache. It's not that bad."

He sat back, inspecting her. "We've overworked your brain."

"What?" Cara's head snapped up while her brows lowered, forming a slash above her narrowed eyes. "We've overworked my feeble brain? Is that what you mean?"

"Don't be ridiculous." He pushed to his feet. "Put pressure on your temples. I'll be right back."

"Where're you going?"

"To make some herbal tea for you," he called while striding into the hall. "It might ease your headache."

When he returned a few minutes later, she seemed more relaxed, indicating the headache had passed. Still, they should stop for the day. He didn't want to hurt her.

"Our brains are physically different." He handed her the tea. "I didn't say yours was feeble. I think you have a beautiful mind, Elire."

"Thanks." She took the steaming mug. "Sorry about that."

"It's all right." He sat beside her on the carpet and inhaled his tea's fruity scent. A hint of orange in the brew reminded him of Cara's shampoo.

"Hey." She paused to blow into her cup. "Can I ask you something?"

"Of course."

"Do you have a girlfriend back home?"

"I've felt some attachments in the past, but no, I don't have what you'd describe as a girlfriend."

Cara cleared her throat and began chewing her thumbnail. "What about Syrine?"

"What about her?"

"Do you . . . um." She stared down into her mug. "Have a special relationship with her?"

The bond he shared with Syrine had outlasted a dozen other friendships, something he'd qualify as special, but judging by Cara's scarlet cheeks, she had another type of relationship in mind. "Define special relationship."

"Well, have you ever kissed her?"

The mental image of putting his tongue into Syrine's mouth made him laugh. "No. I've never kissed Syrine or anyone else, for that matter."

"What?" She glanced up from her tea, her eyes like saucers. "You've never kissed a girl?"

He shrugged. "That's not how we show affection."

"Really?"

"Truly."

"Too bad," she said over the top of her mug. "You don't know what you're missing."

"Not much, I imagine. I researched it, and it sounds bizarre to me."

Cara smiled to herself. "Not if you're doing it right. Nothing's hotter than a good kiss."

"Nothing except *sh'ellam*. It always leads to more."

"So does an amazing kiss."

The challenge in her eyes prompted him to say something he probably shouldn't have. "Care to put it to a test?"

Her pink lips parted in shock.

Was she revolted by the idea? Disappointment knotted his chest. "Don't worry. If you're uneasy—"

"I'm not uneasy." She huffed and set her cup of tea on the floor. "Bring it!"

"You sure?"

"It's on. You go first."

Aelyx hesitated a moment, then stood and carried their mugs to the dresser. He offered his hand to Cara and pulled her to her feet.

"Are you wearing a shirt underneath that sweater?" he asked.

She cleared her throat again, blushing. "Yeah, why?"

"This'll work better if more of your skin's exposed."

After a moment's hesitation, she pulled the sweater over her head, tossed it onto the bed, and stood before him in a cream-colored tank top. "What am I supposed to do?"

"Nothing. Just stand still, close your eyes, and relax."

She took a deep breath and nodded, then shut her eyes and let her arms hang loosely at her sides.

Aelyx's palms had become clammy, and he wiped them

on his jeans, grateful Cara couldn't see how nervous she'd made him. A wave of doubt crested within him. What if she hated it? What if this confirmed that his attraction to her was one-sided?

"What're you waiting for?" she asked.

"Nothing." He stepped forward until their bodies barely touched.

Closing his eyes, he wrapped his hand around Cara's fragile wrist, then smoothed it slowly up the length of her arm to her shoulder. He gulped a breath. Bleeding gods, no substance in his world or hers had ever felt so soft. He skimmed two fingers across her collarbone and rested them at the base of her throat, feeling the pulse of her heart beating through the delicate skin. He'd touched her there a dozen times in his dreams, but it didn't compare to reality.

"Your heart rate is eighty beats per minute," he said quietly, trying not to let his voice tremble.

"Why does that matt—"

"Shh. Don't talk."

With his other hand, he swept Cara's silken hair out of the way, lightly brushing her neck with his fingertips. Her breathing hitched, and he paused for a moment, stunned by her reaction. Had she actually liked that? Was it possible she wanted him? There was only one way to find out.

He nestled his cheek against hers, indulging in the feel of her bare skin. Keeping one hand at her throat, he flattened the other against her back, where heat radiated from beneath the thin fabric of her top. He stroked the length of her spine from top to bottom, his fingertips massaging, teasing, and trailing lightly, leaving her skin covered in goose bumps.

He whispered into her ear, "By monitoring our partner's heart rate, we know how they're reacting to our touch. The body doesn't lie. This is the truest test of physical attraction. For example," he said, stroking the base of her throat with his thumb, "your pulse is ninety beats per minute and increasing very quickly." She *did* want him. He couldn't believe it. The soft curves of her body rose and fell against him as the pace of her breathing accelerated, his own pulse quickening in response.

Aelyx brushed his lips back and forth against her ear and whispered, "One-ten now." But he hoped they could do better than that. He continued to caress her back, pulling her body even closer to his and brushing his lips down her neck to the top of her shoulder. A quiet murmur escaped the back of her throat and fire pulsed through his veins.

More. He wanted more. He traced his fingertips along the outline of her hip, continued across the top of her thigh, and then back up to her waist. Slipping his thumb underneath the bottom of her shirt, he stroked the warm skin of her lower back, then flattened his palm and pulled her hard against him. Her quick, erratic breaths tickled the side of his neck.

"One-thirty now," he said in the faintest whisper.

It was too much. The most deliciously animalistic thoughts filled his head, and he knew he'd lose all control if this continued a second longer. He abruptly removed his hands and stepped back before he did something he'd regret later. He gazed at Cara—sunset hair framing her scarlet-flushed cheeks, lips parted, eyes closed, lost in the moment. By the gods, she was exquisite. His heart swelled inside his chest. This human had captivated him, and her body's response gave him hope that she felt the same way.

"I'd better stop." He tried to hide his elation, but his face probably glowed like a neutron star. "I don't want to send you into cardiac arrest."

Cara's eyes shot open. Aelyx stood there wearing the smuggest expression she'd ever seen. Cardiac arrest? Was this some kind of challenge to prove he could master her body the way he mastered every game in her collection? Like an idiot, she'd thought he was really into her. Suffocating desire transformed into embarrassment. Then anger. But two could play this game. She'd show him a heart attack.

"Well, that wasn't too bad." She cleared her throat and tried to steady her breathing. "I guess I should reciprocate, Earth-style. It's only fair."

"I'm ready," he said with a cocky grin.

Prickles of anxiety spread through her core, but she couldn't back out now. She couldn't let him win again—damn it, she was sick to death of losing. "Let's sit down."

"Feeling weak in the knees?"

"Real funny." But he didn't know how right he was. "Just do it."

Aelyx sat cross-legged on the carpet, and she knelt in front of him with her feet tucked beneath her.

"Okay, buddy." She swallowed hard. "Prepare to have your world rocked."

Oh God, what was she doing? She'd imagined kissing him

a thousand times, but she never thought it would happen. Her heart sprinted, and she was glad he wasn't taking her pulse anymore. A kiss could change their friendship. What if this made things weird between them? Or worse—what if he didn't like it? The humiliation might actually kill her.

"I'm waiting . . ." he said.

"Close your eyes."

He obeyed, and she took a deep, shaky breath. Summoning all her nerve, she inched forward, close enough to smell his warm, spicy scent. She hesitated, and then Aelyx opened his eyes and gave her a look that would set ice water aflame. This was no game to him. That realization gave her the courage to eliminate the tiny sliver of air between them.

She cupped Aelyx's face, stroking the smooth skin with her fingers, and brushed her lips lightly back and forth against his. His mouth was every bit as soft as it looked, the sensation hotter than her wildest dreams. She took his bottom lip between hers and sucked it gently, tasting the orangey tea, and then captured it with her teeth to pull his mouth closer.

When he slid the tip of his tongue between her lips, warm tingles danced across her chest. How did he know to do that? He tilted her face to the side to deepen the kiss, teasing and exploring her mouth, sending those warm tingles spreading out in every direction.

She broke away, gasping. "Are you sure you've never done this before?"

"Yes."

Without wasting another second, he curled his hand

around the side of her neck and pulled her mouth right back to his with a little too much force.

She pulled away again. "Hold up."

"What's wrong?"

"Softer," she said, "like this." Then she showed him how lethal a gentle kiss could be.

He caught on quickly, which didn't surprise her. Like most things in life, he was good at making out, too. The prickly heat intensified with every warm sweep of his tongue. She unclasped his hair, feeling the cool strands between her fingers, and then she slowed things down even further, moving her mouth deliberately, taking her time and focusing on every stolen breath and quiet sigh, cherishing each sensation before it was over.

It felt too good, almost unearthly, and even though his lips never left hers, she felt the kiss *everywhere*. Powerful hands moved to her shoulders, slid down the bare skin of her arms to her thighs, and then tugged her forward.

Heart pounding out of control, she climbed into his lap, straddling his thighs. She wrapped her arms around his neck and claimed his mouth again, feeling his hands on the small of her back pulling her impossibly close. Somewhere in the recesses of her mind she knew things were going too far, but she couldn't bring herself to care.

In a flash, he rolled her to the floor, knocking the air from her lungs. The weight of his body pressed her into the carpet, and she felt his heart hammering against her chest while his hands roamed the length of her rib cage. No matter how tightly she wrapped herself around him, it wasn't close enough. He murmured something in another language and reached a hand between them, tearing at the button of her jeans. Instead of pushing his hand away, she arched her lower back to help him with the zipper. But he suddenly bolted upright and knelt above her, panting.

It took a moment to adjust to the shock of their separation. She cleared her throat and propped up on one elbow, fighting for oxygen. "What's wrong?"

"Listen." He glanced toward the far end of the house. "I think Eileen's home."

The distant groan of the garage door opener proved him right.

"Damn," she muttered. Of all the days for Mom to come home early.

Aelyx drew a deep, shuddering breath. "My sentiments exactly."

Cara sat up and scrambled to button her pants. "Hey," she said, "come here real quick." She gave him a grin that made it clear what she wanted.

He matched her smile and didn't hesitate to kiss her one more time while she pressed her fingers against his throat to count the beats. Fifteen seconds later, she multiplied the number by four and had her answer.

"One-forty!" she said. "I beat your high score!"

Aelyx laughed. "How does it feel to defeat me?"

Cara licked her lips and tasted him again. "Pretty sweet. I've waited a long time to bring you down." Instead of releasing his hand, she laced their fingers together and gave a squeeze. "Listen, I don't want things to be weird between us."

He returned the squeeze. "Me neither."

"We're okay, right?"

"Only okay?" he teased. "I think we just proved that we're quite gifted."

"Oh, totally." She pointed back and forth between them. "The world's not ready for our talent." *Also, I think I'm falling in love with you.*

While her heart rushed, Cara reminded herself that Aelyx wasn't here to stay, and she should probably try pulling back a little. But as she watched him smooth the wrinkles from his sweater and resecure his hair, she realized it was much, much too late for that.

Chapter Eighteen

Aelyx reached out and quickly silenced his alarm before it woke Cara or her parents. Seconds later, his com-sphere buzzed to announce his scheduled check-in with Syrine and Eron, and he stumbled out of bed toward the dresser to retrieve it. While rifling through the top drawer, he noticed his mug of tea from yesterday, still half filled and resting beside his mirror. An automatic grin curved his lips when he whispered "Elire" and set the sphere on his nightstand.

"What are you smiling at?" Instead of two fingers, Syrine greeted him with folded arms and a scowl.

Aelyx stretched and yawned, feigning innocence. "Nothing. Where's Eron?" Usually his image appeared in tandem with Syrine's.

"In China with his *brother*," she sneered.

"You know what I mean."

"He won't join the conversation." Her brows lowered. "Not while I'm part of it."

Aelyx had a good idea what had caused the argument between his roommates, but he asked anyway. "What happened?"

Syrine rolled her eyes, something he'd never seen her do until she came to Earth. "He's punishing me because I won't uproot my *sh'alear*. He's completely lost his mind." Then she tipped her head and studied him. "You didn't uproot yours, right? Eron said you promised to consider it."

"No," he said. "Nothing's changed." Which was a lie. Yesterday had changed everything.

Reflexively, his gaze darted to the wall that separated him from Cara. She trusted him; all the while, he was destroying any hope of a future between their worlds. Maybe Eron was right. Maybe Aelyx should uproot his *sh'alear*. He honestly didn't know anymore. In eighteen years, he'd never felt so conflicted, his thoughts always circling back to the same basic question: would mankind harm the future of L'eihr more than help it?

"That wasn't a very convincing *no*," Syrine said. "Please tell me that flame-haired dolt isn't draining your wits."

Aelyx's spine went rigid, and he ordered, "Watch your tongue!"

Syrine's mouth dropped into an oval. "Why? Because I implied you could be swayed by a human, or because I insulted yours?"

"Cara's not a dolt. She's brilliant and compassionate and—"

"Bleeding Mother." Syrine gasped and pointed an accusing finger at him. "You want to *fash* her!"

Aelyx couldn't deny the statement, so he ignored it. "We're friends. She's loyal and I trust her."

Syrine didn't seem to like that. "Just how much do you trust her?"

"Enough to tell her about the *iphal*."

At his words, Syrine's face went slack. Her eyes widened and she gaped like a dying fish. It took three tries for her to force out the words, and then Aelyx wished she'd remained mute. "You idiot! What if she puts it on her blog? The whole world will know in an instant, then The Way will punish us all!"

"Cara would never do that. She promised."

"I don't trust her!" Syrine shouted. "And the fact that you told her something so sensitive proves you can't be trusted, either!"

"You don't know Cara like I do. She's—"

"This is treason!"

"Don't be ridicu—"

"You've betrayed us!"

Before he had a chance to defend himself, Syrine shut down her sphere. He tried reaching her several times, but she refused to answer.

Spectacular. Syrine wasn't speaking to him, and Eron wasn't speaking to her. They were fostering more drama than the humans at Midtown High. Since arriving on this planet, they'd slowly come to embody the same traits that had always repulsed them. The Elders had hoped to restore their own emotions by living among humans, but for the clones, who didn't suffer the same malaise, would they transform into what they hated most?

Just then, his sphere summoned him with a distinct frequency that indicated the ambassador had finally received his message. Aelyx took a deep breath and attempted to slow his pulse before whispering his passkey.

Stepha's image flickered to life on the bedside table. He barely lifted two fingers, as if he couldn't spare the energy to complete the gesture. "How can I help you, brother?"

"I've discovered a problem with the water," Aelyx said. "Each time I collect a sample, I find plant life reproducing at an unnatural rate."

"That's not possible," Stepha informed him. "I think you mean *Eron* has found plant contaminants in his samples."

Aelyx was confused. The ambassador didn't seem shocked by the anomaly, only that Aelyx had discovered it instead of Eron. "Actually, both our findings are similar. Syrine confirmed it as well."

In a rare display of emotion, Stepha's eyebrows rose in surprise. "You're certain?"

"Absolutely. I repeated the analysis three times because I didn't believe the original results."

"Interesting," Stepha said, sounding anything but interested. "This means the contamination is more widespread than we thought."

"So humans are aware?" If so, why hadn't Aelyx heard of this before?

"Not the general population. This is a closely guarded

secret, so keep your findings private." When Aelyx nodded, Stepha continued in his sleepy monotone. "The World Trade Organization requested our assistance last year. Human scientists rushed to begin experimenting with our nanotechnology without exploring the possible consequences, and they've tainted some of the water supply with growth particles."

"What kind of growth particles?"

"They'd hoped to create a fertilizer to foster crop growth in harsh climates. Their intentions were pure, if naive. The nanoparticles seeped into underground rivers and eventually the Pacific Ocean, causing an explosion in plant growth."

"But if the water in Midtown is infected, that means . . ." Aelyx turned on the light and grabbed his World Studies textbook, then flipped to the world map in the back. "The particles have reached the Atlantic Ocean and the Saint Lawrence River."

Stepha nodded in confirmation. "It's not yet at the chronic stage, but it is increasing exponentially. Within a decade, we estimate the contamination of all water supplies and the destruction of most aquatic life-forms."

"But that would mean . . ." Aelyx hated to say it aloud.

"Eventually, Earth will lose the ability to sustain life at all."

Aelyx could easily imagine the chain reaction that would end the planet. It took surprisingly little to destroy an ecosystem. Thickening plant life would block sunlight and deoxygenize the water, and once the chemical makeup changed, it was only a matter of time before the water became unfit for consumption. Rainfall wouldn't generate enough to support all of Earth's life-forms, and humans would die painfully, battling for whatever drops remained.

"But we can correct the problem," Aelyx said. Ironically, a relative of the *sh'alear* he'd planted would neutralize the growth particles, halting their reproduction.

"Yes, and we will." Stepha's next words nearly stopped Aelyx's heart. "If we approve the alliance."

"If?" Aelyx asked, hoping he'd misunderstood the ambassador. "That sounds conditional."

"Remember when I told you humans and L'eihrs will both benefit when our societies merge? I was referring to this."

Aelyx's whole body flashed hot and suddenly cold. Sacred Mother. The alliance—the one he and his peers had intentionally sabotaged—was the key to Earth's survival?

"The Way would allow humans to perish?" It couldn't be true. "Once they learn what's happening, wars will erupt. Millions of innocents will die, long before the planet does."

With all the emotion of a stone, Stepha answered, "If we cannot coexist peacefully, they aren't worth saving."

Lifting his fingers in an abrupt farewell greeting, Aelyx shut down his sphere and swallowed against the bile rising in his throat.

Oh, gods, what had he done? Bill, Eileen, little Ashley, and Cara—his Elire. He'd sentenced them to a horrific death.

With trembling fingers, he lifted the sphere to his lips and summoned Eron and Syrine, praying they'd answer the call and uproot their *sh'alear* seedlings at once. There had to be a way to undo the damage they'd caused. Any other outcome was unthinkable.

Cara's screeching alarm clock ripped her into consciousness, but instead of slapping the snooze button, she bounced out of bed and reached for the ceiling, rising onto her toes to stretch. Sweeping aside her lace curtain, she gazed through the frosty window at the forest in the distance, where steady rain fell in sheets and a bluster of wind tossed slick, wet leaves through the air. She twirled in place and smiled. What a beautiful morning.

Holding two fingers against her lips, she sighed, remembering how incredible Aelyx's mouth had felt against hers yesterday . . . and wondering when he'd kiss her again. They hadn't exactly talked about it, but she was pretty sure they were a couple now.

After dressing in her warmest sweater and jeans, she practically skipped into the kitchen and sat beside Dad at the table. "Oh, chocolate chip pancakes!" She heaped three onto her plate and drizzled them with melted peanut butter.

"You're in a good mood today." Mom smiled over the top of her coffee mug.

"Yeah, guess I am."

Dad glanced up from the newspaper and grinned to himself. "Think Satan wants to borrow my snowblower?" When nobody laughed, he added, "Get it? Hell's frozen over."

"The only thing worse than a bad joke," Cara said, "is having it explained."

With a grunt and a shrug, he went back to reading.

Cara licked a smudge of chocolate from the corner of her mouth. "Can I borrow the car today, Mom? We'll get soaked if we walk—"

"Hmph," Dad interrupted. "When I was a boy—"

"Yeah, yeah," Cara interrupted back. "You walked to school naked in the snow or something. So can I?"

"I'm leading story time at the library." Mom grabbed another pancake and rolled it up like a burrito. "How about I drop you off instead?"

Abruptly, Dad plunked his mug on the table and folded the newspaper in half. "Listen to this." His cheeks darkened as he read aloud, "In response to Cara Sweeney's proposed L'awareness Day and the nearly unanimous defeat of the Senate bill known as the L'eihr Expulsion Act, HALO leader Isaac Richards has called for an international protest, asking HALO members to assemble in Manhattan, Midtown, Bordeaux, and Lanzhou to demand the revocation of L'eihr visas and end the cultural exchange. 'They're poisoning our water and killing our crops,' Richards said. 'What's next, our children?'"

"Great," Cara said around the food in her mouth. "Just what we need—more crazycake protesters. Why're they surprised the bill failed? The president would give her right boob for this alliance."

"Pepper!" Mom snorted, gently smacking Cara's arm.

"You know she would," Cara argued. "Probably the left one, too. And an ovary."

"Well," Dad said, "it says here the senator from Arizona's already writing another bill just like it."

Mom pointed her rolled-up pancake at him. "Does it say how many people are coming or where they plan to march?"

"No." Dad continued to scan the article. "I'll bet we get a few thousand, probably more." He paused for a moment and took Mom's hand. "I wouldn't worry. The military's not gonna let anything happen to Aelyx. I'm sure they'll send extra troops."

Mom nodded in agreement and glanced at Cara. "Why don't you see if Aelyx is finished with breakfast? We should go soon."

"Breakfast? I thought he was getting dressed."

"He wanted to eat in his room today." Mom shimmied into her coat. "I think he overslept."

Just as Cara stood, Aelyx strode in wearing his jacket. He kept his eyes locked on a copy of *Advanced Biomaterials* while slinging his book bag over one shoulder. When they loaded into the car, he took the front passenger seat instead of sitting in the back with her, then read his book silently for the duration of the ride. After a quick "thank you" to her mother, he jogged ahead of her into the school while Cara ran to catch up.

"You okay?" She tried to lean against him while they walked to homeroom, but he veered off to the side.

"I'm fine."

"Then why won't you look at me?" Grabbing his sleeve, she stopped him in the middle of the crowded hall. "Are you mad? You know, about yesterday?"

Aelyx heaved a sigh and finally turned to face her, but he wouldn't meet her eyes. "I'm not angry."

"So we're all right?"

"Yes, *Cah*-ra. Why wouldn't we be?"

Not Elire. Cara. All the air disappeared from her lungs. She knew a brush-off when she saw one. That sick, swelling feeling returned, the one she'd felt when Tori stabbed her in the back, but even though tears stung her eyelids, she forced them away. She would *not* cry over this. Not while he was watching.

Instead of embarrassing herself any further, she turned on her heel and gave him the space he obviously wanted.

Several hours later, after mindlessly scanning her Dartmouth application for the fifth time, Cara gave up and tried to get a head start on tomorrow's math assignment. When she couldn't focus on that, either, she opened her copy of *Jane Eyre*, hoping to escape thoughts of Aelyx. But no matter what she did, she couldn't quit fixating on him.

With a sigh, Cara glanced around the classroom. Most of the students hunched dutifully over the same history exam she'd finished half an hour ago. The clock on the wall read 11:37, just three minutes later than the last time she'd checked. The day felt so long without Aelyx to distract her. Sliding her gaze to the side, she watched him pretend to read his biomaterials textbook. Although he appeared thoroughly absorbed, he hadn't turned a page in ten minutes.

When the bell finally rang, she asked Blake to escort her to the computer lab and then take Aelyx to the cafeteria. She needed to update her blog and, quite frankly, she couldn't take any more of the silent treatment.

"We'll stay with you," Aelyx insisted. "I'm not hungry anyway."

"Then maybe you should hang out in the library," she retorted. "And *read*."

In true rejectionist fashion, he ignored her, following along with Blake until she reached the lab and settled at the end of a vacant row. "Pull up a chair." *If you can stand to get that close.* "I need a random fact for Trivial Wednesday." He sat at the same workstation but kept twelve inches between them and leaned away like she smelled bad. "How do L'eihrs say good-bye?"

"We touch the side of the throat with our first two fingers."

Wow, they sure had a fixation with throats. "To take each other's pulse, like—" *You did to me yesterday?* She cut herself off just in time.

"Oh." He punctuated the awkward silence with a fake cough. "No, just a simple touch and release."

The central blog site came up, and she entered her login and password. "That's all I need," she said in a cool voice. "You can go."

"I'll wait."

What was his deal? He'd snubbed her, so why was he acting like a stage-five clinger? "There's no reas—"

An error message appeared on the computer screen. At first, she thought she'd entered the wrong password, but upon closer inspection, she found karma had decided to gut-punch her when she was already down. What had she done to deserve this?

This account has been deactivated due to violations of our terms of service.

"Damn it." She hadn't violated anything!

"What's wrong?" Aelyx leaned one precious inch in her direction to read the screen.

"They killed my blog!" Nearly a million followers—*poof*, gone, just like that.

"Yow." Blake joined the pity party, peering over her shoulder. "What'd you do?"

"Nothing."

She hadn't posted about the L'eihrs' weaponry, population size, or anything they might not want to divulge publicly, so the government wouldn't have shut her down. All she'd discussed was L'eihr customs, mutations, and breeding-related advances. That wasn't a big deal, was it?

Apparently someone thought so, and she had no way of finding out who.

CHAPTER NINETEEN

"Culturally speaking, what's the biggest difference between life on Earth and yours back home?" Mr. Manuel absently dealt study packets to the class, busywork to keep them occupied while he focused on his only love these days: Aelyx.

"I could list our similarities faster than our differences, since we have almost nothing in common." Aelyx leaned forward in his seat and rested his forearms on his knees.

Cara wanted to smack him. She was tired of being ignored.

"Basically," Aelyx continued, "our only goal from the moment we're born until the moment we die is to serve L'eihr. We're raised, educated, and trained together for no other purpose. Here on Earth, your only purpose is to please yourselves."

"Nice." She lightly kicked his boot, and it felt surprisingly good. She should've done it harder. "I'll remember that the next time I'm tempted to blow off my plans because you need a ride to the nature preserve."

Aelyx flinched and got that guilty look on his face—the same one she'd seen every day since he'd given her the cold shoulder.

"You're right," he conceded. "I shouldn't generalize."

Aelyx admitting he was wrong? She wished she knew what was going on inside that supposedly evolved head of his.

"You mentioned harsh punishments and executions," Mr. Manuel said. "But if your generation's so flawless—"

Cara muttered, "Aelyx likes to *think* he's flawless."

"—why's it necessary?"

Aelyx tightened his jaw and shot her a look that said his patience was waning. Good. It was about time.

"There hasn't been an execution on L'eihr in nearly two hundred years," he told Mr. Manuel. "But offenses punishable by death include unauthorized breeding, assault, theft, insubordination—basically any crime that goes against The Way."

"So," Mr. Manuel said, "if The Way makes up your central government, who carries out the laws in each district?"

"A military force similar to yours."

"What about corruption?" Mr. Manuel asked. "Who keeps them honest and accountable?"

"Remember," Aelyx said, "it's impossible to lie during Silent Speech."

He made it sound so perfect, like allowing the government inside your head was a good thing. Cara couldn't stay quiet any longer. "What about the right to privacy?"

"What about it?"

"Um, you don't *have* any."

"If you're looking for Utopia, *Cah*-ra," he said, matching her snarky tone, "you won't find it. Not here, and not on L'eihr. Sacrifices are made for the greater good."

"Well," she argued, "how can you justify killing your own people, especially since you're so evolved? Most advanced nations on Earth abandoned capital punishment years ago."

Aelyx shrugged one shoulder. "Execution's a logical solution as well as a punishment. If an individual can't live within the parameters of society, it's best to remove him or her from it. I'd prefer a quick death to imprisonment or exile. I find your system of incarceration cruel."

She had a hard time buying that, especially considering he didn't believe in the afterlife. "What about The Way?" she asked. "Who chooses them?"

"After our assessments," he said, "the most gifted children are selected for The Way, but they don't serve until after their *Sh'ovah* Day. There are always ten members, and each one continues to serve until a more talented citizen's found to replace him." He nodded at Cara and added, "Or her."

She shook her head. What a horrible way to live. "Isn't there anything democratic about life on L'eihr?"

"No." He said it unapologetically, as if equally unimpressed with her government as she was with his.

"And you're really okay with that?"

"Of course."

He had to be lying. "I can't believe it doesn't bother you."

"What doesn't bother me? The corruption within your

system of government?" He tapped his textbook as if the proof lay within its pages. "The inefficiency? The uninformed masses choosing whichever candidate made the most outlandish promises?"

"The lack of freedom, wiseass."

"Ah, freedom." He leaned back in his chair and folded his arms, so cocky and sure of himself. "It's overrated."

"How would you know?" she asked. "You've never tasted it."

"I've sampled enough. The simple truth is most people can't manage total freedom. They make poor use of it."

"There's no such thing as poor use—that's the whole point. *Any* use is good use."

A dry, humorless laugh escaped his lips. "Oh? To bleach insults into your lawn and leave threats in your locker?"

"We're not free to break the law."

"Not technically, but your lax consequences aren't much of a deterrent."

"Oh, please." She flapped a hand. "Those hard-ass punishments didn't keep you from rebelling. You just got whipped for it."

"Which kept me from rebelling further."

She rolled her eyes. What about his late-night trips into the woods? Innocent people didn't sneak around under the cover of darkness. He'd been up to something since he came to Earth—she knew it.

"Anyway," he added, "it's arrogant to assume the democratic method is best because it's all you know."

"Aelyx makes a good point," Mr. Manuel said. "There

are countless systems of government in existence, and none of them is flawless." He pushed his reading glasses atop his head and settled in a vacant desk near his star pupil. "L'eihr reminds me of one of our ancient societies. They were called the Sp—"

"Yes, the Spartans," Aelyx finished. "I knew you'd make that comparison. But you're forgetting Sparta was a brutal warrior nation—quite savage, actually. Slavery, infanticide, ritual murder. L'eihrs aren't aggressive."

"Right," Cara said. "L'eihrs just strip your basic human rights instead."

Aelyx's voice darkened. "They're called *human* rights for a reason. We're not human. Once again, you're being arr—"

"Time out," Mr. Manuel declared, using his hands like a referee to form a *T.* "Maybe we should talk about something else."

She and Aelyx glared at each other.

"I've wanted to hear more about space travel," Mr. Manuel said. "What fuels your ships?"

Cara knew the answer—an element called XE-2—and she had no interest in the new topic and even less interest in her study packet. She needed to get away from Aelyx and calm down before she smacked the *fash* out of him.

"Can I go to the bathroom?"

Mr. Manuel nodded. "Take the pass."

The bathroom pass, a rhinestone-bedazzled toilet seat designed to embarrass students and thus decrease requests to leave, hung on a nail beside the door. When she moved from her seat, Aelyx caught her wrist and released it just as quickly.

"What about Officer Borsch?" he asked. "He should walk with you."

Instead of snapping, *Why do you care?* she scraped together a few crumbs of maturity and said, "I'm going to the bathroom, not to Beirut. What horrible fate do you think's waiting for me in there? Death by toilet swirly?"

"Fine." He folded his arms across his broad chest. "If you're not back in five minutes, I'm coming after you."

"Suit yourself." She grabbed the jeweled bathroom pass, slung it over her shoulder, and stepped into the hall, closing the door behind her.

As she ambled down the vacant corridor, she wondered for the hundredth time what Aelyx's problem was. She knew he'd wanted to be with her that day in his room—the physical evidence was unmistakable. He'd even snagged her in the hallway for another covert kiss before dinner that night. But the next morning—

Movement in her peripheral vision stopped Cara midstride, and she backed up, peering down the side hallway that led to her locker. A girl was standing on tiptoe, shoving a folded note through the door vents.

A girl? She'd assumed Marcus was behind the threats.

Cara pivoted on her heel and charged toward her locker, tightening her grip on the toilet seat in case she needed to use it as a weapon. Heat rose into her face and her pulse rushed with each step, but as Cara approached her locker, she recognized the girl's blond curls.

"Brandi?" *She* was behind the threats? They hadn't been friends in a long time, but Cara thought she knew Brandi better than that. Maybe Marcus had put her up to it.

At the sound of her name, Brandi's head whipped around, gold ringlets slapping her cheeks. Her already wide doe eyes bulged in shock as she flinched back and then lurched forward again, scrambling to remove the folded paper still wedged in the locker vent.

Trying to destroy the evidence? Oh, hell no!

Gripping the toilet seat in both hands, Cara sprinted toward Brandi and used it like a battering ram to knock her aside. Brandi stumbled to the ground, landing right on her moneymaker, but she didn't stay down long enough for Cara to tug the note free. Scrambling to her feet, Brandi charged Cara, crashing into her shoulder, and a full-on shoving match ensued, complete with hair pulling, swearing, scratching, and slapping. Finally, Cara threw the bejeweled hall pass at Brandi, distracting her long enough to push her backward. She faced her locker and tried to push the note all the way inside.

It didn't work. Brandi kicked the backs of Cara's knees, causing her to collapse to the floor while Brandi grabbed the note and shoved it down the front of her skintight jeans.

Ew. No way Cara wanted it now. She'd let Blake retrieve the evidence.

Panting, Brandi pushed a snarled lock of hair away from her face. "That's not for you!"

Cara pushed to her knees and tried to catch her breath. "Then why'd you stick it in my locker?"

"For Aelyx."

"Threatening *him* is just as bad!"

Brandi straightened, her brows disappearing into her bangs. "What do you mean, threatening him?"

"Oh, come off it. I know you wrote the other notes, *Humanist.*"

"What other notes?"

"You know, *traitor bitch, I'm watching you.*" Cara snatched the toilet seat, now missing half its plastic gems, off the ground. "Gotta say, I didn't think you had it in you."

"I swear this is the only one," Brandi insisted, pointing to her crotch. "But I won't write any more." She backed away defensively and added, "I just did it because he won't answer my texts."

"Wait." Cara wasn't following. "What's in that note?"

"I . . . um . . ." Brandi retreated a step and swallowed hard. "Asked if he wanted to hook up sometime."

"That's it?"

Brandi nodded.

"Then why'd you jump me?" Using the battered lid, Cara pointed to the sparkly battlefield where fake rhinestones littered the hall.

Brandi glanced over her shoulder and lowered her voice. "Because you don't know what Marcus would do to me if he found out. And my mom doesn't trust Aelyx. She'd kill me if she knew." She begged with her eyes and said, "Look, Cara. I know we're not close anymore, but please don't tell anyone."

Cara almost felt sorry for Brandi. It must suck to crave popularity so badly that you'd be willing to hang onto a controlling boyfriend just to win a cheap tiara and an extra mention in the yearbook.

"Please," Brandi said. "I'll do anything. Just don't tell."

"Okay." Cara couldn't say no. It was all too pathetic. "I won't."

Brandi pressed a hand over her heart and exhaled in relief. "Thank you. And I swear I won't do it again. I'm really sorry—I know you're into Aelyx, too. That's probably why he won't text me back. He wants to be with you, not me."

"Uh, yeah," Cara lied. "But even if we weren't . . . together . . . you can't get with him. L'eihrs are acidic to humans, remember?"

"Wait. So you two literally can't do it?" She bit her bottom lip. "Not even with protection?"

"Nope. We just cuddle a lot."

"How're you gonna handle it when you go to L'eihr and see him with another girl? I mean, if you can't do it, you can't stay together. Eventually he'll end up with one of his own kind."

Like Syrine, who sees into his soul. "It's no big deal. We're not serious."

"Oh. Well, I'm sorry about the, uh, note." Brandi smoothed her hair and pointed over her shoulder. "I gotta get back to class."

While Brandi sashayed down the hall, Cara considered what she'd said. Aelyx *would* end up with one of his own kind—if not Syrine, then some other pretty L'eihr who could gaze into his eyes to talk. It only made sense. That shouldn't bother Cara, but she couldn't deny it did. A frozen bowling ball settled in her stomach when she imagined spending a semester on L'eihr as Aelyx's third wheel—tagging alongside whichever female his leaders picked for him.

She slumped against her locker, toilet seat in hand, hair in knots, and let herself brood a few more seconds before returning to class.

After World Studies, she and Aelyx stood in front of her locker again, popping open its metal door as Officer Blake looked on.

"What's this?" Aelyx moved to cup her face but seemed to change his mind and instead pointed to the tender scrape Brandi had left on her cheek.

"Nothing. Just scratched myself."

He pursed his lips dubiously, but then his gaze darted to the floor, where a sheet of paper had fallen facedown at their feet.

"Don't touch it." Blake wedged between them, producing a gallon-size Ziploc baggie and a pair of tweezers. Once he'd bagged the evidence, he held it between them all to study its message. With a heavy hand that had pressed the ink nearly through to the other side, it warned: Accidents happen, especially on the stairs. Step on a crack, break your traitor back. —Humanist

"That wasn't here thirty minutes ago." Something about the way the writer had strained his pen with such force against the paper creeped her out. "I checked my locker when I went to the bathroom."

Her gut clenched knowing someone had just been there. What if the person had watched the whole exchange with Brandi, waiting for the perfect time to deliver the note? If she'd lingered any longer in the hall after Brandi left, would he have used the opportunity to take his threat to the next level?

"Isn't your next class upstairs?" Blake must've sensed her anxiety, because with a smile and a gentle nudge of his elbow, he teased, "Then let's make sure we don't slip on any banana peels on the way."

The breath she'd been holding whooshed out in a laugh, and for the first time, she felt grateful for her armed escort. Knowing he'd be right behind her in the dark, narrow stairwell was the only thing keeping her heart from pounding out of her chest. She grabbed her books, and together, the three of them inched through the crowded hall, which thickened into a full-on traffic jam as they approached the door to the stairs.

A buzz charged the crowd, and the students in front of her stood on their toes, peering over the heads of those blocking the way as if a fight had broken out. Which wouldn't surprise her.

"Just great." Blake pushed his way through, disappearing into the sea of bodies. A couple of minutes later, he shouted, "Out of the way! Make a hole!"

There was a frantic edge to his voice she'd never heard before. The students who hadn't already detoured to the other set of stairs inched backward, and Cara peered around shoulders, catching a glimpse of Blake as he kicked open the heavy door. He carried a girl in his arms and rushed her toward the office.

Just before he turned the corner, Cara recognized the girl's orange skin and a glint of metal from the button affixed to her sweater. Though she wasn't close enough to read the lettering, Cara knew the button said L'EIHR LOVER.

Cara rested her chin in her palm and stared blankly across the cafeteria. Blake had promised to call when he knew something about Ashley's condition, but for the past two hours, her cell phone had remained silent.

Shouts of Spanish profanity drew Cara's attention to Eric's table, where Tori shook her finger in front of his face, going off on him for something or other. But Cara was too worried for Ashley to take pleasure in Tori's and Eric's misery.

"Eat something." Aelyx reached across the table and pushed her turkey sandwich until the crust brushed her shirt. "She'll be okay."

"How do you know?" Cara stuffed a bite into her mouth but tasted nothing.

"I noticed she was conscious. In a lot of pain, but alert. That's a good sign."

Cara tried to say *whatever*, but it came out muffled by sandwich. When her cell phone vibrated, she fumbled to swipe the screen before it went to voice mail.

"Heh-wo," she said around a bite of turkey.

"Just heard from Ashley's mom. Broken arm, sprained shoulder, and two cracked ribs. She won't be back at school for a while, but she's okay."

Cara swallowed and took a quick chug of water. "Did she say what happened?"

"Someone pushed her from the top of the stairs, but she didn't see who." Then Blake hardened his voice. "We checked the security cameras, both in the stairwell and near your locker."

"And?"

"Nothing. Someone managed to turn off the system at just the right time. No more unaccompanied trips to the bathroom for you. Like it or not, I'm your new shadow."

"Hey, I'm not complaining." She ended the call and released a sigh. Ashley would be okay. And no Patriot—no matter how brassy his balls—would come after her or Aelyx with a cop by their side.

CHAPTER TWENTY

"You look flushed," Mom said, resting her palm against Cara's forehead. "Feel sick?"

"No, I'm fine." Cara's flush had nothing to do with a virus. Her cheeks burned as she relived scenes from her most recent dream, a particularly steamy one involving Aelyx. She could almost feel his hands on her body and his hot breath on her throat. As if thinking about him all day wasn't bad enough, he had to invade her sleep, too?

"Where's Aelyx this morning?" Mom set a steaming plate of golden waffles on the table, filling the air with the scents of butter and sweet cake. At least the food was good in her virtual hell.

"In his room, I guess." *Where he spends all his time now.*

Aelyx had promised things were fine between them, but Mister "I Would Never Lie to You" was about as honest as a felon. He'd been avoiding her for weeks, acting like her body was surrounded by a deadly force field and holing up inside his room, shouting at his friends on the "phone." Too bad she couldn't speak L'eihr, because whatever they were arguing about sounded juicy.

"Think I'll head out early." Cara held the waffle between her teeth while slipping on her coat.

"You're not going to wait for Aelyx?"

And endure another painfully awkward walk to school? No thanks. Grabbing her bag, she made for the back door before he could join her. "I've got some stuff to do. He can meet me in class."

She rushed outside, where she was greeted by a friendly neighborhood assault rifle.

Gasping, she pressed a hand over her heart. She kept forgetting about the military dudes who'd materialized last night, right on the heels of ten thousand loopy protesters. After releasing a loud breath, she offered a smile to the young blond blocking her way, then waved to a dozen of his comrades. "Mornin'."

The icy blue eyes staring back were not amused. "Where's the L'eihr?"

"We're flying solo today." She pointed past G.I. Jerk, sending an unspoken request for him to move, but instead, he advanced, backing her up two concrete steps.

"We'll drive you both." He puffed his chest like a primate trying to assert dominance. Someone must've sprinkled too much testosterone on this kid's cornflakes. "Together."

She glared right back at him for a moment before hopping over the iron railing that ran along the steps, landing on her feet with a hard *thud* that stung her shins. As she walked toward the trail, she called, "Unless the president's declared martial law since the last time I checked, I'm walking to school."

He groaned and shouted, "Jones! Spaulding! Escort Miss Sweeney to Midtown High and deliver her to Sergeant Baker."

The sound of combat boots slapping the frozen ground approached, but her escorts stayed back, giving her a good ten yards of privacy as they all marched on. A good thing, because she wasn't exactly pleasant company this morning.

The sun rose through dark, heavy clouds, casting a pitiful glow across the forest. Her fingers felt so empty without Aelyx's linked among them, but as much as she ached for his warmth and laughter, she couldn't take another minute of charged silence or empty small talk. She glanced behind her to make sure he wasn't following.

When had she grown so dependent on Aelyx? She couldn't identify any given moment that it had happened. It reminded her of a blizzard from years before, when a surprise cold front had dumped four feet of snow on the town. She'd gone to bed completely unaware of the storm and awoken the next morning to an impenetrable wall of snow surrounding the house.

Or maybe a blanket was a better comparison—the way it gathers warmth so gradually that you don't feel the chill until removing the cover. Yeah, that was just like Aelyx. She'd fallen for him so slowly she hadn't realized the depth of her feelings until he pulled away. But why would he pull away? He was the one who'd initiated the whole let-me-touch-you-all-over-and-take-your-pulse thing. The jerk.

"Miss Sweeney?"

Cara turned to find one of the soldiers, a fair redhead with so many freckles they almost blended together into a tan, pointing his gun toward the end of the trail. "Don't get too far ahead. They told us the crowd's a little wild."

"Wait," she said, "they're *here?*" HALO had announced a march on City Hall, not on the school. This wouldn't be anything like the usual demonstrations. An icy chill snaked up the length of her spine and settled near her heart when she imagined what a crowd of thousands could do to her—Cara Sweeney: L'eihr Lover Extraordinaire. Suddenly, she felt like an idiot for not letting the military play chauffeur. An armored Hum-V sounded pretty good right about now.

The other soldier, a vertically challenged brunet, must've smelled her fear. "The National Guard's handling it. We've got troops up the wazoo, so don't worry."

"Sure," she whispered with a nod. Why didn't that make her feel better?

As they approached the end of the trail, a blazing chorus of sirens began to drown out the crunch of twigs and dried leaves beneath their boots. Red and blue lights flashed through the trees as if the school had caught fire, and then the din of ten thousand voices roared in her ears like a cross between ocean waves and radio static. And what a scene.

The National Guard had blocked off the street with concrete barricades, corralling the chaos at least fifty yards to the left of the school, but rows of armed soldiers couldn't keep protesters from fighting among themselves or throwing rocks and beer bottles. In all her life, she'd never seen a crowd that large assembled in one place, not even at the Women's Health March she'd attended in DC a couple years ago. After a gentle nudge from the redhead, she clenched her teeth and strode forward, sandwiched between her guardians.

Two crimson Midtown Fire and EMS trucks idled near the school's front entrance, and she recognized Dad's strawberry head bent over a long, portly man on a stretcher. The closer she advanced, the more that patient looked like Principal Ferguson . . . because it was.

"Hey," she said, tugging on the redhead's sleeve and pointing ahead, "that's my dad."

"Barry will go with you." That must've been the short brunet. "I need to find Sergeant Baker."

She jogged over, watching Dad bandage a cut above the principal's left eyebrow. When he turned to grab the scissors, she noticed a smudge of blood on the breast of his starched white shirt. When Dad glanced up and spotted her, his eyes widened. "What're you doing here? I left a message for you to stay home."

"I left early." She turned to Mr. Ferguson. "What happened?"

"He caught a beer bottle with his head," Dad answered. "Where's Aelyx?"

"Home." Where he'd probably stay if he got Dad's message. The prospect of an entire day without him at school both excited and depressed her. Mostly the latter.

"I need a word, Cara." Mr. Ferguson sat up and swung his legs over the side of the stretcher, then patted a newly vacated spot on the cushion in an invitation to join him. She settled on the edge and gazed at the crowd, wiping her sweaty palms on her jeans. "I've already talked to your dad," he said, "and he agrees it's for the best."

"What's for the best?"

"If you and Aelyx finish out the school year at home."

"*What?*" Now he had her attention. "As in homeschooled?"

"Just this morning, I lost twenty-six kids to Scott High. Their parents don't think it's safe here anymore with all the fights and protests." He shook his head and apologized with his eyes. "It's nothing against either of you, but I can't disrupt the education of the whole school for one student. I hope you understand."

Hell no, she didn't understand!

"This is crap!" she said, her voice rising above the shouts of the protesters.

"*Cara . . .*" Dad warned from behind.

Ignoring him, she drew in a breath. "You didn't expel Ronnie McPhail after his eleventy-billionth suspension, but you're giving *me* the boot? I'm the valedictorian!" She'd busted tail to hold up her end of the exchange, and this was the thanks she got? "It's true what they say. No good deed goes unpunished."

"This isn't a punishment," Mr. Ferguson insisted. "I even put together an independent study plan, so you won't have to worry about this hurting your transcript."

"This isn't about my transcript. It's the principle. You're required by law to provide me with a free and public—"

"Cara!" Dad barked. "Just go home. I don't want you

anywhere near those people," he said, nodding toward the protest. "We'll talk later."

Cara folded her arms. "Fine. I'll clean out my locker, but this isn't over." She turned to Mr. Ferguson and stressed, "This is temporary."

"Sure." The flatness of his tone did little to reassure her. "I'll e-mail the study plan later."

"Uh, Miss Sweeney?" Soldier Barry tapped her shoulder. "We're supposed to hand you off to the sergeant first."

Of course. Because control of her own life was an illusion right now.

Cara sucked it up and waited patiently while her escorts tracked down Sergeant Baker. They seemed like sweet guys, and if she got them in trouble with their commanding officer, they might have to do a thousand push-ups or scrub toilets with their toothbrushes.

Finally, ten minutes after the tardy bell rang, their contact showed up and signed off on the transfer of goods—her—with instructions to meet Blake at her locker. Then the military finally let her go while they assumed their posts outside the front entrance.

With homeroom already in session, the only sound in the foyer was the slow, careful tread of her boots against the tile. She'd never seen it so placid in here—there wasn't a person in sight. Maybe the classes were on lockdown. It made sense with all the violence going on outside. Each of her squeaky footsteps seemed amplified in the silence, and twice she paused because she thought she heard steps in sync with her own.

By the time she reached her locker, she was ready to take a flying leap out of her skin. Deciding not to wait for Blake, she tossed her book bag to the floor and entered her combination. Seconds later, a crisp leaf of notebook paper fluttered to the ground. It landed faceup, asking in bold block letters, How fast can you run, traitor slut? Not fast enough.

—Humanist

Her palms turned to ice. Before she had a chance to nudge the note aside with her boot, the *click* of shoes sounded from nearby, and with a gasp, Cara whirled to find Tori approaching slowly from the bathroom, wearing a cautious expression. She must have been standing there—watching and waiting—since before homeroom started.

Cara froze. She didn't like this. Something was off.

"Hey," Tori said quietly, inching closer until she reached the locker bank.

On instinct, Cara backed up and put a couple feet between them. "Hey, yourself."

"I've been trying to reach you."

"I know," Cara said. "I didn't have anything to say."

"You shouldn't have ignored me."

Tori's gaze began darting over Cara's head—once, twice, three times. When the hairs on the back of Cara's neck began to prickle, she turned to look over her shoulder, but by then it was too late.

A large hand appeared from behind and clapped over her mouth, tugging her backward. She tasted salty flesh, and she kicked out fiercely, flinging herself forward in a wild attempt to escape. She searched in vain for Tori, who'd vanished from view. Pulse pounding in her ears, Cara sucked a panicked breath through her nose and tried to think rationally. Powerful arms lifted her off the floor and no amount of flailing helped. Noise! She had to make noise. She screamed, but only muffled grunts escaped from her covered lips. A dozen gruesome images flooded her mind, and she kicked her heels against the assailant's shins in panic. It didn't slow him down at all.

He dragged her into a dark room and she heard the door click shut. The scent of wet mops and ammonia told her they were inside the janitor's closet, but the low sliver of light leaking from beneath the door wasn't enough to make anything out. Feeling her eyes widen in the darkness, she tried to scream again, digging her heel into her attacker's foot. He pressed his hand even harder against her face and hissed in pain.

"Shut up, Cara! It's just me, calm down. God damn it, that really hurt!"

Her galloping heart skipped a beat. *Eric?*

"You're safe. I'm gonna move my hand. Promise you won't scream, okay?"

She nodded and Eric pulled his hand away, but then she burst forward, swinging her fists blindly at him. "You asshole! You scared the crap out of me!"

Tori's voice ordered, "Quiet! We're trying to help you, but we've only got a minute."

As Cara's eyes adjusted to the darkness, she was able to identify the outlines of her ex-friends. She and Tori stood nose to nose—or considering their height difference, more like nose to boobs—inside the cramped space while Eric pressed against the door in a futile effort to give her some space.

After Cara caught her breath, she hissed, "You had to ambush me—you couldn't just send an e-mail?"

"Don't be stupid," Tori whispered. "E-mails are hacked every day. The last thing I need is proof that I talked to you."

"Well, what about the cameras?" Cara asked. "Whoever's in the office just saw you two drag me in here."

"No, they didn't," Tori said. "I shut them off after I grabbed the closet key. I'm an office aide during homeroom now."

"So you're the one turning off the cameras?" Cara asked. "Does that mean you two covered for whoever pushed Ashley down the stairs?"

Anger and pain thickened Eric's voice. "You really think we could do that? I mean, I'd kinda like to choke you for almost breaking my shins, but—"

"I have no idea what you could do," Cara told him. "I never believed you'd go after my best friend."

Tori took a step closer. She finally seemed willing to look Cara in the eye. "I'm sorry. I didn't mean for it to happen. He was the only person I knew at the meetings, so we sat together and . . ." She trailed off, looking down for just a second before lifting her gaze again. "Then I realized he was the only sane one there. The others are nuttier than squirrel *mierda*."

"So you're not really together?"

Tori bit her lip. "No, we are." She shrugged, looking helplessly at Eric. "I don't know. He just sorta grew on me."

"Like a fungus," Eric added. "Those were her exact words."

Cara rolled her eyes. "How romantic."

"Moving on . . ." Eric prompted.

Tori nodded. "You have to send the A-Licker home." A noise from the hall startled them, and Tori lowered her voice to an urgent whisper. "I know you wanna birth his alien babies or whatever, but it's gotta stop. The Patriots aren't screwing around anymore."

"I know."

"No, you don't," Eric said. "The meetings are scary now. People talk about declaring war on the government—like full-on civil war. And guess who's traitor number one?"

"Aelyx?"

"Unh-uh." Tori pointed at Cara. "His girlfriend."

"I'm not his—"

"Whatever," Eric said. "It's your fault he's here to begin with, and everyone hates you for it."

"*Everyone?*" she asked.

Tori let her arms hang limp, shoulders slouching like she didn't have the energy to stay angry anymore. She heaved a sigh, and when her eyes met Cara's, they glistened with unshed tears. "You've still got a couple fans. We've been looking out for you."

"That's why we're here," Eric said. "Marcus was running his mouth last night after the meeting. He didn't say who, but HALO's got people following you to learn your routine, and they're gonna try to jump you and Aelyx the next time you leave your house."

"So don't leave your house," Tori said. "You shouldn't even be walking the halls alone."

Cara thought back to that day at the nature preserve. She'd known it wasn't a hiker watching them from the trees.

"Someone's leaving threats in my locker, too."

"Probably Marcus," Eric said. "He hates you worse than jock itch."

Tori hooked a thumb at the door. "I should go soon, or Mrs. Greene will wonder what took me so long in the bathroom."

Eric nodded. "Me, too."

"Be careful," Cara warned, trying not to imagine what the Patriots would do to Eric and Tori if they discovered a pair of moles within their ranks.

Tori started to say something but hesitated, and after one quick wave, she and Eric were gone, leaving Cara alone and a little dazed inside the dark closet. Their exchange seemed surreal, as if she'd wandered in there among the buckets and urinal cakes and imagined the whole thing.

Pressing her ear to the door, she listened for squeaking soles or hushed voices. After hearing none, she stepped slowly into the hall and squinted against the brightness. A quick glance up and down the corridor showed she was alone, so she reopened her locker and retrieved an armload of books.

But wait. Where was the note and, more importantly, where was her bag?

She'd dropped it right there before Eric dragged her into the closet. After scanning the hallway for several minutes, she gave up. Screw it. She shoved the books back in her locker and slammed it shut. After everything that had happened that morning, schoolwork hardly seemed like a priority anyway. And to think scholarship money had lured her into this mess.

CHAPTER TWENTY-ONE

C ara trudged down the steps and waved at Soldier Barry, who sat on the ground by the flagpole, his rifle resting across his lap.

"Hey," she said, "can you take me home?" The parking lot was tranquil again, though the same couldn't be said for the raging protest down the street. Her quiet, cozy bedroom beckoned, and she couldn't wait to curl up in bed, duck beneath the covers, and try to forget what a hot mess her life had become. She wanted to feel normal, even if it only lasted for an hour.

"Yeah, we'll leave as soon as Aelyx is ready."

"What?" The modicum of composure she'd achieved since leaving the janitor's closet vanished, replaced by tensed neck muscles as she glanced around for him. "He's here?"

"Yep. Went inside right after you did. He didn't catch you?"

Catch her? That implied he cared enough to seek her out, which sure wasn't the case these days. "No, he must've gone to the office." She hated the idea of driving home trapped by Aelyx's side. A girl could only take so much awkward. "Any chance you can drive me now?"

While Barry shook his head, something from behind her caught his attention, and he pointed to the top of the steps. "There he is."

Don't spin around! Stay calm. As pseudo-casually as possible, Cara glanced over her shoulder, slowly turning to face the building. Yep, it was him, all right, jogging toward her and holding her backpack.

"Hey!" She reached for her bag. "I looked everywhere for that. Where'd you find—"

Before she could get the next word out, he tossed the bag aside and scooped her into his arms, lifting her off the ground until her legs dangled like a participle. His mouth was at her ear, whispering, "Sacred Mother," and he hugged her so tightly he may have cracked a few ribs.

Just to add to the list of things she didn't see coming today. She pushed against him, struggling to breathe.

"Are you okay?" he asked, lowering her feet to the ground and taking her face between his palms. She pushed those away, too.

"Of course I'm okay! What's your problem?"

"What's *my* problem?" His gaze narrowed, sweeping her from head to toe. "You left me behind, Elire!" She hadn't seen him this pissed since the day he'd nearly liberated one of

Marcus's arms from its socket. "At the most dangerous time possible!"

"Oh, so I'm Elire again?" Striding forward, she jabbed an index finger at his stone chest, but the contact sent a thrill up the length of her arm, so she dropped it to her side. "Unh-uh. You don't get to call me that anymore. I'm *Caaah*-ra now, remember?"

"Blake had to stop a fight on the way to your locker, and you were gone by the time he got there. When you never made it back to the office, we went looking for you and we found this"—he snatched her backpack off the asphalt and shook it accusingly—"on the floor next to your locker with another note. What was I supposed to think?"

"Look, I'm sorry you were scared, but—"

"Scared? I was out of my mind! We tore the school apart trying to find you." He distractedly ran his fingers through his hair and paced a circuit around her as if burning off angry energy. "Why didn't you answer your phone?"

"Because it's in my bag!"

"Wh—" He froze pre-yell, probably realizing he didn't have a counterargument for that. "Well, you know where the first place I looked was?" Aelyx stopped pacing long enough to deliver a scorching glare. "The base of the stairwell. I expected to find you there with your neck broken."

Holding his gaze was like trying to stare at the sun—it burned an imprint of his scathing features into her mind so that she continued seeing him even after closing her eyes. She wanted to strike at Aelyx, scoop together some of the hurt and rejection he'd heaped on in the last week and throw it back in his face, so she squared her shoulders and spat, "Sorry to disappoint you!"

Her words immediately produced the desired effect. "Is that some kind of depraved joke? Because it's not funny."

"It's not a joke. After the way you blew me off, I'm surprised you care."

His posture sank, the muscles in his shoulders rounding forward. "I do care."

"Whatever. You've been avoiding me like cholera since that day in your room."

The crinkle of cellophane caught her attention, and for the first time since their argument began, Cara noticed they'd attracted quite the little audience. A few of Barry's friends had joined him, sitting cross-legged on the ground and leaning forward in rapt attention. One soldier propped against his Hum-V was even munching popcorn from a Smartfood bag. He nodded for her to continue as if she'd pressed the pause button, and now he wanted to resume watching *Romancing the Clone*.

"Sorry, guys, show's over." There was more fighting to do—so much that the air felt thick with the weight of things they'd left unsaid—but it would have to wait. She picked up her book bag and climbed into the armored Hum-V.

When they pulled into her driveway and her knights-in-shining-Kevlar stationed themselves around the perimeter of the property, she unlocked the front door and bolted for her bedroom. She didn't want to argue anymore.

But just as she was pushing her door shut, Aelyx wedged

his foot against the doorjamb and blocked the way. Since it seemed there was no avoiding him, she turned with a resigned sigh and dropped her bag at the foot of the bed while he stepped inside. He closed and locked the door behind him while she crossed to the window.

"The reason I stayed away," he said in a low, tentative voice, "is not what you think."

Pushing aside the curtain, she watched two young soldiers stand guard, weapons at the ready, and wondered what the hell had happened to her life. "How would I know what to think? You wouldn't talk to me."

"I know. I could've handled that better."

Could've handled that better? Was that his idea of an apology? She spun to face him. "Gee, you think?"

He splayed his hands like a beggar and sighed. "This isn't easy for me."

"Love's not easy for anyone! Why do you think the divorce rate's so high?"

"Love?" Turning to her dresser, he idly lifted the tiny porcelain pig Tori had brought back from her last trip to Peru, flashing a sideways glance and a grin that made her belly quiver. "Are you in love?"

Her whole face went up in flames. Had she really said the *L* word out loud? To the guy who'd dropped her like a lubricated dumbbell? "Figure of speech. I meant relationships are hard."

He set down the pig and advanced slowly. "The way I acted . . . It wasn't you."

"Oh, no." She held up one finger and backed away until

her bottom met the frosty windowpane. "You're not even human. You don't get to use the *It's not you, it's me* line!"

"Are you going to listen or not?" He took another step forward, and she inched from the window along the wall. "You were right when you said I was keeping secrets."

Of course she was right. Aelyx was more transparent than Saran wrap. "What does that have to do with dumping me?"

"I felt guilty." He pushed a loose tendril of hair behind his ear, drifting closer as his gaze dropped to her mouth and held there. "I couldn't let things go any further until I was ready to tell you the truth."

She backed into the corner, clinging to the smooth plaster while her heart raced in anticipation of his next move. "You didn't seem so guilty when you practically tore off my jeans."

He shrugged and offered a grin. "A testament to your superior kissing skills." Closing the distance between them, he trailed his index finger across her collarbone and settled it at the base of her throat, where her pulse thumped wildly. "But today, after almost losing you, I made a decision."

She swallowed. "About what?"

"You. Not to waste another second." With his other hand, he lifted her chin, raising her face to meet his. Still watching her mouth, he whispered, "One-ten."

She clenched her eyes shut. "You don't get to do this."

"What?" Lighter than a dragonfly's breath, his lips brushed her temple. "This?" He swept a path to her ear, luring chills to the surface of her skin. "Or this?" Pulling her collar aside, he kissed her shoulder on the magical spot that made her eyes roll back in her head.

With great effort, she pushed him away. "I won't let you mess with my head." *Or my heart.* "I won't be your intergalactic booty call."

He pulled back and cupped her face, his brows pinching together over narrowed chrome eyes. "That's what you think I want?"

"How am I supposed to know? You're running hot or cold all the time." She freed herself and escaped to the other side of the bed. "Why don't we back up to the part where you were ready to tell me everything?"

He hesitated but then nodded slowly and settled on the mattress. "Okay. Let's talk."

That was exactly what she wanted to hear, but Cara's stomach turned cold and heavy. Nothing good ever followed those words.

An ancient human religious figure known as John the Baptist had once claimed, "The truth shall make you free," but if Aelyx remembered correctly, John's honesty had been rewarded with a gruesome decapitation. Aelyx hoped for better results. Before arriving on Earth, he'd had very little experience with deception. Communicating with Silent Speech had resulted in honesty by default among his people, and he'd never understood why humans lied so frequently. Until now.

As Cara gazed at him, those sapphire eyes brimming with doubt, only one thought repeated in his mind: *will she forgive me for what I've done?* As much as he wanted to unburden himself with the truth, the possibility of losing his Elire left him with the nearly irresistible temptation to deceive her again.

"It's okay." She seemed to sense his anxiety. "You can tell me anything."

Could he? Could he really tell her that despite Eron's and Syrine's decisions to uproot their *sh'alear* seedlings—which, due to military escorts, neither of them had accomplished yet—it still might not be enough to save the alliance?

"I'm not so sure," he finally replied.

She softened at that, joining him on the bed. "We have to trust each other, or we're no better than strangers."

"I don't know where to start."

"How about the very beginning?" With a small smile and a nudge, she added, "According to *The Sound of Music*, that's a very good place to start."

He didn't understand the reference, but Cara was right. *Yes*, he could do this—tell her the truth. He needed to have faith, as humans often said. "All right, the very beginning." He took a deep, steadying breath and let it out in a whoosh. "You asked me once why my people ended the breeding program and started cloning new generations from the archives."

She nodded for him to go on.

"Tens of thousands of years ago, L'eihrs were like humans: volatile, greedy, destructive, selfish, violent, ruled by—"

"Enough. I get it."

"Sorry." He laughed, despite the tightness in his chest. "When The Way took control, they started experimenting with selective breeding. Only the fittest, most intelligent, and most emotionally stable citizens were allowed to reproduce. Over time, our technology improved, and scientists started analyzing each citizen's genetic material and creating life in the labs using artificial wombs. They wanted to increase cognitive function and eliminate negative emotions like anger. It worked—a little too well."

"What do you mean, *a little too well?*"

"You've met our ambassador, right?"

"Mmm-hmm," Cara said. "At the gala."

"Did you notice anything . . . different . . . about him?"

"Besides the fact that he's old?" She shook her head and shrugged. "Not really."

"He didn't seem lethargic to you? Like a machine running on half power?"

"Oh, sure. My grandpa was like that the last few years before he died."

"Right, but Stepha's only fifty."

"What?" She turned on the bed, shaking the mattress when she bounced to face him. "He looks like a relic!"

Aelyx chuckled. "I'll tell him you said so."

She shoved his shoulder, sending him rocking back. "So that's what you meant about working too well? They bred the life out of themselves?"

"Pretty much. But it wasn't until Stepha's generation that they began to see negative effects—the depression, lethargy, decreased life span, dependence on medication. Our scientific advances suffered, too. Emotion is what drives creativity and discovery, and the Elders had gone too far in trying to subdue it."

"So they backtracked using clones."

"Exactly. But they still don't think it's enough."

The skin on her forehead wrinkled into three distinct zigzags. "What do you mean? You seem pretty normal to me. Well, now, anyway. When we first met, you kind of reminded me of a zombie."

"A zombie?"

"You know, the walking dead."

"But I've changed." Scooting closer until the outside of their thighs touched, he took both her hands. "You brought out a lifetime of dormant feelings in me, and that's where humans come in." Squeezing one hand for emphasis, he added, "The Way wants to join our two societies. What's happened with me, they want the same for the other clones, maybe even for themselves to some extent. And eventually, they want us to interbreed. That's the real reason for the exchange program—to see if it can work long term. They want to form a colony where humans and L'eihrs can coexist."

She tipped her head while considering what he'd said. "So it's like an experiment? A test to see if we can play nice?"

"Basically."

"And that's it?"

He nodded.

"But that's not such a big deal," she said. "Why the guilt?"

A rush of panic surged inside him. The time had come, but could he really admit what he'd done? Would Cara forgive him when he might have doomed the future of her entire race? He wasn't sure. His resolve faltered until the last drops of it evaporated completely. Maybe she didn't need to know.

He could take his secret to the grave and find a way to save mankind if the alliance failed, even if he had to steal the technology and bring it back himself. But he had to tell her something—she was waiting.

"I discovered a problem," he told her, "two weeks ago—something your government has been hiding from you for years. My ambassador asked me to keep it to myself, but I think you deserve to know." He quickly clarified, "Only you, though. Nobody else can find out, or it would incite panic."

While Cara pulled a pillow onto her lap and hugged it, he told her everything he'd learned about the growth particles affecting Earth's water supply . . . with two major omissions: that mankind's survival was contingent on the alliance and that the contamination had spread worldwide.

She sat there in silence a while, then asked, "Are you sure? I mean, I can't believe nobody else has noticed."

"Some humans *have* noticed. It's just been covered up." He took her hand, which had grown cold, and pressed it between both of his to warm it. "At first, I didn't believe it, either. I took two more samples before I contacted the ambassador."

"And you're positive L'eihrs can fix it, right?"

"Absolutely," he promised. "It'll be easier than manipulating the weather."

"Are they going to start working on it soon?" With her free hand, she rubbed the cotton fabric of her pillowcase between her fingers. "Ten years might sound like a while, but why not nip it in the bud now?"

"They've already put together an action plan." Which,

Aelyx supposed, wasn't a total lie. "There's nothing to worry about, but we can't tell anyone." He delivered a pointed look. "You understand, right?"

"Totally." And then she said something that twisted his heart. "You can trust me."

If only the reverse were true.

"Wait." There was one thing Cara didn't understand—why did Aelyx's guilt cause him to push her away? "In a nutshell, you blew me off because you felt horrible over a small contamination that L'eihrs can fix with a snap of their fingers?"

A flicker of surprise sparked behind his gaze. When he parted his lips to speak and nothing came out, she knew he was stalling for an excuse.

"Don't," she ordered. In the past few months, she'd suspected he was in trouble. What about all those trips into the woods? Maybe he'd gotten caught breaking a rule. Maybe his leaders were waiting back home with that horrible electric whip. "Tell me what's going on. No more hiding. What did you do?"

He shook his head frantically and swore, "Nothing. I told you—"

"Just stop." She tried blocking his words with her palm. "I'm tired of your lies."

"They're not lies," he argued. "Why can't you believe me?"

"How do I know what to believe?" As long as he was keeping things from her, she had no way of trusting him or knowing how he really felt about her. If their brains were more compatible, she could delve inside his mind for the truth, but so far, all she'd managed to do was hear his painfully loud voice inside her head. That was no help to her now. "I'm not a L'eihr. I can't just use telepathy and know what you're thinking."

Realization dawned in his eyes and he scooted forward, reaching for her.

She tensed. "What're you doing?"

He took her face between his hands and refused to let go. Peering deeply at her, he whispered, "This is how I feel every time I'm with you."

She wasn't prepared for what came next. A split-second rush of chest-swelling desire inflated her lungs, lifting her rib cage until her body felt melded with his. Sensations of devotion and tenderness flashed through her in an instant, forcing her to exhale or burst. Every inch of her skin flashed hot and prickled into gooseflesh while her heart fluttered like hummingbird wings. Her limbs lightened, and she grasped two handfuls of his shirt to stay grounded. It was both terrifying and glorious in its intensity.

It was love.

The dull ache at her temples barely registered. All her doubts vanished. *Oh my God, he loves me.*

"You love me," she repeated aloud. The breathy words tasted sweeter than icing on her tongue.

"Is it really that hard to believe?"

"Do it again!"

"No." He smiled and kissed the tip of her nose. "It's your turn."

She let out a snort that would have embarrassed her had

she not just catapulted over the moon with joy. "I love you, too, but that's pretty anticlimactic compared to Silent Speech."

His answering smile lit him up so beautifully it almost hurt to look at him. "Not to me."

"Then I love you." She twirled one finger around a loose tendril of his hair and unfastened his leather cord to comb her fingers through the soft strands. "Now show me more."

"But you might get a headache."

She reclined against a heap of pillows and turned her body to face him. "Do it again."

He nodded, peering deeply into her eyes while his warm breath stirred against her lips. Soon she felt the same rush of emotion as before, the same warm tingles bubbling across her flesh.

"Mmm." Closing her eyes, she held on to the sensation, treasuring it before it melted away. "That's worth a thousand headaches."

When she glanced at Aelyx again, he was watching her with a new hunger that loosed a swarm of fireflies inside her belly. She'd seen that look before, and she knew what it meant. Curling one hand around his neck, she pulled him down, expecting a slow kiss. Instead, his mouth came hard against her and melted her bones.

They picked up where they'd left off weeks ago as if no time had passed, and within minutes, both their shirts lay in a heap on the floor.

She wrapped one leg around his waist and let her hands explore the smooth planes of his back, and he responded in turn, moving his palm up the length of her ribs.

His breaths were deep and shuddering now. A few moments later, he tipped their heads together, squeezed his eyes shut, and chanted, "Silicone, phosphorous, sulfur, um . . . chlorine." Then, wrinkling his forehead in concentration, "Um . . . argon . . . um . . ."

"Potassium?" she offered, raising an eyebrow.

"I'm sorry." Eyes still closed, he shook his head. "We have to stop for a minute."

"Why?"

"Because there aren't enough elements."

This was nothing like the times with Eric, who was always pressuring her for more. For the first time she *did* want more—but she wanted it with Aelyx and no one else. She'd never felt so desperate to be close to someone.

"I don't want you to stop," she said, then kissed his chest. "But we probably should. It's too soon, don't you think?"

He wrapped one arm around her shoulders and drew her nearer. "I don't know. It's kind of hard to think right now."

She understood the feeling. "It's just, I've never . . . uh . . ." *Done this before, and I'm a little scared.* Why was it so hard to say it out loud?

"Me neither." He hesitated a moment before adding, "Do you think . . ." He met her gaze, a question in his eyes.

She shook her head. "Not yet."

"Okay," he replied simply. No pouting, no whining, no guilt trips.

God, she loved this boy. She hugged him tighter to show how much.

They lay in contented silence a while, Cara listening to

the slow, steady beat of his heart and Aelyx raining occasional kisses atop her head. Eventually, the recent sleepless nights caught up with her and she drifted off, wrapped in his arms.

She dreamed of floating in black space, hand-in-hand with Aelyx as the pinpricks of distant stars winked all around them. She snapped her fingers and an angel nebula swirled into view, tentacles of twinkling light permeating the darkness like a glowing specter. At her command, a sleek ship appeared, a floating colossus to jettison her to a new home, but just as she reached for the hatch, a thumping echo pulled her back toward Earth. Aelyx disappeared, and then she was falling, falling, falling while the noise grew louder inside her head. Cold wind whipped her hair in her face and she spread her arms wide, watching the verdant grass rise up to meet her at a thousand feet per second.

Just before hitting the ground, she awoke with a start to the sound of her father pounding on the bedroom door and calling, "Cara?"

Chapter Twenty-Two

"Cara!" Bill shouted, startling Aelyx out of a dead sleep. Bill jiggled the doorknob from the outside and knocked again. "Why's the door locked?"

It took a moment for Aelyx to free his mind from the haze of deep slumber, but when he did, he bolted upright in bed, squinted against the afternoon sun, and whipped around to face a petrified Cara, half naked beside him and clutching one arm over her chest.

Oh, leaping gods! Bill was going to kill him!

"Pepper?" Her father's voice sounded closer, as if he'd pressed his lips to the crack between the door and the wall. "You okay?"

"I'm fine!" She leaped out of bed, but Aelyx didn't give her exposed body the slightest glance. He was too busy scrambling to find his own shirt. Curse it all, where was it? "I just fell asleep."

"Where's Aelyx?"

Their eyes met in panic from opposite sides of the bed. "Uh," she stalled, pulling her sweater over her head while he snatched his shoes from the floor and crammed his feet inside. "He's right here. We were studying and we dozed off."

"With the door locked?" Bill turned the knob with more force, and Aelyx thought his heart might actually beat out of his chest.

Cara hurled his shirt at him, and he pulled it on with one hand while helping her smooth the comforter.

"Cara Mary-Katherine Sweeney," Bill said in the most bone-chilling voice Aelyx had heard in two galaxies, "open this door now!"

While Aelyx fluffed the pillows, Cara Mary-Katherine Sweeney faced the mirror, frantically finger-combing her tangled hair.

"Okay, Dad." She tried to use a carefree, singsong voice, but it cracked on the last note. "Coming." She turned to scan the room one last time and flinched, pointing to the bedside table and silently communicating with her widened eyes.

Glancing down, he noticed her tank top, but when he tried to snatch it off the table, he wound up knocking it to the floor with his trembling fingers. Kicking it under the bed, he nodded for Cara to open the door, and then he leaned casually against the far wall, trying to look like he'd just been doing homework.

Cara opened the door, and Bill glowered from the other side, his body stiff and trembling with all the pent-up rage of a bull ready to charge. He stepped inside and scanned the room, taking in the rumpled bed before his burning gaze settled on Aelyx.

"Fell asleep studying, huh?" The control in Bill's voice brought chills to the surface of Aelyx's skin. This wasn't a man who'd lose his mind and attack in the heat of passion. He'd premeditate the murder and carry it out with a steady hand and clocklike precision.

"Yeah," Cara said. "We're homeschooled now, remember?"

Bill swept his hand toward the polka-dotted comforter, crooked and draped across the mattress at an odd angle. "Where're your books?"

"At school," Cara said without missing a beat. "We used the Internet." Thank the gods she was such a skilled liar, because his own tongue had decided to play dead in the interest of self-preservation.

"I see." Bill walked slowly to Cara's dresser and leaned on the edge, folding his arms as the pine creaked under his weight. Even the furniture feared this man. He studied Aelyx for a few interminable seconds before asking, "Do you usually study in bed? With girls?"

Still unable to speak, Aelyx shook his head.

"Da-aad!" Cara charged ahead, standing toe-to-toe with her father. "Leave him alone. You're making a big deal out of nothing!"

"Fine." Bill's voice was smooth as cream, but he couldn't conceal the redness rising up his neck and seeping into his cheeks. "Just two questions and I'll go."

Cara gripped her hips, mirroring her father's stubborn stance.

"First," Bill began, "what were you studying?"

"The periodic table."

"And second." He stood, rising to his full height like an angry bear and flicking the tag that protruded from the front of Cara's sweater. "Why's your shirt on *inside out and backward*?"

Midtown's debate champion couldn't produce an explanation for that. As Cara would say, they were busted.

"I'm calling your mother." Bill stalked to the door and paused, glaring at them one last time. "You two stay in your rooms until she gets here. Your *own* rooms."

Aelyx and Cara shared a commiserating glance, and then he joined her father in the doorway. Bill stepped aside, barely allowing Aelyx to pass, remaining close enough for him to feel the heat and scarcely contained rage rolling off his body. Slowly, Aelyx made the walk of shame to his room, closing the door behind him and leaning against it to steady his breathing.

Sacred Mother, short of Bill catching them "making out," that couldn't have gone any worse. But despite the heaviness in his lungs, a smile spread across Aelyx's lips, and he pressed a hand over his mouth to muffle a laugh. He didn't understand his body's reaction—there was no humor in this predicament—but his smile wouldn't fade.

Two hours later, he wasn't smiling as he sat beside Cara on the living room sofa facing Bill and Eileen, who'd perched atop chairs they'd brought in from the kitchen. Aside from Sharon Taylor's absence, the scene reminded him of their weekly interviews, minus the friendly banter. Minus *any* banter, actually. The only sound in the room was the distant hum of the refrigerator and occasional laughter from the soldiers stationed outside.

Finally, Bill broke the silence. "How far did it go?"

"Gross, Dad!" Cara covered her face with one hand. "This is sick! I'm not discussing my sex life with you!"

Bill shook an accusing finger at his daughter. "There better not be anything *to* discuss!"

"I'm practically an adult, and it's none of your business what I—"

"Stop." Eileen held one palm forward, and Cara clamped her lips together. Resting her elbows on her knees, Eileen spoke to her daughter in a firm but gentle voice. "It doesn't matter how old you are. You'll still be our little girl when you're eighty."

"Nothing happened, Mom. And even if it did, this isn't just some hookup." Cara linked her arm through his, and Aelyx noticed her father's grip tighten on his chair's wooden armrest. "We love each other."

"Okay," Eileen said with a nod. "But it has to end sometime, and then what? I don't want to see either of you get hurt."

"But it doesn't have to end." Cara turned to him and whispered, "Can you tell them?"

Nodding, he entwined their fingers in a show of solidarity. He wanted to send a clear message to Cara's parents that this was no game—he'd chosen their daughter to be his *l'ihan,* if she'd have him.

"It's true," he said. "If the Elders approve the alliance, we'll recruit colonists. Then Cara can come be with me on L'eihr."

"Wait." She stiffened beside him on the sofa. "L'eihr? I thought you'd stay here."

"On Earth?" he asked. And spend every moment of his life guarding against attack? Out of the question. "No, they want to set up the first colony on our planet." Her stunned silence told him this wasn't welcome news, so he added, "But we could visit every couple years." That didn't seem to help, either.

He glanced at her parents—Bill, whose flushed face drained of color right before his eyes, and Eileen, who'd frozen in place with her head tipped in contemplation. The idea of losing their only daughter to a foreign galaxy obviously disturbed them, and he understood. He couldn't bear parting from Cara, either.

"W-well," Bill sputtered, "we'll talk about that another time. She can't even go until she graduates. Till then," Bill continued, "no fooling around in my house. Are we clear?"

"Of course, sir."

As Bill and Eileen returned their chairs to the kitchen, arguing over which of them would be responsible for supervising "the kids" during the day, he studied Cara's blank expression and tried to discern her thoughts.

"You all right?" he eventually asked, stroking her forearm.

She jerked to attention and shook her head as if to clear it. "Yeah, sorry. Just thinking."

"About?"

When she nibbled her thumbnail, her gaze flickered up and down, never holding his own.

"Talk to me," he pressed, smoothing his palm over her hair.

"It's just . . . We didn't even discuss it. Why do I have to be the one to leave everyone behind? Why not set up the first colony here? It kind of makes sense."

He dropped his hand, feeling a prickle of shame. It was selfish to assume she'd follow him to an alien planet and leave behind everything familiar. Most humans her age wouldn't make a commitment of that magnitude for at least another five years. Cara was mature beyond her chronological age, but of course she would worry. However, the colony was already under construction. He couldn't relocate to Earth, even if he wanted to. If Cara refused to leave her home, they couldn't be together. The thought left him cold.

"Hey." She squeezed his knee. "You're almost as pale as I am, and that's saying a lot." Reaching up, she tapped one finger against his forehead. "What's happening in there?"

"I'm sorry. I thought you understood." The words sounded distant to his own ears. "I shouldn't have—"

Two sharp knocks rattled the front door, and a stern-faced soldier rushed inside without waiting to be admitted. "Turn on the TV," he ordered Cara. "Channel Five, and hurry."

While she crawled to the coffee table for the remote control, the soldier, a middle-age male with cropped gray hair, began calling for the Sweeneys. In seconds, they ran into the living room, and then everyone turned their attention to the sixty-inch screen mounted on the wall, where a national news reel showed a HALO protest twice the size of what they'd seen in Midtown.

". . . coming to you live from Lanzhou," a woman's voice reported, "where the Patriots of Earth have claimed responsibility for the murder of a L'eihr exchange student, an eighteen-year-old boy known only as Aaron . . ."

"Eron," Aelyx whispered, standing from the sofa.

". . . after he evaded military escorts and wandered from his home. According to unnamed sources, the boy was found contaminating the soil and taken by Patriots to an undisclosed location, where he confessed under torture to blighting the local wheat crop . . ."

Aelyx gravitated toward the television, his limbs heavy as if moving underwater.

". . . when an armed militia stormed the boy's home, they found scientific equipment and samples to indicate he'd tampered with the water supply . . ."

Oh, gods, Eron must've snuck away from his guards to uproot his *sh'alear.*

". . . no news on the whereabouts of the female student in Bordeaux, who fled her home and disappeared after learning the news . . ."

Syrine had evacuated to her shuttle and Eron was dead.

". . . the L'eihr ambassador has ended alliance negotiations and called for the immediate removal of the two remaining students . . ."

And without the alliance, mankind would perish. Aelyx's stomach churned, and he bolted to the bathroom just in time to heave into the toilet.

Beads of sweat covered his forehead and upper lip while dry sobs racked his whole body. Every one of his muscles ached from holding the grief inside. Sacred Mother, what had he done? Turning to the sink, he splashed cool water on his face and rinsed his mouth of the sour taste of vomit, flinching when a fist pounded on the bathroom door.

"Aelyx!" Cara rushed inside, half hysterical, with tears streaking her cheeks, her parents following closely behind. "You have to take me with you! They're getting ready to—" She sobbed, choking on the next words, and he grasped her upper arms to steady her.

"Getting ready to what?"

Bill leaned one shoulder against the doorjamb. "They're taking you to the nearest post. Right now. Another mob's on the way."

If Aelyx listened over the pulse rushing in his ears, he could barely discern soldiers barking frenzied orders and the sound of armored vehicles roaring to life.

"The alliance will never happen now," Cara said in a blubbering rush. "If you don't take me, I'll never see you again."

Eileen wrapped one arm around Cara's waist, but she pushed it away and threw herself at him, grabbing his shirt with both hands. "Please." Her eyes brimmed with terror. "Take me with you."

"Think about it," he told her. "Everything's changed. If you go with me, you might never come back." He bent low until they were level, delivering a solemn look. "Is that really what you want?"

Tears leaked down her face, dripping from her chin in great turrets, but she didn't hesitate to say, "Yes."

"Pepper, you don't mean that." Bill's imposing form lost

six inches as he deflated and turned to his wife for support.

Cara spun around and buried her face in her father's chest, her body quaking with sobs and apologies. "I want to go."

"No," Bill said, still in a stupor. "Just . . . no."

"It wasn't a question." Cara's voice hitched, but she met her father's gaze. "I'm going, one way or another. At least I can make sure Troy's okay."

Aelyx couldn't let the Sweeneys think there was any danger of retaliation. "He's safe. I give you my word."

"The sergeant wants to take us somewhere else," Cara told him. "To a safe house."

And Aelyx knew Stepha would never allow Cara to board an official transport. That left only one way to bring her to the main ship—his emergency shuttle. "Do you remember what I said a couple weeks ago? Where to meet if we ever got separated?"

She nodded vigorously.

"Go there now and wait for me. It might take a while, but I'll get away and meet you."

While Bill clutched his daughter tightly with one arm, he studied Aelyx in disbelief, scanning his face and surely calculating whether to trust him with her future. In the silence, Aelyx noticed the distant roar of frantic voices. The mob was approaching—they didn't have much time.

"Let's go!" shouted a voice from the hall. A soldier shoved Bill aside and threw an oversize camouflaged coat and a black ski mask at Aelyx. "Put that on and get outside!"

"Give us a minute to say good-bye," Bill said as he ushered the whole family completely inside the bathroom.

"I'll give you five seconds."

Bill shut the door and held one hand out for Aelyx's ski mask. "Gimme that. The coat, too." He rummaged through the drawer beneath the sink until he found a pair of scissors and told Cara, "You're not stuck there. If you change your mind—if there's even one second of doubt—I want you to come home with your brother. Understand?"

Cara nodded while the din of the crowd drew nearer. "They're coming," she said in a surprisingly steady voice. "Just like in Lanzhou."

"Sweeney family!" a soldier yelled from the hall. "Outside now, or we *will* take you by force!"

"Coming!" Bill called over his shoulder while shrugging into the heavy coat. He tugged the ski mask over his head and motioned for Aelyx to turn around. As soon as Aelyx faced the other direction, his head snapped back as Bill yanked at his ponytail. Then with a few quick tugs of the scissors, his head lurched forward, free from Bill's grasp and lighter by six inches of hair.

Aelyx spun around in time to see Bill tuck what remained of Aelyx's brown ponytail into the back of the ski mask so it dangled past his shoulder blades. Bill would easily pass for a L'eihr if he kept his freckled hands concealed.

"Love," he said to Eileen while zipping his coat, "I'm gonna run for it. That'll stall 'em while the kids slip out the window. Make sure they get out, then you stay with the soldiers."

The noise was deafening now, the crowd nearly upon them. Gunfire popped from outside the house, and Aelyx darted to the window, hauled it open, and used both hands to push the screen to the ground below. An icy breeze frosted his cheeks. He pulled the fresh oxygen into his lungs so deeply he felt it in the soles of his feet.

Eileen kissed Cara's forehead and pushed her toward the window.

Without wasting a second, Aelyx helped Cara out and then climbed through, joining her in crouching low among the shrubs along the back of the house. He heard the bathroom door open and the heavy *clomp* of shoes retreating down the hall. Outside, the setting sun sliced through the bare trees, illuminating the woods in its orange radiance and offering no concealment for at least another twenty minutes. More gunfire rang out, along with shouts of *Stop!* and *Stand down!* that led him to believe Bill had fled, enticing the soldiers and crowd to follow. Aelyx tried not to consider how far Bill would get or what the mob would do to him in the end. Now was the time to move.

But his limbs froze. Cara's parents had just risked their safety for *him*—an arrogant stranger who'd stolen their daughter away. Had he really once considered them ill-mannered and inferior?

Thankfully, Cara brought him to his senses with a jerk of his hand. "C'mon!" She linked their fingers, and together, they bolted into the barren forest without looking back. From his periphery, Aelyx saw the first cluster of bodies rush the house.

Chapter Twenty-Three

Cara ran like hell.

Her lungs screamed for air, and each icy breath stung her nose as if she'd snorted glass shards, but she pushed through the pain, desperate to put more distance between herself and the machine-gun fire crackling in the background. When the staccato chop of helicopter blades whirred overhead, she pumped her legs even harder and clenched her teeth against the acid burning through every muscle in her thighs. Soon, adrenaline took control, physical pain fading until nothing existed but the rhythmic clap of her boots pounding the frozen soil.

Aelyx patiently matched her stride, barely winded, but his death grip said, *Faster!* He quickened his pace and propelled her forward until she was no longer running but stumbling at the speed of sound. At any moment, more than a thousand rabid Patriots and hundreds of soldiers would realize the masked man hauling ass in the opposite direction wasn't Aelyx, and then they'd fan out and scour the woods. If they hadn't already.

She couldn't dwell on what might happen to Mom and Dad—there wasn't time. She focused on survival, pushing aside all thoughts except, *Run harder!*

Shouts echoed from ahead, and Aelyx veered left, towing her off the main path and into the underbrush. A deep carpet of decaying leaves clutched her boots like mud, and the minefield of twigs, brambles, and fallen branches cracked so loudly beneath each step, they might as well send up a flare to announce their position.

"Slow down," she implored with a gasp.

He gave her a brief reprieve, pausing to step over a rotted log and pushing chin-length locks of hair behind his ears before urging her on. "We're almost there."

Soon, they reached the stream. As they plodded onward, two other landmarks came into view: the kidney-shaped bolder and the charred tree, cleaved in half by lightning. Cara breathed a sigh of relief but immediately wrinkled her nose at the musky reek of algae thickening the air. The green slime had completely taken over since the last time they'd been there. She tiptoed and hopped over patches that crept out of the water and onto the mucky soil and wondered how this stuff managed to thrive in the dead of winter.

"I see what you mean." She slipped on a green-coated stone and flailed her arms to steady herself. "It's like a science experiment gone wrong."

Aelyx muttered something unintelligible and jogged to the tree where his "getaway car" hovered high among the branches. Peering up, he patted his back pockets and froze, wide-eyed, before frantically patting his front pockets and the ones on his shirt that didn't even exist. Cara's stomach sank. This was universal body language for, *Oh, crap, I lost my keys!*

"*Fasha!*" he shouted. "My electron-tracker's at the house. My com-sphere, too."

Those sounded pretty important. And judging by the distant shouts of angry men and the whir of approaching helicopter blades, the head start Dad had given them had officially expired.

"We can't go back," she said.

"I know." He cursed again and returned his attention to the sky.

"Please tell me you've got an extra set of keys stashed somewhere."

"The tracker's not a key, more like a remote control. It brings the shuttle down and into view."

"So you don't need it?" Maybe they weren't screwed after all.

"The shuttle's programmed to respond to my touch. If I can reach the damned thing, I can get inside and pilot it." A twig snapped from about fifty yards behind, and Aelyx crouched low. "How good are you at climbing trees?"

Her only experience with the act had resulted in two sprained ankles and a bruised tailbone. "Not very." Automatically, she scanned the small clearing for a place to hide, coming up empty. Winter had stripped the trees and shrubs of their leaves and flattened the tall weeds that typically covered the ground, offering no shelter.

"Then you'll have to wait here." Their thoughts must've traveled on the same wavelength, because he darted a glance in every direction and scowled. "Just do your best to stay low." He found a pebble and threw it into the air to gauge the shuttle's position. It bounced back after about thirty feet—a long way to climb considering he'd be exposed, too, but he didn't waste another second deliberating.

The ease with which he scaled the tree both impressed and annoyed her, mostly the former since their lives were at stake. While he continued his slow-but-steady ascent, she knelt on the ground and hugged herself as a shiver rolled across her body. The adrenaline rush had worn off, and her sweat-dampened clothes leeched the frost from the air like a suit of ice cream.

She'd just wrapped both arms around her knees when crunching footsteps caught her attention. Her head snapped up. As the footsteps drew nearer, she could make out snippets of conversation.

". . . freezing my ass off . . ."

". . . shoulda brought my other coat . . ."

The voices were deep, male, and very familiar.

". . . starvin' to death . . ." She'd know that voice anywhere—Eric.

". . . I'd kill for a basket of wings right now . . ." And Marcus Johnson.

A female voice joined the conversation. "Seriously? Is food all you ever think about?"

Cara craned her neck and glanced at Aelyx, halfway up the tree. His frozen posture told her he'd heard the voices, too. When she peered in the direction of Eric's voice, a few glimpses of his blue jacket flashed through the trees. If she could see him, it only stood to reason he could see her—and Aelyx.

The boys shared a laugh and Marcus said, "No, I think about lacrosse, too. Oh, and ass."

"Male or female?" the girl teased. "Not that I'm judging or anything."

"Chillax, Brandi," Eric said. "I'm pretty sure it's your ass that's on his mind. Though I *have* caught him staring at me in the locker room a couple times . . ."

Brandi?

Cara held perfectly still, watching Eric and Marcus pick their way through the woods. The girl closed the distance behind them, and Cara squinted at a familiar puffy white coat. It *was* Brandi . . . with her hand curled around the iron shaft of a golf club. She linked arms with Marcus, who toted a hunting rifle. Eric gripped a wooden baseball bat, and the three of them slung the weapons casually over their shoulders like kids strolling to the local fishing hole.

Without moving an inch, Cara turned her eyes to Aelyx, whose black shirt and dark jeans camouflaged into the scorched wood, but his arms were trembling from holding still in such an awkward position. He'd pressed his forehead against the bark as if trying to become one with the tree. Just then, one of his shoes skidded against the charred bark, sending debris raining down on her and pelting the dried leaves on the ground.

Eric's gaze immediately fell on hers and locked there for

one eternal moment. Her breath hitched and she bit her lip, praying that Marcus and Brandi hadn't heard it, too.

With a barely perceptible shake of her head, she asked him to keep walking.

"Hey." Marcus halted, bringing one hand up like a defendant swearing an oath. "You hear something?"

"Yeah." Eric broke eye contact and pointed to a ravine in the opposite direction. "Over there. Sounded like a squirrel."

"Naw, man. It came from that way." Marcus nodded ten yards ahead of her position, and Cara held her breath, willing herself invisible. She'd picked the wrong day to wear a pink sweater—it was a miracle Marcus hadn't spotted her yet.

"You wanna split up? I'll check over there"—Eric hooked a thumb toward her—"and you two head that way." He pointed to the ravine.

"No," Brandi said. "If our team's gonna bag him, we should stay together. It's the only way to take him down."

"She's right," Marcus said, absently rubbing his upper arm. "That bastard's crazy strong."

Eric laughed dryly. "Scared? You're the one with the gun, for chrissakes."

"No, dickweed." A tremor in Marcus's voice betrayed his fear. "I was trying to help you, but whatever. Good luck with your pansy-ass Louisville Slugger." He stalked in the other direction and Brandi reluctantly followed.

Once they'd moved out of her line of vision, Cara released the breath she'd been holding and watched as Eric made his way to her in slow, deliberate strides. He crouched down and pretended to study tracks in the dirt, sliding his gaze to the side to observe Marcus as he whispered, "You can't stay here. There're more coming."

"Is my dad okay?"

Using his baseball bat as a walking stick, Eric pushed to standing and stepped around her, making a show of inspecting a patch of thistle. "Guess so. Got the crap beat outta him, though."

She started to ask about Mom when more chunks of burned wood pelted her head, and she shielded her eyes and glanced up to see Aelyx resuming his climb. Eric flinched, noticing Aelyx for the first time.

"What's he doing up there?" Even in the lightest whisper, Eric's unadulterated loathing for Aelyx came through loud as an air horn.

"Getting his ship down."

Brows pinched together, Eric crouched low again, tipping his head and scrutinizing her face as if she'd grown a second nose. "Do *you* see a spaceship?"

"I'm not crazy," she hissed. "The cloaking device makes it invisible."

"You're not screwing with me? He's really got a ship up there?"

She nodded.

"Where's he gonna drop you off? The base?"

"He's not dropping me off, Eric."

It took a few seconds for him to figure out what that meant. When the realization hit him, he rocked back on his heels and landed on his backside. "No effing way! They're evil, Cara—they've been poisoning our water! Our crops, too! That kid confessed to it." He turned his glare on Aelyx, and it didn't escape her notice that his hand tightened around the bat with white-knuckled force.

"It's a lie. He was killed for no reas—" She bit short her reply when the hairs on the back of her neck stood on end. The winter air had long since covered her skin in goose bumps, but something else had chilled her deep inside. She'd been so caught up in her conversation with Eric that she'd stopped monitoring Marcus's and Brandi's distant footsteps, and pure instinct paralyzed her once again. They were close. She sensed it.

Eric must've felt it, too. Springing to the balls of his feet, he swept the forest with his wide-eyed gaze. He crept toward the ravine, calling, "Johnson! Greene! Find anything over there?"

Cara's heart pounded so hard her fingertips throbbed. She peered into the branches as if she could lift Aelyx to the top through sheer will. He was so close—just a few more feet. Flexing her fingers to restore feeling, she silently moved onto all fours and then crawled around the tree to reposition herself out of sight.

That's when she noticed Marcus's size elevens planted right in front of her.

With a gasp, she glanced up just in time to see Marcus draw back his rifle and slam the stock into her left cheek-bone. White-hot sparks exploded behind her eyelids while the crushing force sent her head slamming against the frigid ground.

"Damn, baby," Brandi said from nearby. "You don't mess around."

Cara's lips parted in a silent scream. When she curled onto her side and covered her face, Marcus used the opportunity to kick her squarely in the ribs. She heard bones crack within her chest, her lungs emptied, and pure pain blinded her.

"Stop!" Eric demanded. His shoes scuffled and scraped right beside her ear, but the sensation flew to her mind's periphery as she struggled to breathe. Nothing existed but her need for oxygen—even pain gave her a temporary reprieve while she opened her mouth wide, coaxing air into her flattened lungs.

That first glorious breath tasted sweeter than ambrosia, but relief lasted only a moment before agony returned with the fury of ten nuclear bombs. Eyes watering, she cried out and pushed backward, away from the grunts of the boys fighting inches from her head. Each movement sent barbs skittering across her raw nerves, but she scooted across the soil until her spine met the resistance of solid oak.

The second her vision returned, her eyes found Aelyx. He'd reached the shuttle and held one palm against its invisible hull, but his gaze darted back and forth between her and the violent shoving match nearby. She didn't need Silent Speech to understand his dilemma: should he stay with the ship or come down to defend her?

Cara shook her head, scraping her temple against a pillow of dried twigs. *Don't do it*, she silently implored. *Get the ship down!* Before long, more Patriots would find them, and she couldn't run anymore. She couldn't even sit up.

Suddenly, Eric's body hit the ground and skidded to her

side, spraying her with dirt and cracking her shoulder with his discarded baseball bat. Before he could scramble to his feet, Marcus cocked his rifle and pointed it at Eric's chest.

"Just stop, man," Marcus said, panting. "She's the enemy. You're thinking with your wang!"

Brandi pointed her golf club at Cara. "She's been banging Aelyx for months. You think she gives a damn about the rest of us? My mom says we'll end up as slaves to the L'eihrs, cranking out their half-breed spawn, and she'll be safe on the other side like the traitor she is."

"Exactly," Marcus said. "She's not human anymore."

"Take your head outta your ass!" Eric pushed off the ground and charged Marcus again, shoving aside the barrel and then pointing at her. "That's *Cara*. The same girl who let you cheat off her in sixth grade. My girlfriend for *three years*! She's one of us!" He turned to Brandi and said, "You used to be friends."

Brandi joined her boyfriend and raked a disdainful gaze over Cara. "Not anymore. She's been up the alien's ass since he got here."

Cara couldn't draw enough air to say, *You're one to talk*, but it must've shown on her face because Brandi made a disgusted noise and sneered, "I was never into him. As if I'd let an alien touch me."

Eric muttered, "Her mom's head of intelligence for our chapter."

It seemed so trivial now, but Cara remembered the day she'd caught Brandi trying to shove a note in her locker. She really was behind the threats—she'd probably followed her and pushed Ashley down the stairs, too. And for what? To gain her mom's approval and to date the homecoming king?

Marcus hocked a loogie and spat it at Cara's feet. He pointed his rifle at her. "Where's the L'eihr?"

Cara shook her head against the ground and wheezed, "The army took him."

"I think she's lying," Brandi said. "Or she'd be with them, too."

Marcus slid his hand along the rifle stock. "I'll get it out of her."

"No." Eric scrambled in front of her and did something far worse than kicking Cara in the chest. He pointed to Aelyx in the treetop. "He's up there!"

When Marcus tipped back his head and spotted the left half of Aelyx's body disappearing into thin air, he didn't stop to question the validity of what he'd seen. Instead, he tucked the rifle stock into his armpit, raised the weapon, and squinted one eye to take aim.

Cara didn't hesitate, either. She curled her hand around Eric's fallen bat and pushed onto all fours. She gritted her teeth, ignoring the flames lapping at her ribs, and swung with all her strength at the side of Marcus's knee. His leg cracked and he collapsed, skewing his shot as he pulled the trigger.

Gunfire pierced her eardrums, followed by Marcus's screams of agony. Dropping the bat, Cara crumpled into a heap and began dry heaving. How was it possible to suffer this much without passing out? She curled into the fetal position and darted one last glance into the trees—seeing nothing. Aelyx had made it into the cloaked shuttle.

"You idiot!" Brandi raised her club to strike Cara, but Eric shoved her aside and bent low to snatch his bat off the ground. He should have gone for the rifle. By the time he realized his mistake, Brandi had beat him to it. She raised the barrel in line with Eric's belt buckle while he dropped the bat and held both palms forward.

"She dumped you for an alien," Brandi told him. "And you're still defending her?"

Eric backed away. "Jus—"

Before he got a word out, the air around them warmed to the temperature of a scorching July afternoon and vibrated so thickly Cara's teeth rattled. Brandi scrunched her forehead, darting narrowed glances in every direction, while Cara and Eric exchanged a knowing look. She wished she hadn't told him about the ship, but there was nothing she could do about that now.

Cara's left eye had begun to swell shut, so she used the right one to scan the clearing for a spot wide enough for Aelyx to land the shuttle. There was only one place—right on top of the stream ten yards behind Marcus's now-limp body. Oh, sure, *he* could pass out.

"What's that?" Brandi demanded, hands trembling as she cocked the rifle and pointed it at Cara's face. "What's the L'eihr doing to us?"

Cara floundered for a lie—something so clever it would send Brandi running—but apparently, the simple act of remaining conscious had drained all her brainpower.

"Make him stop!" Brandi screamed, half hysterical. If

she shuddered any harder, she'd pull the trigger whether she meant to or not.

Shaking her head, Cara held up one hand in surrender. "I don't—"

"I'm gonna count to three," Brandi cried, "and if it doesn't stop, I'll kill you. I swear to God!"

"Whoa, whoa, calm down." Eric approached Brandi, but she stepped back and pointed the rifle at him in warning before turning it on Cara.

"One!"

"It's just the ship!" Cara said.

"She's right," Eric echoed. "You can't see it 'cause it's cloaked."

"Two!"

"Jesus Christ, Brandi, I'm telling the truth!"

"You gotta chill out." Eric inched toward Brandi like she was a wounded animal. "You don't wanna shoot her."

"Three!"

Clenching her eyes shut, Cara curled into a ball and wrapped both arms around her head as if she could block the bullet with her sweater. Her life didn't flash before her eyes like she'd expected. Instead, her heart pounded painfully against her cracked ribs and her whole body flashed cold, despite the sultry air. She heard Aelyx call her name and then a shot, and she flinched, waiting to feel the bullet's impact.

But it never came. After several seconds, it occurred to her she hadn't been hit. Tentatively, she peeked out from under one arm.

Eric had Brandi pinned to a tree, but he struggled to hold her as a bright spot of blood blossomed out from a hole in his shirtsleeve.

Aelyx dashed into view, kneeling on the ground and gently brushing back her hair. "Can you move?" he asked.

She pushed him aside, whispering, "Eric's shot."

"The bullet just grazed him," Aelyx said in a rush. "We have to go. Hold on to me."

The slightest movement brought searing pain, but she wrapped her arms around Aelyx's neck and held her breath while he carried her past the scuffle to the spacecraft and set her gingerly atop the passenger seat. While he strapped her in with the greatest of care, she peered out the open door at Eric, who'd managed to wrestle the rifle away from Brandi. Clearly outnumbered, Brandi turned tail and bolted, leaving her injured boyfriend behind.

Aelyx climbed over Cara and into the pilot's seat. Placing the pads of his fingers lightly against a steely panel that reminded her of a dashboard, he whispered something in L'eihr and the doors began to hiss closed.

She watched Eric nod good-bye. With half a smile and watery eyes, he mouthed something she couldn't quite interpret, and for just one second, she saw a flash of her old friend.

And then she was gone.

CHAPTER TWENTY-FOUR

Cara gasped when a pair of cool metal shears brushed the skin on her abdomen, causing the L'eihr medic who wielded them to pause and offer a questioning glance.

"Sorry," Cara said, "it's just cold."

The medic, a soft-spoken girl with the longest eyelashes Cara had ever seen, continued cutting away Cara's sweater, sending a tiny pearl button clinking to the examination table. When the last remaining wool scraps had fallen, Cara's chest broke out in goose bumps. The air—or, rather, the lack thereof—sixty miles above Earth was brutally frigid, despite the heated ventilation.

Cara picked up the button and rolled it between her thumb and index finger while glancing around the immaculate gray-walled exam room. A variety of foreign instruments hung on the walls, and she tried to guess their purposes. Tilting her head, she leaned to the side to inspect a polished metallic rod. Aside from delivering a good bludgeoning, she couldn't imagine how it was useful.

"Please be still," the girl said in a thick accent similar to French-Polynesian. "This will be uncomfortable, but traveling at light speed will widen the fissures in your ribs if we don't mend them first."

"We'll reach light speed?" That surprised Cara, since they weren't going directly to L'eihr. Aelyx's leaders were bringing Troy and meeting them halfway for an emergency hearing.

The girl smiled, but her eyes were vacant. "Yes, now hold still."

Vacant stare or not, Cara welcomed and reciprocated the smile. It was the first she'd received since Aelyx had smuggled her aboard the main ship an hour ago. Even the withered old ambassador with dead eyes had straightened his spine and puckered his mouth when he'd caught a glimpse of her. He and Aelyx had engaged in the most intense staring match she'd ever witnessed, and though she hadn't been able to sneak a peek at their thoughts, she'd felt the message loud and clear: she wasn't welcome. She just hoped nobody flushed her out the airlock like people did to their enemies on *Battlestar Galactica*.

"Sit up straighter, please." The medic placed a hand on Cara's back and helped her lean forward on the exam table. Then she wrapped a flexible pad around her chest and secured it in the front. Moving to a control panel on the wall, the girl warned, "This is slightly unpleasant, but try to relax."

Cara nodded, preparing for the worst, but to her surprise,

the wrap warmed like a heating pad. Tipping back her head, she closed her eyes in rapture and groaned, "Ah, that feels aweso—"

Suddenly her fist clenched around the pearl button. The warmth shot from soothing to unbearable in an instant, as if the medic had turned a stove burner from low to volcanic. Her skin burned while scorching heat filled her lungs, forcing up ripples of nausea. She swallowed down bile as beads of sweat dotted her upper lip.

Then an ungodly tightness squeezed her chest like a blood pressure cuff, stealing her breath and forcing the heat into her face, where it settled inside her throbbing cheek. *Slightly unpleasant, my ass!* She closed the one eye that hadn't already swollen shut and tried to stay calm, but the pain was too intense. Just as she was about to cry out, the pressure released and the wrap cooled just as suddenly as it had flared.

Relief was instantaneous, but Cara inhaled deeply through her nose to clear away leftover queasiness. The medic removed the wrap and encouraged Cara to stand. "Move around and tell me if you feel any pain."

She hopped down from the table and twisted her torso from side to side—tentatively at first, but then with more enthusiasm. "Wow, that's amazing! I feel perfect." Whoa, almost. The walls began to blur and swirl around her. She grabbed the edge of the table and cupped a hand over her swollen eye. "I'm still a little dizzy."

"I haven't scanned your head yet," the girl said, reaching for the metal rod Cara had noticed earlier and then holding it to the back of her skull. "Just a fracture of the lateral orbital rim. It won't take long. Then we'll start on your bruises."

"Oh, the bludgeoning stick's an X-ray machine." She'd never have guessed it.

"Pardon?" the girl asked, looking from the instrument in her hand back to Cara.

"Nothing, just talking to myself."

After using a less painful, headband-size heated wrap to mend Cara's fracture, the medic pulled a clear gel pad from a drawer beneath the exam table and filled a hypodermic needle with milky fluid. She shook the gel pad, and it began to emit a purple glow.

"This," she said, holding up the needle, "will help your body reabsorb the blood from your bruises. And this"—she nodded toward the pad—"will heal the underlying tissue. Watch."

She began with a softball-size bruise above Cara's waist, injecting the white liquid until a pocket bubbled up from her skin. It stung, but this was a mosquito bite compared to getting dropkicked in the chest. Then the medic rested the glowing purple gel pack lightly atop the bruise and applied gentle pressure, pushing down a little harder as the seconds passed. When she lifted the pad, all traces of the bruise were gone.

"Wow," Cara whispered.

After healing her cheek and puffy eye, the medic concluded Cara's treatment with a *fahren* wrap: tingling, muddy goop that smoothed every last cut and scrape from her skin, leaving it soft and flawless. Maybelline had nothing on the L'eihrs. After sponging off and changing into a tan and gray uniform, she pulled her hair into a low ponytail and grinned at her reflection in the mirror—the ultimate L'annabe, minus the spray tan. Ashley would've been proud.

"Thanks." Cara hesitated, then touched the medic's forearm. The girl might feel the same aversion to contact Aelyx once did, but Cara needed to express her gratitude, not only for the medical care but for her kindness.

The girl did flinch beneath Cara's fingers and pulled away, but she softened the rejection with a gentle smile. "I'll take you to Aelyx. I know he'll be glad to see you."

Flutters tickled the inside of Cara's belly at the mere thought of him. She followed her guide along the winding corridors, finally taking the opportunity to study her surroundings. When they'd first approached the main ship, she'd been too busy trying to stop dry heaving to spare a glance out the shuttle window, and Aelyx had whisked her away to the medic right afterward. Honestly, though, there wasn't much to see, at least not at the moment. Everything—halls, floors, doors—was a monotony of metallic gray. The transport was like a floating labyrinth, a maze of sleek and simple silvery passages. She wondered how she'd ever find her way alone.

"There." The girl pointed to the end of the hallway, where Aelyx stood, locked in Silent Speech with a petite female Cara recognized as Syrine. Considering the rigid set of their folded arms, this wasn't a friendly gab session. After a quick two-fingered touch to Cara's throat, the medic left her and returned to the clinic.

Suddenly chilled again, Cara leaned against the wall and chaffed her hands while studying Aelyx and his best friend, the lovely emotional healer who saw into his soul. Not that she was jealous or anything.

Aelyx's honey-brown hair, now too short for a ponytail, fell over his brow, and he shoved it behind his ears before resuming the "argument." They were fighting about her. She knew it. After what'd happened to that poor boy in China, she couldn't blame the L'eihrs for icing her out, but at the same time, she hadn't expected such an evolved race to hold her accountable for a murder she didn't commit. She'd stood by Aelyx even after her community shunned her—didn't that count for anything?

Judging by the way Syrine had just shoved Aelyx's chest, the answer was no.

Maybe she shouldn't interrupt. Cara hugged herself, shivering against the wall as she worked up the courage to keep moving.

Help you? Syrine pounded her fists against Aelyx's sternum, reminding him of the time he'd taken Cara to the boxing gym to help her get back her "fight." It seemed Syrine had returned from Earth with a little too much of it. *You're delusional if you think I'll help you save the cretins who killed Eron!*

So you'd punish billions for the crimes of a few?

Yes! This wasn't the same Syrine he'd known for a lifetime—not this girl with snarled lips, her teeth bared like a rabid animal. *I hate them all! Even your precious Elire!*

He shrank back at the dark undertones in her thoughts. *She's part of me.* Aelyx closed the distance between them and gripped Syrine's upper arm. He had to make her understand. *A threat against her is a threat against me.*

Suddenly, Cara's porcelain fingers curled around his hand, startling him into relaxing his grip. "You okay?" Tilting her head, she regarded him with wide eyes, her face radiant and healed and so stunning it made his breath catch.

He stepped back and took in Cara's uniform as an involuntary smile played on his lips. The simple tan tunic seemed more out of place on her shoulders than the jewels on Mr. Manuel's toilet seat back on Earth, yet the sight made his heart swell until it bumped his lungs. He loved seeing her in his people's clothing. It was a reminder that she'd chosen a life with *him*, impossible as it seemed.

"Oh, this?" She posed like a fashion model, lifting her collar and shifting her weight to one hip. "Guess I'm an official L'eihr now. I'll blend right in."

"Aside from your skin, eyes, and hair, yes, you'll blend right in." He opened his arms and she rushed inside, locking their bodies together. "How're your ribs?" he asked.

Resting her chin on his chest, she blinked up at him, smiling. "Hug me as hard as you can and we'll find out."

He cupped her cheek and kissed her softly before encasing her in his arms again and crushing her closer. Just when he thought there was no space between them, she found a spare molecule and eliminated it by returning the embrace with all her strength. His blood warmed, spreading the tingling heat through his veins until his whole core hummed with loving her.

Syrine made a mock retching noise, but he ignored it. When Cara pulled back, she reached up and ruffled his hair. "With a little gel, you'd look like half the guys in school. You're more human than me right now."

"Which explains his asinine behavior," Syrine retorted. "But don't stop now. I'm sure you can mold him into the perfect companion."

Cara's fist tightened around his shirt, but she concealed her frustration, maintaining a blank expression as she turned to Syrine. "I don't want to change Aelyx—I love him just the way he is."

Syrine scoffed, her laugh so dry it tainted the air with the stink of loathing. "He doesn't feel the same about you. Your kind disgusts him." She raised her chin in contempt. "Did he tell you what we've done?"

"That's enough!" He locked eyes with Syrine and delivered a stern warning. *No more! She's mine, and I won't let you ruin her with your hate!*

Ruin her? Syrine asked. *Or ruin you? Afraid your sweet Elire won't forgive you for what you've done?*

Syrine had always been able to pinpoint Aelyx's greatest fear, but this was the first time she'd ever tried to use it against him. *Please don't.* He couldn't hide his desperation. For the briefest of moments, Syrine's resolve faltered, but in the end, her rage took control.

"You mean the water?" Cara said. "I already know about the contamination."

Syrine turned and gave him a look of reproach. "Is there

anything you *haven't* told her? Thank the Mother I had the forethought to delete her site."

"You shut down my blog?" Cara demanded.

Syrine ignored the question as a wicked grin curved her lips. "I'll bet there are some things you didn't share with our sweet Elire." Then she practically sang, "Like the *sh'alear*."

"What's that?" Cara asked.

"Nothing," he said. "Syrine's out of her mind with grief. She doesn't know what she's saying." He grabbed Cara's hand and tried to lead her away. "Come on. I'll take you to your room so you can rest."

"Don't do that." She jerked free. "Don't lie to me again. I can tell something's going on."

"Lie to you *again?*" Syrine gave a teasing *tsk-tsk-tsk*. He pleaded with her, but she blocked his thoughts. "What's he told you?"

Instead of answering, Cara faced him and waited for several agonizing beats, offering him a chance to confess. He remembered what she'd said that morning, though it seemed a lifetime ago: *We have to trust each other, or we're no better than strangers.* He shook his head, silently begging her to let it go.

Cara finally turned back to Syrine. "He said the exchange was a trial," she told her. "That your leaders want us to intermarry because you're missing emotional depth or something. They want humans to colonize L'eihr."

"Wanted," Syrine corrected. "Past tense, but yes, that's right. What he didn't mention is that our generation detests the idea." She paused to curl her lip and scan Cara from head to toe in obvious disdain. "As if we need your inferior genetic material. So we sabotaged the experiment. Aelyx planned everything. The whole time he's been living with you, he's been killing your crops to incite panic so he could keep you and your foul race away from L'eihr."

Cara released a humorless laugh as if the words were too ludicrous to believe, but when she glanced at him he could only gape at her in shame.

Slowly, her brows rose. "Is that true?"

"It started that way," he admitted, taking her hand again, "but then I began to care for you, and I realized we couldn't be together if the alliance failed, so I uprooted my *sh'alear*."

"Wait." Cara held one hand forward. "What's that?"

"The *sh'alear* is a parasitic tree," Syrine told her. "It robs the soil of nutrients and destroys most fruit-bearing vegetation until it's uprooted. Aelyx showed us how to smuggle the seedlings to Earth and how to plant them. He said it would fuel human paranoia."

"That's why you kept going into the woods," Cara said to him. "When did you pull it up?"

This was the worst part—the most damning. "A few days ago," he said.

Cara shook her head and stared at him in silence. When she spoke again, the pain in her voice prickled his flesh. "So, up until three days ago, you were trying to make sure you'd never see me again?"

He didn't have a response for that. How could he make her understand how conflicted he'd felt? How afraid he'd been that mankind would destroy his planet and his people?

Just look at the way humans had transformed Syrine from a compassionate healer into a black hole of malice.

"But I killed my seedling," he objected. "And Eron tried to do the same."

"Getting him murdered in the process!" Syrine shouted.

"He knew it was the right choice, long before we found out—" *The alliance would save mankind.*

"Oh, gods," Syrine said, clapping a hand over her mouth to stifle a giggle. "I forgot the best part! Without the alliance—and our technology—your planet's as good as dead."

Cara continued to shake her head absently. "They won't help us unless the alliance goes through?" She glanced at him once again for a refusal he couldn't provide.

"I didn't know until a few days ago—I swear it on the Mother." He couldn't let her think for one second he'd plotted to destroy her people. As he explained how the growth particles had infected all of Earth's major water sources, Cara's chest rose and fell in shallow gasps.

"We've got ten years?" she whispered. "And L'eihr won't help us?"

"But I fought to save the alliance as soon as I found out."

"Oh, well, that makes it all right." Cara freed her hands and backed away from him.

All his nightmares had ended in some variation of this—losing her once she learned the truth of what he'd done. But unlike the dreams, he wouldn't stand frozen and watch her disappear from his life.

Giving her space, he held up his palms like a man in surrender. "Please listen. I was wrong, but as soon as I realized—"

"Stop." She shut her eyes, sealing them tightly as if to block out reality. When she opened them again, tears spilled down her cheeks. "I sacrificed everything for you, and you were screwing over my *whole planet* the entire time."

"Not the entire time."

"Till three days ago!"

"But I love you. I showed you my feelings—you know they're real."

"And that's why I can't trust you." She paused to drag her shirtsleeve beneath her nose. "Loving me didn't stop you from lying or playing God. And now you expect me to fly away with you and leave everyone behind to die?"

"No! I'll get the technology somehow, even if I have to steal it."

"Damn right, you will. And then I'll take it home with my brother."

Syrine shoved him aside and held one finger in Cara's face. "You won't take a single grain of sand off L'eihr. I already told the Elders what Aelyx was planning."

"Then I'm glad the experiment failed," Cara spat, "because you're monsters. All of you!"

Before his brain could register what was happening, Syrine slapped Cara across the face, hard enough to send her stumbling into his arms. He held her protectively, but she recoiled and pushed free.

Syrine gasped, staring at her palm in disbelief as she backed up a pace, while Cara advanced, blood surging into her cheeks, fingers flexing, muscles coiled and ready to strike back. She stilled her hand and stopped within an inch of Syrine's nose.

"And you called *my* people barbarians," Cara said. "You're no better. At least humans can love."

"Don't talk to me about love," Syrine whispered, her back against the wall. "I loved Eron all my life—even when he chose someone else. I never stopped."

"I didn't know Eron very well," Cara said, "but I bet he wouldn't want a whole planet to die for him." She whipped her head around and locked eyes with Aelyx, her gaze cold and empty. "I'm going home. I never should've left."

"Wait." Lurching forward, he grabbed her shoulders. "I can make you understand. Just let me show you how I felt . . . how much I struggled with the choice."

"No!" She closed her eyes.

"Just this once, and I'll never ask you again."

Cara pushed him away, screaming, "I don't want your poison inside my head!" She turned on her heel and fled down the hall, her ponytail swinging to and fro.

Her words sent him stumbling back like a blow to the chest. Aelyx's eyes welled until she blurred into a collage of red and beige, then she turned the corner and disappeared.

He had to fix this. But how? Stepha had promised a dozen lashes for bringing Cara aboard the ship, and the Elders would watch him too closely for him to steal the technology and escape.

Whatever it takes, he decided. It didn't matter what he had to do—the end would justify the means. He'd find a way to save Earth or die trying.

CHAPTER TWENTY-FIVE

Cara swore she'd never travel at light speed again. Never ever ever. Not even if astronauts discovered a chocolate and peanut butter planet and claimed it for the US of A.

Oh, God, she shouldn't have thought about food! Ripples of nausea turned her stomach as her mouth flooded with saliva. Clutching the steely rim of her toilet with one hand, she rose onto her knees, tugged her hair aside, and hurled for the third time that morning.

She moaned to herself. Outer space sucked. Why hadn't the L'eihrs warned her this would happen? Oh, yeah, because everyone aboard the SS Buzzkill hated her with the fire of a thousand supernovas. Except for Aelyx, who'd holed up inside his own room, which explained why their paths hadn't crossed.

With a groan, she curled up against her bathroom wall, too weak to even wipe her mouth. She'd never felt so miserable, not even when she'd caught the swine flu in kindergarten and wound up in the hospital with secondary pneumonia. Of course, she hadn't lost the love of her life at age six.

Childish as it felt, she wanted her mother. Mom would know all the right things to say to make her feel better, but Cara's parents were galaxies away, and she didn't even know if they were safe. If she weren't so dehydrated, she'd break down and cry again, but she knew the tears wouldn't come, and crying without tears felt too much like dry heaving.

A light knock sounded from the door to her quarters in the next room, but she didn't budge. Whoever it was could come back later, maybe collect her dead body and ship it back to Earth. A loud *hiss* told Cara someone had opened the door, and she prayed to God it wasn't Aelyx. The last thing she wanted was for him to find her on the bathroom floor with dried puke in her hair. But when the medic poked her head through the doorway, disappointment tugged at Cara's heartstrings. Part of her *had* hoped it was Aelyx. She missed him so much it hurt.

"Sacred Mother," the girl said, twisting Cara's heart with another reminder of him. "You look awful."

"Can't. Stop. Yakking."

She gave a sympathetic smile and nodded. "Speed sickness. Why didn't you come to the clinic?"

"Because I couldn't take the toilet with me." It sounded better than, *I'm a wussy coward who was scared of running into*

Aelyx in the hall. She'd had all her meals brought to the room for the same reason, not that she'd been able to keep most of them down.

"Well." The girl blinked her mile-long lashes and set her bag on the floor. "I'm glad someone asked me to check on you."

There was only one person on this godforsaken spacecraft who cared if she lived or died, and as much as she hated it, she still cared for him, too. "Is he sick like me?"

"Sicker than I've ever seen him." The medic crouched down and rooted around inside her bag until she found a hypodermic needle and a glass vial filled with clear liquid. "But not like you." She tapped one finger against her temple. "He suffers here." After scanning Cara's face a moment, the girl pressed two fingers over her heart. "And here."

"I'm sorry to hear that." Despite all his lies, she hated the idea of Aelyx hurting. It'd been so tempting to let him use Silent Speech to explain away what he'd done. There was no point denying that she ached to be with him. But she couldn't trust Aelyx, and without that, they had nothing worth saving.

"Do you understand why you're so sick?" The girl filled her needle with clear solution and motioned for Cara's arm. As she injected the medicine, she explained, "It's all in your mind."

Sucking in a sharp breath, Cara clenched her teeth as the icy liquid swept through her veins.

"Your brain doesn't believe your body is capable of light speed," the girl continued as she massaged Cara's arm, pushing the medication toward her heart. "How can your mind understand something you've never experienced? So it assumes you're hallucinating—that you've poisoned yourself—and it induces vomiting to rid your body of the perceived toxins." She pulled what looked like a metal thermos from her bag, unscrewed it, and handed it over. "L'eihrs are no different, *Cah*-ra. Our brains are resistant to change. How can we understand what we've never experienced and adapt without making mistakes?"

Cara's hand froze in midair as she reached for the cup. She had a feeling they weren't talking about motion sickness anymore. So, if she understood the subtext correctly, the medic was suggesting she cut Aelyx some slack for wrecking the alliance because he'd never been in love before? That was the lamest excuse she'd ever heard.

"Well," she said, regaining use of her arm, "if L'eihrs are so evolved, they should be able to figure it out."

"We can." She nodded for Cara to drink. "But it takes time. And patience."

Cara studied the girl over the top of her cup as she finished the sweet liquid—electrolyte supplements, no doubt—in three eager gulps. Why did this L'eihr give a fig about her relationship with Aelyx? Out of the hundreds of crew members aboard this transport, why was she the only one to offer comfort and gentle smiles? "What's your name?" she asked the medic.

The girl screwed the lid on her container, peeking through a fringe of dark lashes that seemed suddenly familiar. "Elyx'a," she said, pronouncing it *e-licks-ah*. "But call me Elle."

Cara's heart raced. "By any chance, does that mean *daughter of Elyx*?"

Face expressionless, the girl nodded.

"You're his sister," Cara whispered. Aelyx had never mentioned brothers or sisters. Just add that to the long list of secrets he'd kept from her.

"Genetically, yes," Elle said. "From what I understand of human culture, you'd consider us more friends than brother and sister." She stood and extended her hand to help Cara to her feet. "But I care for him."

Propping one palm against the wall for support, Cara gripped the girl's hand and pushed to standing, waiting for nausea to catapult her stomach into her throat. But to her surprise, nothing happened. Her stomach stayed right where it belonged.

Elle wrapped a supportive arm around Cara's shoulder and guided her into the main chamber, a gray room the approximate size of a postage stamp, vacant with the exception of two metallic bunk beds. Cara remembered how comfortable Aelyx had felt in his boring gray room back home. It finally made sense.

"He's different," Elle continued. "More empathetic than most of the clones. I think that's the real reason the Elders chose him for the exchange, not because of his language skills."

Cara quirked a skeptical brow, recalling how cold and unfeeling Aelyx had seemed when they'd first met. "*He's* the best you've got?"

"No," Elle whispered, turning her gaze to the floor. "That was Eron. I suspect they'll clone him again."

"I'm so sorry." Cara squeezed the girl's hand and sat on the edge of her bed. "Were you two close?"

Nodding, she stood on tiptoe to pull a clean uniform off the top bunk. "He was my *l'ihan*." She dropped the clothing into Cara's lap and explained, "The Way wants us to emulate the human method of reproduction."

"To make babies the old-fashioned way?"

She nodded again. "And for the first time, they've allowed us to choose our own mates."

"Oh, no." Cara studied Aelyx's sister—really paid attention for once—taking in the redness that rimmed her silvery eyes, the dark circles beneath her lashes, the smiles that never reached beyond her lips. Though she'd done a stellar job of hiding it, this girl was grieving the loss of her . . . "*L'ihan* means husband?"

"No, more like betrothed. The literal translation is *future*."

Dipping her head in shame, Cara clutched the clean clothes to her chest as if to hide behind them. "You must hate me."

"Quite the opposite." Using one finger, she tipped Cara's chin up until their eyes met. "I hope you'll stay." She gestured to the uniform and added, "Get dressed. We'll meet the other transport soon, and then the three of you will appear before The Way."

"The three of who?"

"You, Aelyx, and Syrine." Elle glanced around the tiny room until she found her bag. "You'll have a few minutes with your brother while Aelyx receives his reckoning. It won't take long. Our leaders will summon you then."

"His reckoning?" Cara didn't like the sound of that.

"Yes. He needs to account for disobeying the Elders by bringing you here."

The *iphet*, then. That horrible electric lash. Cara told herself she couldn't wait to get away from these sadistic bastards, but in reality, she had to grip the mattress to keep from bolting out the door to Aelyx's room.

He lied to you for months, she reminded herself. *You can't trust him, and he's not your problem anymore.*

Before Elle left, she asked, "Will you think about what I said?"

Cara wished she could say no, but she couldn't have stopped the words from turning over in her mind if she'd tried.

After she'd washed the vomit from her hair and scarfed down a meal that really *did* taste like Mom's roast, Cara heard Troy's knuckles rap on her chamber door. She knew it was him because he always knocked three times, each strike punctuated by a sweeping beat of silence, so it sounded like the intro to that old song their dad loved so much. *Thump, thump, thump. Another one bites the dust.*

She opened the door for her brother and completely fell apart at the sight of his welcoming smile and outstretched arms.

She collided with him at full force, locking her arms around his neck and shaking his chest with the force of her sobs.

"Damn, Pepper." It took her brother three tries to unglue her from his body, but he finally held her at a distance. "You missed me that much?"

She wiped a sleeve over her eyes to bring Troy into focus, noting at once the changes in him. The wavy black hair he'd inherited from their mother nearly touched his shoulders, which seemed odd when contrasted against his military uniform, but that wasn't what struck her. It was his eyes—still vividly blue, but no longer sparkling with carefree wanderlust. He studied her face deliberately, in a way he'd never done before, pursing his lips in concern.

Sweet mother of God, Troy had grown up.

"What happened?" he asked. "When Mom e-mailed, she said you were happy to leave."

"Mom's okay, then?"

Troy nodded. "Dad, too. More or less."

Cara led her brother inside. After taking about a dozen deep breaths to calm herself, she told him everything—starting with how she'd fallen for Aelyx on Earth and ending with what Syrine had said a few days ago.

"So," Cara continued, her breath still hitching, "somehow I have to convince them to give us the technology so we can take it home."

"You're sure about this? *Ten years?*"

She nodded, and Troy gaped at her in disbelief.

"I don't have much time before they call me in. I need to know what's going on back home—anything that might help. Did they catch the guys who killed Eron?"

He dragged one hand over his face, seemingly struggling to absorb what Cara had just told him. "Troy?" she pressed.

"No." He shook his head. "And they probably never will. Tracking terrorists isn't like busting civilians. They're networked. They operate as one, and they never give each other up."

"I was hoping at least—"

A quick series of knocks interrupted her, and she answered the door to find Stepha, the L'eihr ambassador, observing her with indifference.

"If you'll follow me," he said, tipping his head toward the hallway.

Troy promised to wait there, and after a quick good-bye, she followed the ambassador to what she assumed was a conference room.

When Stepha pressed his palm against an identification panel, both doors retracted into the wall and Cara stepped inside, taking a moment to orient herself. Dominating the space were ten plush, vacant seats arranged in a soft arc, a single glass podium glowing beneath an overhead light in the center. Three metallic stools faced the panel, two of them already occupied by Syrine—who slouched forward, cradling her head in her hands—and Aelyx, who sat ramrod straight next to her.

As Cara moved to the seat beside him, she scanned his back, expecting to see a crisscross of welts raising the uniform's fabric but finding none. The skin on his neck appeared smooth and unmarred, too, but when she took her seat and examined him more closely, she noticed a thin sheen of sweat glistening on his face. He gripped his knees with trembling fingers, and Cara could almost feel his agony. Her own flesh prickled, and heat flooded her cheeks when she imagined the pain he'd endured.

She stewed in silence for several long minutes before turning to him. "You okay?"

Not returning her gaze, he spoke in the detached voice of a stranger. "When The Way enters, it's crucial you don't talk until you have permission—the previous speaker will hand you a small baton. To interrupt is considered the height of rudeness, and while the Elders might have admired your passion at one time, they won't look kindly upon it now. Not after what happened to Eron. Do you understand?"

The coldness in his tone made her throat tighten. She nodded and whispered, "I'm sorry you had to go through that because of me."

"Just remember what I told—"

"Don't worry." Whether on Earth or in another galaxy, if there was one thing Cara knew, it was the rules of debate. She couldn't salvage her heart, but maybe she could save her people. It was time to put Aelyx out of her mind and focus on the speech she'd been mentally rehearsing all morning.

She took a deep breath and prepared for the fight of her life.

CHAPTER TWENTY-SIX

Aelyx couldn't look at her, not even through his peripheral vision. Because one glimpse of Cara would send him to his knees pleading for forgiveness, and he didn't want her to remember him that way—weak, pathetic, filling her mind with "poison."

Using the hem of his tunic, he blotted sweat from his brow, wincing when the fabric tugged against his back. The ghost of the *iphet*'s lashes throbbed so severely he felt it in his teeth, but he embraced the pain. It helped him focus on what lay ahead instead of on the girl brooding to his right. He only hoped she'd control her temper. If she insulted The Way, nothing he said or did could help her.

As he tried to ignore the anxiety twisting his gut, the doors retracted once again, and the same Elder who'd administered Aelyx's reckoning a few minutes earlier strode to the podium and placed the gleaming metallic speaker's baton lightly atop the illuminated glass. They shared the briefest of glances before Aelyx broke eye contact, rubbing his nose to expel the scent of singed flesh.

Turning his head toward Cara but careful to avert his gaze, he whispered, "Stand when The Way enters, and don't sit until they do."

"Got it," came her terse reply.

A few moments later, soft, controlled footsteps clicked inside. Aelyx stood and glanced up, expecting to see the same ten Elders who'd composed The Way since his youth: six males, four females, all withered and slumped with age. But his brows rose in shock when two young clones—one male, one female—accompanied the Elders and took their places among the panel, standing before the cushioned seats of honor with stiffened spines, both wearing haughty expressions of authority. They must have come from another precinct, because he didn't know them. The girl couldn't have been older than eighteen, while the male possessed the tall, lanky build and the defined jaw of a twenty-year-old.

While Aelyx openly gawked at his new leaders, Cara left her place by his side and approached the panel before he could stop her. His heart leaped painfully, but he resisted lurching forward and wrestling her back to her seat. That would only create more of a spectacle, and The Way demanded order above all things. Great gods, what was she doing?

Cara stopped at the podium only long enough to grasp the baton before squaring her shoulders and marching right up to the first Elder and pressing her fingers against the side of his throat in her misinterpretation of a L'eihr greeting.

The Elder's dormant gray eyes widened in surprise, but instead of chastising Cara for her brazen act, he returned the gesture.

One by one, she greeted each leader, letting her fingers linger far, far too long, not understanding that she'd given them the human equivalent of an intimate embrace instead of a handshake. When she touched the young male, his lips twitched in an amused grin before he regained his mask of cool superiority.

Cara returned to her seat, taking the baton with her, and the male locked eyes with Aelyx.

It's my understanding, the boy communicated, *that you've brought her here as your* l'ihan.

Aelyx made no effort to conceal his heartbreak. *Not any longer.* He noticed the male's posture sag in response to the pain. *She wishes to return to Earth.*

"Point of order." Cara held the baton in the air.

"Yes, Miss Sweeney," the young male said as he stood tall once again.

"I respectfully request that all communication during these proceedings be verbalized in English for my benefit."

A laugh escaped the male's lips before he had a chance to stifle it, reminding Aelyx of his own first interaction with Cara.

"Agreed. I apologize for my rudeness. My name is Jaxen." He gestured to the young girl at his side. "Aisly and I are new to the order and are still learning proper procedure." After a bow that seemed almost playful, he smiled at her and sat down.

Aelyx didn't particularly care for Jaxen's flirtatious behavior, but he decided to give him the benefit of the doubt instead of hating him on sight.

The rest of the panel lowered to their seats, and Aelyx followed suit. The chief Elder, a woman named Alona, waved lazily at Syrine and droned, "The girl will speak first."

Syrine stretched her arm across him, demanding the baton from Cara, who surrendered it with a quiet sigh. Then Syrine stepped to the podium, leaning her elbows on the glass as if standing required too much effort.

"I'd hoped for a better outcome," Syrine said to the panel, "but our trial living among humans has failed. My interactions with them were torturous, and I found them deceitful, dishonorable, violent, and hedonistic." For the next fifteen minutes, she went on to tell stories of schoolboys crawling beneath the dinner table to fondle her legs; provincial French villagers who crossed themselves when passing her on the street; and how, in the end, death threats had escalated until she required constant military protection. "I don't need to remind you of Eron's murder." Syrine now spoke directly to Alona, who'd raised Eron for two years before sending him to the Aegis. "Let his death prove beyond all doubt that we cannot live in peace among the human race, and more importantly"— glancing over her shoulder at Cara—"that they don't deserve our mercy."

Alona stared blankly ahead, her voice devoid of feeling when she ordered, "Let the human represent her people."

Cara inhaled deeply and released a trembling breath before standing and retrieving the baton from Syrine. Instead of hiding behind the podium, she stood to its right, resting one elbow atop the glass in a casual stance, as if sharing an anecdote among friends.

"Thank you for allowing me to speak, especially considering the tragedy that ended Eron's life. Your willingness to listen shows how evolved you truly are." A far cry from *You're monsters, all of you!* Leaving the podium, she lowered to one knee in front of Alona.

"I only met Eron once, at the exchange gala, but I remember how he shook my hand and smiled so warmly. I could tell Eron had a gentle spirit. Elle, his *l'ihan*, told me he was the kindest among you." She paused a moment, peering directly into Alona's eyes. "I don't think he would want The Way to sentence my people to death as retribution for his own."

Cara stood and paced a slow circuit around the room. "It's easy to assume humans are depraved when that's all you hear on the news. Let me tell you the stories you haven't heard."

She shared tales of human kindness: a terminally ill child who'd spent her last days raising money to provide clean drinking water for strangers on another continent; a man who'd harbored a wounded enemy soldier, then healed him and risked his own life to smuggle him out of his war-torn country. Cara's fluid articulation stunned Aelyx; her radiance and passion stole his breath, and all the while, she never mentioned that he'd set out to sabotage the exchange. He didn't know why she kept his secret, not after what he'd done, but her loyalty warmed his fractured heart.

"Violent extremists," Cara continued, "have robbed mankind of some truly gifted and passionate visionaries: Mahatma Gandhi, Medgar Evers, Martin Luther King, Jr., John Lennon. But in the end, peace and logic prevail because, at their core, most humans are good. Look at the nearly unanimous defeat of the Expulsion Act—Americans support the alliance, and they've made their voices heard.

"The necessity of an alliance still exists," Cara concluded. "You need our spirit of humanity, and we need your scientific advances. If we work together, we both win." She approached the podium, turning the baton over in her hands before resting it atop the glass. "You can coexist with humans—I know it. If you'd be willing to try again, I think we can learn a lot from each other."

Jaxen tipped his head and studied her in a way Aelyx didn't like at all, with one corner of his mouth turned up appreciatively and a curious gleam in his eye. When Cara took her seat, Jaxen's gaze followed, and Aelyx stood, blocking his new leader's view until their eyes met.

I understand why you brought her. Jaxen quirked a brow. *I'd have taken twelve lashes for this one, too. Pity she won't stay with us.* There was no sympathy in the young man's thoughts, just a dusting of envy. Aelyx blocked his thoughts to conceal a surge of jealousy and took his place behind the podium.

"Last year you charged me with a task," Aelyx told his Elders, carefully avoiding Jaxen's gaze and gripping the smooth glass until it squeaked. "But I was too arrogant to carry it out. I didn't believe we needed humans—their influence, their culture, or their DNA—so instead of trusting the wisdom of my Elders, I conspired against you from the very beginning, even before I arrived on Earth." He paused a moment, waiting for them to gape at one another in disbelief, but aside from Jaxen and the girl at his side, they didn't seem the least bit surprised, which stunned him into a beat of silence.

"Um," he continued clumsily, "I . . . didn't think the experimental exchange would succeed, and more importantly, I didn't want it to succeed." Then he confessed to planting the *sh'alear* and manipulating mankind, ending with his accidental discovery of Earth's water contamination and his love for Cara. "Eron wanted to uproot his *sh'alear* weeks ago, but I wasn't ready. When we found out the alliance was necessary for human survival, we agreed to destroy the seedlings right away, but Eron was under armed guard by then. He had to evade them to accomplish it, and that's when he was captured. It was my fault, completely. If it weren't for me, we'd still be on Earth right now—all of us, safe among humans."

The baton had grown sweaty in his grasp. He took a moment to wipe his palms on his tunic before gripping it tighter than ever, as if he could draw courage from the warm brushed metal. He allowed himself one glance at Cara, who stared back, openmouthed, shaking her head.

"What I did was criminal." He faced his Elders, heart pounding with the gravity of his admission. "Eron's blood is on my hands, and I ask that you punish me, not mankind. You need them—you need their compassion and love, humor and folly . . . even their anger. Please reconsider the alliance and take my life in exchange for theirs."

Cara gasped from behind him, and Aelyx knew he had to act quickly before she bolted to the podium. He turned and locked eyes with her, then pushed a hurried thought into her head. *Don't move. Don't speak. You'll ruin everything.*

Tears spilled from her lashes as she pulled her brows low and burned a glare into his mind so fiercely it stung, and then something happened he couldn't believe. He felt her emotions. No words broached the veil between their minds, but his blood chilled with a fear so acute he had to close his eyes to break the connection, because he couldn't bear it.

He'd felt her fear of losing him. Not only that, but an aftertaste of her love, so strong and real he could almost reach out and pluck it from the air. Sacred Mother, she still loved him. She'd forgiven him. Nothing else existed in his world beyond that truth.

If only he hadn't just demanded his own execution.

Alona stood from her seat, declaring, "We will discuss this privately." Aelyx scanned her face for any betrayal of emotion, a hint of what she was thinking, but found none. The Elders filed quietly out of the room, Syrine on their heels, no doubt to make one final appeal for the destruction of mankind.

Cara wasted no time in rushing to him. He drew her close and buried his face in her hair.

"I can't believe you did that," she whispered. "You idiot. I love you."

"I felt it." He flattened one hand over her heart. "You looked in my eyes and I felt you."

Her lips parted with a soft *pop*. "I used Silent Speech?"

"Without words, but yes. You did it." He hoped he'd survive long enough to figure out how. "I'm so sorry, Elire. If they let me live, I'll spend the rest of my—"

"Don't." She pressed an index finger to his lips and whispered, "If they say no, we'll steal a shuttle."

"And go where?" Linking their hands, he towed her back to his seat, where he gathered her into his lap.

"As far away as we can get."

Her voice was so full of hope. He didn't have the heart to tell her a shuttle's fuel supply would only take them as far as the nearest transport. Instead, he tucked his thumb beneath Cara's jaw and lifted her lips to his, lightly at first, parting them and tentatively exploring her mouth with the tip of his tongue. Her sweet taste loosed a thousand white-hot sparks that tingled over his flesh, inexplicably burning and healing him all at once. She laced her hands behind his neck and returned the kiss with so much force he had to back away an inch.

"Oh!" She gasped. "Did I hurt your back?"

Yes, but he didn't care. He fisted her shirt and pulled her in again, savoring the feel of her soft, wet lips against his. He didn't know what the Elders would decide, and if he only had minutes to live, he wanted to spend every last second kissing her. He brushed her face, forcing his fingertips to memorize each gentle curve before moving to her throat and settling his thumb at the base, where her pulse hammered for him.

"One-ten," he whispered against her lips.

She kissed her way to his ear. "Still can't beat my high score."

She was probably right. He'd only had her in his arms an instant and already he was on the verge of reciting elements. Taking her face in his hands, he tipped their foreheads together and tried to steady his breathing. He couldn't stop planting tiny kisses on her nose, her cheeks, her eyelids, anywhere his lips landed. It felt surreal to have her back, and he half expected to wake up any minute, alone in his bed.

They sat like this, silently soothing each other, until the doors whispered open and Jaxen stepped inside. He paused for a moment and eyed them like a visitor at the zoo, face pressed to the glass of an exotic birdcage.

"Well?" Cara pressed.

Aelyx felt her heartbeat quicken through the thin tunic, and he continued stroking her back, both to calm her and to reassure himself she was still his.

Jaxen announced, "I understand that on Earth it's typical to offer a choice when delivering both good and bad news. So, which would you like to hear first?"

Chapter Twenty-Seven

"The good news." Cara always wanted the good news first. It tempered the bad, though if the Elders had decided to make Aelyx pay with his life, there'd be no softening that.

She tugged Aelyx's bicep so he'd stand beside her. If she understood correctly, he wasn't supposed to sit in the presence of an Elder—even if they were the same age. Jaxen seemed like a nice guy, but why tempt fate?

"Please," she added.

"Certainly." Jaxen leaned against the podium and crossed one foot over the other. "I'm happy to tell you The Way will continue alliance negotiations."

Interesting choice of words. He hadn't said The Way would give Earth the technology to decontaminate the water supply, only that they'd negotiate, which involved give and take. She didn't want to imagine what kinds of concessions her people would have to make in the deal.

"And the bad news?" She backed against Aelyx's body and pulled both his arms around her waist. He hugged her tightly, and she covered his hands with hers, bolting them in place. If his leaders had decided to execute him, they'd have to take her, too.

Jaxen turned his gaze on Aelyx and held it there. "Both you and Syrine will be punished for what you've done, a consequence harsher than the *iphet* but less unpleasant than death." His lips twitched in a grin as if he'd amused himself. "I convinced the others to let the punishment fit the crime. Since you worked so hard to destroy the alliance, we're sending you back to Earth to help repair it. You'll have to admit to humans what you've done and find a way to earn their forgiveness."

That didn't sound so bad.

Jaxen nodded at her and continued. "But Miss Sweeney will return with me to L'eihr, followed by the other two human exchange students."

Cara felt her eyes widen. "But," she objected, "I haven't graduated yet." *And I don't want to go without Aelyx.* She kept the last bit to herself, hesitant to rock the boat—or spaceship, as it were. "Why don't you send me back to Earth? Then I can help get more people onboard with the alliance . . . maybe even recruit colonists."

Jaxen grinned. "Persuasive as you are, I'm sure you'd be an asset to Aelyx and Syrine. But completing the exchange now is a show of good faith—a sign that humans trust your safety on L'eihr as we trusted Eron's safety on Earth."

Translation: *you're a walking insurance policy.* She felt Aelyx tense behind her. He asked, "How long until I can come home and join Cara?"

"As long as it takes," Jaxen said simply. He studied Aelyx for a few silent seconds before his voice turned smooth and teasing, like they were old friends. "Don't worry, Aelyx. I'll take good care of your *l'ihan* while you're gone."

Aelyx didn't say a word, but the tremor rolling through his rigid muscles spoke volumes. Clearly they weren't friends at all.

"I'll leave you two alone." Jaxen stepped toward her wearing a disarming smile. He pressed two fingers against the side of her neck in the standard good-bye, then yanked his hand away and strode briskly from the room.

She spun to face Aelyx, melding their bodies together. "Well, that could've gone better. But it could've gone a lot worse, too."

Ignoring her sentiment, Aelyx rubbed a thumb over her throat as if to erase Jaxen's touch.

"It's not so bad," she insisted, trailing one finger along the smooth edge of his jaw. "Think about it. If we were still on Earth, you'd go home in the spring, and I wouldn't be able to see you again till the fall semester. This way is better." She kissed the triangle of skin above his shirt collar and breathed him in. "It'll go by fast. Then we'll have all the time in the world."

"Mmm." He slipped his thumbs beneath the front of her

tunic and captured her waist in his palms. "That *is* something to look forward to."

"And we still have a little time before you leave." Which she intended to make the most of, starting now. "I don't want to spend any more of it in this room."

"Hey," Troy said, "you know what'd be really awesome, *Alex*?"

Cara plopped onto her bed and stretched out, surrendering to a sudden yawn attack. "His name's Aelyx."

"Whatever." Troy rolled his eyes and went back to snooping through her cabinet, which someone had stocked with clean uniforms, toiletries, and silvery gadgets she didn't know how to use. When he stumbled across a small white packet, he whispered, "Score!" then tore it open and started eating the contents.

Patiently enduring her brother's assholery, Aelyx smiled and joined her. He pulled her into a chaste cuddle. "What'd be *really awesome*?"

"If you stopped touching my sister."

Cara couldn't help laughing at that. After hightailing it across the globe when she needed him most, then disappearing to another galaxy and never e-mailing, Troy thought he could suddenly resume his role as the protective big brother? "Bite me," she told him with a single-finger salute.

"I'm serious, Pepper. It's grossing me out." He shook a metal golf ball at her, identical to the one Tori had found in Aelyx's underwear drawer all those months ago. "And maybe you can forget what he did, but I can't."

"That's how forgiveness works, nimrod." Cara nestled her cheek into a magical spot between Aelyx's chest and shoulder that seemed custom-made for her face. "Kind of like when your brother ditches you for two years, and you keep loving him anyway."

That shut him up for a few minutes.

While Troy continued perusing her things, the steady rise and fall of Aelyx's chest and his fingertips stroking her hair lulled her into a trance. She was just drifting to sleep when an obnoxious buzz filled the room. She waited for it to stop, thinking maybe this was the L'eihr equivalent of an alarm clock, but it kept getting louder.

With a groan, she pushed to sitting. "What's that?"

Aelyx raised one brow and darted a quick glance around the room. "What's *what*?"

"Um, the annoying buzz that's rattling my skull?" She turned to Troy. "You don't hear it?"

Troy shook his head and smirked, probably gearing up to make a snide remark, when he suddenly said, "Oh," and gave a slow nod. "Does it seem like someone shoved a beehive up your nose?"

"Yeah." It kind of did.

"That's your com-sphere," Aelyx said, laughing. "You're the only one who can hear it."

Troy tossed her the metal golf ball.

"Say your name," Aelyx told her. "That's always the default password. You'll have to reset it later."

She closed her fingers loosely around the vibrating metal and brought her hand to her lips as if playing an imaginary trumpet. "Cara Sweeney." Instantly, the humming stopped, and the sphere quit tickling her palm.

"Now set it down." Aelyx patted a spot on the bed.

She obeyed and backed up a few paces, just in case. Then her jaw dropped and she glanced back and forth between Aelyx and Troy for confirmation that she wasn't tripping on some weird alien drug. On a scale of one to ten—one being normal and ten being whompass crazy—seeing Mom and Dad flash to life in miniature form right beside her pillow rated a twenty.

"They were cleaning out Aelyx's room and found his sphere," Troy said. "I had it reset so they could use it."

"So they're real?" She knelt on the floor and gripped her mattress, leaning in to study her tiny parents the way she'd scrutinized bacteria under a microscope in science lab. If she squinted, she could barely make out the living room sofa's tacky magnolia pattern.

Six-inch Dad scratched his nose. "You're making me nervous, Pepper."

"Unbelievable." Sinking back on her heels, she took a moment to absorb what she'd seen but didn't believe. "Intergalactic video conferencing." She extended her palm toward Six-inch Mom, who did the same, giving the illusion of their mismatched hands joining in midair. "I was worried I'd never see you again."

Mom tried to respond, but her voice hitched, and she tucked her forehead against Dad's shoulder. Cara's heart sank as she realized how much pain she'd caused her parents. Now both their children were gone. Aelyx knelt by her side, interlacing their fingers and giving a reassuring squeeze.

He smiled at her parents. "I hope you're not tired of me yet, because I'm coming back to Earth while Cara takes my place on L'eihr."

"And it looks like the alliance will go through," Cara said, "so I can come home to visit when the program's over."

Mom took a few moments to let that sink in. "But it's so sudden—you didn't even get to pack. Can't you come home first?"

Cara shook her head but tried to stay upbeat for Mom's sake. "Lucky for me I'm good at traveling light." Before she forgot, she added, "Will you tell Tori I said good-bye?"

"She called yesterday," Mom said, "to let us know Eric's okay and to see if you'd really left, because she didn't believe it. When I told her, she did a lot of cursing in Spanish."

That made Cara smile. "Tell her about the sphere, Mom. She'll keep it a secret." Cara wanted to hear her best friend call her a *pendeja* so badly her chest ached. She wanted to see Tori's miniature form stamp her high-heeled foot and grip her hips like Wonder Woman. Maybe flip her the bird, too.

Mom promised to invite Tori over for a "conference call," but because the name Sweeney was still synonymous with traitor, she didn't know how long it would take for them to arrange it. Tori didn't want to give the Patriots any reason to doubt her loyalty, and Cara didn't blame her.

When they finally said good-bye and disconnected, Troy begrudgingly left her alone with Aelyx, but only because it was time for supper—*l'ina*, his favorite. Nothing came between Troy and a good meal, not even the possibility of his kid sister getting lucky during his absence. But before shutting the door, he pointed at the top bunk and announced, "I won't be gone long. And I'm crashing here tonight, so don't get your hopes up, *Alex*."

Cara grabbed the lump of fabric she'd been using as a makeshift pillow and hurtled it at her brother, but he easily slapped it aside and danced into the hall. Right before disappearing from view, he laughed and called her a dorkus. Maybe he hadn't matured so much after all.

When she turned to rejoin Aelyx, she noticed a distant glimmer of light winking through the glass porthole behind him, a twinkle that wasn't there before. The ship must have rotated since they'd returned to the room. She moved closer to identify the source of the light.

Aelyx followed and wrapped both arms around her waist, resting his chin atop her head. He pulled her close, and she felt the steady beat of his heart against her shoulder.

"It's a planetary nebula," he said. "A dying star."

"Wow." Stars really knew how to go out in style. It was stunning—illuminated wisps of orange and pink clouds forming an oval around a center of cornflower blue, like the eye of God staring back at her. "And me with no camera."

She wished she could enjoy the moment, but a circuit of worries and what-ifs played inside her head like credits at the end of a film. Was she really ready for this—to pack up and move to another galaxy? Unlike Aelyx, she hadn't researched her new home, and she didn't know an edible root from a parasitic seedling or how to behave in polite society. Of course, Troy had managed not to single-handedly end alliance negotiations between their planets, so maybe L'eihr standards for manners weren't as high as Aelyx had led her to believe. But either way, she'd have to navigate this new life without him, and the prospect left her tingling with a mixture of fear and anticipation.

"There's one visible from L'eihr, too," Aelyx said. "Bigger and twice as spectacular."

"Really?"

"Mmm-hmm." He tightened his hold around her waist. "Every time you see it, I want you to think of me. I'm going to mend that alliance in record time, and soon we'll stand together, just like this, and we'll watch the L'eihr sky from our colony."

It'll go by fast, Cara repeated to herself. *Then we'll have all the time in the world.*

Decades from now, this brief separation would seem like a hiccup. Now wasn't the time to sulk, not with so much at stake. Once L'eihr and Earth sealed the alliance, she and Aelyx would be together again.

They'd survived so much already—a few measly light-years couldn't keep them apart.

Acknowledgments

I have many people to thank for helping *Alienated* make it into your hands, so kick back and get comfy. This might take a while.

To my editor, Laura Schreiber, thank you for being my very first L'annabe. You fell in love with my characters and took a chance on their creator, for which I am infinitely grateful. Working with you has made this book stronger than I ever imagined possible, and I've felt your enthusiasm during every step of the process. It's truly a privilege to be your author.

A thousand thanks to my agent, Nicole Resciniti, who cheered me on through *one more* rewrite, then went on to sell this book to Disney. You found the perfect home for the book of my heart, and that makes you my hero.

Big hugs to my critique partners, Carey Corp and Lorie Langdon, who have also become incredible friends. I don't know what I'd do without your companionship and support. I'm grateful to have you in my life. Next time we schedule a writing retreat, I'll bring the peaches. Additional thanks to my sisters at the OVRWA. You ladies rock.

A giant shout-out to the NaNoWriMo community for helping me see that I had the power to finish a novel—even if it was a hot, ungodly mess at the end of those thirty days. *Alienated* exists because of you. Write on, friends!

Many thanks to my early readers: Heather, Shannon, Olca, Jamie, Zoe, and of course, my mom. I'm mortified that I sent you guys the second draft of a book I wrote in thirty days, but your encouragement helped me push through five rewrites. Well, that and my own obsession. But let's give you the credit, because that sounds better.

To the NBC writers, thank you for helping me with everything from brainstorming to query advice. Nesties rule! A special thanks to YA writer Shana Silver, whose detailed critique of my first six chapters taught me more about fiction writing than any instructional text I've read.

Thank you to Carol M. Stephenson, Ph. D., for patiently explaining to me the dangers of nanotechnology . . . and for being an excellent neighbor.

Much love to my friends and family. You continue to amaze me with all you do to help spread the word about my books. Thank you! To my children: Ashley, Troy, and Blake, thanks for your patience. I know it's hard when Mom is chained to her laptop every day, but, hey—you're in my book! I hope that makes up for all the nights we've eaten grilled cheese sandwiches.

Finally, to my husband, Steve, thank you for being the finest human I know. The L'eihrs might not elect to clone you, but I totally would. Love you, babe!

Turn the page
for a sneak peek:

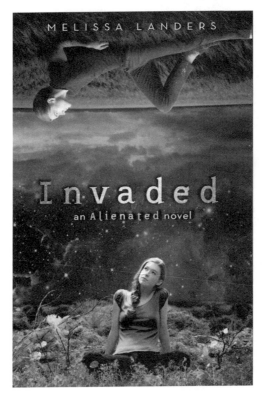

PROLOGUE

Cara frowned at the starched gray duffel bag at Aelyx's feet. It was identical to the one he'd brought to Earth last fall when he'd traveled from L'eihr to stay with her for senior year.

"We only have a few minutes," he said, taking her hand in both of his.

She glanced out the spaceport window to the ship that would jettison Aelyx back to Earth—without her this time—while she continued on to his planet. A shiver of anxiety skated down her spine. The exchange wasn't supposed to happen like this, without Aelyx there to guide her. As much as she wanted to go home, that wasn't an option. The Elders had made their demands painfully clear. Her chest tightened and heat prickled behind her eyes, but she refused to cry. Repairing the alliance between their worlds could save the human race.

That trumped a broken heart.

She summoned a smile and met his silvery gaze. If they had only one minute left, she'd make it count. "I love you."

The corners of his lips quirked in a grin. "Show me."

"I've been trying to show you for days," she said suggestively. "You'd think on a ship this big, we could find someplace to be alone."

Her lame joke didn't deter him. "Do it."

"Right here?"

He checked over both shoulders to ensure no one was watching. "Go ahead. It's safe."

They'd kept her ability to use Silent Speech a secret, but Aelyx made her practice every day. It didn't come easily. Communicating with her mind was more grueling than advanced trig.

"But it's our last minute together," she objected. "Don't I get a break?"

"No." He took her face between his palms. "Show me."

Of course she couldn't deny him, not when she knew how good it felt to experience his emotions, to know on a cellular level how much he loved her.

"Okay."

Closing her eyes, she pulled in a deep breath and released the tension in her shoulders. Aelyx used his thumbs to lightly brush her temples, helping her relax and reminding her to clear her thoughts. That was the hardest part—banishing her inner voice.

She rested a hand over Aelyx's heart, feeling its rhythmic beat against her palm while she focused on the rush of sentiment she felt for him in the moment—attraction, respect, adoration, and, more than anything, need. She let the feelings multiply until she couldn't contain them any longer, and when she opened her eyes, she channeled her passion through his wide pupils and into the consciousness beyond.

He felt it—his expression left no doubt. He closed his eyes for a moment as if to savor the sensation, then locked gazes with her. *That was amazing*, he communicated. *You're getting better.*

"Now it's your turn," she said.

Aelyx tapped her forehead. *Ask me the right way. From up here.*

"Slave driver."

You'll thank me one day.

Cara heaved a sigh and restarted the process of clearing her mind. When she was ready, she gazed through Aelyx's pupils and formed two simple words in her brain: *Your turn.*

But nothing happened.

Try again, he encouraged.

She did—three more times—but without success. For whatever reason, she could share her emotions with Aelyx but never her words. But on the bright side, she didn't get the headaches anymore.

He caressed her cheek. *Be patient and keep practicing. Ask Elle to help you while I'm gone. She should teach you to block your thoughts as well as share them. I trust her, but don't tell the other clones about your progress . . . especially not the Elders.*

Just as she opened her mouth to reply, the steely travel band around Aelyx's wrist buzzed, alerting him that it was time to board. They shared a desperate glance before he pulled her mouth hard against his.

It didn't take long for the kiss to transform from benign to scorching—it never did. The signature tingles only he could summon danced across her chest. Cara crushed their bodies together, clinging to his broad shoulders like she could stop him from leaving if she got close enough. But it didn't last. Just as she captured his lower lip between her teeth, he groaned and broke away.

"I have to go," he murmured, tilting their foreheads together. His wristband buzzed again, a final warning before it would heat against his skin and cause him physical pain.

She pushed his chest, refusing to break down. "Hurry. Before it burns you." She smiled and added, "I don't want anything making you that hot unless it's me."

With a grin, he grabbed his duffel bag and jogged across the metal grating that led to the boarding corridor. When he reached the doorway, he stopped and shouted, "I almost forgot. I built a new blog for you, to replace the one Syrine deleted. Same login and password as before."

"Thanks," she called with a wave. "You're pretty awesome . . . for an alien."

He laughed as he backed into the corridor, leaving her with five final words.

"Actually, *you're* the alien now."

Chapter One

MAY THE SOURCE BE WITH YOU

MONDAY, DECEMBER 24
I'm Dreaming of a Beige Christmas.

Happy Holidays, earthlings! Welcome to INVADED, your exclusive sneak peek into my one-woman invasion of planet L'eihr. I don't know how 597,350 of you found my new blog so quickly, but I'm glad you're here. Pull up a chair, kick off your boots, and grab a steaming mug of *h'ali* (the closest thing to hot chocolate on this sugar-hating spaceship).

It's Christmas Eve, and if the stars align—not to mention the intergalactic transmissions—you should see this maiden post by morning. It's an icy absolute zero here in space, but we should arrive at my balmy home away from home by lunchtime.

I have to say, it's a little weird being one of only two people on this vessel to celebrate Christmas. My new friends think it's crazy to believe that God's spirit impregnated a virgin, but they think it's totally logical to accept that a Sacred Mother birthed six gods and goddesses who created L'eihr from meteor dust and starlight. Because that's a lot more feasible.

But I digress. L'eihrs celebrate the birth of their deities each spring, but instead of exchanging presents, they fast for two days to bring them closer to the Sacred Mother by way of collective suffering.

Talk about *bah humbug*!

To all my friends and family back home, guzzle some eggnog for me, and while you're at it, choke down some fruitcake, too. You'd be surprised how much I miss that stuff . . . and you. Always you, dear readers.

Merry Christmas and Happy New Year!

Posted by Cara Sweeney 2:07 a.m.

No comments had posted, but that didn't surprise Cara. Sometimes there was a twenty-four-hour delay sending and receiving electronic data from the L'eihr ship stationed above Earth's atmosphere. Still, that wasn't too shabby, considering how many galaxies those poor bytes had to travel.

She pushed aside her brother's laptop and set her com-sphere on the polished cafeteria table, where Mom and Dad would soon join her for Christmas dinner, hologram-style. Her life felt like a futuristic holiday special: *A Very Virtual Christmas.* If only she could summon some digital decorations for the ship's sterile, empty dining hall. It was as festive as a death-row prison cell in here—bare gray walls, rows of meticulously parallel metallic tables and benches, dead silence, and nothing illuminating the darkness but the computer's backlit screen.

At three in the morning, not a creature was stirring, not

even a *harra*, the L'eihr equivalent of a mouse. But instead of nestled all snug in her bed with visions of Reese's Cups dancing in her head, Cara was running on Midtown time, day versus night, waiting for the "phone" to ring. As she often did during these quiet moments, she wondered what Aelyx might be doing in Manhattan.

It'd only been a week since the L'eihr Elders had sent him back to Earth to help rebuild the alliance, but it felt like a year. Aelyx was the reason she'd left Earth in the first place— so they could build a life together on the L'eihr colony. She never imagined she'd be alone when she glimpsed her new home for the first time.

Well, not literally alone.

Her brother, Troy, was here to serve as a human mentor, but truth be told, he was a real horse's ass—the kind of guy who would point and laugh at her misery instead of warning her not to touch a flesh-eating alien plant . . . assuming those existed on L'eihr. She hoped they didn't.

The sound of dragging footsteps turned her attention to the doorway, where Troy shuffled into view sporting unlaced combat boots and the same rumpled military fatigues he'd worn to bed last night. He yawned loudly, not bothering to cover his mouth, and used both hands simultaneously to scratch his chest and butt.

Yep, that was her mentor. She was *so* screwed.

"They call yet?" he grumbled, taking the seat across from her.

Cara slid an extra nutrient packet at him. "Merry Christmas to you, too."

Instead of answering, he rubbed one eye and plucked his offering from the table. He loved those protein bars, though Cara couldn't understand why. They smelled and tasted exactly like boiled cabbage.

"Merry Christmas," he said eventually. Then followed it with, "Dorkus."

Flipping him off didn't seem very "yuletide gay," so she rolled her eyes instead. "When are we supposed to shuttle down?"

"Dunno."

She rested her chin in one hand and sighed.

Their transport had reached the L'eihr solar system hours ago, but for reasons she wasn't privy to, the Elders had held off on shuttling them planet-side. Cara had a raging case of cabin fever—or starship fever, as it were—and if she had to listen to Troy's chronic snoring one more night, she'd smother him in his sleep. He'd insisted on bunking with her while Aelyx was on board, because God forbid she got lucky for once, and he'd refused to leave her side ever since.

She narrowed her eyes at him. "I hope you don't think we're sharing a dorm at the Aegis." Or on the colony, or wherever they ended up.

She expected him to cop an attitude, but he dropped his gaze into his lap. An emotion she couldn't place darkened his features. It looked a lot like guilt, which didn't make sense. Troy was too self-absorbed to feel guilty.

"What's going on?" she asked. "There's something you're not telling—"

She was interrupted by the buzzing of a thousand hornets

inside her skull, her com-sphere's irritating-but-effective way of alerting her to an incoming transmission. Cringing, she snatched the gadget into her fist and whispered her password against its cool metal shell.

Mom's and Dad's six-inch holograms flickered to life beside her nutrient packet while Troy hopped onto the table and slid across its slick surface to occupy the spot next to her.

"Merry Christmas!" Mom called, waving from her seat atop Dad's lap. They had settled on the magnolia-festooned living room sofa, and Dad wore a jolly red sweater that clashed with his orange hair. It was a cornucopia of tackiness, but Cara had never beheld a more beautiful sight.

If she listened closely, she could just make out Bing Crosby's buttery voice crooning "I'll Be Home for Christmas," which was kind of ironic, considering. She returned the greeting along with Troy, then held up her nutrition bar. "Did you finish dinner? I thought we could eat together."

"Oh," Mom said, "we got takeout from the Szechuan place down the street." Her cherry lips curved in a smile, but she couldn't hide the sadness in her voice. "Didn't seem right, cooking a big meal for just the two of us."

Cara wilted and tossed aside her packet. "I hate these protein bars anyway."

"I can barely see you," Mom said. "Why are you sitting in the dark?"

Troy pulled his laptop closer and adjusted the settings to brighten the screen. "They're pretty frugal with energy here."

"Good for them," Dad piped up. "Now lean in so I can get a closer look." Cara and Troy obeyed, pressing their cheeks together to let Dad scrutinize them. Dad nodded in approval until his gaze settled on Troy. "When're you going to cut that hair, Rapunzel? I can't believe your CO lets you wear the uniform when you look like that."

Troy's hand darted to the loose black curls—identical to Mom's—that brushed the tops of his shoulders. His hair was almost long enough to wear in a low ponytail like the L'eihrs did. Wrinkling his brow, he argued, "When in Rome . . ."

"Get a trim," Dad said, then turned his attention to Cara. A grin broke out across his face. "Pepper, I can't get used to the sight of you in that L'eihr getup. You remind me of those little fan girls who wear costumes and dye their skin brown."

"L'annabes," Mom supplied with a soft snort.

"Yeah, that's it."

Self-consciously, Cara smoothed down the front of her tunic. She couldn't get used to wearing the uniform, either, or pulling her auburn waves into the same low braid every day. She missed her jeans and scoop-necked sweaters, not to mention her leather riding boots and double-barrel curling iron.

But saving Earth was worth the sacrifice. And so was Aelyx.

Clearly Dad's thoughts traveled on the same wavelength. "You hear from Aelyx lately?"

"He called a couple days ago," she said. "He's staying with the ambassador in Manha—" She cut off as a miniature white ball of fur pattered into the hologram and hopped onto Mom's lap. It looked like an overgrown hamster. Cara extended a finger. "What's that?"

Mom cuddled the fluffball against her cheek and made

smoochy noises at it. "Say hello to your new baby brother, Linus. He's a German-Malty-Doodle-Poo." Then she spoke directly to her furbaby. "Who's Mommy's little sweetums? You are! Yes, you are!"

What in the ever-loving hell was a German-Malty-Doodle-Poo?

"We adopted him from the shelter," Dad explained, not sounding pleased. "I think your mother's got Empty Nest Syndrome."

Mom elbowed him in the ribs while Cara exchanged a puzzled glance with Troy.

"But I'm allergic to dogs, remember?" Cara said. "What happens when we come home to visit?"

Mom waved a dismissive hand. "That won't be for ages."

"Uh, actually . . ." Troy began, then stopped to clear his throat. "I'll be home sooner than I expected. Colonel Rutter's calling me back to Earth. I got orders yesterday."

Cara almost sprained her neck whipping around to face him. *"What?"*

Troy took a defensive tone. "I only came to L'eihr because of the student exchange program, and now they're saying it's over. The other two humans won't come because they're scared. The Marines want me to report back to—"

"When?" Cara demanded.

He couldn't meet her gaze. "Two weeks."

Cara wiped her sweaty palms on her pants. No, this couldn't be right. The Marines had agreed to station Troy here for two years, until the original exchange students—herself included—returned home. If he left now, she'd be alone. The only human on a planet full of mankind-loathing L'eihrs. She had exaggerated on the blog when she'd referred to her "friends." Only one clone aboard the transport gave her the time of day, and that was Aelyx's sister.

Troy was undeniably a horse's ass, but he was *her* horse's ass, and she loved him. There had to be a way to keep him with her. He could go AWOL. What were the Marines going to do, court-martial him from Earth?

"No," she told him with a firm shake of her head. "You can't go. The program isn't over. I'm still here, and . . ." *I need you.*

"But that's the thing," Troy said. "You're an official colonist now, not an exchange student. When the year's over, you're staying on L'eihr. Like, forever."

"Pepper," Mom said tentatively, "if you're not happy there, you can come home with your brother."

A light *ding!* chimed from Troy's laptop as the incoming electronic data began delivering comments to Cara's blog post.

Subscribe [Archive] [Recent Entries] [About Me]

MAY THE SOURCE BE WITH YOU

Ashley said . . .
So jealous. Seriously, I wanna go. Take me to your leader!

Eric said . . .
Glad to hear you're safe—FOR NOW—but you're an idiot for leaving Earth over some guy, especially after he poisoned our mothereffing water!!!

Cara tapped the touchpad and closed her webpage before any more discouraging remarks popped up. She'd committed to this life, and she wasn't turning back.

A shrill *yip!* forced her attention to Mom, who held Linus over one shoulder and patted his back, burping him like an infant. It was official—Cara had been replaced by a German-Malty-Doodle-Poo. In two weeks, she'd lose her brother, and once they landed on L'eihr, she wouldn't have a friend in the world.

This was the worst Christmas ever.

"This is the best Christmas present ever!" A L'annabe danced from one foot to the other, nearly slipping on the icy sidewalk while Aelyx autographed her copy of *Squee Teen.*

"Not a problem." After scrawling a quick signature, Aelyx returned the girl's magazine.

She stared at his glossy eight-by-ten photograph and sighed dreamily while her friend thrust a copy of *Fangasm* at him and asked, "Did you and Cara really have a secret wedding? 'Cause that's *sooooo* romantic!"

"Excuse me, miss." A young national guardsman named Sharpe extended one palm toward the girl. "I need you to step back."

She nodded and obediently retreated a pace, joining a dozen other girls, each dressed in mock L'eihr uniforms, their hair fastened into low ponytails. The only threat they posed was admiring Aelyx to death. But while he found his guard detail overzealous at times, he was grateful for their presence. His last visit to Earth had ended in an attempt on his life, and he wished to return to Cara with all his parts intact.

"No," he told the girl, forcing a smile. "Humans and L'eihrs can't legally wed." He added with a wink, "Yet."

"Oh, gods," groaned Syrine, his former best friend. Emphasis on *former*. They'd barely exchanged ten words since she'd tried turning Cara against him on the transport. Syrine shoved him aside and jogged up the front steps leading to the penthouse apartment they shared with the L'eihr ambassador. Two armed guards followed her inside.

"You should probably wrap it up," Private Sharpe whispered. "You're exposed out here."

A frigid gust of wind stung the back of Aelyx's neck, sending a shiver across every inch of his flesh. He'd never felt winter's bite until his travels to Earth, and gods willing, he never would again after this mission ended. A warm fireplace beckoned from upstairs, and Sharpe didn't need to ask him twice.

"Just one more," Aelyx said to the girls, eliciting a chorus of disappointed moans. He was poised to sign his name when a sudden movement in his periphery caught his eye.

Glancing to the side, Aelyx noticed a uniformed guardsman approaching quickly from an armored Hum-V parked at the curb, his boots loudly crunching over the salt and slush that carpeted the street. A pink scar stood in contrast against the man's ivory forehead, his brown eyes fixed straight ahead at no one in particular. Aelyx scanned the soldier's jacket but found no nametag.

Why didn't he have a nametag?

When the soldier broke into a jog, Aelyx's body tensed, his instincts on high alert. Before a question could form on his lips, the man drew his pistol and aimed it over Aelyx's heart. In a voice colder than morning frost, the man rasped, "This is from the Patriots," and pulled the trigger.

Adrenaline surging, Aelyx reacted, but not quickly enough. As he dodged right, a deafening crack pierced his eardrums and two hundred pounds of force knocked him to the frozen asphalt. A cocktail of screams, shuffling boots, and counter-fire flooded his senses.

It took Aelyx a moment to realize that not only was he alive, but that Sharpe lay atop him. Aelyx freed himself and propped on one elbow in time to see the rogue gunman tear down the street and vanish between two townhomes. Several guardsmen followed in pursuit while the rest of their unit scrambled to secure the area.

Sharpe rolled onto his back with a deep groan and asked, "You all right?"

Aelyx patted his chest and moved his arms and legs in a brief inventory. "Yes." A glance at Sharpe revealed a wet patch of blood slowly spreading across the outside of his shoulder. "But you're not."

Sharpe followed Aelyx's gaze to the wound before he gave a frustrated grunt and rested his head on the ground. "Just a scratch. But it's gonna sting when the rush wears off."

Up close, Aelyx realized for the first time how young the man was, likely no more than twenty. They might even be the same age, which surprised him. Sharpe's bravery and quick reflexes rivaled that of a seasoned warrior. "You took a bullet intended for me."

Sharpe shrugged his good shoulder. "Part of my job."

Aelyx couldn't help smiling at the boy's stoicism. They could use more like him on L'eihr. "Well, thanks for doing it so thoroughly, Private Sharpe."

Sharpe chuckled, then grimaced in pain and extended his opposite hand. "Call me David."